WILD BOY

Also by D. J. Etchell

Sonnets from the Iliad
Sonnets from the Odyssey
The Lych-gate
Not to be Read by your Wife and Servants
Mckinley
The Falling Leaf Does Not Hate the Wind
A Twilight Tale

WILD BOY

AN ODYSSEY

D. J. Etchell

Published by
Burghwallis Books

Publishing services by
Mushroom Publishing Services, Bath UK
mail@mushroompublishing.com

Printed and bound by Lightning Source

Thanks to Brian Smith for assistance with the manuscript

For all the Wild Boys

'*You cannot connect the dots looking forward; you can only connect them looking backwards.*'

Steve Jobs

Prologue

If you were born into a Northern working-class household, none of the first four decades of the twentieth century had anything to recommend them. Poverty, malnutrition and disease were always around. All the kids got chickenpox and measles, and often mumps and whooping cough as well. Some perished or were irrevocably damaged by these diseases. Vaccines for polio were not available, and tuberculosis was common. The first antibiotic—Penicillin G—was first used just after the Second World War. Although it had been available in 1944, all the first supplies were directed to the various theatres of war for use on injured servicemen.

In mining communities like the one I was raised in, the working conditions underground had slowly improved from horrendous to merely awful. With hindsight, it is amazing that anyone put up with them. But none of the workers had the sort of overview which would have permitted radical or revolutionary changes. In the house, women's work was drudgery, polishing, cleaning and washday, all undertaken by hand and with none of the modern aids.

There were brief periods when pay was good, principally due to the two world wars and the need for every ton of coal which could be produced to power the factories, trains and the huge British mercantile and Royal Navy battle fleets. As soon as the First World War ended, demand dropped, and then dropped further due to the great slump of the thirties. Most miners were working a two- or three-day week, on reduced pay until the second war started to loom. After the Second World War, demand for coal continued to be strong for a while, mainly because the UK was bankrupt and could not afford to

1

import the more convenient to use oil-based fuels in any quantity. Wages were good but there was little to spend the money on. The boozers, bookies and tobacconists managed to account for much of the surplus cash. However, by the sixties the economy had improved to the extent that the planners were now thinking in terms of a considerably reduced mining industry. This was given further impetus by the move away from coal to diesel for fuelling ships and trains.

My memories begin from about 1948—I would have been about three years old. There was always a coal-fire in the small and cramped kitchen, even in summer. This was necessary because there was no gas or electric cooker. Meals were cooked using the single gas ring, the fire and the coal oven. Two pans were left bubbling in front of the fire and one above the gas ring, sited next to the sink above the metal tub which had a fire lit beneath it on wash days.

In the metal tub, clothes were boiled with soap flakes and then laboriously rinsed in cold water using the zinc plated bathtub or the large stone sink. The excess water was removed by putting the clothes through a large manually operated mangle or wringer, with items often handed to my grandfather or an uncle to have the last drops of water wrung out of them by the hugely strong forearms which they all possessed.

Meals were basic in the extreme. Rationing in 1948 was more severe than at any time during the war. If God had been on our side in obtaining victory, he must have left shortly after VE day because torrential rain during the summer of 1946 ruined the wheat crop. This resulted in bread rationing, which had been avoided all through the war. If that wasn't bad enough, the severe frosts of 1946/47 ruined much of the stored potato crop and potato rationing was introduced in 1947. The late forties were a grim time to live through, especially after six years of war and the decade of poverty caused by the slump preceding that.

Clothes were virtually unobtainable due to their huge cost and the number of clothes rationing coupons required for each item. It was a time of make do and mend. Socks were made of wool, and when they developed holes they were darned. This was done with a large needle with a blunt and curved tip to weave wool into the existing fabric until the hole was filled. Other clothes were patched up or re-sown until they were virtually falling apart. Men's garments, as they reached the bottom of the line, became 'pit' clothes.

Items such as cups and plates, bedding, pots and pans were virtually unobtainable, as were light bulbs. These usually hung bare in each room with no lamp shade. Electrical goods were far too expensive for most people. Electric kettles, fires, toasters, refrigerators, washing machines, telephones, hoovers, and so on, were owned by a few middle-class households. Freezers were non-existent. Indeed, they probably could not have been used due to the absence of the ring mains and thirteen-amp sockets which modern houses have. If an electric iron was owned it would be plugged into a light socket served by the lighter duty wiring which usually runs near to the roof and serves the lower amperage needs of light bulbs in modern houses. The only universally owned item of electrical equipment was a radio or 'wireless'. They were generally large affairs, in a wooden or 'Bakelite' cabinet. Bakelite was the first plastic and was used for light switches, electrical plugs, telephones and similar. It was the only plastic available for the three decades before nylon and the new polymers were invented.

Almost no one had a television, and these were hugely expensive costing the equivalent of two to three months wages. They were small, unreliable, usually with a nine- or twelve-inch screen. Only one BBC channel broadcast for a few hours each day in black and white, and many areas of the country did not get a signal from the BBC transmitters. The beginning of the huge explosion of electronic goods based on the transistor or microchip was twenty years away. Any entertainment came from occasional visits to the cinema or reading the papers, which were hugely influential and virtually all Tory leaning. Pubs and working men's clubs were the hub of village life. Churches had extremely poor attendance, their influence was minimal, and they were resented for keeping Sunday holy, which meant they were miserable.

No sport was permitted on TV on Sunday and light entertainment on radio was limited to an early mid-afternoon slot consisting of 'Two Way Family Favourites'. This had replaced 'Forces Favourites' which had been popular during the war and was thus hard to get rid of. The BBC was determined to raise the 'moral tone' of the show. Thus, mention of 'girlfriends' was taboo and noisy music like jazz was forbidden. We were allowed an innocuous mix of records stretching back to the nineteen-thirties or even earlier. They usually included just one record from 'the Hit Parade', as the top ten was then quaintly named. It seemed to be BBC policy that any type of music could be broadcast as long as it was bland. 'The Billy Cotton Band Show' featured around midday on Sundays, with a couple of mediocre singers, a light crooner called Alan Breeze and a woman called Cathy Kay, both churning out melodious, lifeless, polite, low impact stuff with absolutely no beat.

A half hour of comedy was allowed. *Hancock's Half Hour* was hilarious. *Educating Archie*, featured Archie Andrews—a ventriloquist's dummy—on the radio! Wasn't bad. There were a few others such as *Meet the Huggetts* and *Life with the Lyons*; millions listened, but jollity was severely restricted on Sundays. Huge swathes of time were given over to serious, moral productions, religious discussions, church services. Frankly, the public were just not interested. During these broadcasts, millions turned their wirelesses off.

On 1st January 1947, known as Vesting Day, a little less than a thousand pits were taken into public ownership, along with the huge coking and chemicals industry, eighty brickworks, and other ancillaries owned by the colliery companies. Nationalisation is portrayed as a socialist and inefficient initiative. It often is. However, in this case, the mines had been starved of investment for years and they were poorly equipped. Coal was vital to the national interest and thus public investment was the only way the necessary production could be secured in the absence of the private capital needed to re-equip them.

Despite the poverty and food shortages, the atmosphere in

the home was surprisingly cheerful. Things had got better or would get better because there was a Labour government in power. Major nationalisations were taking place: railways, steel, electricity generation, gas production. And, most importantly, the health services. The National Health Service is one of the great achievements of this nation, or in fact of any nation anywhere in the world.

So what was a boy born into one of that broad swathe of very tough mining villages which ran above the South Yorkshire coal fields to make of life in this grey, impoverished, brave new postwar world?

Chapter 1

Dreamtime

'Dreaming when Dawn's Left Hand was in the Sky'
The Rubaiyat of Omar Khayyam

I can just remember the late forties. Fragments of memories linger of slow and dreamlike days, but above all I remember the hunger and the ever-present smell of tobacco smoke. We all lived in a pit-house, built by and rented from the colliery company. It was small, with three bedrooms, a small kitchen, a bathroom and an indoor lavatory, which was a bit of a luxury because many houses still had them outside. The house was crowded: two grandparents, two uncles, two aunties, and Jed and Liz and their two kids. Jed was still finishing his naval service, having signed on in 1932 for sixteen years. He was absent most of the time and did not take up full-time occupancy in the house till his demob in 1948. Crowding was normal; one family on the street had twelve kids, and another had fourteen.

The village had grown up next to the pit. What had been a rural hamlet expanded as the colliery company bought land and then the council stepped in with houses and schools. Followed rapidly by the big breweries who built large pubs to cater for the thirsty thousands who made up the workforce. The workers did not like paying the monopoly prices charged for the beer and thus set up working men's clubs. These often started in large sheds with basic tables and chairs or stools. They rapidly made money by selling beer cheaply and slowly expanded into much plusher premises.

Other vital small concerns followed, such as a dairy and rows of centrally located shops. The mining settlements were always called villages but in reality they were urban townships each with several thousand houses. The inhabitants were generous spirited, with small horizons. They were also fiercely tribal.

I didn't like getting washed! Standing in my vest next to the large stone sink while a flannel was rubbed round my face and neck. After that it was a bit of fried bread or bread and jam or bread and dripping for breakfast. Time moved so slowly. There was nothing to do—no books, no drawing materials, no source of stimulus apart from the adult chatter and the blandness of the radio, or the lack of comprehension if the BBC symphony orchestra was playing a serious bit of music. I have never liked the late Beethoven string quartets ever since then because of that experience.

As a parent, Liz didn't have a clue and wasn't too bothered either. Kids were just an unfortunate consequence of hasty and unprotected sex. If the chore of bringing them up could be shuffled off onto someone else, she was delighted. Nothing seemed to be her responsibility, life just happened to her, and she merely adjusted to events in a manner that required her to expend the least effort possible. She had worked as a maid before the war and clearly did not like hard work. Having seen the other side of the coin, she would much prefer to have been one of the served rather than one of the servants. She was never happier than when she sat with a fag in her mouth doing nothing in particular.

A few things hang in memory of my pre-school years. One late February day, when I must have been almost two, I can remember the great excitement as my grandad opened the back door to reveal that the opening was two thirds filled with snow which hung in a long arc above the drift which had blown in overnight from one of the huge 1947 snowstorms. Excitement was unusual in grandad. He was usually very taciturn, sitting smoking his pipe in the corner of the kitchen, probably thinking about his four years in the Great War as a private in the Tyneside Scottish regiment, or about his fifty-one years in the mines. He had joined the army as a volunteer in 1914 and was pleased to be alive and warm. He had worked and fought in unpleasant conditions, but he was through it, he was small and tough. He had seen lots of death and severe injury. He was grateful that apart from a few blue scars, which characterise all mineworkers due to the coal dust trapped in the cuts, he had escaped unscathed and had also survived both the Somme and the third battle of Ypres. At the Somme he had been lucky, sustaining a minor wound a week before the big attack which resulted in him needing hospital treatment. Thus, he missed the first of July slaughter. After three weeks he was returned to light duties and that may well have saved his life.

He was pulled off the coalface late due to the Second World War. He was in his early fifties. The usual practice was to pull men off the coal face in their mid-forties because by then they had spent thirty years underground and would usually be physically knackered due to spending years shovelling ten, fifteen or even twenty tons a shift into the low tubs which ran behind the face line. He now worked as a packer, which would have been regarded as hard physical work by anyone not brought up in the mines. It was steady work building and repairing the roadways which ran to and from the coal faces using the rubble extracted during the mining operations.

That snowy morning, I had been sent downstairs to be washed by my youngest aunt, Polly, while Liz and Jed, who was on leave, had a lie in and enjoyed a woodbine following early morning sex. My granny was making the fire in the living room because it was winter. The fire in the kitchen had stayed alight overnight and was now burning brightly after being refreshed with coal from the bucket that always stood ready at the side of the ash spattered and burned peg rug which lay on the hearth. The burns were caused by a coal rolling off the fire or a large cinder leaping from it. Often, my grandad would pick the coal up and toss it back and then spit on his fingers. The cinders were too hot for that and needed the shovel to scoop them up so they could be thrown on the back of the fire.

As soon as I and my younger brother were old enough, which was three in my case, we were allowed to hang around with the other street urchins, wandering round adjacent streets or down to the swings, slides and roundabouts in the park at the bottom of the long terrace which our road led into. Liz thought it was normal for kids to do this and was glad to get rid of us for a few hours so she could get her feet up, read a magazine and have a cup of tea and enjoy a fag. That seemed the pattern. It didn't seem to occur to her that she bore some responsibility for her life's actions.

When my youngest brother was born, she couldn't wait to suggest that I might like to look after the new arrival and push him up and down the road in his pram while trailing my middle brother alongside. As a five-year-old, I found it difficult to push an old and heavy pram which towered above me. When I said this to her, I received a petulant and bad-tempered outburst about how disappointed she was because I wasn't willing to help out. After being ganged up on by Polly and Grandma, she backed off, but I could tell by the glint in her eye that she was not pleased.

Revenge followed shortly after that. When returning from the local town a brief and boisterous squabble broke out between my younger brother and me on the bus. A quick admonition would have ended it, but she sat there as if it was nothing to do with her. However, after some woman made a comment about rowdy ill-behaved kids, she got off the bus and marched down the road, head held high and obviously in high dudgeon. When we got in, she rushed upstairs and grabbed her hairbrush and gave us both a good hiding, shouting that she would teach us not to show her up. I got the worst of it, and we were both sent straight to bed without anything to eat. Polly just looked on, shaking her head at the hysterical behaviour of her elder sister.

Later that night, Liz got her coat on and insisted that Jed take her out for a drink to calm her nerves down. Jed wasn't all that keen because the unexpected midweek expenditure ate into the money he had available for his beer and fags. After they left, Polly came upstairs with glasses of milk and a biscuit and read us a bedtime story. She told us to forget about it, that Liz was upset but loved us really. We were also told to say nothing about the milk and biscuit, or Liz would be annoyed again.

After that, I was wary of Liz and kept out of her way if I could. In the following few days, Polly, who had a heart of gold, made it clear what she thought about the incident, but Liz just brushed it off. The last thing she was ever going to do was take her responsibilities as a mother seriously.

When I started school, aged four and a half, I remember her running out into the street to talk to one of the girls in the last year at secondary. Liz asked if she wouldn't mind if I walked into school with them on my first day and for a few days until I got used to it. I was got ready and pushed off and trailed along, walking behind the giggling teenage girls to the strange and somewhat Victorian styled school building about a mile away. One thing that sticks in my memory was the fondness of the girls for a recent record with the opening line 'Put another nickel in, in the nickelodeon.' By the standards of the time it was a lively tune with a sort of honky-tonk piano background. Decidedly not the sort of thing the BBC types would allow on Sundays. By today's standards it is so banally bad it would never have been released.

The woman in charge of the nursery was known to the kids as 'Miss Custard' because her name was similar: Custant, I think. She seemed to spend an awful lot of that first day saying 'Jesus loves you.' This left me nonplussed as I did not have a clue who Jesus was, having been brought up in a household where absolutely no one had any time for religion of any sort. No one in the family ever swore, but I had heard Polly use the term Jesus H Christ during moments of extreme exasperation. So, I supposed it must have something to do with him, but I never bothered to ask. I suppose I was fortunate; no Christopher Robin type prayers were imposed on me before bedtime, and no grace was ever said before meals. There was no bible in the house.

Grandad came back from the war hating clergymen, especially the Church of England types who had been useless and overly timid in the forward areas of the trenches and in seeing to the needs of the dying and injured at the front. All the family had negative experiences of various sorts of clergy, so religion played absolutely no part in my young life.

When I got back after my first day at school, Liz asked me about it. Apparently, she had read an article in a woman's magazine about how important it was to show an interest in your child's education. She was willing to go along with the fantasy and role play for a few minutes. When I told her that the teacher had told me that Jesus loved me, her eyes glazed over, and she rapidly lost interest. I would have liked some sort of explanation as to who this Jesus bloke was and why he took an interest in the grubby and undernourished kids at the local infant's school, but none was forthcoming.

The teaching that followed helped extraordinarily little. One afternoon, we had a story about this Jesus chap, saying, 'suffer the little children to come unto me.' But the archaic language and the seeming inability of the teacher to explain it in terms comprehensible to under-fives left us all baffled.

Lots of what happened at school left us baffled. In my second year at infants, we had a fat teacher called Mrs Smith whose chief preoccupation seemed to be rushing down to the staff room as quickly as she could at breaks so she could smoke. She showed a profound disinterest in education. It was an imposition for her to be there with us in the classroom for several hours a day. I cannot remember a single thing about anything she taught. My only memory was of her looking out of the staff room window drawing heavily on a Park Drive with a look, almost of fear, on her face which seemed to say, 'oh fuck, in ten more minutes I will have to be back in there with the little bastards.'

The curriculum, I suppose (I say suppose because I can't remember any of it), must have been little different to the three Rs of the pre-war years.

Adults continued to amaze me, on one occasion I developed

some boils on my leg and was sent off to school with a bandage on the affected area. The headmistress noticed it and hauled me out in front of the assembly and delivered a little homily about 'this brave boy' coming to school while suffering from this condition. I wasn't too sure what it was all about. The boils were minor and did not hurt. The bandage was an inconvenience, but the antiseptic ointment applied was working nicely. I stood there sheepishly while all the other kids looked at me as though I was some sort of oddity. I mentioned it when I got home and Liz looked quite pleased, but Polly said acidly, 'You ought to have got him down to the doctors, boils can be nasty.'

Another thing which sticks in my mind was the hot summer towards the end of that term. It must have been 1950. I would have been five and a few months. My shoes wore out and I had holes in each. There was a flurry of activity and a huddle with much smoking and worried looks and wails of 'there's no money in the house.' Jed was back from the navy by then but had not been able to get a reasonably paid job. He worked on a farm for a bit and did some window cleaning. My uncles had offered to get him a job at the pit, but for some reason that did not appeal, despite assurances that he could get a pit-top job or on the haulage underground and be nowhere near the dangers of a coal face. Grandad told him that working in the roadways was a doddle, but Jed didn't want to know. He seemed to be afraid of going underground.

Anyway, it was decided that I would go to school wearing wellingtons, in high summer. Gran wasn't pleased about it. She had refused to pay for my footwear, pointing out Liz and Jed were both managing to smoke, and he was down at the club every night for a couple of pints, or so he said. She had by now experienced several years of Liz's pleas of poverty and in the early days had helped out. This time she felt it needed to be spelled out—'Your kids, your responsibility.' Liz airily replied, 'Oh, lots of kids wore wellingtons in summer when I was at school.' Thus, I was sent off to school wearing the tight and unsuitable footwear. After a couple of days trailing the mile there and back, I complained about sore feet. Gran had a look and said to Liz: 'His feet are badly blistered!' This produced more flurries of concern, more smoking, until it was decided that Liz would buy me a pair of plimsoles. These were the cheapest footwear available. They cost about the same as a pack of twenty Players. They were OK for hot summer days but totally unsuitable if it rained.

It did rain eventually; the pumps were then dried out on the hotplate which accelerated their deterioration. They rapidly became scruffy due to constant wear during the summer holidays. Liz moaned about it. She had hoped I could have gone to school wearing them during the warmer autumn months without eating further into their fag money. Gran and Polly got their heads together and saved sixpence a week between them. Before autumn term started, I was taken into town and bought a pair of stout hobnailed boots. They were slightly too large, but gran knew what she was doing—I would soon grow into them. Liz, once again having been relieved of her parental responsibilities said, when I returned with Gran and the new boots, 'Aren't you a lucky boy.'

School policy in the area regarding hitting kids varied enormously. At one local school the headmaster had a seriously sadistic streak and was noted for saying he caned kids if he thought they were going to be naughty. We were lucky it was frowned on by the head at our school. The staff had strict instructions that in a case of serious misbehaviour the child was to be sent to him. This virtually never happened. It was great psychology by the head. It meant the staff had to use people skills, and could be authoritative, persuasive, humorous, pleasant or in one case extremely nasty, probably as a result of that teacher being a dried-up old spinster who probably had no other sexual outlet apart from raging at some unfortunate child. All the staff realised that sending a kid to the head showed they could not control their class—it was a mark of failure. Delinquent pupils were only sent to the head as a last resort.

The day started with an assembly. None of the kids in our class could read then, so the previous afternoon we would practice the hymn which would be sung the next morning, accompanied by the poorly tuned piano in the hall. Those with retentive memories could join in for some of it. Eventually, most of the words sunk in, but the thicker kids just looked blank. We also spent lots of time learning something called the Lord's prayer—again it meant little, the language was of three centuries earlier and there was no explanation of its meaning. It was just something strange which we had to say every morning. Years later I was talking to Tommy Powell, a kid who went on to Grammar school with me. He said, 'For years in assembly, I said "which chart in heaven." That prayer was just gobble-de-gook to me. I didn't understand it, and nobody had ever explained it to me.'

I remember learning to read. In class we were faced with a wall of incomprehensibility and impatience from a teacher who just expected us to magically see it and then start to read. She and most other teachers of that time had little grasp of the science of teaching infants, of the slow and necessary gradations which needed to be integrated and progressed through to impart the needed skills. Thus, it was a battle. I can remember none of the detail of what was taught but remember words being written on the board which we had to copy down using pencils. It was the final year of infants—six-year-olds, turning seven as the year progressed. Few could read. Those who could were the brighter ones who had been coached by parents or older siblings at home.

I could not read; I was approaching seven. At Christmas, my Gran bought a Brer Rabbit book for us. A few weeks later Liz said to me quite sharply, 'Why can't you read? Your younger brother Bob can and he's a year younger than you.' This took me aback, but Polly and Gran were there and said, 'If you had spent as much time with him as you have with Bob and that book, he probably could read it!' This produced a look of consternation and after that a 'look at me, aren't I the virtuous mother' phase resulted, as she sat down with me and went through the book when other people were about.

Amazingly, I could read almost instantly. A beneficial effect of this manifested itself in class, because I was now grouped with the readers and given simple reading material whilst old Tinsent carried on her battle with the non-readers, becoming increasingly sharp and unpleasant with them as the group got smaller.

I began to realise that Liz didn't like me too much and favoured my younger sibling. There were never any hugs, kisses or other signs of affection. If she ever spoke about us it was always – 'Oh, Bob's the clever one, he could read when he was five.' Later on, I must have been eight or nine, Liz was ill and advised that walking in the fresh air would be good for her lungs and her health generally. One day she trailed me off on a walk down the local bridle path. I remember her pinched white face and heard her say things which didn't quite seem to connect with reality, seeming to presuppose knowledge which I clearly did not have. As we walked to a stone church, she smoked several cigarettes, oblivious to the fact that this was heavily polluting the beneficial fresh air she was sucking in.

We walked round the graveyard and she looked intently at one spot with no grave marker. As we were walking back, she took on an intense manner and asked me if I knew who was buried there. I didn't, which was not surprising as I had never been there before or been told anything about it. The reply was an emphatic 'I do,' with the tone and strange demeanour and air of superiority that contained the strong underlying assumption that I should have known that. After a bit she decided to share her special knowledge of the place, saying 'That's where your great Grandma is buried.' After that I was even more wary of her as in addition to her hysterical impulses, she seemed to me to be not quite rational.

Later in life I occasionally ran into hysteria and the opportunity it presented for the gratification of those types of urges. You could spot the girls or women prone to it working themselves up towards it. My reaction was always one of very forceful disapproval. Amazing how that brought them back down to earth when they realised that they were not performing to a sympathetic audience. I read later that one of those 'trick-cyclist' johnnies was of the view that hysteria had a strong sexual component and that working oneself into that sort of state provided relief for sexual tension. Having experienced people indulging themselves in the practice, I can well believe it. I always wondered if the girl who eventually chose me for marriage appealed because she was eminently sensible, hardworking, and had an exceptionally low opinion of girls who shrieked a lot and were prone to having attacks of the vapours, as the Victorians described them. My wife to be was also an extremely attractive blond with an eye-wateringly voluptuous figure, but these attributes were of course only a minor consideration.

Chapter 2

A World Without Love

'Please lock me away and don't allow the day here inside where I hide with my loneliness.'
Peter & Gordon, "A World Without Love"

The drab grey of the forties shifted into the slightly less-grey fifties. Some consumer goods started to become available, clothes were no longer rationed but they were expensive. The austere men of the Labour government were replaced by a less able bunch of Tories who wanted to get back to business as usual with the haves having even more and the lower orders allowed the minimum possible. In earlier times the moral and parsimonious Labour cabinet would have been spearheading Calvinism or some similar soaked-in-misery religious movement. The Tories found it much harder to govern than in the twenties and thirties when the gaffers had the whip hand because of weak unions and mass unemployment. After the war, the unions were powerful in a heavily industrialised country and unemployment rates then were remarkably low.

Jed eventually got a job with the fire service. It was twenty-four hours on and twenty-four off. The shift would sleep at the station fully clothed in basic beds, hoping there was no night callout. Usually there was not. If there was a callout, it would often be late evening because somebody had got back from the boozer and decided to smoke in bed. Occasionally, during harvest time, a corn field would catch fire. It turned out that all the ordinary firemen had second jobs, working cash in hand as gardeners, window cleaners, as pall bearers or as builder's labourers on a 'beat the taxman basis.' Jed built up a window cleaning round, working for a few hours during each of his twenty-four-hour off days.

At grandad's house, one of my uncles had left by this time, as had one of the aunts, both having struck up relationships and found accommodation in other less crowded houses. In 1951 the bombshell dropped when Polly announced she was leaving home to join the RAF nursing service. This meant that the only remaining sources of affection in the house were gran and grandad. But they were old and tired, due to lifetimes of hard physical labour. They were in their sixties, but gran looked ten years older. A weak heart due to rheumatic fever as a child meant that she got out of breath easily if she did hard physical work. Thus, the burden of being a loving and guiding parent fell on Liz, who used the kids as a captive audience, often playing one against the other or creating cruel scenarios to gratify her own need to make us dependent on her.

One vivid memory was the tale of her own grandmother's death in 1941. It was winter and there were no flowers to be had because of the war, so the hearse went to the church with a lone holly wreath on top of the coffin. I had asked about the cause of death and Liz said, 'Oh she was old. One night as she was going to bed, she said, "Oh, I do feel tired tonight," and she died in her sleep.' Of course, a few weeks later, when Jed was doing one of his twenty-four-hour shifts and we were all climbing the stairs to bed, she had a look on her face which was difficult to describe—cunning but not quite that. When we were about halfway up the stairs she said, 'Oh, I do feel tired tonight.' I turned and could see the look of triumph on her face as she caught the look of consternation on my face. She had achieved exactly the effect that she had wanted. After a fitful night, I was relieved to wake and see her up and still alive. She repeated the remark from time to time but as I got older, she could see that the expected reaction was not forthcoming, and she packed in that source of her amusement.

Eventually, after an eight year wait, we moved to one of the new council houses being built in the next village. There was no planning or thought about how they would manage, no realisation that now they had left her parent's home they would have to pay for coal and gas and electricity and bear all the full household costs.

Grandad, as a miner, had received free coal. This was a recent concession. Up to the start of the war, they had to pay for it or scrabble for it amongst the spoil dumped on pit tips. At the start of the war, Churchill was writing pamphlets exhorting miners to 'stand behind their brothers in arms and cut more coal.' The mineworkers universally hated Churchill for sending troops in to help break a strike in the Rhonda in 1911. They killed two men when they opened fire. In 1941, he used a cabinet minute to grant concessionary coal in perpetuity to the miners as a recognition of their magnificent efforts in producing the material without which the war could not have been won. A contribution conveniently forgotten by Thatcher forty years later when the miners became 'the enemy within.'

Jed was just cold. No affection, ever. No treats, just the mean look on his pale face as he counted his change and calculated how much money he had for that week's beer and fags. I never ever had a conversation with him. He used to give orders and say things to us like: 'Help your mother with the washing,' or 'Get the lawnmower out and cut the grass.' He never played games with us inside or outside the house. His orders were often relayed through Liz—'Your dad wants you to cut the hedge,' etc. I did cut him some slack until I was about twenty, because he had gone into an orphanage at eight-years-old with his younger brother. His dad deserted the family after the general strike. They were living in near destitution in a caravan in Blackpool at the time. His departure forced his mother's hand, and she contacted the social services. His six years in the institution were followed by entry into the Royal Navy at 14 in 1932 and service throughout the war.

I have met people who did coastal patrols in the war and who never saw action. One said, 'The most danger we were ever in, in our MTB stationed in Scotland, was when the pressure cooker blew up in the galley.' Jed got the lot—North Atlantic convoys, 1939-41, Malta 1941-43, Russian Convoys 1943-44, then one of the first destroyers in on D-day to bombard the beaches. I assumed he was like he was because of his early life. However, I later met someone who had almost identical experiences—orphanage followed by harrowing experiences during the war—but this bloke could not have been a warmer or more caring family man. I realised that with Jed, that's just how he was.

Of course, you evaluate things. There were other families in the locality where the fathers worked every shift possible and skimped and saved to get a child through grammar school and college. This was unusual because until the 1944 education act, secondary schools were fee paying. Even if you got a scholarship place to cover tuition, the other fees meant that for most working-class families, taking up a place was beyond their means. There were other families where the dad was a shirker and got just enough shifts in at the pit to get by. Usually, the wife was unhappy as she bore the constant brunt of the scrimping and making do. I became aware that even in these situations these waste of space dads could have good and warm relationships with their kids.

I realised that we were just unfortunate. Near the bottom of the pile, but not quite at the bottom. That was reserved for the real lowlifes. The drunkards who were wife beaters or who were having sex with the daughters. There were those who drank, smoked and gambled. Sometimes this applied to the women, who's undersized kids were always dressed in patched or ragged clothing and who had that blank look which you get with a very poor-quality low protein diet, of bread or chips, with little in the way of eggs, milk, meat or fruit and veg.

For the house on the new estate, some essentials had been purchased. A couple of old beds and a wardrobe came from grandma's. A second hand, three-piece-suite was donated. Curtains were made, a few rugs appeared, bits of lino were laid. A gas cooker was bought on the weekly plan from the gas showrooms and an old washer was bought. It was operated by hand with clothes, some hot water and soap powder put in, and the mix turned by hand using a lever on the top of the machine. The front room remained empty till I left home and was used as a dumping ground for old toys and other unwanted items.

Life could have been poor but cheerful, but the latter was missing.

The new house was a lot colder than grandad's. Coal had to be bought and was used frugally. Except for the coldest winter days, a fire was usually lit in the late afternoon to cook with in the adjacent oven and on the hot plate. The coal was not from coal merchants, it came from the blokes who took it to the mineworkers' houses. The outfit who delivered it was called 'The Home Coal'. The deliverers were well known to be very poor at arithmetic because they often delivered only 19 or 18 hundredweight bags rather than the twenty which made up the full ton. Somehow, they never delivered 21 bags. In addition to the purloined coal, some miners, who got ten tons a year and did not use it all, would sell any surplus to the drivers who sold it on.

In those days breakfasts were always porridge, cornflakes or a similar cereal, or a boiled egg, and dinners were school dinners or those on Sunday served when Jed got in from the club. He always smelled of beer and cigarettes because of his own smoking and the fact that in the early fifties all clubs and pubs were dense with cigarette smoke. After dinner, he went to bed, and we were told to keep quiet.

Liz was a master at spinning food out and producing low-cost meals, something she had learned during the war. Sandwiches made of thinly spread meat paste, or thinly sliced corned beef or chopped pork or eggs usually greeted us when we got in from school. It could be soup made from ham hocks or potatoes baked in the coal oven. As long as it was cheap. Everything had to be cheap. Sausages and mash, tinned stew, corned beef hash, all frequently appeared. The arrangement was that Jed would pay the rent and provide money for the gas and electricity meters. Liz was given as little as he could get

23

away with to pay for food and her cigarettes and for items of furniture or clothing, usually on the weekly plan. This further decreased her ability to provide, due to the large percentage taken by the firm providing the credit for the stuff she bought on hire purchase.

Jed's long shifts meant he ate at the fire station when he was there. If he intended going window cleaning, he would take a sandwich with him or grab a meat pie followed by a couple of pints. If it rained, he looked miserable and stayed in the house working at some household job or other with a fag in the corner of his mouth. We kept out of his way. We ate together sometimes if we were home, but often we were at school and saw little of him. During meals he rarely spoke but ate his food and then hurried off to have a smoke. He always had bacon and egg when he returned from work just after nine. That was an understandable post war treat, having gone for years without seeing bacon and real eggs. In those days, they seemed to be reserved for aircrew prior to missions. The rest of the population managed on one egg per week and on powdered egg if they could get it.

I realised as I grew up that other kids were treated differently. Taken to circuses, football matches, fairs, pantomimes, and the like. It never happened with him. It was always work, boozer, fags and beer. He was more like some disinterested lodger than a dad. A few fathers, usually the very stupid, were little better than animals and prone to violence when they got back from the boozer. At least we didn't have to put up with that, but there was the constant coldness and meanness. Never an 'I'll treat you lads.' Every penny possible was going to be used on beer and cigarettes, with the pale unsmiling face matched by the pale unsmiling blond hair and a physique of average size and height. Perhaps that is why he avoided a job at the pit. My uncles were both physically powerful, with big shoulders and muscular arms. Perhaps Jed thought he wouldn't be up to it, or perhaps eight or nine hours underground without a cigarette was too much for him to bear.

Chapter 3

An education of sorts

'The whole educational and professional training system is a very elaborate filter, which just weeds out people who are too independent, and who think for themselves'

Noam Chomsky

My experiences at infant and junior schools had left me singularly unimpressed with education until my very last year. Then we had a teacher Mr Bryant, who was stimulating, clued up, and who knew what was what in the educational world and determined to get as many as possible of his working-class charges through the eleven-plus and on to grammar school. He was from the same background as us, from an earlier generation and obviously a bright lad who had managed to get to grammar school. There he had matriculated and gone on to do the two-year course at teacher training college. We were lucky because more than half of his forty or more classes got through the exam. I realised later that it was a lottery with bright kids having bad days and failing and duller types managing to guess the right answers and get through.

That lottery was further compounded by the ability of the teachers who taught the final year in the various junior schools of the area, some being cleverer than others and much better at gaming the system or realising how it worked. It became apparent when I got to the grammar school that three junior schools from the ten that fed into it had sent the bulk of the pupils there, with the others only managing a handful each. It was nothing to do with the ability of the kids at these schools, it was all down to the bad luck of having inferior tutoring. In some schools, the heads would not enter those who they thought would not pass, to avoid having to pay the exam fee. Obviously, some stood no chance, but attitudes varied, and it was left to the head at each Junior school. At ours, the head insisted that everyone be entered, including those who could barely read or write. He felt it was his moral duty not to deprive any student of their chance of a grammar school place.

There was a second chance when the kids were a year older, with late developers given the opportunity to take the eleven-plus again at secondary modern school when they were twelve. Few bothered, because they would go into the first form as twelve-year-olds and complete the fifth as seventeen-year-olds. This additional two years of educational expenditure compared to a kid who just did the four years at a Secondary Modern school placed a considerable financial burden on parents in those days of comparative poverty; in the fifties, most parents would not contemplate it.

These days it is difficult to imagine how tight things were. In each year there were several who passed the eleven-plus and who declined the place offered due to the cost. This arose from the extra year at school and the uniform. This dawned on Liz, when, after racing round all the friends and relatives to tell them I had passed the exam and would be going to grammar school, she received a list of the clothing required. Blazer from an approved supplier, satchel, plimsols, shorts for P.E., singlet, football boots, shorts, socks, shirt. Whites for cricket in the summer term. Fountain pen, ink, geometry set, etc, etc. She lit a cigarette and said, 'I can't afford that!'

What Noam Chomsky, quoted above, says about the educational system is true but he looks at it too narrowly. The major initial filter in obtaining a half decent education in the UK in the fifties was family poverty. Fortunately, as I came to realise later, Mark Twain's wry observation, 'don't let schooling interfere with your education' was far more pertinent in the very big world outside education.

To go back a while. I was amazed that I had passed the eleven-plus for three reasons. The first of these was repeated bouts of tonsillitis, which meant I had lost a huge chunk of my junior year's education. The second was absolutely nothing in the way of parental encouragement or assistance, and the third was a very disjointed few years at various schools.

I had changed infant school on moving to the new council house and then changed up to junior school. However, due to the shock of them having to bear the full household costs rather than the partial ones when we lived with my grandparents, everything was pared back on, including food. Jed continued to smoke and drink, and Liz still smoked, but she skimped on her own food and lost weight until she became ill due to self-inflicted malnutrition. The doctor was called, and she was taken away in an ambulance and spent three months in a convalescent home on the east coast. This meant that Jed had to arrange for us to go back down to live with our grandparents, which meant a move from my new junior school to another one near to Gran's and then three months later a move back when we got home. Thus, I had five school moves in about two years. I liked it at Gran's, and was sad when I had to move back to the emotional void of the parental home.

The equipment for the grammar school was obtained slowly. I saved my pocket money and bought the fountain pen and geometry set, and did some odd jobs and picked peas in the late summer and bought a second-hand satchel. Gran bought me the plimsols and shorts. And Polly, who was back on leave from the RAF, bought me the football boots. The major item was the blazer, which Liz bought at five shillings a week from the local drapers; the five-pound blazer cost her seven pounds. I was almost set.

In early September I was introduced to education for the elite. The elite of that mining area of course, not the real elite who ran the country. It was my first real introduction to class division. In that small pool which I grew up in, all the kids had Yorkshire accents. They dropped the H from word beginnings. At the end of words, ing became in, hurrying thus becoming 'urryin'. Two-word groupings ending in 'not' were contracted. 'Would not' became 'wu'nt', 'should not', 'shu'nt', 'could not', 'cu'nt', 'do not', 'du'nt'. Vowels were pronounced as written and not subjected to the strangulated alterations affected by the upper class. Accents varied markedly across Yorkshire and those of Barnsley in the west and Hull in the east were almost mutually unintelligible to the natives of those towns. In my area the accent had the broader edges taken off it due to the huge influx of mineworkers from other areas in England and from Wales and Scotland. To southerners, it was as hard on the ear as all the others. The language pattern also was very direct and sometimes disturbing to those of the languid south because it often sounded aggressive.

There was none of the 'I say old chap would you mind awfully if I asked you to take this parcel to the post-office, the matter is rather urgent I would appreciate it if you could do it with all possible urgency.' It would be, 'Tek this parcel to t'post office and be bloody quick about it.' The latter form of discourse was expected and perfectly normal and given and taken without the slightest offence. Later in life I realised that the terseness of expression derived from the working environment in the locality. It was almost battle language. If an emergency occurred in a foundry or underground, flowery language was the last thing you needed. Rapid communication was the order of the day. I also found out that if a southerner heard a northern accent they would start to patronise by reflex. It could be a toff or a worker on a whelk stall, but as soon as you opened your mouth you knew what to expect.

The same thing applied with most southerners who had moved north. Teachers, clergy, etc, anyone who spoke with what was called 'received pronunciation,' or 'with a plum in their gob,' as the natives described it, would automatically adopt an attitude of hauteur when encountering the Yorkshire accent and address the locals as though they were talking to benighted savages. They knew that their world view on politics, society, sport and religion was of a superior nature to that of the cap doffing masses. It was not even worth debate—it was axiomatic. Intelligence did not come into it. It was not needed. The superior ones possessed what was needed—'the voice of authority'—and the local inferiors were supposed to obey.

This led to an endless and prolonged piss-take by the cap-doffers at the expense of that small elite group, who were blissfully unaware that they were being slow timed or having rings-run round them at every turn. And, to add insult to injury, this was being done by the unwashed lower orders who should have known their place. It was particularly hard for those kids whose parents had decided that they would leap the great accent-determined class barrier by making them take elocution lessons. After a few weeks of 'how now brown cow,' recited walking down to the fish and chip shop in one case, and a slow but noticeable shift towards received pronunciation, they were ribbed mercilessly by their classmates. One brother and sister were put through it particularly fiercely. The brother doggedly persisted in all circumstances with his new vowel sounds and by the fifth form had a cut glass accent or, as he would say, 'ket glarse'. The sister adopted the strategy of maintaining the local patois with her mates at school and youth club. At home and on holiday she spoke with the same accent as her brother. I always wondered if her parents, who had marked northern accents, felt inferior to their progeny.

But back to my first day at the grammar school. Two things struck me immediately. The first was the plain black academic gowns worn by the teachers. These were the daytime garb of all the graduates. The P.T. teacher, and the metalwork and woodwork teachers, did not have degrees. Thus, they did not wear these garments. On one day a year the staff wore the full gown with hood and cap. This was at the annual prize giving. The second thing which struck me was the accents. I had never run into so many people who used received pronunciation. I had heard it on the BBC, but otherwise it was totally alien to my world. Some teachers spoke with an accent which I call 'polite northern.' The H was never dropped and word contractions such as wun't, were never used. A slight northern twang was evident because of vowel usage, but the accent was homogenous and hard to place. Some of the teachers who had joined the 'posh' club via elocution, made slight mistakes in pronunciation or just overdid it a little. The kids were very acute in picking this up and when they did the currency and authority of the teacher became devalued because they had been revealed as one of the elocutionistas.

P.T., or physical training, eventually became known as the P.E. of today. As one very ancient member of staff said, 'I could never work out why they changed it from drill!' The grammar schools very much aped the public schools in what they did as sports—there was no rowing of course, or any exotic sport such as squash. There was a basic fare of cricket and athletics from easter till summer term. In the autumn and winter, we had cross country runs or time in the gym and a double period each week playing football. Most public schools did rugby, or rugger as it was known, as did many grammar schools. In our area there was almost no amateur rugby union played and thus football was pursued as a somewhat inferior alternative. It seemed to me that the whole purpose of the exercise was to produce a level of fitness which would be useful when we entered the army at eighteen as National Service recruits. In our case, this was rather wasted as National Service ended just before our year would have been called up.

Although I didn't realise it at the time, we were on the cusp of a massive change. The upper classes still held the reigns of authority, but the traces were being considerably loosened by the increasing wealth and full employment of the time and by the need for higher education. The increasing spending power of the teens drove the new phenomenon of pop stars, some of whom were being paid insane amounts of money. This was also changing. The first pioneers such as Tommy Steele and Cliff Richard had rapidly morphed into popular entertainers, making bland films such as *Tommy the Toreador* and *The Young Ones*. They had been swallowed by the professional management machine at the top of the music industry and regurgitated as wholesome non-threatening nice boys who could be watched safely by grannies and vicars. Then along came the Stones, Beatles and Kinks and progressively even wilder outfits who caused severe concern to the establishment.

A little later, in 1967, the establishment made itself look ridiculous by sentencing Mick Jagger to three months in prison for the possession of four amphetamine tablets. A public outcry followed and after a night in jail and an appeal the sentence was reduced to a conditional discharge. The cracks were growing, and the old moribund establishment was losing the easy control it had long enjoyed. The masses were becoming alarmingly less deferential. They were earning and spending, taking holidays in places like Spain. Some of them such as footballers and pop singers were being paid enormous amounts of money. Due to the increase in education with Comprehensive Schools starting to come in and a huge increase in sixth form and university places, the children of the lower orders were being equipped with the intellectual tools which enabled them to question and challenge the status quo.

Chapter 4
Starting to make sense of it

'When all makes sense, and you start to understand how things work you become unstoppable.'

Cristina Imre

Things started to make sense when I was about twelve. The dribs and drabs of education were starting to help slightly, and some subjects such as science helped much more than others. The thing which probably did it more than anything else was the huge amount of reading I did via the local library. But the Mark Twain thing was kicking in and it was information and observation integrating with my reading which was making the difference. It was the realisation that I was a tiny cog—a small and insignificant part of a huge number of interrelated systems—which was seminal. I realised it was not what teachers taught but how they taught, and how the school and schools generally were organised. This was vital. It was also the realisation that kids were just different. Some were naturally athletic because of the legacy bestowed by their genes; some were good looking and others had spots. Some were very bright while others were just bone thick. It was all part of life's lottery.

On the home front I was starting to make comments and ask questions which Liz was uncomfortable about. When I found out about the large interest paid on hire purchase and on the Provident checks she used to buy major items of clothing and suggested that she would get far more for her money if she put money in the post office and bought them using cash, she said, 'Oh, we can't afford to do that.' The stupidity and lack of logic in her reply left me non-plussed. Jed was very secretive about what he earned. They both smoked and I estimated that about a third of the total household income was going to pay for cigarettes. All of Jed's part-time window cleaning earnings went on his beer.

We never went on holiday. Our trips to the seaside were restricted to the annual bus trips to the coast via the local working men's clubs. Members paid into an outing fund for each child and the proceeds of some events bolstered that money. Perhaps ten shillings was paid in by the parent, but a pound or twenty-five shillings was drawn out for each child. The club hired all the available coaches for miles around, with often sixty or seventy of them setting off at 8am on the slow crawl of the 60ish mile journey to the east coast, returning at about 8pm in those days before motorways. We always took a big flask of tea, and egg or meat paste sandwiches. The kids on the coaches were all given a bottle of pop and a bag of crisps on the way in. When we got there, we ate the food then trailed round the amusements which we had been given tokens for. As young kids we always had candy floss and an ice cream, and a penny was invested in the laughing policeman to entertain us. Jed took us on petrol powered speedboats at a lake near the seafront after some cajoling by Liz. It was the only activity he ever did with us. It perhaps reminded him of his time in the navy.

As we got older, we were allowed to wander off on our own, with stern injunctions to be at the coach park before departure at six. We must have been ten or eleven by then. This meant that after the food they brought had been consumed, they could spend the afternoon in the boozer on the seafront and then have a snooze on the sands or in a deck chair till it was time to leave. I remember a discussion about the envelopes for the kids, which each contained twenty-two shillings that year. The question came up as we readied to go off on our own: 'How much should we give them?'

Gran, who was with us that day, said, 'The money is for them to have a good day out.'

Liz said, 'Well, we have to pay for other things like chips and rock for them,' which would have been about a couple of shillings.

Gran said, 'In that case, at least 10 shillings!'

A mean look passed over Jed's face. He said, 'Five shillings will be enough.'

Liz looked for a moment like she might try for more but then decided to stay silent. We were given five shillings each and told: 'Get yourself some chips out of it.'

We wandered up the sea front looking at the amusements, occasionally putting a penny in a slot machine and much less occasionally winning and then putting the money back into the machine. Five shillings comprised sixty pennies. Perhaps ten or fifteen of them would go in the slots or into the machines with cranes which picked toys up. I stopped investing in the latter after a few attempts, because I never won or saw anyone else do so. I learned to be entertained by observing people and listening. Couples would row, kids would be yelled at. The older teen girls would make eyes at the boys, who were usually smoking ostentatiously and being loud. Unmarried twenty-year-olds would take their young men off somewhere quiet to engage in the mysterious practice described as 'doing a bit o' courting.'

Many of the kids with me at the grammar school were taken on a week's holiday. The school was a place of differences. The education given was far from uniform. It was well known, for example, that if you got a certain teacher your chances of getting an O-level pass were low, but if you got another in the same subject it was almost guaranteed. The amazing thing was that in my day nothing was done about the crap teachers. They had an almost divine right to be there, untouched by years of dismal results which must have been glaringly apparent to the head and the local authority advisors, and in some cases the governors.

At some grammar schools, in middle class areas, the Governors were mainly clever and supportive and would usually ask the headmaster the right sort of questions. My school had been set up a few years earlier due to laudable efforts by some leading lights in the Labour Party. A few of the governors were intelligent but uneducated and with little insight into how the education system worked, but many were just dense, long serving party members. None of them had been at school beyond fourteen and none of them had the education which bestowed the analytical overview which would have enabled them to challenge a system which was just not delivering for many pupils.

The grammar schools had changed somewhat, in that slightly more emphasis was now given to science and foreign languages than previously. It was only just over a hundred years since the grammar school act of 1840 had introduced English and Science into the curriculum. Prior to that, the Quadrivium—initially pronounced quadri vium the four ways (roads)—and Trivium, (the three ways) had been taught, these had been mentioned in an early lesson but no explanation of the word meanings was given to us. I resorted to a copy of the Encyclopaedia Britannica: The Trivium established grammar, logic and rhetoric, and this foundation was built on to teach the geometry, astronomy, music and arithmetic of the quad-rivium. The arithmetic involved teaching about numbers as abstract concepts and the grammar of the trivium was Latin and Classical Greek grammar.

I managed to tease out the essential facts from those tomes but found it difficult. It seemed to me that they were written in such a way as to make them difficult to understand. It seemed more about the various authors showing how clever they were by the use of obscure academic language. As time went on, I realised that this was the case in many textbooks of that time. If your chemistry or maths teachers were incompetent or not willing to show you the full picture, you could not fill in the gaps by reading the books available. They had omissions when it came to imparting essential key facts. They were really only any use as a complement to what a teacher could tell you. I did find the Britannica useful in one respect, when at twelve years old I first heard of venereal diseases. I found the stuff about them with difficulty and used a dictionary to work out the meaning of the words in the text, but at the end of my study I was the class expert on syphilis and gonorrhoea.

Much of the ancient syllabus had been retained in the newly constructed curriculum, but new pressures were driving us towards science and technology. Industrial competitors in Japan, Germany and America were moving ahead and the government, which was always loth to spend money, was half-heartedly responding to it by increasing university places. Many of these were in the sciences, engineering and medicine. Though the first BSc was awarded in 1860, it has never been awarded at Oxford university. In 1940, only about 1% of the population went to university. By the time I got to grammar school it was approaching 3%. In 1940, very few women made it to university. They were still very much in the minority in 1955. In the majority of cases, those women who did get degrees went into teaching in grammar schools or girl's high schools. A few went into medicine, science and some of the other professions.

During my third year I realised that the allocation of places within the school was a cosy little middle-class carve-up. It worked like this: The head seemed to regard his success and that of the school as being measured by the number students he could get into Oxford or Cambridge. This was usually between one and three each year. The head, who had bushy eyebrows which were raised from time to time and were one of his very-effective weapons of control, had a passing resemblance to the actor Bela Lugosi. The dark shadow under his eyes and severe look meant that you would not want to encounter him in a graveyard late at night. The head operated with almost no input from the school governors. He presented his plans to them, and they almost invariably agreed. He seemed to have developed a self-image of the head of a minor public school. He was not keen on caning, but he was well up on the power of the psychology of a system built on esteem. Thus, he let the senior boys know that he regarded them and expected them to behave as decent chaps. He often used the phrase 'I would have expected better of you' to devastating effect, making any transgressor of his rules feel bad about themselves if they overstepped his bounds.

The school ran five forms, and rather than number them throughout the years as A B C D and E, they were cunningly disguised after the first year as 2AS 2AL 2X 2GA and 2G. 2AS translating as top stream with science or maths aptitude, 2AL indicating highest language ability. The X indicated those in the middle and the G streams indicated general lower ability. What actually happened was that an exam was held at the end of the first year and those with the highest marks went into the A classes and those with the lowest into the G streams. Thereafter, it was virtually impossible to move! No account was taken of the well-known educational fact that late development occurs. The methodology was crude and can only be judged by its effects. Generally speaking, those who were sifted into the higher classes were the brightest or those with middle class parents, who knew what was going on and made damn sure that their kids studied extremely hard for that vital end of first year exam. Vital, because it would determine your place in the school for the next four or six years, and would also have huge influence on your career prospects when you left.

I never found out whether Bela was just incompetent or a cynical class warrior who was determined to further the interests of middle-class types like himself. Whichever it was, it was undeniable that the best teachers were given to the top streams and the less able or incompetent were aimed at the lower orders. Sometimes a G streamer got a good teacher by accident because there was a gap in the timetable which needed to be filled.

I was particularly unlucky. Besides having clueless parents and no place to do homework or study apart from a freezing bedroom lit by a forty-watt bulb, I got the flu the fortnight before the exams at the end of my first year. This period was devoted to revision. I got back and remember being asked what I felt about taking the exams, having missed the vital revision. What did I know? They clearly knew how vital it was.

I did not have a clue. I murmured something about feeling alright about taking them, which absolved them from responsibility. My results were not good, and I ended up in the bottom form and there I stayed. At the end of the second year, our geography teacher, who happened to have taught all classes in that year, set us all the same exam. I gained the highest mark in the school. I found out later that he had told Bela I should be in a higher class. The response was the usual heavy dose of raised eyebrows.

The system the head had put in place did eventually rebound on him. Some poor teaching combined with the waste of talent caused by the rigid streaming and low expectations of the lower forms produced results which were noticeably poorer than other grammar schools in the area. Concerns were finally raised, and in a desperate attempt to improve things, the number of O-levels which could be taken was restricted to six for the lower forms and seven for the higher. It was felt that having more periods in fewer subjects would intensify the focus on each subject and produce more passes. In fact, it made things worse because it meant that subject choice was more limited. For example, I was lumped with metalwork, which was poorly taught and of little interest to me, instead of English Lit, which I would have sailed through.

In my case I was further disadvantaged by the lordly head's decision that the kids of the lower orders would be offered General Science rather than have a chance at Chemistry, Physics and Biology. I would have easily passed all of them, and in fact did easily pass them by dint of night-school classes in the eighteen months after I left the school. I dropped metalwork as being no use to me. I was looking at the prospect of leaving with four particularly useless O-levels when it came to pursuing my career choice and trying to get a job in a lab.

Maths was the other O-level that I was certain to fail. The maths teacher was peculiar. He was known as Jake throughout the school. He had a broad Yorkshire accent and must have been particularly brilliant at maths to have gained a place at university back in the 1930s. However, he had the strangest class-based attitudes, and lacked vision and intelligence. He lived in a world which had changed little since he was a young man and which, according to his world view, would never change. OK, the King had just died and unfortunately been replaced by a woman, but she would obviously be kept in line by her husband and an all-male cabinet until the natural order of things resumed. His misogyny emerged during one lesson when he started to express disapproval at the fact that women teachers had recently been awarded equal pay to male teachers on an equal work for equal pay basis. He didn't flesh his objections out but made it clear that males were obviously superior to females and thus should be paid more.

It seemed that he was unwilling to teach us mathematics, or if he did it was just in incomplete fragments. I don't know what his motivation was, but from various oblique remarks it seemed that he saw himself as some sort of upholder of the status quo. A status quo which was only admitting 3% of the population to university. So it was his job to limit access at all costs via the vital subject which he taught. He saw to it that it was, and no one in my class gained a mathematics O-level. I passed it about eighteen months after I left the school and subsequently went on to do a lot of university level higher maths, which I found no difficulty with due to the excellence of the tuition I received. I have never worked out whether Jake's attitude was encouraged by the establishment or condoned by it as being necessary, or if it was just the product of his own deluded world view. His dismal results must have been obvious to the head and to the LEA maths advisor and others in the town's education department. Perhaps they didn't care. Perhaps they condoned what he was doing.

At the end of my five years at the school I went into Bela's office. He looked down the lists of exam results, found my marks, which were high, and then said, 'These are surprisingly good results.' The cheeky bastard! Not to me they weren't, nor would they have been to anyone who had kept his eye on the ball in respect of pupil performance and development at the school which they were responsible for running.

I was now cast out into the world of employment, ill prepared for it by anything my parents had done or said to me and fitted up wrongly by my school for what I wanted to do. But I had observed. I was beginning to realise how the huge interrelated systems of control and vested interests worked in Britain and I now knew I could rely on only myself. I was lucky in one respect; I had managed to stay at the school for the full five years and the O-levels I had obtained gave me just enough of an 'in' to progress and to drag myself upwards. I managed to stay there by the skin of my teeth.

One evening, quite late, I heard a furious row downstairs. I crept out of bed and leant over the banisters. Jed had returned from the boozer where he had been 'advised' that I could leave school at fifteen. His advisors occupied the saloon bar of the local pub, which was just over the road from us. They were always offering him useful advice. I remember the time he came in just after the union had got them a big rise. He rather sheepishly lit up a Player rather than his usual Woodbine, saying 'I've been advised that these will be better for my chest.' It was all I could do to stop laughing out loud.

When they had accepted the school place for me, Liz and Jed had given a written undertaking that I would complete the full five years. The argument was that if I didn't, I would be depriving someone else who would have benefited from that place at the school. His suggestions unleashed a tirade from Liz. 'What will the neighbours say! What will Gran and the other relatives say! Your name will be mud by the time I have finished with you!' She went on and on. Jed finally surrendered. It was nothing to do with maternal protection, it was everything to do with what people on the street would say. Some of their kids had followed me to grammar school, as had my younger brother. Her fear of what the neighbours would say if I 'had' to leave early, with its connotations of family poverty, were a powerful motivator for her. This trumped Jed's cold meanness. He would have to wait another year before I could contribute towards his fag and beer money.

Chapter 5

The Big Boy's World

He that would eat the fruit must climb the tree

I left school as an undersized sixteen-year-old weighing nine and a half stone and was about five feet nine in height. The diet at home had done nothing for my size or general health. In the growth spurt at fourteen during puberty, Liz, hoping for more housekeeping money, had said to Jed, 'The boys are eating me out of house and home.' This was because, to fill ourselves up, we had started to eat a lot of bread. Jed said, 'Ration 'em, just two slices with each meal.' The result was that I developed abscesses. Liz, as hapless as ever, suggested kaolin poultices. When this did not work, she said, 'Jed will have to squeeze the stuff out.' I endured the considerable pain of this for over a week. Finally, she said, 'Oh, you'll have to go and see the doctor.' Something she didn't like, because she was frightened of authority, and she had a feeling that my poor state of health might be laid at her door in some way or other. I went to see the doc. He took a quick look, sighed, and then gave me an injection of penicillin and prescribed some pills and vitamin supplements. I was fine after a couple of days. Liz looked guilty, probably because once again it had shown that, as a parent, she was inept. Jed, in that respect, was just non-existent.

When I turned fourteen, he said to Liz, 'I want him down there with me on Saturdays.' This was to help with his window cleaning round. It was peculiar; there was never any direct communication with him. He said things, but I can never remember having a conversation with him. I suppose in other households it would have been, 'Look son, I would like you down there on Saturdays with me. There will be some extra pocket money for you.' But the order came indirectly through Liz. It was made clear that I would be paid, but rather than saying, 'Look, I do about sixteen houses and charge two and six for each and you will get sixpence for each one,' which would have meant him giving me eight shillings for the work, when we finished each cleaning session a sort of mean look always came over his face and he would jingle the change in his pocket and eventually give me four or five shillings, which was probably the least he thought he could get away with. Thus, he usually left with about one pound and fifteen shillings, which in those days would buy him about twenty-five pints or the equivalent in cigarettes, which were about four shillings (twenty new pence) for twenty. I was doing the downstairs windows and thus doing half the work. If Jed had been left to do the upstairs and downstairs windows, he would only have managed seven or eight houses.

The world outside was getting slightly brighter, with most households having televisions by the early sixties. There were two channels in black and white and TV was dull. There was some light entertainment—variety shows with singers who were OK but not exactly top notch. A new breed of comedy arrived based on the radio shows and teams of script writers. Most of the older comics who had been touring the variety halls for forty years with the same act could not cope. After they had appeared once they were finished because all their material had been used—seen by millions. Occasionally there were some hugely popular American imports such as the Lucy show and Bilko, but these were of limited availability, especially on the BBC, because of their expense. These were the shows which usually filled the peak viewing slots on Friday or Saturday evenings.

The BBC continued on its mission to be worthy. It had Children's Hour, from five to six, with shows like Crackerjack and Blue Peter and serialised children's dramas. There were

44

hour long plays on Armchair Theatre which went out just after Sunday Night at the London Palladium. The style was topical, but controversial subjects such as Apartheid and Black comedy were avoided. In the early days it went out live as did most TV, but after a young actor dropped dead halfway through one play, it moved to a pre-recorded format.

During the week there were long dreary interludes with anodyne time fillers. Lots of local news and the very solemnly delivered national news at 6 p.m. and 9 p.m. Generally dullish current affairs programs like 'Tonight' filled the gap until something livelier arrived at seven-thirty or eight. The thing was given a lift when 'Coronation Street' arrived in the early sixties. It was the first time that working-class lives had been portrayed by actors from those backgrounds and with genuine working-class accents rather than the awful stage school northern accents we usually saw on TV and on British film. The episodes of the first couple of years were full of social realism.

Lots of time was still given over to religion, where topics such as the differences between Anglican and Methodist doctrine or the sanctity of marriage were explored by clergy and academics. These were the hours when people turned the sets off and went to do something else until the boredom had finished. Despite the incredibly low ratings of these programs the BBC persevered with them due to pressure from the churches and the broadcasting acts, which said 110 hours of religious broadcasting must occur each year. After years of flogging a dead horse and miniscule audiences, those programs largely disappeared. 'Songs of Praise' is now about the only survivor. Here, hymns are sung enthusiastically by large congregations, bussed in for the most part from surrounding churches to fill the church used for the actual broadcast.

Most adults then gained some relief from the tedium in the evenings by visits to the clubs, pubs or cinema. For those in that twilight world inhabited by the teens, who were below drinking age, there was little to do. Youth clubs operated on some weekday evenings but not at weekends. Early on in life I had eluded the tedium by reading voraciously. I read most of Dickens and the other greats, such as Walter Scott and Robert Louis Stevenson. I read all the science fiction in the library and some stuff on science and chess. Jed did not like me reading—it was not useful. Useful involved physical work for him or around the house. However, it proved the foundation of my later success in life, because from junior school on I always came top in vocabulary tests and had an intuitive grasp of English forms of literary expression.

I had learned that I was largely on my own, that I could not count on my hapless parents who managed a hand to mouth existence on a week-by-week basis. I was less than impressed with the educational system I had encountered, but had a high regard for some teachers who had done their very best for us within the limits set for them. I had little regard for those who were running things because strict control of all aspects of working-class lives was in operation. Pubs and clubs closed at ten-thirty, and at ten on Sunday. Entertainment was limited. It seemed that the rulers wanted the masses to be church going, law abiding and obedient. Gambling was discouraged. Betting shops were reluctantly legalised in 1961, recognising that there was a huge underground network running off-course betting and that it might as well be legalised and regulated and taxed. The strongest opposition came from those involved in on-course betting and from the religious groupings who specialised in purveying misery to control their congregations.

Sex and sexuality were heavily controlled. The pleasure-reducing condom was available. It had been made available with reluctance, but to control disease rather than hold back procreation. Only dangerous back street abortions were available for the masses. The pill was yet to come—it arrived in the mid-sixties. Fear of pregnancy before marriage held back sexual pleasure and pleasuring to a huge degree. Consumer goods were more expensive than they should have been due to a nice little carve up called 'retail price maintenance.' This meant, for example, if Cadbury supplied a 6d bar of chocolate, it had to be sold at 6d. This was anti-competitive and the margins, which could be twenty-five or thirty percent, guaranteed small shop keepers a very good living. Their demise was signalled by the 1964 act which made the arrangement illegal. After that, the supermarkets were able to bulk buy and discount heavily. Most of the small shopkeepers who had been leeching off our local mining communities for years slowly went under and disappeared during the seventies and eighties.

The whole thing was underpinned by huge hypocrisy. The media portrayed the upper crust as being largely self-sacrificing, noble in intent and of high morals. The reality was that the higher classes gambled heavily in their clubs, shagged whoever they wished, and had none of the restrictions on their lives which were viciously applied to the lower orders. They were not subject to the legal strictures which held the working classes down. The lower orders had to be kept in line at all costs. After all, they were the fodder who fed the factories and mines and armed services. Iron discipline and subservience were two of the cornerstones of the system. For those of the upper-classes, abortions were no problem, they had the contacts and the money which gave them access to the top-drawer Harley Street surgeons who would do the operation because the physical or mental health of the mother was endangered in their opinion. An opinion more than somewhat influenced by the large fees they pocketed. For the working-classes, an attempt to procure an abortion, as the law quaintly described it, meant imprisonment.

In football the players, who were all working class, amazingly, were subject to a maximum wage, something which obviously never applied to anyone in professions which were almost exclusively reserved for the middle and upper classes. One or two players who signed on for foreign clubs and much higher wages were subjected to vilification in the press and excluded from national sides if they dared to break ranks and go for decent money. Players were getting a wage which was little better than average earnings, but all this ended in 1961 after the players union threatened a strike which would have meant huge losses for the clubs and for the gambling industry.

Top players quintupled their earnings overnight, but then were only getting the equivalent of £2000 a week. Ten years later, George Best was getting the equivalent of twelve to fifteen thousand a week but was still way behind the hundreds of thousands a week earned by the top players today.

Thus, I was out there slowly putting things together. I was grasping the big picture and realised it was going to be all down to me. I could have got a job at the pit and started on the route to being an electrical or mechanical engineer. A friend had done it, but a part-time three-year craft course and then a bridging year followed by four years getting an ONC and then a HNC and then two or three years doing the professional exams of one of the institutions, just did not appeal to me. All my time for ten years would have been spent working or studying. And I found mechanical engineering unimaginative and boring. Electrics had never appealed either. I wanted to do what I was good at and interested in, and that was chemistry. I tried for a few jobs when I left school but could tell at the interviews when I explained I had an O-Level in General Science that they were not interested. All the other candidates from the other grammar schools in the area had O-Levels in Chemistry and Physics.

I had an interview for a job as a quantity surveyor, but the company was going bankrupt, the interviewer had just had a nervous breakdown, and I was not interested. Thus, I bummed around for a bit working on a demolition site and earning as much in a day as some of my ex-classmates were getting as clerks on the railways for a week. The work was dangerous, with a couple of near fatalities and near serious injuries occurring while I worked there, so I moved on. The best I could get was a job in a dairy lab. I had words with the manager who said the job would come up soon, but I could work in the dairy for a few months with the other lads if I wanted to. I did that but was going to night school. I bought a new biology text by somebody called Mackean. It was the first textbook I had ever read which contained the full picture and was readable. I realised I could pass the exam without a teacher.

I took the Biology O-Level in the November and sailed through and took the maths and physics O-Level the following summer. I signed up for Maths and had a wonderful teacher who was an ex-insurance salesman. He had real insights and interest in the subject. I had read Teach Yourself Algebra and Geometry over the summer and Polly had sent me a copy of Hogben's *Mathematics for the Million*. All were incredibly helpful in filling in the gaps left by Jake. I swopped over to the alternative syllabus, which included Calculus, and I found it easy. I passed the maths O-Level in November with a good pass result.

My next step needed to be enrolment on an ONC Chemistry course. I left the dairy lab behind and got a job as a lab technician at a school. The money was worse, but the real prize was day release. They would have liked me to take the lab technicians' course, which included things like glass blowing. Fortunately, the local tech college did not do it, so I enrolled the next year for ONC Chemistry. At last I was on my way. I could see light at the end of the tunnel.

Having completed the first year of the ONC it was now easy to get a job in a lab. I had a think about things. I had tried to join the Parachute regiment when I was old enough, but although A1 in every other respect, I was turned down for having defective eyesight, being half blind on one side due to a lazy eye. I applied for a job with British Rail labs but was turned down for the same reason. Then I applied to the National Coal Board lab and was welcomed with open arms. When blundering around underground in very poor light, one eye was as good as two as far as the National Coal Board was concerned.

I had realised that no one was going to give me anything; it was all down to me. I now had a decent diet; I had started to weight train and did some boxing. My weight increased to twelve and a half stones, and I was fit and strong. I was ready for anything.

Chapter 6

The Wild Boys

'Rejoice, O young man, in thy youth?'

Ecclesiastes 11:9

'Eyup Twat.' The voice rolled through the dim light in the Old Barrel Café.

I looked over past the Juke Box. I could see three of the reprobates who I had worked with briefly at the Dairy. It was early on Friday. I walked over and Big Danny said, 'What are you doing here!'

'Same as you I suppose,' I replied. 'Nothing to do, bored. This place is the only one near the bus stop that has a Juke Box. I thought it might attract some birds.'

I pulled a chair round and sat down. Jase said, 'Who invited you to sit down?'

I said, 'Don't worry Claud, I won't tell your mam.' Jase shut up and coloured up. He had been christened Claud Jason—he hated his first name. Baz, the third member of the trio, just sat and glowered. Glowering was his speciality; he was big for his age, broad shouldered, and was good in a fight.

We sized each other up. Big Danny said, half approvingly, 'You look bigger.'

'It's all that school milk,' I replied.

He grunted. 'What you been doing?'

It was the second summer after leaving school. I had bought a second-hand set of Spur weights and a barbell for £3 and had been training in the shed at home. There was just room amongst the mower and other junk to put the weights. I had been given a few old copies of Health and Strength and had worked out a basic routine of presses, curls, and standing and bent rowing. I was doing lots of press ups and dips with chins on a crude apparatus I had built in the corner of the shed. I had put nearly three stone of muscle on since leaving school and I had grown and was now just six feet tall.

Physical Culture, as it was called in those days, fascinated me. We had done nothing about different body types at school. The natural differences between huge men such as the best British shot putter, Arthur Rowe, and the slim long-distance world record holder runners like Gordon Pirie, became clear to me. Both were excellent at their sports, but not because they had decided just to do them. It was because their body types, endomorphic in the case of Rowe and very ectomorphic in the case of Pirie, ideally fitted them for those sports. But these were still those pre-steroid days of the gentleman amateur and the naturally talented. Steve Reeves was still a top body builder, ex Mr Universe and latterly film star. He had won the Universe with a forty-eight-inch chest, twenty-six-inch thigh and eighteen-and-a-half-inch bicep. Figures which today wouldn't get him into the final of Mr Barnsley.

There had been nothing about this sort of thing during the P.T. lessons at school. It was more or less just football, cricket, and cross country runs—which few completed. Numerous shortcuts were known, and some pupils even dropped into a local transport café for a tea and a fag on the way round. There was equipment in the gym to vault over or climb—the routines were boring and there was no coaching, we just did them by numbers, mostly half-heartedly running at the vaulting horse and getting over or in the case of the fat boys not managing it. There was no recognition that for some pupils a vault was impossible—you were lined up and expected to run at the thing and get over or face the humiliation of not being able to. No explanations were given about body type, muscle groups or cardiovascular or strength workouts. I suppose somebody at the top of the tree had some sort of idea that we needed to do all that stuff to get us halfway fit, ready for National Service. But now National Service had gone, I was working out ten times as hard as I had done at school because I could now see a purpose to it and enjoyed it.

I also started to do a bit of boxing. The coach was an ex British Empire champ. He was incredibly knowledgeable about the sport and knew a lot of dodges which were very useful in a boxing match. He had also been in the colonial police in the Far East and in the rough African ports. He showed me a couple of moves which were decidedly not Queensberry rules. He said, 'I shouldn't show you this really, but I know you are bright enough not to use them unless you are really up against it, against three or four.' He liked me. I was a natural 'southpaw' which surprised him because it was rare in a right hander. He wanted me to go on to a local top amateur club. He could see that I was strong and fast with a long reach and had what he called a boxing brain.

I liked the sheer exhilaration of boxing and was good at avoiding a head punch. He made me do work with a medicine ball to harden my mid-section and said, 'If you get that area tough most body shots won't hurt you, then you just need to avoid the knockout punches.' He would have liked me to get involved in local matches and then in area championships, but I drew back. I knew one bloke who had a flat boxer's nose, who worked on the pit top at the local pit. I found out eventually that he had over four hundred contests as an amateur and had won a junior ABA championship. I heard one of his work-mates say he was now so punch-drunk that he usually had to be told which bus stop to get off at when he went home from work. I didn't want to end up like that. My brain seemed to be one of the better ones, and I did not want my most useful asset damaged.

The three at the table were known as youths who were not to be messed with. In the occasional bouts of fisticuffs which erupted from time to time in the village they would come out on top. Fist fights were amusing to watch. There were those who were useless with little strength and little idea how to fight. Drink often caused the fights; it also made the useless even more useless. They would go straight down against a good opponent. If both were good, after a certain amount of punishment equally matched opponents were usually sensible enough to realise that the fight would produce no winner and it was sensible to walk away. Sometimes the combatants even shook hands. I had been involved in a few fights and had won all of them, and news gets around. Also, I had been told that one of the local hard cases had been threatening my younger brother. I had walked up to him at a local beat-night and offered him 'outside' to settle the matter. He backed down in front of a big crowd which pushed my reputation up no end. He told me that whoever had said he had been making threats had been talking bollocks and I should check them out.

I realised that I had been set up with respect to the local hard man; it was a good object lesson—a trap to avoid in future. I eventually got hold of the youth who had set me up, in an alley at the back of some local shops. No doubt he thought I would have got a good hiding had I been so foolhardy as to make a challenge. It didn't turn out as he expected. I could see he was sweating and shitting himself, probably because I had one hand round his throat. I considered giving him a pasting, but it was just not worthwhile. It would have been like punching a woman. I explained to him that if I ever ran into him again, I would pound his slimeball face into pulp. I only ever saw him in the distance after that. Whenever he saw me, he would rapidly move off in the other direction. After a while he got a job in Birmingham and left the area.

Back in the café, Big Danny was holding forth. 'It's all bollocks!' he said. 'Schools, churches, royalty, courts, the police, the forces. We need bits of it, but it's all there mainly to keep us in our fucking place. We are stuck at the bottom of the shit heap, what chance do we have of getting out of it? They let us work in shit jobs for shit money. At the dairy when you get close to eighteen the manager tells you to fuck off and find another job because at eighteen you got the full adult rate.' I was well aware that this was common practice in the local area in the smaller firms, warehouses and similar, which depended on cheap unskilled youth to do the work. If you had an apprenticeship, you were protected and usually stayed with the firm after twenty-one if you were any good or were related to a foreman or similar at the works.

I agreed with what he was saying. He hadn't thought it through, but his gut feeling about the way things worked was right, apart from the fact that you could get out of the shit if you set your stall out to do that. It wasn't easy. What was easy was to drift with the crowd, to smoke and drink and maybe have an occasional bet and moan about things. To do what my parents had done and meander, living with just enough to get by on week by week and with no financial reserves. I think the final indication that they were pathetic in this respect came when Gran died. I was eighteen.

The insurance that she had paid into all her life paid for the funeral and we all went back to her place for some sandwiches afterwards. There were a couple of crates of beer and some feeble attempts to cheer my Grandad up. He just seemed stunned by it all, sitting there in misery in the poorly furnished house that he had shared with her for more than forty years. He was small and still had that wiry strength which characterised miners. He sat puffing at his pipe, smoking the acrid smelling black twist which he had used since he was in the trenches in the Great War. He didn't seem to be quite coherent. Later on, they realised he had suffered a minor stroke due to the stress of her death and would be a semi-invalid for the rest of his life.

Several months later I wandered down to the cemetery. It was Gran's birthday. I had picked some wild daffodils in a local wood. When I got there, I found a small posy which was from Polly and Grandad. I laid my small bundle next to it. What surprised me was the lack of a gravestone. When I got back home, I asked when one would be erected. Liz responded sharply and seemed guilty in some way. 'We can't afford a gravestone,' was the reply, with the emphasis on the 'we', and then rapidly closed the discussion. A few months later she told me with a serious look on her face, 'Your grandma has got her gravestone.'

I was curious regarding who had paid for it, but she brushed my questions aside, repeating, 'Your grandma has got her gravestone!' and that was it, conversation terminated. It was obvious that the other members of the family had paid for it, and she wanted some credit without having to lie about what her and Jed might have contributed out of the holy fag and beer money. These were obviously an essential household expense, which could not be reduced or diverted to other uses under any circumstance. If she had been clear on the contribution made by them it might have emerged later that she had been dissembling, something she would not risk. I noted what had happened as another example of her behaviour in trying to massage facts or to give as little information away as possible, to put herself in the best possible light. She had been wary of speaking to me since I turned fourteen and the trivial incident in which I had exposed her in a direct lie. The response then was a temper outburst, and then she stormed off in a nicely manufactured fury at having been found out.

I just spent more and more time out of the house. Riding round the country lanes after work on a bike I had bought for a fiver. I just rode and thought, sometimes stopping at some secluded spot or in summer lying on flattened corn with the bike hidden, just looking up at the blue sky and the clouds drifting by. It was certainly all bollocks, but how did you get out of the ground-down, non-thinking, hapless and inept ranks of the masses? How did you avoid the petty snobbery of the small minded, two up two down inhabiting, Daily Mail reading, pursed lipped, Tory voting, rigidly permed, working class matrons who seemed to infest the next layer up? How did you get past the barrier which consisted of those who had some status and a little money, the comfortably off shopkeepers, teachers like Jake, the clergy I had met? Those who thought a clerk or council worker was superior to a mineworker, even though he could be earning two or three times what they did. There had to be a way out. I needed a plan.

Back in 'the Barrel' big Danny had wound down. We all sat looking morosely at the last inch of coke in the bottom of the bottles. Part of the game was to sit there as long as possible with just one bottle in front of you, brooding. We were world class at it. On one occasion we had managed two hours with just one bottle in front of us. The woman behind the counter occasionally looked across with some anxiety. She would rather not have us in the place. We were potential trouble. Her anxiety increased noticeably when we all started wearing our uniform, which was a leather jacket, black tee shirt and jeans. This was the dress mode of the juvenile delinquent. They knew this because it was portrayed like that on TV and film. A few years earlier potential hooligans wore Teddy Boy suits, but they had mostly disappeared. The leather jacket was the uniform of bikers, who also has an unsavoury reputation thanks to the media. But bikes cost a lot of money, which was something we lacked.

Occasionally, a shopper or worker dropped into the place and had a cup of tea and a slice of cake. Even more occasionally, the older ones would put sixpence in the Jukebox and the mechanism would slide into action and choose a record. Usually something bland by one of the crooners of the late fifties or early sixties. Pat Boone or Ronnie Carrol or similar singers. I thought they were dire.

Sometimes a young temptress, or a group of them, would call in to the place on the way to the pictures or congregate there before going on to one of the pubs which got quite lively after about seven on Fridays and Saturdays. They were universally known as 'birds' in those far off days. I remember one young bird. She walked into the place with her hair up in the big bouffant style which was popular then. She was quite heavily made up and wore very high heels. She looked round and lit a cigarette and moved to the counter and got a coffee and then sat down near the window. She was looking across at us while pretending not to. After a bit she got up and leaned over the Juke Box and selected a couple of records. This time it was Elvis, 'Jail House Rock'. Thank God! Something with a decent beat. Followed by 'G.I. Blues' from the 1960 film of that name.

I could see her moving sensuously to the beat. Big Danny, seeing my look of interest, leant across and said softly, 'Jailbait'. I took a harder look. She was smallish and with not much in the way of breasts. Danny said softly 'She's twelve, thirteen in two months. My cousin is in her class at secondary.

I said, 'Never.' I sat back, thinking. Being with these three was hugely educational. After that I spent much more time looking below the surface appearance if a piece of promising totty got anywhere near me.

Danny said, 'She's a spoiled brat. Her mother runs a hairdresser, and her dad works the clubs with a singing and comedy routine. She had lots of money and can afford to smoke and buy make-up and nice gear. She is ready for it but avoid at all costs! I don't think we would qualify anyway. We look OK, nice builds, but she will want a bloke with money and a car.'

After a while we drifted off, but not before arranging to meet every Friday from then on at 'the Barrel' and then move on to see if anything else was happening around the town. I got back to the youth club. My main interests there were the boxing group and the little side room with some weights in it. Most of them had been cut out of plate or manufactured from discarded machinery up at the pit. The youth club had been set up the Miner's Welfare Organisation. It was the usual thing; a couple of table tennis sessions were going on and some of the younger girls were jiving to the music scratchily emitted by an old record player. The girls were experiencing the first full flood of hormones and growing tits, some very noticeably so. They were all about one thing, getting a boyfriend. Once that object had been achieved, they spent much less time in the club because that's where the competition hung out and they did not want their boyfriend straying.

One notable feature was the groupings. Some of the girls had jobs. These had mostly gone to the local secondary modern school and worked in local factories, shops, or hairdressers. Another group had left school with two or three GCE O-Levels in arts subjects. This lot had gone to college and made a big thing of it. In this case it was the local Art College which was incredibly easy to get into. It ran a number of basic City and Guilds courses, in design, window dressing and similar, in addition to some more advanced stuff. After leaving they almost all ended up working in Marks and Spencer or similar outfits rather than setting up as interior designers or graphic artists. The cleverer girls from the Grammar who had left school armed with four or five O-Levels, including English, usually went to work in the various Coal Board or Council or similar offices. They, very noticeably, generally did not attend the youth club.

There was another group of girls who did not bother with the youthie. I worked it out later that these were the big fit and good-looking ones with the high sex drives. They almost universally had older boyfriends and most of them were out drinking with them from fifteen or sixteen. They always smoked and all looked nineteen or twenty. They wouldn't be seen dead in a place full of juvenile females and spotty youths playing ping pong. Maybe it was me, but the hot ones always seemed to have big tits. Height didn't matter.

One of that group had been christened 'Little Queenie' after the Jerry Lee Lewis record. She fitted the lyrics perfectly—short with black hair piled high, very black eye make-up and the highest high heels it was possible to get. She smouldered, drooling sex when she walked into a pub, usually with a cigarette dangling from the corner of her voluptuous lips. Only seventeen when I met her, she had been just about killing her twenty-eight-year-old boyfriend, whom she had been ravishing for at least three years. If he was aware of the illegality of it when they started having sex when she was fourteen, he did not seem to care. He was the son of a local bookmaker, drove a sports car and had lots of money. The 'respectable' girls in the area hated her. She was having lots and lots of what they would have loved to have been getting. She didn't talk about it, but they all knew exactly what the score was, she was the one who always carried a couple of packs of Durex in her handbag. If they had dared to do that their mothers would have killed them. But she had done the cost benefit analysis of not being respectable and had decided early on what her priorities were. I had also determined that the sex, but certainly not the smoking, was going to be high on my list.

Lots of the local youth were similar to the girls. Tie wearing clones of respectable dads and respectable mothers, the cloning often going as far as wearing sports jackets with leather patches sewn at the elbows and smoking pipes. They were usually physically weak, or weak by my standards. They were going to end up exactly like their parents twenty years down the road. That was the last thing I was going to do. I hadn't worn a tie since I left school—it was a symbol of conformity, of servility or regimentation. It was a relic of when serfs wore iron or leather collars to show their station in life. As far as I was concerned, a tie was for the brown-nosing gaffer's lads who were trying to get the foreman's job.

Chapter 7

The facts of life – Theory and practice!

'Sex is like money; only too much is enough.'

John Updike

I didn't realise it at the time but apparently the male sex hormones peak at about eighteen and then slowly decline. This is fine if you have a low sex drive; if its high you are just about going crazy thinking about it all the time. Another thing about sex in the early sixties was the lack of information about it. There was nothing about contraception, abortion or the venereal diseases. What little information there was circulated via gossip. The information was often wrong.

I returned frequently to the *Encyclopaedia Britannica*, which was my bible for sexual information, persevering with the difficult language until I had a decent picture of the mechanics of sex. It was useful to know, for example, that the female usually ovulated about fourteen days after the end of her period. It was the pre-pill era, but I worked out that this probably meant that unprotected sex, which was the best sort as far as I was concerned, could probably be indulged in during the seven days after the period ended and the seven days before the next one started. The middle fourteen days were the danger area in which unwanted pregnancy could occur. Avoiding pregnancy using this knowledge was known as the rhythm method, the rhythm being that of the female menstrual cycle. I later learned that some Catholics used this method. Any attempt at artificial contraception was frowned on by the churches and especially by the Catholic Church. Some wag had later described the method as 'Vatican Roulette.'

I also knew from some old army types that sex with prostitutes, which was generally looked down on by them, could only be contemplated if the male wore a Durex. I also learned subsequently that prostitutes came in different varieties. It was rare for one of the higher-class ones to catch a venereal disease or pass it on, because they made sure that French letters were always worn and were wise to other infection avoiding measures such as douching with weak solutions of antiseptics. As far as they were concerned, 'Pro' meant professional. VD was usually the preserve of the low life, bottom of the rung tarts who had little intelligence or who were too screwed up or drunk to care. I knew from one of the lads who worked in the local pathology lab that syphilis was rare in our area. If it occurred, it was almost invariably from a lorry driver who had picked it up from a prostitute in Hull or Liverpool and who had done a delivery from the port and made an overnight stay in the town while driving across country.

Despite the best efforts of the churches in opposing the sale of condoms and the dissemination of any information regarding prophylaxis, condoms were sold in chemists and in some barber shops. The realisation had slowly come to the powers that be, that despite the moral dimension, practical steps had to be taken to reduce the disease after it was discovered that throughout the Great War between forty and fifty thousand men were constantly out of action due to them catching venereal diseases.

Those growing up in the twenty-first century would find the huge sexual repression of the 1950s and early 1960s extremely hard to understand. Despite the strict laws preventing abortion, and contraception being frowned on, an undercurrent of salaciousness was always present in the press. The Sunday tabloids were inordinately fond of articles about Call Girls and similar, especially if they were attractive. The dangers of Soho strip joints and similar red-light areas featured frequently in juicy and detailed articles. Nothing graphic could be written about sex, but the journalists writing the stuff were masters of suggestion and inuendo via pretending to describe the pitfalls in great detail and by similar pseudo-moralising.

Similar strict censorship controlled what could be shown on film or TV. Nudity was available in the theatre, but only in unmoving statuesque poses in theatres such as The Windmill, which had done a huge amount to keep up wartime morale with its shows. This stretched the censorship laws to their limits. Anodyne and non-sexually arousing nudity was permitted in some health and efficiency type nudist magazines. Teenagers and many adults operated almost in an information vacuum as far as sex was concerned. There were snippets of distorted facts circulating, such as the idea that pregnancy would occur only if both male and female orgasmed at the same time. Or if the woman didn't orgasm, she couldn't get pregnant. A few were very worldly wise about contraception and knew about douching and permanganate solutions to stop infections, but generally ignorance ruled.

My initiation into the mysteries of sex had started when I was approaching sixteen. A babysitter used to look after the four-year-old next door so that the parents could get out to the pub on Saturday night. I got chatting to her as she sat on the porch having a fag. She was big and ordinary looking, but after a while she invited me in when the kid had gone to sleep. We sat on the sofa, and she started to kiss me and pushed my novice's hands towards her breasts. The experience was mind blowing. She started to rub my crotch and then pulled my zip down. She seemed pleased with what she saw and while continuing stroking with one hand she deftly removed her knickers with the other and then pulled me towards her open legs.

Wow! Bliss! Ecstasy! She was writhing almost instantly as I thrust my virgin apparatus deep into her deliciously moist vagina, then she started to orgasm and couldn't stop. I rapidly followed. She grinned and said, 'We will do more later; I will show you what I like.' I learned an awful lot about the mechanics of sexual pleasuring from her, things which for some reason didn't seem to warrant a write up in the Encyclopaedia Britannica. It turned out that Christine was very highly sexed. Not a nympho but she had made her mind up by the time she was fourteen that the two things she really liked in life were cock and nicotine. She wasn't particular about the order in which they arrived as long as she got plenty of both.

My education at her hands continued for several weeks, but one Saturday she didn't turn up and much to my disappointment the new babysitter was the middle-aged auntie of the bloke next door. I heard later that Christine was knocking off one of the local miners. He had plenty of money and I heard she married him a year later. I liked Christine. She wasn't too bright, but she knew what she liked and had none of the hang-ups about sex which beset most of the local maidens.

After that it was months of quick fumbling in the back seats in the pictures or round the back of the youth club. Full intercourse just never happened. I was always willing to indulge the local girls who needed to be pleasured, and although I could tell they were exceedingly needy it never seemed to get there. I worked out that it was partly the age of the group. Their older sisters seemed to be indulging as far as I could tell, but that was on the basis of an engagement ring and the imminent prospect of marriage. For the younger set the terror of pregnancy in those primitive and repressed days was inimical to the huge pleasure which could be found in sex.

Unwanted early pregnancy before marriage occasionally happened. The burden of shame fell largely on the girl involved. Sometimes a rapidly arranged 'shotgun' marriage could retrieve things. Sometimes, one or both prospective parents was too young to marry. In those cases, the girl was sent away when birth was near, to homes, invariably run by churches, for 'naughty' girls. Those running the places, often nuns, had the warped idea that the pain of childbirth was punishment for the sin which had been committed by giving way to carnal desires. The babies were whisked away for adoption with the young mothers unable to do anything to prevent it. The children almost invariably went to people with church connexions.

'The Barrel Boys' continued meeting on Fridays. Sometimes we just walked around the town in our uniform of leather jacket, blue jeans and white tee shirt. On other occasions we would walk down to a small funfair which had a permanent camp on waste land near the river. The fair was open on Fridays and Saturdays. 'The Waltzer,' a large roundabout with big rotating cars on its deck, was a permanent fixture. There was a hot dog stall and a few side shows. During weeks when the big fairs operated, they packed up and went off to make some money, but during the quite weeks they were satisfied with just ticking over in their semi-permanent location. The fair attracted mainly teenagers. Groups of youths on their way into the town's boozers met there, and some of the more wayward girls of the area. It was centrally located on three main bus routes and near a picture house and a couple of pubs. Teens coming out of the early showing often drifted down to the amusements and had a look around, a hot dog and coke before getting the bus home.

The fair represented excitement. The Waltzer blurted out some heavy pop music. Usually American and chart toppers of the sort that the BBC just didn't play. The dynamic was interesting. The fair was run by a tough crew from the travelling families. They were used to dealing with trouble which was probably why it rarely occurred. Sometimes a drunk would kick off about the side shows being fixed so you could never win. They were, but we all knew that and never bothered spending on them. The ride operators looked fairly bored most of the time as the fair was quiet compared to the huge hustle and bustle of crowds which happened at the big events.

One evening it was drizzling lightly, and no one fancied the fair or a stroll round the town. Big Danny said, 'Let's go down to the market square.' Jason wasn't too keen because of the reputation of the place. The marketplace was the location of the towns rough boozers and a couple were known to be active haunts for some of the town's prostitutes. I was curious and Baz grunted assent. It was just a couple of hundred yards to the first of the pubs, which was called The Bull. We set off, unconcerned about the fact that we were all under the age which permitted buying drink in a pub. We were all big lads however and anticipated no difficulties. We had one acquaintance who was short, baby-faced and twenty-one, who was always asked if he was old enough to drink if he entered a strange boozer. On one occasion when he went for a drink with us, we were all seventeen, but he was the only one challenged about his age, much to his fury.

We got there just after eight. It was just starting to get dark. We strolled into the place and were the subject of curious stares from the much older clientele, most of whom seemed to be regulars in the place. Big Danny had got our money from us before we went in and went to the bar and asked for four pints. He was six feet five, blond haired and with that square jawed rough look which deterred trouble. We were all unusually broad shouldered and tall for our age. He was served by the landlady who sounded him out. 'Not seen you boys in here before.' The comment was a question which invited a reply. 'Yeah,' said Danny. 'A bit out of our territory. We heard about the place and thought we would look it over.' She seemed reassured and stood back, looking around, then pulled out a pack of cigarettes and inserted one into a shortish holder. She lit the cigarette and took a long drag. She must have been about fifty. Very dark hair and make-up with a low-cut dress and phenomenal tits which seemed to be pulling my eyes towards them.

We wandered towards an unoccupied table and sat down. After a while, Jimmy Jones walked in. He was a few years older than us, small and sharp featured. Girls in the village avoided him for some reason. He got a drink. We could see that the barmaid knew him and rapidly realised he must be a regular. He turned around and when he saw us, he came over and sat down. The landlady on seeing that he knew us seemed further reassured. Undoubtedly, she would be pumping him for details about us later, but she was thinking that we were probably not tearaways looking for excitement, which with young men was often accompanied by trouble.

Jimmy looked around furtively then leant forwards and started to explain the setup in the place. I had noted one or two rough looking tarts but had no idea if they were on the game. Jimmy said, 'Glance at the long seat along the wall next to the bar—don't stare, don't all look at once.' I had noticed it when I had walked in. A bloke in his early thirties was sat there with a woman of similar age. They were both drinking large whiskies. Occasionally he broke out into wild, almost half deranged laughter. It looked like he had a cleft palate or some similar defect. She had false teeth and a dingy looking mouth. She smoked constantly and periodically hurled abuse at him or was pointedly unpleasant. Two women sat next to them, probably in their late twenties, both had a sort of on the game, tarty look about them. Two other women in black leather coats stood near them, conversing. One looked young and the other was plump and about forty as far as I could tell.

Jimmy said, 'The two stood up are mother and daughter. The daughter was brought up on the game and has been getting it since she was about thirteen. The two women sat down are a pair of thick, crude-mouthed tarts. Not quite bottom rung but heading there. Those two are being pimped by a Pole who came here during the war. The older one handing the abuse out has been at it for over twenty years. She works solo and has had some good hidings for turning pimps down. She is a real nasty piece of work. She really has her hooks into the bloke next to her. He is a clerk on the railways. He comes here every Friday night and spends all his weeks wages on her. He tells everybody that she is his girlfriend. She really knows what pulls his strings and he loves the abuse. I was told he has never fucked her, but she makes him shoot his load in other ways and then throws him out till the following Friday.'

Jimmy said, 'Don't ask about the other ways—nobody knows, but whatever she does to him he keeps coming back for more and seems keener than ever. If he had the money, he would be here every night.' Occasionally, one of the whores would get up and disappear and then come back twenty minutes to half an hour later. I couldn't work out how it worked but some signal was arriving telling them that they were needed. Jimmy, 'They need to be a bit careful; the police know the score and usually turn a blind eye, but soliciting for the purposes of prostitution is still illegal.'

I asked Jimmy what he was doing in the place. He looked at his feet and said, a little sheepishly, 'I feel comfortable here, I fit in. There is something about me, the girls in the village don't want to know. It's like I've got some sort of invisible disease they can all see, but I can't. There are quite a few similar get in here, older men mainly. They get a kick out of being near the girls, a couple of them supply Durex to them, some are clients some not. One of them is an ex-Methodist retired police inspector from Norwich. He must have been tortured by his "un-natural" desires for sex during most of his life. When he retired, he came to live here, he packed the church in and surrendered to his nature. He hires one of the older pros every week for a couple of hours. She has to dress up in long leather boots with high stiletto heels and then piss on him and abuse him.'

I was wide-eyed in amazement and spluttered, 'You're joking.'

He replied, 'No. I've seen the pictures!' Jimmy looked at me and said, 'One thing I have learned over the years is that sex involves every activity that you can possibly imagine and many more that are way beyond imagination. Most young lads like you think that sex is all about sticking your cock into some willing maiden and then rapidly emptying your balls. Its far more than that. As you get older you might learn. Most never do, though. They live in that buttoned-down world of the older generations, repressed, frustrated and miserable. And often wanting to take that frustration and misery out on somebody else. I have chatted to the retired police inspector. He worked with the Met CID for a bit. He says at the top end of society they do exactly what they want when it comes to sex. Usually with each other. They tend to be intelligent and have lots of imagination when it comes to sex. Also, lots of the blokes from that class are warped and emotionally stunted by being sent off to public schools from the age of eight.

'Anything goes. Drugs, underage, homo stuff—lots of that—animals, anything you can think of.' One senior police officer told him, 'That lot would have fitted in fine during the decadent days in ancient Rome.' He had no time for them, but they had the money, and all the top lawyers and judges were from that class in any case. If they didn't do anything silly or in public, they were fireproof. Even if they did, a pay-off could usually shut the complainant up. Lots of women would prefer that rather than be ruined reputationally by people knowing she had been raped.

He went on, 'Even up here there are lots of seemingly respectable middle-class types who very discreetly indulge their pleasures and perversions. I know of one vicar who is a client, a couple of solicitors and a bloke with a PhD in chemistry who teaches somewhere. He's a portly, pipe smoking overly hearty, rugger type, never married. You know the sort.' Actually, I didn't, but nodded as though I did. 'That last bloke was picked up by one of the girls while he was scrabbling through the dirty magazines on a market stall. She took him for a drink, he paid, and then back to her place. From their chat she had an idea of what would turn him on. She used the old trick of leaving for a few minutes and then getting changed and walking back in, in some interesting gear. She told me that he came into his pants as she was unbuttoning him. After that he was hooked. He is still a regular, in his sixties and a lot happier, apart from the nagging fear that somebody might find out.'

Jimmy looked up. The matronly type was looking at him impatiently. He got up and went across. He looked across at me, winked, and they turned and left. I wondered where to. I found out later that the woman had been a pro and now had a big Victorian house in the decaying centre of the town. Several of the girls rented rooms there. Jimmy wasn't interested in doing sex, but he got turned on by talking about it. He had a regular Friday night date with the woman and after a few drinks at one of the towns posher pubs he used to take her for a meal. In return, he got lots of juicy titbits about what was happening in the local sexual underworld.

I found what Jimmy had to say wonderfully enlightening. It filled in a big blank in my rapidly developing picture of how things worked. It was becoming clear to me that sex was one of the big drivers of society. It was used to control people; it was a key commodity, exploited directly or indirectly in most human activities. It sold papers, sado-masochistic parts of it were exploited in activities ranging from prostitution to religion. Amazingly, most people just could not see what was going on. I realised that Jimmy, far from being some sort of pervert, was actually one of the enlightened. I later realised that many were tortured by their sexuality and tortured to the point of desperation or near madness. Desires were dulled by smoking or drinking or diverted by substituting other sorts of excitement such as gambling for those deeper desires.

I failed to understand why prostitution was not legalized and controlled, with regular compulsory testing of the girls.

Jimmy said, 'Just think who makes money out of it.'

I said, 'You mean the girls and pimps?'

Jimmy smiled and said, 'Don't be daft, what about the lawyers who get paid to defend them in court, the police who get backhanders to turn a blind eye, the moral crusaders who make money out of the repressed through donations, the churches, the newspaper men who peddle sleazy stories about prostitutes in the Sunday papers, pubs like this where the trade goes on, the drug companies who supply the antibiotics, the blackmailers. If a politician sensibly suggests that brothels should be legalised and regulated, he will lose a lot of votes from those with vested interests in keeping things just as they are. They don't want it ended, they want to keep it just as it is and keep on getting nice little earners on the back of it.

'The religious types pretend to be concerned about the girls but underlying that is a deep-seated hatred. I can't quite work it out. A hatred of sexual pleasure? A hatred of women as descendants of Eve who started sexual sin off? It's very deep, but they are psychotic about prostitutes. Some preachers rail about sin, immorality and work themselves and their congregations into a religious frenzy, to the point of orgasm apparently.'

He grinned and continued, 'It's a sort of hobby of mine. Some blokes collect beer mats, I soak up information about sex. I ought to write a book.

'It's a weird thing with pros. The girls don't enjoy the sex. After hundreds of blokes a year have used them the thought of intercourse makes a lot of them feel disgusted. Some women hate prostitutes, the tightly buttoned up types, who think that the pros are getting lots of what they have never had: sexual pleasure. They should see the reality. I could show you some of the old pros and the states they are in after a life of disease, abortions, and being attacked by customers or beaten up by pimps for not earning enough. Some are ravaged, others are mental, quite a few commit suicide. Their world is sleazy, sordid and harsh, and often driven by poverty. Lots of the girls who come into it have been abused as kids. Some are stupid, some are idle and make the calculation that they would sooner be laid on their back taking cock rather than working eight-hour shifts at the sweet factory. Just occasionally one gets it right and makes enough to retire on, but they are rare. It usually needs a fair bit of intelligence to do that. Most girls settle for enough to pay for their fags and booze and pay the rent and support their kids if they have any.'

He went on, 'The important thing to remember about sex is control. The ruling classes do whatever they like but the lower orders need to be kept in line. Sex within marriage is allowed —though somewhat reluctantly by the churches. They are a bunch of perverts. They don't believe sex should be enjoyed— just performed to procreate. Sex is just about the most pleasurable activity ever invented; the orgasm excruciatingly pleasurable for those that have them. Some don't. It might be physical or because they are so sexually repressed by their upbringings that they are repulsed by it. I just don't understand it.'

Just then the heavy-set matronly woman came into the pub. She looked across and saw Jimmy and waved. 'Got to go,' he said, 'but if you ever want to know anything about the marketplace and the girls, come and talk to me. I'm a bit like a sponge. I soak all the local sleaze up.'

I had always thought that Jimmy was a bit weird and none too bright. After chatting to him I realised he was very astute and articulate in his special area of interest. After that I always made a point of acknowledging him when I saw him and having a chat about the latest happenings in the town's sexual underworld.

Danny finished his pint and said, 'Drink up, this place is boring. Let's try somewhere else.' We all did so. I noticed that Claud had been casting furtive glances towards one of the pros. She was heavyset, severe looking, and must have been about forty. She periodically glanced back at him with a look of seeming dislike, but he couldn't stop looking. We all drank up and left and wandered round the square. There was some sort of folk band at one pub, but we didn't fancy that.

We moved on and drifted into the Woolpack which was another of the town's pubs of dubious repute. There was a small snug which was crammed full of drinkers of all types. We looked in but it was packed, so we went down a corridor into a larger dark and dingy room. No one was behind the bar. The only occupants were a pair sat facing each other. She was about thirty with a black jacket and skirt on and a wide brimmed black hat. She had good legs and a good figure. She was drawing heavily on a long cigarette. Her companion was short, in his fifties, and wore a trilby hat. I knew by now that this almost inevitably meant that he was bald. The short man had both hands on the woman's thighs, inside her skirt, which had moved up due to his attentions. She kept on trying to deter his advances, but his hands seemed set on moving higher and higher.

The pair ignored us. After a minute or two Danny said, 'This is crap, let's piss off.' We turned and left. In the middle of the town, we split up. Danny and Baz wanted to have a look at a newly opened pub. I had no money, so I made my way back to the bus stop. Claude looked a bit furtive and set off back towards the marketplace, muttering, 'I've got to meet somebody.' I wondered if the fascination lay in the severe looking woman he had been staring at in the Bull.

I dropped off at the youth club deep in thought. One of the girls giggled when I walked in and said, 'Where have you been, its nearly closing time.'

I growled back, 'You wouldn't believe it.' She looked a little crestfallen. I smiled and said, 'Ask no questions and I'll tell no lies.'

She brightened up at that, but I really wasn't in the mood for silly-teen chit chat. I had experienced a most educational evening and had gained more insights. This time into the hot and seedy world of adult sex. I walked on down to the weights room to see if anyone was still there.

Chapter 8
All the fun of the fair

The boredom of life at or near the bottom of the human pile continued. Baz and Danny got jobs on a building site. Claud had gone off to work as a steel fixer which amazed me because he was the least physical of the four of us. When I asked about the job, Danny sniggered and said, 'He needs the money, he has got an expensive hobby.' The work, which involved placing and fastening the steel bars in large construction projects, was often at heights, was hard, and could be dangerous. I was working in a lab now and had just completed the first year of an ONC in chemistry. Almost everyone knows about A-Levels but very few know what these courses entailed.

The national certificates, Ordinary and Higher, were run at technical colleges under the supervision of the many engineering and scientific institutes and institutions. In our case the supervising body was the Royal Institute of Chemistry. The system seemed to have come about due to the desperate need to train competent professionals without the huge expense of building and staffing the universities which would have been needed to produce them otherwise, and which existed in countries such as Germany and the USA. The system was there primarily to serve the needs of industry. It hoovered up bright working-class kids and trained them as industrial chemists, electrical and mechanical engineers and the like.

Entry to the courses was only possible with O-Levels in chemistry, maths, physics, English language and one arts subject. Attendance at the 'tech' was one full day, 9 am to 9 pm, and one evening from 6 to 9 pm after work. The course was designed to produce competent analysts. Three-hour practical sessions were run in both organic and inorganic chemical analysis. In addition to this there was theory which took the students well on the way to A-Level chemistry. Some related physics was included with maths taken as a separate endorsement which covered a fair part of an A-Level maths course. All this was possible via the extensive readings and exercises set as homework in addition to the day release and the rigid discipline imposed. Attendance of less than 85% meant failure, and a large number of set practicals had to be completed during the year. If you didn't manage to do them, you were invited to repeat the year or leave. There was no messing about during theory lessons, which were quick fire and with intensive note taking. After a one-hour session I remember emerging with ten pages of notes. Many years later I taught some A-Level chemistry and realised how poor it was in comparison to an ONC. It wasn't the syllabus content; it was just the difficulty of imbuing the pupils with the same kind of poverty driven urgency which had pushed me through my courses. With us, there was none of the silly I can only be half bothered, and I'm doing you a favour being here, attitude of the A-Level kids. The industries sending us on the courses wanted the goods delivered in terms of competence and kept a keen eye on what was happening and helped to keep the pressure up. In terms of ability as analysts, those doing ONCs were generally streets ahead of their A-Level counterparts.

We rarely saw Claude. I ran into him a few years later though, and he had hardened up incredibly due to the hard-physical nature of his work. All the boyish softness around his face had disappeared and he had acquired a few facial scars which looked like they were from fist or even 'bottle' fights. His hands had hardened and roughened. I reckoned that if it now came to a fight, he would have been up there with the best of us rather than at his previous number four position in our crew. I reinstated him as Jason rather than Claude in my classification system.

One Friday before he left the group, we decided to visit the local fair. This was one of the biggest held in the North. It always ran for a fortnight around the big race meeting at the local course. The races attracted thousands of punters and with them came the scum of the earth. Thieves, con men, travelling prostitutes, booth fighters and the various side show and ride operators. These were often crewed by criminals on the run, deserters from the army and similar types. We had arranged to meet outside the fair at seven—it was cloudy and would soon be dusk. The darkness always enhanced the magic of the fair ground. The bright lights from the rides blazed into the gloom and the music was mostly the latest hits. Groups of excited girls drifted around in flared skirts, chattering loudly and looking round at the boys. Sometimes they could be heard shrieking as they crammed into cars on rides and were spun manually by one of the youths who always rode the decking.

The operators took money and looked warily on at what was happening around them. They always looked swarthy and had greasy hair if they were blokes. Their women who worked on some of the smaller attractions, such as the 'land a ping pong ball in a goldfish bowl to win a goldfish', were usually dark and frequently smoked heavily as they circled, taking the money. I could never work out if the showmen families were of gypsy descent or not. I knew that some of the important fairground family names were Doubtfire, Waddington, Scott and Shufflebottom, which were certainly not gypsy names. I also knew that the Smart family who now ran a big circus had come from the fairgrounds originally. There was a minor police presence consisting of a couple of large and portly constables who strode round at the regulation pace of two and a half miles an hour, but in those days that was usually enough. Everyone knew that a big police station was just five minutes away and that if anything serious erupted dozens of officers with dogs would be rapidly on the scene. Some groups, consisting of father, mother and kids were still there, but they drifted away as the night fell. Families generally visited the fair in the afternoon when the leather jackets were absent and the atmosphere was less edgy. That was the thing about big fairs, it always seemed that something exiting was about to happen. Occasionally it did, but we usually just missed it. I noted a few of the well-known petty criminal and hard cases from the town circulating, and a group of Teds. Although the teddy boy mode of dress was drifting out, a few die-hards still clung to the drainpipe trousers, crepe shoes and long jackets with velvet collars. Their heyday had gone though, and the days of gang fights at dances with bike chains, flick knives and cut-throat razors had vanished after a spate of heavy borstal or jail sentences in the fifties. They rarely carried weapons now as they knew that even carrying one was a serious criminal offence and that if they were part of a teddy boy group the jail term would be longer. If they got into bother their favoured weapons were fists and the boot. Even so, if they walked into a place they would cause the same sort of concern as a group wearing leather jackets. But really, they were a spent force.

After a long slow tour of the side shows we followed the group of Teds into the boxing booth. The offer was £20 for anyone who beat one of their pugilists. Danny always fancied his chances—he was big and powerful and a natural hothead, but I always held him back. I had done some boxing and with a 38-inch reach, no one could get past my guard, and I was also one of those very awkward southpaws. I showed him how easy it was to block a punch and position yourself for a counter punch. I also knew an ex-booth fighter who explained the game to me. He had done some pro boxing and had continued as a booth fighter till he was nearly fifty. He said, 'It was just a matter of watching out for the wild swings, which were usually telegraphed way in advance anyway, and then clipping 'em on the jaw or in the gut and winding them. Most bouts didn't last more than a couple of minutes.' If he didn't manage to put his man down, the opponents rarely laid a glove on him, and the prize money was never paid out. Most people don't realise that after years at the game the avoidance skills become instinctive. You move out of the way without thinking about it, responding to the position of the arms and body of the opponent. He said, 'At this level the last thing you are going to get is a feint. They can be big strong miners, but they need to connect. They usually end up punching thin air.' We watched, and after a couple of bouts a big Ted strode forward. He had been saying that he could 'do' that fat little fucker, who happened to be the shows best fighter. He was egged on by the rest of his group. He took his jacket and bootlace tie off and had gloves put on and then stepped into the ring with a three-quarters smoked cigarette still dangling from the corner of his mouth. The referee deftly removed it and dropped it through the ropes. He brought the two to the centre of the ring and then allowed the slaughter to begin. 'How long do you think he will last?' said Danny. 'Not more than a minute or two I should think,' was my reply. The Ted was square jawed and looked tough and broad, but I could see after he had removed his heavily padded jacket that he had no shoulder development and thus no power. His arms were big, but they were fleshy with little evidence of muscle.

After the bell he charged forwards and took a wild swing. The booth fighter side-stepped it and punched him hard in the ribs. I saw the Ted wince. After that he was wary and tried some more controlled punches, which missed their target by a mile. After each one the booth man came in with a counter punch or sometimes a one-two. After about a minute the Ted's nose was bleeding and his face looked red from the punishment it had taken. He tried again, and to avoid more punishment after throwing his punch he dived forwards and went into a clinch. The booth man clipped him on side of the head and the Ted saw red and stuck the nut on the boxer. The ref started to move in but the booth man ignored him and stepped forward and released a torrent of powerful punches to the head and body. I could see that the Ted was out on his feet. The ref tried to stop the bout, but the booth fighter pursued him along the ropes and delivered a punishing left hook to the jaw. The Ted slid down the corner post, into oblivion. The ref raised the winner's hand as the seconds picked the loser up from the canvas and helped him out of the ring. Ten minutes later, he was still looking dazed. After that no one seemed very keen to take the boxer on and we drifted off.

Our next stop was the strip show. I had seen a couple of heavily made-up women in dressing gowns having a cigarette round the side of the big tent in which the strippers worked. They looked older than my mother. Danny and Jason were keen to have a look, but Baz and I said we were off for a hot dog. The two paid their five shillings and were allowed into the tent.

We met up about twenty minutes later and Baz asked, 'What was it like?'

'Crap,' said Danny. 'They got undressed as fast as they could to music from a record, but they were all saggy tits and stretch marks. It put me off sex for about five minutes. They ought to advertise it as "the granny strippers." It was about as erotic as going to mass. They came on looking bored and slightly sleazy. They took stuff off till they were wearing stockings and sus-penders and then whipped their bras off to show us their saggy tits for a few seconds then the curtain came down. What a waste of five bob. That could have bought me three pints.'

We continued to wander but it was getting late and the crowds were drifting away, some to get a last drink in before closing time and others to avoid the late busses which were often full of drunks. As we neared the end of the ground, we could see an argument developing between one of the neanderthal town hard cases and a group of bikers. The hard case stepped forward and kicked one of the bikes over. Its owner, who was a fresh-faced youth, looked crestfallen and said, 'What did you do that for?' The leader of the group stepped forward and said, 'We don't want any bother.' The thug turned on his heel, and I could hear him say 'Bunch of fairies' as he strode away. Danny said, 'If he had done that to my bike, he would have had bother, hard case or not.' I didn't say any-thing but noted it as another of life's lessons. Bikers had a reputation, some of 'em were undoubtedly tough nuts but obviously many were not. They liked to share the notoriety of the group by having the bikes and the leather gear, but the fighter's temperament was something that did not appear when you put the leather jacket on. Some youths could be trained to fight but others were born fighters and frequently in brawls which they found enjoyable because they almost always came out on top. Those who went in for boxing or wrestling or the Judo, which had come into the UK in a big way after the war, were usually the strong robust types who had the natural gifts which would make them good at those very physically demanding sports. I was learning to judge and sift who had that fighting temperament and who did not.

Chapter 9

The Wild West

I had seen fights at local dances which were usually pathetic affairs with the combatants so ale-ed up they couldn't connect or fell over after swinging a punch. There were others who wanted to build a reputation as hard cases, this was often done by taking a swing at some unassuming and unsuspecting youth in a bar. The punch was often thrown without reason at the unsuspecting victim, and I thought deep down the man involved had a cowardly streak and problems with his masculinity. Nine times out of ten the floored youth was so deflated that nothing more happened. This of course enhanced the reputation of the cowardly instigator. I saw a couple of such incidents where the lad who had been hit stood up and started to throw punches back. Those fights got stopped by the landlord, but I could see that the head case who started it starting to look worried as he started to get the worst of it.

The behavioural code in those villages did not come out of any respect for the law. The law was for the middle classes. At grunt level, down at the bottom, behavioural norms usually derived from watching John Wayne westerns or something similar. It was almost always fist-fights—bottles or boots were a rarity; they were frowned on by the code. A beating provoked resentment but the police were never called by any of the participants—the view was that it was none of their business.

Society was tribal. If you walked into a dance in a village where you were not known, you were asking for trouble. There was a pecking order, with a few individuals in each locality who by temperament and physique were at the top of the pile.

If you messed with them, you usually came off second best. If a fight broke out, they would jump in, often for the sheer thrill of it, and sort it out. These hard men knew each other and generally avoided getting into bother with each other. The rest of the herd knew their place. Occasionally some hot-head would try his chances, usually after a bit too much beer, and would regret it later. Serious injury was rare but black eyes, thick lips and wounded pride were the usual outcome of a fight which usually stopped when the loser was down or too dazed to continue.

I was a keen observer of physical attributes. I noticed that the best fighters were rarely the barrel-chested big bicep types. They were too slow. It was almost always the broad shouldered, lithe athletic builds such as mine, around the twelve to thirteen stone mark, who came out on top. Lots of the opposition was puny and avoided confrontation like the plague. There were others, big and with a powerful punch such as rugby union types who thought they were hard but who were too slow and generally did not know how to fight. Throwing a punch at someone who can't see it coming in a scrum is a very different kettle of fish to facing someone on a one-to-one basis in a serious fight.

There was usually one pub in each village which attracted punch ups, usually on a Saturday night after too much beer. Mostly swift affairs which brought a landlord rushing out to prevent damage to his property. Mayhem broke out one night at a local pub, called 'the Swinger' because it had swing doors. We had arrived late due to our usual shortage of money and had managed to get a table in the corner. A couple of the local girls were dancing to a record on the juke box which the owner had installed after they shut his venture into strippers down. The girls could have a dance without the need to get into town and pay to get into one of the nightspots which were just starting up because the law had relaxed. If you lived in an outlying village, it was expensive as it always meant overpriced drinks and a taxi back. Here you could dance for the price of a few halves of bitter.

We were discussing the state of things in our small world and Big Danny was pursuing his usual theme: that everything was bollocks. In the big world outside, the Profumo Scandal had just erupted, with him resigning from the Commons after lying about an affair with a high-class tart called Christine Keeler. Inconveniently, one of her other lovers was a naval attaché at the Russian embassy, and as Profumo was Secretary of State for War, a security breach was an obvious danger.

We were innocents in those days and had no idea of the convoluted sexual world in which the upper crust operated. Various Royals, and even the then Prime Minister Harold Macmillan, were not above it. Years later we found out that the bisexual Lord Boothby, who could conceivably have become Tory leader and Prime Minister if the political dice had fallen right for him, had a long-standing affair with Macmillan's wife and was supposedly the father of her youngest daughter. He was also involved with the Kray twins and with various rent boys. The facts were known by the press but not published due to Boothby's connections. Both men had gone to Eton and Oxford and were part of the tight-nit circle at the centre of Conservative/establishment politics. Both portrayed themselves in public as serious and honourable statesmen of unimpeachable standards. Danny was saying that what they were and what they stood for was all bollocks, purely by his instincts, which were heavily coloured by the prejudices of the working class. It turned out that his instincts were absolutely spot on.

The atmosphere in the concert room was gloomy due to the dim lighting which was a legacy of its days as a strip joint. The heavy fog of tobacco smoke did not help things. The relative quiet was broken by two young blokes bursting through the double doors in the middle of a fight. One tripped and the other jumped on him. One of the dancers looked across and then jumped on the bloke on top because the bloke underneath was her brother. Another group of fighters spilled in. Then a table went over and the men whose beer had been spilled joined in and others rushed in. We grabbed our pints from the table and pushed it forward standing next to the wall to watch the action. Several tables had gone over and there was broken glass all over the floor.

One of the women picked a pint bottle of beer up and flung it at someone's head, it missed narrowly and hit the Juke Box. I had never seen a fight like this, it was like a saloon fight in a Western but with real blood and hard punches thrown, chairs being flung about, and tables knocked over. More than twenty of them must have been at it and most had drunk a lot of beer. After a couple of minutes, the landlord rushed in and shouted, 'the police are on their way.' Nobody believed him but slowly the fight wound down and the dazed and bloodied limped off muttering threats of the 'I'll get that bastard,' sort. The landlord came out with a brush and shovel and started to sweep the broken glass up. A few minutes later somebody put the Gene Vincent classic, *Be-Bop-a-Lula* on and a couple of girls got up to jive. We had nearly finished our pints when a police sergeant pushed his head round the door and surveyed the peaceful scene.

I realised that fights were a rarity and that few were really good at it. Almost none of the combatants had done any boxing or wrestling or judo, and if they could fight it was usually what they had learned during brawls in bars and at dances. One or two men in the village were notably powerful due to their work underground, but they never seemed to get involved. It was always drunks and a handful of others who had reputations, usually gained by downing very inferior opposition. Booze was often the cause of punch ups with a few who seemed to want to fight the world after five or six pints. After eight or nine they seemed to become happy again.

I could never work the psychology out; it was almost like the rutting rituals of deer at one level. At another it seemed that the ones who constantly sought the opportunity rarely had girlfriends. Perhaps it was some sort of deep seated need to gain female attention or even repressed homosexuality with a need to prove masculinity. It was clear that many of the regulars at the brawling game were disturbed in some way and often fearful of losing reputation. I learned early that if you dressed hard and acted hard you were invariably not. What you were, deep down, was insecure about your masculinity and probably yellow if it came down to it and came up against some real opposition. I saw a couple of these types come off worse because they miscalculated.

On one occasion a vicious case called Tiger, because of a tiger tattoo on his shoulder, took a swing at an unassuming, smart looking youth after he was told to wait his turn by him in a crush at the bar. He grabbed the youth and swung him round, throwing a punch at the same time. The youth was at least a couple of stone lighter than Tiger, but he sidestepped the punch and landed a couple of short hard jabs in Tiger's face. The response was a look of bewilderment and a wild flurry of blows, none of which connected. By now a circle had gathered round the two to watch the fun. The slighter youth, who could obviously box, blocked and evaded, and each time came back with precise shots to the head or body. Tiger couldn't back down but by now was looking round desperately for support from his gang of toadies. None was forthcoming. His face was looking red and bloodied and he was puffing and blowing heavily. His opponent was unmarked, cool and not out of breath in the slightest. In desperation, Tiger lurched towards the bar and grabbed a bottle which he smashed and thrust forward to keep his tormenter back, a murmur of disapproval went round the audience.

The smart youth seemed unconcerned, but blood started to pour from Tiger's hand. The idiot had smashed the bottle, but the glass had split and cut the inside of his hand badly. The smart youth stood ready and said in a quiet and deadly voice: 'Come in with that bottle and I will ram it up your arse.' Tiger looked at the blood and turned pale and dropped the bottle. Clutching his hand, he turned and made a dash for the door. I heard later that he had needed twelve stitches in the cut. Later on, I heard him muttering to his acolytes. 'If I hadn't cut my hand, I would have done him.' I smiled walking past wondering how many stitches he would have needed with the broken bottle up his arse. He was involved in another incident later which was even less impressive.

One of the regulars on the fight scene was known as Silver. This was because he had a head injury which had resulted in a silver plate repair to part of his skull. He was intelligent but a bit on the wild side. He had passed the eleven-plus but at grammar school had thought it would be rather a good jape to set off a firework in the quadrangle. It exploded with a loud bang and unfortunately a diminutive French teacher had just walked by. She had fled German bombs during the invasion of France, where she had been holidaying. The loud sound resulted in her having a fit of the vapours and she had to be revived by concerned colleagues. Young Silver was dragged off to see the head, given six of the best and expelled on the spot.

His treatment had rankled because he and many others thought it was unjust. Everybody had expected people to be startled as the firework went off, but no one had the least expectation that the teacher would be affected in the way that she was. It was an unfortunate accident, but he was a working class oik from a mining family and he had upset the authority structure of the school and thus had to be made an example off. If the same sort of jape had occurred at a public school he would have been heavily admonished and perhaps caned, but never expelled. After that he went to the local secondary school and was constantly in trouble for not attending and for challenging the teachers, a class of people which he now hated. In fact, he hated all authority. He had made up his mind that he was not going to play, he would not accept any aspect of authority except at the pit. That was necessary in order to provide the money he needed for booze and fags. His work on the coal face also resulted in a powerful pair of shoulders and a punch to go with them.

His deep anger frequently boiled over into fights, especially after he had been drinking. After three years brawling round the village, he got his national service call up. He turned up as requested but once he got there and NCOs started to bawl at him, he kicked off. Nobody was going to shout at him. He told one lance corporal to fuck off and a burly corporal stepped forward and got right in his face and started to scream at him. Bad mistake. Silver belted him hard on the jaw and floored him. This resulted in the guardhouse and threats, but nothing made any difference. After a bit, the army admitted defeat and awarded him a dishonourable discharge, telling him that as a result he would never get a job in civvy street. Silver didn't give a fuck. He got back home and started back at the pit the following Monday. The industry was so desperate for men back in the sixties that a small thing such as a 'disgusting discharge' as he proudly called it was not going to stop the NCB employing him.

It was back to the old pattern, working hard. He was soon on a face earning a lot of money. He was down at the local pubs every night drinking and fighting. After a while he was barred from all the clubs and pubs in the area apart from the Swinger. There, you could get barred, but it was difficult. A fight was just an almost everyday occurrence. I got barred once but the landlord was elderly and couldn't remember who he had had kicked out. I left it for four days and walked back in and ordered a pint. Nobody batted an eyelid.

I was having a drink with Silver early on, before his wild fighting tendencies kicked in (I tended to avoid him later on because he would start to mutter and then kick off at the slightest thing). Most of the other youths in the village gave him a wide berth all of the time. He said, 'I heard you got barred. Fuck me, I've never been barred here, it must have been bad. What did you do? Stand on the bar and piss on the piano or something?' I laughed and said, 'Just a small misunderstanding.'

As time went on the drinking increased and so did the fighting. He started to get arrested and fined for drunkenness. He was always the same in court, truculent and defiant. When asked if he pleaded guilty or not guilty, he always said, 'I can't remember what happened.' If the magistrates pushed it and said he must plead guilty or not guilty he would say, 'How can I do that if I can't remember what happened?' The magistrates would look at the clerk and Silver would be told, 'We will take it as a plea of not guilty.' The policeman who had done the arrest would be sworn in, the evidence would be read, and he would be found guilty and asked if he had anything to say. He would be as awkward as possible, typically saying 'About what?' The magistrate would say, 'About the fact that you have been found guilty.' His usual reply was, 'How can I say anything about something I don't remember?'

The first few times in court he was fined, the amount increasing each time. Eventually they got fed up and gave him a fortnight in prison. Then a month. Then six week and then three months. Each time he came out, his hatred of authority increased. Each time he came out he went back up to the pit and was set on straight away. Inevitably he was arrested again but this time they were a bit rough with him, so he belted a policeman. In court his temper got the best of him when admonished for daring to strike a policeman. He replied, 'What about them fuckers? They kicked the shit out of me!' The Chair of the Bench told him that such language was unacceptable in her court. Silver retorted, 'You all piss in the same pot. You are a joke. You would find me guilty whatever I said.'

The Bench retired to confer, returned, and delivered the guilty verdict and asked the defendant if he had anything to say before sentence was pronounced. By now Silver could not sensibly contain himself and said, 'Yes—Fuck Off!' The magistrates who would probably have given four or six months referred him to crown court for sentencing and the judge gave him a term of imprisonment of nine months. Inside it was explained to him that in future he was looking at an increasing term every time he came to court. After that he did some thinking and was just about able to contain himself, it was difficult. On one occasion I saw him walking home after a lot of beer swearing and boiling up in rage as he walked past some young constable, who sensibly shrank back into a shop doorway looking worried. But he walked on, encouraged by the rest of us. He did not like long periods in prison—it interfered with his drinking.

Silver hated everybody in authority apart from the deputies who supervised him underground. Some of us tried to talk some sense into him but he was a lost cause. Every night he was on the piss, and it wasn't doing him any good, but at least he managed to stay out of jail. One Saturday he joined a Swinger trip to a low life club in Leeds. By the time he got back on the bus he could hardly stand. Tiger was on the same trip with a few of his bootlicking buddies. He hardly drank all night and just sat most of the evening glowering. We neared home and stood up as the bus slowed. Tiger rushed forward, pushed past Silver, and then turned and shouted 'Cunt' and hit his inebriated opponent several times. It was no contest as Silver was incapable of self-defence. Tiger climbed out of the door and down the steps with a swagger—he was a hard man. He had done the most dangerous man in the village.

I saw him the next night in the Swinger and heard him bragging. I told him there was no glory in downing a drunk. He didn't like it, but he didn't fancy his chances with me. Silver was nowhere to be seen. Two days later Tiger was somewhat chagrined to find Silver hammering on his door shouting. 'Come out here you yellow bellied cunt, I'm not drunk now.' The hero of the bus trip decided that perhaps a return match against a fully capable opponent was not a good idea. Silver had kicked a door panel in by then in his desire to get his hands on the yellow belly. Tiger's response was to block the door with a table and kitchen cabinet. Silver smashed several windows and shouted to his assailant that the next time he saw him he would smash him into a pulp. The next day Tiger packed a suitcase and caught an early bus into town, he left the area and was never seen again.

I lost touch with Silver. Some years later I saw him leaning over a wall being sick. It was the last time I saw him. I offered to run him up home, but he said he would be alright. A few months later I heard he had gone; he had been out of work and spent his dole on beer and fags. After a few months of eating almost nothing it was too much—he got pneumonia and died. He was only thirty-six.

Chapter 10

The pleasures of sex and its avoidance!

Women, that great mystery! The only thing I can say, is that Charles Bukowski gives much better advice about them than Saint Augustine.

Anon

I could never work women out. Who can? The centuries roll by and places different constraints on the female sex. I suppose the sixties were unusual in the West because for the first time ever most girls were healthy due to scientific advances and were well nourished. This had some interesting effects. A few decades earlier it wasn't unusual for girls to go through puberty at seventeen or eighteen. Now it was happening at thirteen or fourteen.

Hormones began to rage but virtually no advice was given. The churches hung like a dead weight around the neck of a sensible and human approach to the problem. Hatred of sex and of women seemed to colour their thinking. The only acceptable female sexual behaviour in their eyes was to be a virgin bride, who was never inflamed by lust and who indulged passively in sex occasionally, with a view to producing children. Sexual pleasure was frowned on and sex outside marriage and divorce were reprehensible and shameful acts. No information from any official source was available on topics like contraception or venereal disease. What was available came down unofficial channels and the taboos and embarrassment surrounding the topics was huge. With hindsight, it seems to me that lots of the clergy then were misogynistic, homosexual or just warped. The 'supposedly' celibate Catholic clergy indulged in excessive violence in the classroom, the Freudian ideas on sublimation, with sexual urges often transformed into violent or sadistic urges had blithely passed them by. Sadistic violence against female sexual transgressors continued late into the twentieth century in the guise of the Magdalene laundries and in the institutions where unmarried mothers gave birth and then immediately had the child taken from them for adoption with the mothers then kept in the laundries as slave labourers.

Sexual repression was still very much the order of the day amongst those working-class parents who had been brought up in the thirties and forties. The middle classes were better informed and freer, with sexual affairs often indulged in—the main worry was people getting to know about it. The fact that a spouse was having sex with someone else was of far less concern than friends and colleagues getting to know and gossiping about it. The upper classes continued their long established and unfettered practice of shagging whoever they could get into bed with complete freedom and absence of censorious comment, unless juicy details emerged during a divorce case, such as the notorious case of Margaret Duchess of Argyll, reported with glee by the tabloids in 1963.

Big Danny was skimming through a copy of the Daily Mail, which was covering every salacious morsel, immune from prosecution because they were just writing what had been said in evidence in court.

Danny suddenly exploded, saying, 'What the fuck's fellatio?'

Baz looked blank, but I chipped in and said, 'That's the posh word for cock sucking.'

Danny's rejoinder was 'Dirty bastard'.

He read the bit out to us: the husband of the Duchess had broken into a cabinet at her flat and discovered a polaroid of her, nude apart from pearls, performing the act on a man, though the shot only showed his torso. Divorce resulted and with it much speculation about who the man had been. Duncan Sandys who had been Winston Churchill's son-in-law was a front runner because at the time there was only one polaroid camera in the country and that was on loan to the ministry of defence to which he had considerable connection as a former minister. Such activities would be unusual among the working classes, whose sexual practices were notably unadventurous largely due to total lack of information about what was available.

I realised that with women it was impossible to generalise when it came to sex. All kinds of influences went into the pot which made them what they were. There were a few broad categories such as the 'prim-miss' who seemed to show little interest in sex, and 'the repressed' who could often be identified by constantly going on about how dirty and disgusting sex was. I always got the feeling that beneath all that was a boiling cauldron of rampant desire. Their objective was—boyfriend/ marriage and then lots of sex. Then there were the types who liked sex and were determined to get plenty of it; they usually had few inhibitions and were very matter of fact about being pleasured. I liked the last group best.

Even then it wasn't easy to work out but most of them seemed to end up getting what they wanted and the blokes they ended up with seemed willing to go along with it. Trading in the boozy nights with their mates for domestic bliss and three-piece suites on the hire purchase. In just a few cases some serious thought was given to what they wanted out of life in the longer term. I admired the women and the occasional man who had gone for the non-conformist pathway, but these were few and far between. A huge enemy to the free spirit was convention and gossip, often vicious gossip if you did not conform to the norm.

One or two blokes I knew had worked it out. They got themselves room and board with widows. It was all very formal with the woman always addressed as Mrs. This arrangement had the wonderful benefit as far as the men were concerned of a responsibility free life. There was no pressure to work weekends or do extra hours underground to provide new televisions, curtains, fridges, and so on for the wives. Children were not a constant drain on the pocket. They always had enough money to have a few pints or smokes and a bet at the bookies. They could please themselves as far as holidays or leisure went and visit London or coastal resorts for weekends, watch football matches or just lounge in front of the TV watching racing or cricket. Men like this seemed to attract the all-round disapproval of the female classes, but they were insulated from any gossip or other attempts to get them to conform because they just did not interact with females, other than their landladies. It was a life choice. I could see the logic. It was not for me though; I found the female of the species far too alluring.

The rigidities imposed by a culture in which virtually all males had either fought in the war or done two years national service were still there. Conscripts were still going into the army as late as 1960. The norm as far as haircuts were concerned was very much the army style—short, back and sides. The Teddy boys who had arrived on the scene in the mid-fifties started to kick against it with long sideburns and large quiffs at the front, but these were a small minority. The style, though derided by most of the older generation, was still masculine and linked to aggression and aggressive behaviour. Long hair was considered to be effeminate. It took the breakthrough by the Beatles in 1963 to cause a radical change in hairstyle norms. But at the end of the day, it was all about display—being the flashiest peacock in the bunch, in order to attract the females.

I observed that some women were attracted to the nice, neat, suit wearing mummy's boy types. My early cynicism led me to think that was probably because these were the ones who would do what their wives told them to do. Others liked those with highly paid jobs or cars. Some liked the broad-shouldered leather jacket wearing types such as those in our group. Some went for Teds, but not many for some reason, perhaps because they were seen as inviting trouble. Quite a few Teds ended up with the windfalls because by virtue of their own looks or personalities the choicer fruit higher on the tree was not available. Right at the bottom of the pile were the unfortunates, the dregs, usually thick as pig-shit and sometimes borderline bonkers.

It wasn't that they were unattractive. Quite often they were, but the clothes and make-up used were chosen by a sort of instinct rather than thought. Often, they got it wrong with combinations which clashed or looked odd. They were usually loud, with very limited conversation and they smoked and drank too much. I avoided them as did most others. I was in the Swinger one evening waiting for the lads. The other tables were full, and a woman sat down. She had obviously had a lot to drink. She was slim and quite tall with jet black hair and very black eyebrows which looked over exaggerated to me via too much eyebrow pencil. She lit a fag and proceeded to smoke it, but she seemed to be putting the end too far into her mouth. She looked round the room for a while, and after a bit she spoke:

'Do I know you?'

Noncommittal grunt from me.

'I like that leather jacket, where did you get it?'

'A leather shop.'

'What did it cost?'

'Eight quid.'

'It suits you.'

The problem for me was that with each sentence she shuffled her chair a little closer round the table towards me. She was drinking a Cherry B. which was advertised as 'the drink with a kick'. It was strong, at about 14% alcohol. It was sweet and cherry flavoured and supposed to be cherry brandy, but it could have been just ethanol and water with colour and flavourings added.

She finished her Cherry B and looked at me and said, 'What are you drinking?' That was fairly clear as I was near the end of a pint. The comment was an obvious invitation to ask her if she wanted a drink. She obviously did, but I wasn't buying her one. By now she was really close—about a foot from my face. I

could smell perfume—Woolworth's Number 5 by its fumes—
and stale cigarettes.

She leant forward and put a hand on my thigh.

'What's your name?'

God she was so old (she must have been about twenty-six or
twenty-seven). I might have been rampantly in need of sex at
that age, but there were limits.

I waved to an imaginary person at the door, saying, 'Got to
go.' She looked startled, but I got up rapidly and walked out of
the main doors then round to the posh end of the pub, which
was a separate bar with a separate entrance and used by
respectable people. I took a quick look in—three middle aged
to elderly couples were sat there having a staid conversation
and a Friday evening drink. One of them seeing a leather
jacketed interloper looked uneasy. I turned and walked down
to the bogs, had a slash and then left the premises after looking
round from the door to see if the Cherry B swigger was about,
but she was nowhere to be seen. Fortunately, as I walked down
the row of shops, I could see Danny and Baz walking towards
me. They suggested a bus ride down to the little fair. It was
Friday and I thought it might be lively, so I agreed.

There wasn't much happening there. The lads running the
Waltzers looked bored because most of the time they were
letting it run with only a couple of cars full. They much preferred it jam packed with people with some drink inside them.
I had got to know one of them very well. I had given him some
backup at the pub down the road from the fair after he had
been threatened by three youths from my village. The three
making the threats backed down after seeing that I was in the
bloke's corner, saying 'We don't want any bother with you,
mate.'

He had said to me in one of our chats later: 'It's amazing
what you find after they get off the cars. Sometimes its loose
change or a bit of jewellery. Sometimes they leave purses or
handbags. I have had a few wallets left. It's amazing how care-
less they are, they just drop out of a pocket. I always pick them
up then move round the back of a car and flip it underneath

towards the runners at the centre where they couldn't easily be seen. They sometimes came back when they realised it was missing. Half the time they can't remember which car they were in, but we go through the pantomime, and I let them look in each one. I am sympathetic but thinking, stupid twats. When we shut up for the night I get under the car and rake the wallet out. There was twenty-three quid in one and a few betting slips, with a couple of winners among them. I didn't try to cash them though, somebody at the bookies might have recognised me. I dumped the wallet near the bus stop. It might have got back to its owner, minus the money of course. Twenty-three bloody quid, it takes me a month to earn that on here.'

A regular fixture at the fair was a couple of young women, late teens I would have said. One was attractive, the other had a severe sort of face, not ugly but not one most men would be attracted to. They were always sat or stood next to one of the stalls run by an older woman. I never saw them on any of the rides, but they were a regular fixture, looking around or chatting and usually smoking. I couldn't quite work them out. Whenever I walked on site the attractive one used to look at me with a sort of wistful expression on her face. She never smiled at me or gave me any sort of come on but there seemed to be some sort of yearning for contact. I came close to chatting her up a couple of times but never quite got there as I was always at the fair with others of my exclusive group.

I saw the severe looking one a few years later working at a fish shop and got chatting. I told her I remembered her from the fair and asked about the other girl that was always with her.

She told me that a few years previously she had taken an overdose of sleeping pills and died. She said, 'She was always sad. If only she had got a boyfriend, it might have helped; it was in the papers, didn't you see it?'

I replied, 'I might have but I never knew her name!'

That was a real shocker, what a waste! It was the first suicide of someone that I actually knew. It made me feel guilty. If I had taken her out perhaps things would have turned out better.

Later I chatted to a nursing sister who worked at a mental hospital. She said, 'Often it's in 'em for some reason, they are on that track, always focused on themselves and how they feel. The only solution that they can see to their unbearable melancholy is to end it. It's a pity though because they have some new drugs now which help people cope. I used to see others when I was in general nursing, real fighters. They were just the opposite—they were in very bad states with cancer or similar but would do anything to stay alive.'

It was a strange week, one of those that feels disjointed. Besides working I had spent a lot of time in the little weights room at the youth club really blasting at it and then pounding an old heavy punch bag which was a permanent and little used feature hung in the corner of the room. It helped with my feeling of foreboding, but that was just probably the gloomy weather. Perhaps it would be better and brighter next week.

Chapter 12

Sorting out a slander

The trouble with scum is, they don't feel shame, what they do feels normal for them because they live at the bottom of the shit heap.

Anon

Something was up. I called in to the swinger to meet Baz and Danny, feeling relaxed and having the usual jokey conversation. I could see a group of girls who worked at the local sewing factory and could see they were talking in low tones and with occasional hostile looks cast in my direction. There was definitely an atmosphere. I waited my chance. I knew one of them slightly and when she got up to go to the lavatory, I followed her out and grabbed her arm. She turned round and then tried to pull away.

I said, 'You're not going anywhere Maggie till you tell me what all the dirty looks are for.'

She said, 'Its Mona and what you lot did to her.'

'Is she the tall dark one, a bit gormless?'

'Yes.'

'You tell your little crew in there that I didn't do anything to her. She sat at the same table as me one-night last week, she was three quarters pissed, and after a few words with her I left as fast as I could and then went to town with Danny and Baz. Ask them. I was with them all night.'

She said, 'She remembered talking to you, she thinks you were one of them, but she says everything is hazy.'

'So what happened?' I asked.

'It was disgusting,' she replied. 'She thinks Ronnie Barwell was one of them as well.'

I answered with some anger, and she could see it, 'Well just get this perfectly straight—you and your mates—I wasn't involved in any way!'

I knew the Barwells, they were about as close to living specimens of the Neanderthals as it was possible to get. The whole family was noted for being brutishly stupid. They could barely read and any writing they did was confined to filling betting slips out. I said, 'Don't worry, I will get the whole story. In the meantime, you lot watch your gobs, find out the facts before you start bad mouthing people.' She turned away but I could tell by the look on her face that the anger when I had said my piece had registered. If there was one thing which got to me above virtually anything else it was being tried and convicted on the basis of self-righteous, vicious gossip. I had seen it happen in the village. One bloke had been vilified for child abuse; the problem was, it wasn't him, but even after that had been established the gossip wasn't totally quashed, it still circulated and arose occasionally amongst the loose mouthed classes.

I had a word with Baz and Danny and asked them to report back to me if they heard anything. I thought I could find out what had happened. One youth called Jimmy Beard always hung about with the Barwells—he wasn't as dense as them but was related through marriage, so he knew them all. He was spindly, balding and worked for the council. His dad was a councillor and had managed to get him set on as a groundsman working in the local parks. There were lots of better candidates but that was how it seemed to work when it came to council jobs. It didn't pay a lot and the work was boring; I thought he was welcome to it. Danny had known him at school and called him beardo the wierdo. He said 'That dim twat was about fourteen before he could tie his own shoelaces. I always thought he would end up on the dole or shovelling shit in a sewage works, but there you go, it's all the usual bollocks, dad a councillor and now a nice cosy number, weeding flowerbeds.' A couple of nights later Danny said, 'I heard that the Barwell crew were seen walking down the shop fronts on that night we went to town, they were with that dopey Mona bird, she was well pissed.'

Jimmy was the obvious target to get the facts out of and I knew he occasionally played darts down at the Woodsman's Arms on the other side of the village. I looked in there on a couple of nights, but he wasn't about. On the third evening I called in I could see him at the end of the bar waiting for a game. I sat, slowly drinking a small bottle of Guinness, not looking at anyone in particular and certainly not at my prey. Jimmy got through a couple of pints, finished his game and eventually decided to go for a slash. I followed him. The gents was a primitive affair, just outside the pub's back door. I waited for him to come out and then grabbed him by the neck and dragged him down the alley next to the pub. It was quiet and ill lit, and people didn't like using it after dark.

I said, 'Now then Jimmy, tell me what happened with the Barwells and that Mona bird from the sewing factory.'

He spluttered, 'I don't know anything.'

I had no sure knowledge of what had happened but decided that a bluff might get the truth. 'Not what I've heard. You can tell me exactly what went off and walk away or I will beat the shit out of you.' I pushed him up against the wall and lifted him up by his neck onto his toes and gave him a hard stare. 'Your choice,' I grunted.

He swallowed hard and said, 'OK, I was there but I wasn't involved. I shot off as soon as I could, I didn't want to get blamed.'

'So what happened?' I asked.

'Well, we had all had a skinful and that Mona tagged along. She could barely stand up. One of us, Les Barwell, had the keys to his uncle's house. It was being emptied because the old bloke had just died. We sort of drifted there. It was me, his two brothers, and their cousins Les and Don. He said there was still some booze in the cupboard, and we could have a party. We got there, and it was mainly whisky and vodka and a big bottle of sherry. One of 'em gave mona a big glass of sherry, but he had poured a lot of vodka into it. They sat round drinking, and after about an hour Mona was so pissed that she passed out.

'Billy Barwell had the idea of getting her arse up in the air on one of those big cushion things and taking her knickers down. He did that, and they all had a peek and thought that looking at a big hairy pussy was funny. One of 'em said, 'Should we shave it?' Then Billy slapped her pussy a couple of times and said, "Talk to me then." They all howled with laughter. He took a long look and said, "I might as well fuck it." He leant down and said, "OK by you Mona?" She just moaned. He dropped his pants and tried, but he had so much booze he couldn't get a hard on. They all started laughing at him. Then he decided he would piss on her pussy. They all thought that was hilarious and they stood there and watched him. When he had finished, she was drenched, it was all over her legs and belly and skirt and bottom of her jumper. He finished off by saying, "Don't worry duck, I'll fuck you next time." They all drank up and left her there. She must've come round after a bit, wet through, with her knickers round her ankles and with no real idea what had happened. She was treated like a piece of shit. I've kept away from them since it happened. If she had been sober and could have told people what had gone off, the police might have been involved.'

'So, it was mainly Billy then?' I said.

Jimmy replied, 'Yes. The others watched. They were well pissed and thought it was funny, but they didn't do anything.'

'Right ho,' I said. 'If I were you I would give the Barwells a wide berth. Some of Mona's mates think that I was involved, and I don't like my name being dragged down. Something nasty is going to happen to some of that crew.'

Jimmy scurried off with a very worried look on his face.

I knew what I said would get back to Billy and he would be ready, but I didn't care and could choose the time and place of our encounter. I left it a few days, thinking I would let him stew and then start to think I wasn't going to show. I knew that the brothers and a few others always went down to the local dog track on Thursdays and then dropped into the Swinger for a few pints on the way back. It would be quiet. I knew that I was more than a match for any of that crew. Billy was brutish and strong but not fast and certainly not fit. He worked hard on a coal delivery round, but he was far too fond of booze and fags to last long in a punch up.

I walked in through the swing doors and saw the Barwells and their two cousins. Jimmy was nowhere to be seen. I could tell by the looks on their faces that they expected bother. The place was half empty, which suited me. I strode across to Billy. He stood up and started to say something, but I wasn't in a mood to listen to excuses. I just belted him very hard in the mouth and knocked him flat. The rest of his clan stood up but seemed reluctant to get involved. Billy just lay there looking dazed with blood pouring from his mouth.

I picked his pint up and another and poured them all over him, and said, 'How do you like to be drenched, you cunt! You're lucky it's not piss.'

Billy groaned and got up on one elbow and spat a tooth out. I found out later that I had knocked four out. I had also hit him so hard that I had cracked a knuckle. I glared at the rest of his clan, turned on my heel and walked out just as the landlord came rushing in.

After that, three things happened. The Barwells started to drink in a low-life pub in the next village. Maggie saw me a few days later outside the Swinger. She grabbed me and put her arms round my neck and pushed herself in close, very close, her body language obviously sexual and very invitational. She said, 'We all want you to know we are sorry for what we were saying about you.' She looked at me. 'You're a real man, aren't you. There aren't many about.' The third thing was that other regulars in the pub started to be very respectful. They probably thought I was some sort of psychopath.

I took Maggie for a drink in the posh end, and she invited me back to her place. She had married early and got a colliery company house, but her husband was more interested in booze than work. After a couple of years, she had kicked him out and with the rapidly reducing workforce at the pit she managed to keep the house and now shared it with her cousin who did the late shift at a transport café just up the road. Maggie said, 'Don't worry, she gets back after midnight and goes straight to bed. We have loads of time.' I could tell she was hot; it might have been the time of the month or something else – she perhaps liked violence or being in bed with someone who could dish it out. It was abundantly clear that she was in the driving seat and much more sexually experienced than I was, but I didn't want to seem to be a novice, so I held back on my instinctive urges to rip her clothes off and have violent and inevitably brief sex.

I left it to her to lead while I sat on the sofa with a cock-bursting hard on. She started to undress in a matter of fact but sexually provocative manner. She seemed to be watching carefully to judge how I reacted. Her dress slipped to the floor, then her underskirt, leaving her standing in black nylons and suspenders with bra and panties and high heels. She moved almost as though she was performing some sort of ritual, which she obviously was, one of the oldest rituals around, the seduction ritual. As a relative novice at the game, I was spellbound. She slipped her bra off revealing firm, forward pointing tits. Next, she dropped her panties to the floor and stepped out of them and moved forward to assist in undressing me. I was naked in about ten seconds, and she slid her deliciously wet pussy down around my urgently throbbing member.

Maggie said, 'Not too fast, big boy, I don't want you coming until I'm ready. Put your fingers round the base of your cock and squeeze.'

I did as I was instructed! The effect was one of excruciating pleasure. I was bursting to orgasm but the pressure from my fingers just prevented it.

She slid up and down, taking the whole of my cock and then riding up it until the end was out and rubbing against her clitoris. She was controlling the love fest beautifully and doing just enough to prevent my orgasm. She was moaning now and obviously needing my cock to be inserted and used more violently and vigorously. I acted by instinct and did what her moans were telling me to do. All of a sudden, she started to scream. I paused but she moaned, 'Don't stop, don't stop.' She was in the throes of a massive orgasm. I ejaculated massively and an earth shuddering spasm seemed to wrack her whole body. She collapsed on top of me.

The feeling of total satisfaction was immense. She got up slowly and walked to the bathroom. I could hear the taps running for a bit and wondered what she was doing. She came back in slowly and lay down next to me and reached for a cigarette which she lit and then took long slow drags. She said, 'You weren't bad for a young bloke, you did it just right.' She seemed thoughtful and eventually said, 'Let's get this straight. That was all about sex, I don't want a permanent relationship. I certainly don't want putting up the stick, that's why I raced off to the bathroom.' I looked quizzically at her. She laughed and said, 'Precautions, you don't want the details.'

We had sex after that quite frequently for about eighteen months. She took care to not get too involved with me emotionally. I grew to like her and respect her an awful lot. She was unusual, not one of the running with the herd giggling types. She was level-headed and had worked things out and was going to have things on her terms. Her dad had been badly injured at the pit and was still in pain and had to use a stick when he walked. Maggie had an elder sister who had buggered off in the Air Force as soon as she could to escape the straightened circumstances at home. Her dad got a piss poor invalidity pension and her mother worked on school dinners. Maggie had got a job at the sewing factory as soon as she could and now worked on piece work as a skilled machinist. The money had helped a lot at home but when she was eighteen her parents moved into a small council bungalow in a development built for pensioners and those with disabilities. After that she married young and then divorced.

Maggie knew exactly what she wanted now that she was a little older—a high earning steady bloke. A face worker would

do fine because they fitted that bill. There were other con-
tenders such as the group who worked at the local ICI factory.
Their earnings were almost on a par with face men. I liked her
because she was very straightforward and knew exactly what
the score was in respect of what life would give her. I knew that
as soon as she found someone who fitted her husband specifications that I would be given the fond farewell, but that was
alright as the no-strings sex we were having was terrific.

Chapter 13

Sex and the single boy in the nineteen sixties

It was past New Year now. The Tories were still in difficulties due to the Profumo scandal. Macmillan had packed it in as Prime Minister and passed the job on to a mate called Alec Douglas Hume. Hume had been the 49th or 94th Lord Home or something, it was all very confusing. The Tories seemed to operate in a feudal way. Macmillan and Home or Hume had similar backgrounds, aristocratic connections, considerable wealth and both had been educated at Oxford and Eton. Macmillan had prostate cancer and thought he was dying, so he anointed Hume as his successor saying about his choice that he had 'taken soundings within the party', probably from a few other mates from the same educational and social spheres. He just handed the job over and amazingly, got away with it. His lordship then ditched the peerage so that he could get into the House of Commons.

Hume had a skull like face and talked like a ventriloquist with sounds coming out of his mouth without his lips moving very much. After a year in power in which he failed to impress he lost the General Election to Labour after clinging on until virtually the last day allowed by law for a parliamentary term. After that he became a Lord again but this time he had a different title. In the middle of it all he had become Sir Alec Douglas Hume—like I said, it was all very confusing.

Big Danny wasn't interested—'it was all bollocks.' He grabbed me one Friday and said 'Does tha' want to make a few quid.' I asked how. He said, 'A mate of mine is in court next week and expects to get at least six months. It's Johnno Simonds—you know him. He's got a part time winder-cleaning round at weekends. Johnno says we can use his ladders. He just wants us to keep it going till he gets out. He has showed me how to clean the windows using a wash leather and a scrim, but you've already done some, so you know what to do. He says he can take over when he gets out.'

I agreed and the next Saturday morning we went down to his mother's and picked the ladders up. It turned out that her son got fifteen months so we would probably be doing the job for at least half a year.

The round had over two hundred houses scattered within the streets near Johnno's Ma's place. We split it up and arranged to do sixteen on the Saturday and sixteen on the Sunday, thus completing the round about every six weeks. We charged half a crown a time and took turns doing upstairs and downstairs windows. I was quite a bit faster than Danny at first, but he soon got into it. The arrangement meant that by the end of each weekend we had a couple of extra quid each and it was tax free. In those days that was about a third of a week's take home pay for youths such as us. As time went on, I realised that the job had other perks.

Most of the customers were older women, often elderly widows, but a few were youngish. One in particular kept on looking at Danny when we did her windows. She was in her late thirties, blonde and attractive. She came out when we arrived at her house carrying a bucket of warm water and with a cigarette hanging salaciously from the corner of her mouth. I wasn't exactly Errol Flynn but the sexually provocative body language oozing out of every pore of her told me exactly what she wanted. She obviously liked big boys and Danny was big. We came to an arrangement where I did both the upstairs and downstairs windows when we did her house. This gave Danny a good twenty minutes in which to pleasure Norah, that mature Nympho. As time went on Danny's services were called on more and more and in addition to the occasional fuck during the round, he was going back there late in the evenings three or four times each week when the husband was at work.

Her old man worked a permanent night shift at the pit on both weekdays and at weekends. He slept during the day. It was a strange relationship. Apparently, the husband wasn't keen on sex at all, but she was absolutely drooling for it all the time. I wondered why they had got married, but it transpired that she had got pregnant at seventeen. He was five years older than her and rapidly decided that he would sooner work ten-hour nightshifts than stay at home with an insatiable bride. Danny eventually found out, much to his chagrin, that he was the latest on a very-long list of those who had been invited to pleasure her, but for now he thought he had won the sex-pools.

I was beginning to realise that sex was a very subtle thing, that complex visual signals occurred as well as the spoken ones which would draw people together. I realised that with Norah an instant sizing up had occurred. My look was probably one of disinterest, despite the huge come on her body was giving out, but Danny was a big raw-boned lad who did not do refined or sensitivity and in all aspects of his life was fond of quantity rather than quality. She seemed to pick up on those qualities in an instant and all her attention then focused on him.

Norah was also amongst that smallish minority of women, or so it seemed to me, who had decided that lots of cock was one of life's top priorities. I had run into the frigid types but there were lots of others who were either terrified of their parents or of what the neighbours would say to loosen the sexual reins. I had run into middle aged and older women who seemed to talk about sex all the time but who obviously were not getting much. Also, there were the miserable older crones who seemed to be viciously anti-sex. This group seemed to include a lot of heavy smokers. I wondered if nicotine substituted for or reduced the need for sex. I couldn't quite work it out.

Our arrangement worked fine and although I had received a few obvious come-ons, I was still seeing to Maggie's needs and none of the women pointing their loaded tits at me were worth the hassle. Towards the end of our stint, I was doing the upstairs and a bedroom window opened. Inside was a nubile seventeen-year-old called Carmel. Her parents were out but her younger sister was in the next room. She kept on looking at me and especially at my crotch. After a couple of minutes, she was stroking me, and I was overcome with strong urges. She then started showing me her superb tits and was sat on the sill and reaching out to try to get my zip down.

The flesh can only withstand so much temptation. I said, 'Give me a minute.' I whizzed down the ladder and adjusted it till the top of it was just level with her sill. I went round to where Danny was doing the lower fronts and said, 'Have a fag and a cuppa when you've done, I have an inside to do.' Danny grinned and I went back round to the rear of the house and climbed the ladder and said to Carmel, 'Get your knickers down and get over here with your arse on the windowsill. She cottoned on quickly. It was a bit precarious, but the level was just right, and I could just get nicely up her pussy from the top of the ladder with her clinging round my neck and sitting on her windowsill.

The sex was intense and furious. She was incredibly hot and started to moan and orgasm as soon as my cock thrust into her. I had a huge orgasm, and she took the lot deep into her pussy moaning with pleasure. I pulled out and zipped up. She was giving me longing looks and could probably have gone on all day. I said, 'Later babe, when we have more time and space.' I looked down and could see Danny looking up. I shinned down the ladder and carried it round the front to finish off. Danny sniggered as I walked past. He said, 'dirty bastard', obviously in total approval of the quickie.

I was a bit worried about Carmel being pregnant, but I saw her a week later down at the local post office. She explained that her dad was a Catholic and thought that using birth control was a sin, but her mother wasn't, and she had decided to stop at two kids rather than at the ten or twelve of some of the other families of the faithful, by using a Dutch-cap and spermicides.

She explained to me that her mum knew that her eldest daughter was highly sexed and was likely to get into trouble. Thus, she had gone to a contraceptive clinic in Leeds and had been prescribed the birth pill for herself which she had passed on to her daughter. The pill had become legal in 1961 but could only be prescribed to married women until 1967. The happy arrangement meant that Carmel became exceedingly popular amongst the youth of the area. Her parents were spared the shame of having to send their daughter off on a holiday for several weeks, to a home for unmarried mothers.

The local priest wasn't overly happy because of the lack of young Catholics being produced by the household, but it was a 'mixed marriage,' always a mistake as far as he was concerned. Those women brought up in the faith tended to be fearful of their priest and usually did what they were told, especially when it came to breeding. Carmel seemed to pop up more and more in my life. It was as though she had some sort of tracker following my movements in the village. Whenever she appeared she was immediately giving me the strongest of come-ons. Her looks and body language constituted a constant and lascivious invitation to have sex. Danny said, 'Watch out boy, she's got you lined up for the altar.'

Marriage was the last thing I had in mind. Carmel was great when it came to sex. I fucked her senseless in most of the quiet spots of the locality and at her parent's place in the evenings when they were down at the pub. She was always gasping to get my cock into her hot and lubricating pussy, always gasping with pleasure during the act and always yearning for more afterwards. All that was great, but the only problem was that sex was all she could think about. I started to vary my routine to avoid her after a few weeks. A few months after that the problem was solved for me by the whole family emigrating to Australia on the assisted passage scheme. Carmel's dad had been offered a job and couldn't believe how much it paid compared to what he was getting in the UK. After the family left, I wondered how Carmel would be greeted by those big, bronzed Aussies—probably with huge enthusiasm, I thought.

By the summer we had both saved a few quid and Danny had an idea. He had been talking to some lads at the pit and they said they had a great holiday the year before on a boat on the Norfolk Broads. I had a vague idea that they were a series of linked rivers and canals somewhere near Yarmouth, but I was doubtful. I had no experience of boating and neither had Danny or Baz. Also, I had no experience of holidays apart from the annual day trip to the coast organised by the working men's club that Jed belonged to. We had a chat to Baz and Jase and they agreed. Jason's dad was a big help because he had been stationed down there during the war and knew the area and agreed to drive us down in the battered old Bedford van that he used to move second hand furniture round in. He also found an address and some prices for the boats and sent a cheque down as a deposit for us.

He explained that the broads were shallow lakes which had formed after peat had been cut by monks in the Middle Ages. They were interconnected by several rivers and canals. The four of us paid a quarter each to hire an old narrow boat. The plan was to set off early on a Saturday morning and Jase's dad sent the balance off a fortnight before we arrived. It had been suggested to us that we take lots of tins of soup, stew, corned beef, tinned beans and tomatoes along with lard, tea and sugar and cheese and cream crackers. The lads who had travelled down the previous year had said, 'Tha' dun't want to eat out down there, its bloody expensive.' On their advice we also took four crates, each containing a dozen pint bottles of Sam Smith's Bitter. They had said, 'When tha' gets down there buy some bacon, eggs, sausage, bread and milk. Tha' can start off every day wi' a bloody big fry up.'

I didn't smoke, which was unusual in those days in our area, and cut down on my drinking because I was determined to have a good holiday which could have been spoiled by a shortage of cash and started to save. I even managed a couple of pairs of jeans and a few tee shirts and a black donkey jacket. The four of us had chatted about money and agreed that it would be a four-way split on food and we would drink in rounds. If anybody had a big thirst they could top up at the end of the night. We all looked at big Danny when we arranged that because we all knew he could easily do a gallon. Jason couldn't take a lot and three or four was easily enough for me. Baz could drink but he had to watch it because he usually wanted to fight after about five pints.

We talked about money and the other three said they would have a week's pay because none of their mothers would be taking the weekly board while they were on holiday. We had chatted about board previously and I found out that Jason was paying two pounds a week. Baz and Danny paid two pounds ten shillings and I was paying four pounds. Baz said, 'Tha's being robbed.' I know blokes that tip up and get clothes bought who don't pay that much after they get their pocket money back. In my case I asked about keeping the week's holiday pay but was told: 'Oh, the rooms there for you, if you don't want to use it, it's up to you.' Liz even had the nerve to suggest that I bring her a present back from my holidays. I put their grasping attitude as one of life experiences. I knew the occasional youth who was worse off than me. There weren't many though, and it was usually in circumstances where the father had been killed at the pit or didn't work for some reason. My dislike of the pair grew, and I became more determined than ever to escape from home as soon as possible.

Spring seemed to drift by incredibly slowly, but finally we entered June and the week of departure loomed. We loaded the van up the night before and arranged to be at Jason's place for six. His dad had explained that if we got off early it would be a big help in missing the Saturday traffic. We were all in the van and on our way just after six. To my surprise Jason was driving. He had passed his test a few months earlier and his dad said: 'It will be good practice for him on the empty roads.' The plan was to do about halfway and then let Jason's dad take over before we got to Kings Lynn. He said the trip was about 200 miles. He knew the area well due to his war service.

Jason was a ropey driver but seemed to get better as we chugged along, sometimes hitting fifty-five or sixty on the straight stretches of the A1 and then the A17. Just after eight-thirty we pulled in at a transport café and Jason's dad bought us all a breakfast. It was a big fry up with lots of brown sauce and fried bread. 'My treat,' said Bill. 'You are all growing lads, and it will set you up for the day. I was taken aback; parental generosity was just something I wasn't used to.

After the breakfast, which was washed down with pint mugs of hot strong tea, Jason's dad got into the driver's seat, and we set off on the last leg to Potter Heigham. The road was getting busier, and we really slowed down driving through the small villages. Though we had covered well over a hundred miles before the stop, we were now plodding along averaging about thirty. The Bedford was a big old reliable diesel. I had been in the back during the first leg but was now at the front in the big double passenger seat. With Baz, Jason and Danny had decided they would stretch out in the back until we got there.

Bill pointed out places of interest as we drove through the North Norfolk landscape. I had never seen anything like it. There seemed to be no towns, just pretty villages. There were no pits, factories or slag heaps, just mile after mile of the sort of scenery which I had only seen previously on the lids of biscuit tins. We drove past a sign to Sandringham. Bill said 'That's where the big royal estate is. It's about twenty thousand acres. There's a massive house that they live in occasionally and the estate has five villages on it which they own. The Royals certainly know how to pick good places to live. They have that huge place at Windsor, Buckingham Palace and a fifty-thousand-acre estate up in the highlands at Balmoral. I knew one of the Grenadier Guardsmen; he said they have a couple of dozen other places with various relatives parked in 'em. Not the sort of thing that gets much publicity.'

'None in Yorkshire then,' I said. 'You must be bloody joking,' he replied. 'I doubt if any of 'em are within a hundred miles of a spoil heap.' 'Not a royalist then,' I added, laughing. Bill replied thoughtfully. 'Put it like this. I don't like the bullshit— the pap that we get fed by the BBC and the press about them. Also, I got some inside info about how they carry on from my guardsman friend. They all know what goes on, but they keep their gobs shut. But to be fair the old king did a good job through the war and his daughter, and the Duke of Edinburgh seem to be on that path, but you can never be sure. But it comes and goes. That Duke of Windsor who was king for a bit before her dad was a spoiled brat twat who liked wine women and cigarettes. He got all that he could handle and possibly more. He put his personal pleasure before his duty. I have no time for the bloke, and he was a bit too keen on the Nazis in the thirties for my liking as well.'

After that he was silent for a while until we passed a large field with a bedraggled copse at one end. 'See that,' he said. 'A Lancaster came down there in 1943. It had a 2000 pounder stuck underneath. The release mechanism had been damaged by flack, as had his engines. He just made it back at low altitude. He ordered the crew to parachute out. Two did, but two were badly wounded so he tried a pancake landing in the field. He nearly made it, but the jolting released the bomb at the last minute and blew everything to bits.' It was my turn to be silent. 'The Skipper was twenty-two, and the crewmen who died with him were twenty. Makes you think, don't it.' It certainly did.

Chapter 14

An introduction to the country life

Willows whiten, aspens quiver,
little breezes dusk and shiver
through the wave that runs forever
by the island in the river.

Tennyson

After that the countryside got even flatter with numerous dykes and occasional flashes of open water. The day was warm for mid-June at well over seventy Fahrenheit. Bill said, 'I think tha's going to be lucky wi' t' weather.' We eventually rolled into the boat yard at Potter Heigham. There were two caravans, which had been drawn up close and linked. The front one was the office and the rear the owner's living quarters. Bill led us into the office and did most of the talking. The elderly bloke who ran it was a retired bargee who had bought a few of the old narrow boats cheaply when their use had declined after the war. His accent came as a surprise to me as I had never heard anybody with the rounded rural accent of a Norfolk man.

He took us across to the boats which were moored side by side in twos. We had a tour of the craft. There were four single bunks in two small rooms at the front. A bathroom in the middle containing a shower, a sink and a lavatory. There was a small kitchen and seating towards the front of a small cockpit at the rear with the tiller. The vessel was surprisingly spacious and two of the flat couches converted into small beds. The boat could sleep six at a pinch, but the two smaller beds were really just for kids.

The bargee was called Joe. He took out an old briar pipe and cut off a few small pieces of 'black-twist' tobacco from a six-inch length of the material. I recognised it because it was a strong, cheap pipe tobacco favoured by a lot of the older miners from my village. He crumbled it between his fingers and pushed it firmly down into the bowl and struck a match and held it just above the black mass and drew through the pipe, pulling the flame down onto his twist until it started to glow and smoulder. After that he puffed contentedly as he showed us round the boat. He asked about our ages. The boat was supposed to be under the charge of an adult, so we told him that Danny was twenty-two, which as a big and raw-boned lad he certainly looked. Joe said, 'Well, you're in charge then,' and showed us the engine and how to add the diesel. He explained that the craft was very reliable and we should be able to chug on forever at a steady three or four miles an hour. He showed us how to fill up with fuel and said 'Make sure you don't run out. You can pick some up at any garage and the boat yards along the broads sell it in two-gallon cans.'

He spent a few minutes explaining the shower and cooking setups and then said, 'We'll just do a circuit and I will show you how to steer and berth.' He skilfully went through the basic manoeuvres, and then said to Danny to try. Steering was easy but berthing more difficult, however we berthed alright. He said, 'Just cut the engine a little earlier and let it drift in, then one of you jump off and moor it.' There were a couple of tyres cut in half and mounted on either side of the boat as shock-absorbers. He explained, 'It's a big old boat, robust. It would take a lot of mishandling to damage it, but be careful, you don't want to end up paying for it.' He then pointed us to a big map mounted in front of the tiller.

He said, 'You can go wherever you like but there are suggested routes marked out on the map. Most people like to motor along for a bit and enjoy the scenery but there are lots of stopping places. If you look at the map, I recommend the red route, which will see you berthed near a pub every night. Just follow the river traffic and stick to the main waterways, and you will be fine. One other thing, the boat can get hot. You can drop those clips and the side panels can be lifted up out of their slots and laid on the top of the barge. Make sure you put 'em back at night, because it can get cold, and it might rain.'

He went on, 'The main thing you need to remember is that the boat must be back here and tidied out by ten in the morning next Saturday. Most people like to be back here by Friday night and have a last night in the big village pub here. There is always a folk group on through the summer. There are a couple of smaller places if you want a quiet drink. If you don't get back on time you lose your deposit.'

With that we loaded our gear onto the boat and set off with Danny at the tiller. Danny said to me, 'You can look at the map and tell us where to go. I haven't got a fucking clue about maps.' I took a quick look at the routes recommended by old Joe. There were three marked on the map, one in red, one in black and one in blue. I chose the red route and set Danny off across the broad stretch of water.

After a while I told him to fork left, and we chugged along up a pretty river. Danny soon got bored as tiller man and I took over while he moved forward for a fag. Jason and Baz took their turns and we moved on slowly through pretty countryside.

'Not like the bloody pit villages, is it?' said Baz.

I knew exactly what he meant. The pit villages, like most northern industrial towns, were usually constructed cheaply as grim barracks for the working classes and their families. The houses were functional, often with outside washhouses and lavatories. Those dwellings lined roads which were devoid of greenery. If there were gardens, they were usually sparsely attended to if they were attended to at all, for the simple reason that after five and a half days working down a pit the men were just too knackered to bother. The older men usually spent Saturday afternoons resting after they got back from work. They might take a stroll down to the local park or bowling green, or a sports club if there was a cricket match on a fine summer afternoon. Some of the younger men raced home and got the bus to the local football or rugby stadium. Lots of them would finish their Saturdays down at the working men's clubs.

In the immediate post war years there was a hell of a buzz at those clubs. The men were earning a lot, and due to rationing, there was little to spend it on apart from beer and cigarettes. With only radio entertainment available, and most of that wasn't entertaining as far as the workers were concerned, the clubs were the natural focus for social life. There were churches in the district but most of them were in severe decline. The move away from them, which had started in the Great War, had accelerated after the Second World War. Although most people still got married, christened, and had a funeral service in a church, fewer and fewer people attended the Sunday services. Eventually the Baptist churches started to fold then the Methodists. The Church of England with its huge rental and investment income hung on as did the small Catholic enclaves.

I thought about it later and it was obvious that Christianity had lost that driving energy and with it the huge authority which it had possessed during the nineteenth century. Its wealth was also slowly ebbing away. Income from collections at services was down and declining year by year. More and more people were getting married in Register Offices and independent spirits were arranging for humanist readers and the like to officiate at the funerals at the crematoriums, which were becoming more and more popular. Beliefs like the resurrection of the dead were fading and the whole shaky theological foundation of the religion was crumbling under the assault of science and the socialist analysis of religious belief.

The establishment tried to hang on like grim death to the control of the masses that religion had afforded them. But the masses were having none of it. Those who ran the religious hierarchies shot themselves in the foot by their determined policy to keep Sunday miserable! Commercial sport such as horse racing and football was not allowed. TV on Sundays was as dull as a drizzle-filled winter's day, with lots of worthy and moralising discussions, usually involving notable clergymen.

In those days of course there were no clergywomen apart from a few at the lowest level in the Church. Some areas of the country still banned drinking on Sundays. The licencing laws elsewhere were severely restricted, and they would probably have liked no drinking at all on the Sabbath but for the fact that thirsty miners and steel workers and similar would probably have rioted. The silly twats who ran things didn't seem to realise that after a week's hard graft in miserable conditions the last thing that the workers wanted was a day of misery. Final defeat came during the latter part of the twentieth century, but even in the twenty-first, repressive organisations such as 'the Lord's Day Observance Society' were still fighting a determined rear-guard action, but to no avail.

As we drifted along, I continued to be delighted by the beauty and greenery which lined the waterways. I could recognise weeping willows and a few other trees but there were also numerous other flowers and shrubs, most of which I had never seen before. Like most other kids of my village, I could recognise buttercups and daisies and dandelions and not much else. This seemed lost on Danny who spent a lot of time thumbing through the collection of dog-eared western novels he found in a drawer. Jason had brought a recent copy of the racing information manual called Time-Form. In it there were tips on trainers and horses and supposedly recent information about horse performance obtained by blokes armed with binoculars hiding in bushes with stop watches near training establishments. I asked Jason if he believed all that guff and pointed out that there were hundreds of racehorse trainers, and that the Time-form organisation would need to employ a small army of spies in order to get comprehensive coverage. But Jason had faith. He knew that you could get rich by betting, all you needed was to pick the right horses. The trouble was nobody ever did, and those who had the occasional big win via an accumulator bet or similar were invariably queuing up at the bookmaker's to lose it at the next available race meeting.

I eventually realised that there was no point in talking about things like that. The irrational always ruled. Early on I could read graphs and understood statistical tables. I realised that I understood scientific data, many just could not grasp it. They had read the same stuff as me about things like smoking, but they were convinced that they would be one of the few who had the pass-out which gave them exemption from its huge number of death-causing effects. These lucky ones went blithely on, puffing away until the stroke or heart attack. I became aware that even when smokers got to the stage where they were struggling to breathe, many persisted. Even when they started coughing up blood due to lung cancer, they were still at it, even while in hospital being treated for it. It was just the same with gambling and heavy boozing—the need to do it far outweighed any rational thoughts about outcomes. But it was up to them, I had enough with sorting my own life-problems out.

As we moved serenely along the quiet and verdant waterways, lines of poetry from school and words which had never meant much to me such as 'idyllic' surfaced in my brain. This area was indeed a place of quiet serenity, almost a natural beauty reservation. All of us saw things differently. We all liked the novelty of being on the narrow boat and I could happily have drifted on for hours drinking in the sights of different birds, insects, stretches of water and the magically changing verdure of the riverbanks. Baz rapidly got bored and wanted to moor the boat as often as possible whenever we got into any place of any size. Jason had borrowed an old camera which his dad had obtained in Germany after the war. It was a Voigtlander, and apparently had excellent lenses. Jason took a few snaps of us round the boat and of the landscape and waterways as we chugged through them.

We soon got into a routine of a big fry up for breakfast, with sausage, eggs, bacon, tinned tomatoes, beans and fried bread. Later in the day it was tinned soup or stew and big chunks of buttered bread. At stops along the way we grabbed pork and meat pies and sausage rolls. Lots of snacks such as cheese and biscuits and ordinary biscuits were on hand. Danny's mum had contributed a carrier bag containing some big packs of salted peanuts and oranges and tins of pears and plums. She knew very well how ravenous young men could be at our ages.

We always planned it so that we got to a mooring by five or six. We had a wash and shave, then a shower occasionally and then had a look round. Our first stop was always a pub. On the first night we got into a large village and spent an hour strolling round, looking at the pretty cottages and lanes. There was a village shop which was shut, but there were three pubs. We drifted into the first which was half empty. We looked at the labels on the pumps. The landlord said, 'It's Woodfords, that's the main brewery round here.' We sampled a pint but were not impressed, having been brought up on the bitter beers of South Yorkshire, including Barnsley bitter, which was reputedly the bitterest beer in the country. The landlord was built to the standard pattern, about fifty-five with a big fleshy face and matching gut. He had noted our harsh accents and was obviously sizing us up.

'Where you lads from?' he intoned in the rolling Norfolk accent.

'Donny' Danny grunted.

'Oh, Doncaster,' he replied. 'On holiday?'

'Yeah,' I replied. 'Narrow boat. We are moored near the others.'

The landlord said, 'We don't get many strangers in here, it's mainly locals. The tourists usually head down to The Fox. It's bigger and they do food.' I got the distinct impression that he would rather we did our drinking elsewhere. I picked those vibes up quite a few times down there. Perhaps it was the Northern accents, perhaps it was the fact that we were big lads who looked like we could enjoy a punch up, especially after a few pints. Perhaps it was memories from the war with northern squaddies picking fights with locals and American airmen. The pub was dingy and looked like a hard-drinking-man's place. I wondered about it being packed with thirsty farm workers and door-locked drinking sessions into the early hours like one or two of the boozers near us. It had that sort of air, with basic, solid furniture. No fripperies, everything geared to having the beer as cheap as possible. I might have been wrong because farm labourers were on shit wages. Face-workers had loads of money in those days and lots of 'em liked lots of beer.

We drifted down to The Fox. It was a lot bigger than the first pub and had resisted the early sixties trend of refurbishment and modernisation. It looked like a pub and smelled like one. Beer, cigarette smoke and sweaty bodies were much in evidence. The clientele was weirdly non-homogenous to my uneducated eyes. Up round us you could go into most boozers, and you would find everybody dressed the same and talking the same. There were a few drinking establishments in the more prosperous fringes of my hometown where the clientele was solidly middle class. They usually wore suits and ties and stood around drinking halves. The drinks were always more expensive, and they didn't make nearly as much money as the pubs and clubs in the mining areas. There, you always had a hard core of drinkers who could easily do a gallon a session and did it seven nights a week, and Sunday mid-day sessions but usually only three or four pints then. In addition, there were others who got in most nights and who did half a dozen pints, and the retired mine workers who got into the public bars, which were almost exclusively male preserves, and who had their steady four pints a night while playing dominoes or cribbage. In The Fox it was every type you could think off, I was fascinated.

There was a group of big lads stood round one corner of the bar. From their slow accents and soft vowel sounds I placed them as farm labourers or similar. There was a group who were obviously on boating holidays. Some wore flannels and blazers, often with cravats the neck. Others had roll neck sweaters and peaked caps giving a nautical appearance. Some of the conversations drifting across the room were about boats. I heard snatches about engines, rigging, waterproofing and the like. The wives made much less effort to dress like experienced mariners. They were mostly in summer dresses and Marks and Spencer cardigans or similar.

A red-faced bloke came in wearing a flat cap and tweedy

jacket. He walked across to the big lads and bought them a drink and left some money for a second round. After some jovialities he downed his pint and made his way out. I heard the word gaffer a couple of times and concluded he was a farmer probably buying his farm hands some Saturday night beer. A few harassed looking dads were in with their families, sat in the big porch. Now and again, they would come to the bar and then depart with a tray full of bottles of pop and crisps to feed the squalling brats and satisfy the equally harassed looking wife with a Cherry B or similar alcoholic concoction, which the breweries were now pushing via the newly arrived TV advertising.

After a while the folk group arrived and started to churn out favourites like 'The Barley Mow'. The audience loved it and sat in semi reverential silence while the woman in the group got through 'A Bold Young Farmer Courted Me.' I could tell that Danny was less than impressed and I had hated the jingly-jangly music of this type ever since my early youth when the only lively music allowed on the BBC was a Scottish country music group called Jimmy Shand and his Band. I still, even now, have a strong urge to strangle anyone I hear playing an accordion. After a bit they left with the dire promise to be on later. One of the locals then started to circulate selling raffle tickets so we went outside.

We stood in the late evening sun finishing our pints looking around at the rural greenery and at the broad expanse of water beyond the moored boats. I could see a group of girls who were giggling and looking at us. From the conversation and looks I estimated that they were seventeen to eighteen-year-olds. It was always difficult to estimate ages from appearance. I knew one incredibly well-developed girl back in my village who looked nineteen but was only in fact fourteen; her immaturity showed immediately though whenever she opened her mouth. A couple of them were smoking and one of them, an attractive blond, started to look in my direction in a very juicily wanton manner. The signals were so obvious that even Baz said, 'She fancies you.' I looked back in the direction of the blonde. She was about five feet six and had a pair of rather large tits, always a magnet to someone of my tastes. She was blond with the bouffant hairdo which was then fashionable, blue eyed and with a wide and generous mouth which turned down at the corners giving her an impish expression.

I had discovered early that in the sexual chess game it was always a good strategy to feign indifference and to let them make the first move. It was fatal to appear to be over eager or in fact to appear interested. After a few minutes, the hot humming hormones in the blond won and she drifted over and said, 'Hello, I haven't seen you round here before. You on holiday?'

I was still finding the soft yokel-ish Norfolk accent a bit strange, but I grunted a reply, 'Yep, we're on a narrow boat moored down there.' I nodded in the general direction.

She said, 'You're from up north. We get all sorts on holiday down here.' It looked as though the tourist trade meant that my accent wasn't nearly as strange or new to her as hers was to mine. She continued, 'I've always wanted a ride on a narrow boat.' Her salacious smirk indicated that the sort of ride she wanted wasn't exactly a slow meander down the river.

Big Danny said drily, 'We're off back in the pub then, see you later.'

I then found myself walking slowly back towards the narrow boat with Lana. She explained that her parents were fans of the Film star Lana Turner. I wasn't too interested in film stars but remembered this one as not so long back there had been big headlines about her fourteen-year-old daughter stabbing a gangster called Johnny Stompanato, who had been Turner's boyfriend.

We eventually got back to the boat. There was no one around and I ushered the Norfolk lovely aboard. She walked straight to the bedroom and slipped out of her dress. We moved together and started to kiss as she reached down and fondled my bulging cock. I dropped my pants as she pulled her panties down and pulled me towards her.

Her actions were even more urgent than mine. She gasped

as my pulsating and rigid member slid into her wet and welcoming cunt. After a furious burst of action with her legs pulled back as she lay across the bed, I had a huge orgasm and relaxed on top of her.

She said, 'That was bloody quick. I've been gagging for a good hard fucking all week.'

She pushed her tits towards my mouth, and I started to suck and bite her nipples. She started to moan again and pulled my hand down towards her pussy. I knew enough about the female anatomy to feel for the swollen area at the top of her slit and then I started to finger it gently. She was really moaning now and pushing up against my fingers.

After a few minutes she started to writhe with pleasure, almost screaming, and then she went limp, also having had a huge orgasm. She lay back eyes half closed and eventually reached for a cigarette. She lit it and inhaled deeply and said, 'God, I needed that. It's months since I had a decent shag. At least you knew how to make me come. With most of the farm boys round here it's like being in a farmyard, they don't have a clue.' She giggled and said, 'I suppose that now you've had your wicked way with me you will want to get back to your mates. I will get back to the girls I was with. They will want to know what happened, all the dirty details, so they can get off and finger themselves silly in bed tonight dreaming about somebody doing it to them.'

We dressed and got off the boat. I could see a red-faced, stout, middle-aged bloke glowering at me. I stared back at him, hard, and he looked away and then went below deck on his launch. The look said everything; disapproval marked with jealousy, probably born of sexual frustration. We slowly made our way back to the pub.

Lana asked me if we would be back later in the week, saying, 'I wouldn't mind a repeat of that. With a bit of tutoring you could be a real sex machine.'

'I will do my best. It'll probably be the Thursday if I manage it.'

'Good, my parents will be in Norwich at her sisters. They

always have a few drinks and get the last train back here. It gets in at ten past eleven so we could have a nice long evening together down at our cottage. It's on a smallholding on the outskirts of the village.'

I asked about the place, and she explained it was about eighteen acres.

I said, 'That's a bit small. I wouldn't have thought you could make much of a living from that.'

She laughed. 'The black alluvial soil round here is some of the richest in the country. We can grow crops round here that you can't get anywhere else. My dad has about an acre covered in cold frames and greenhouses. He is a tight bugger; his brother-in-law is a builder and over the years he has built them himself using old window frames and bricks from building sites he has helped with. My mum raises chickens, and they sell the produce over the summer at local markets, and he delivers to hotels with his van. They do a roaring trade. Lots of it is cash in hand so it doesn't go through the books or have tax paid on it, and he buys up surplus stuff from the other small holdings and allotments to sell on. He has a cottage he lets out to holiday makers through the summer, and very cheap to a couple of artists who come down here to paint over the autumn and winter.'

I logged the information, mentally comparing the lives portrayed to the tough lives lived in the mining villages. It seemed that it wasn't all rich farmers and landowners and impoverished farm labourers down here, there was a lot more scope for a good life than I had imagined. In addition, the place was beautiful. There was none of the soot and grime from the coal fires of the towns and large urban huddles which made up the mining villages, and none of the huge grey spoil heaps dotted every two or three miles or the ugly pit chimneys and head gears and washeries and other buildings. If you lived there, it was something you were attuned to—you didn't particularly notice it. Being in these surroundings brought my home environment sharply into focus and sharpened my desire to escape from it.

I walked Lana back to the pub. I could see her friends giggling and giving us that 'we know what you've been doing,' sort of look that teenage girls are prone to. I thought, 'I bet they can't wait to hear the full juicy details.'

I wandered back into the pub and found Danny and the boys.

Baz said. 'Ho! just in time, it's your round.'

I drifted to the bar and ordered four pints. We sat chatting and Jason said, 'Come on then, what was she like?'

I said, 'Oh, a well brought up young lady. She enjoyed looking round the barge.'

Baz grinned and said, 'Lucky bastard—you attract 'em like flies round rotten meat.' Shortly after that the folk group started to make their way back onto the small stage, so we drank up and strolled back through the balmy summer air to where the narrowboat was moored.

Chapter 15

On the beach

'Most Gods throw dice, but fate plays chess!
You don't find out till too late, that he has been
playing with two queens all along.'

Terry Pratchett

The following morning was a glorious June day with hardly a cloud in the sky. I got up early and got the breakfast going. The other three emerged reluctantly from their berths when they smelled the bacon frying. I found out that the best way to manage things was to put the sausages in the oven and fry the bread after the bacon and put that above the hot plate while I buttered bread. Beans and tomatoes slowly warmed up in a pan while I did scrambled eggs after the fried bread.

After a while we all sat round eating and planning what to do.

Danny said, 'Tha's the brains of the outfit. What do you think.'

Pointing at the map, I replied, 'We can head up here and choose a route to Honing or Coltishall. If we do that its up and then back the way we came and there are a couple of low bridges which might best be avoided. I think we should take this route down to Yarmouth. We can spend a day there if you want. After that we could chug on down towards Lowestoft or towards Norwich, but I don't fancy a big city somehow. We can ask around when we stop. I think we will get lots of help. One thing we need to keep in mind is getting back. We ought to start back on the Wednesday. I don't fancy getting back late and losing our deposit—that's half as much as we paid for the whole week.'

The three readily agreed and half an hour later we were on our way. I soon got used to handling the slow and cumbersome craft. It was supposed to do four miles an hour but that was obviously a maximum. I got the impression that against the current upstream it was only about half that. I enjoyed the gentle and ever-changing scenery on the river. I was amazed at the variety of wildlife, especially the birds. Where we lived you might see the occasional soot encrusted sparrow or robin or blackbird and not much else. Here I was seeing woodpeckers, jays and numerous small birds, often in attractive plumage. Waterfowl of various types were always about. On the riverbanks I was aware of quick and wary eyes and a sudden flash of activity as an otter or water-vole or similar became aware of us and darted for cover.

There was a small booklet on boating etiquette which I had read. The main points seemed to be to reduce speed on narrow stretches, slow down when you are passing moored boats and to be careful when using locks and to ask for help if you are a novice. I made a mental note and encouraged the others to slow down if we passed a mooring.

As the morning drew on, we took turns to steer and pulled in anywhere that looked interesting. Usually, we were back on board quickly as the small shops containing trinkets for tourists, and the tea rooms, had little attraction for us. But it was interesting, and I was getting a feel for the place. I noticed that the locals looked healthier than most round us back at home. Gone were the pallid faces and the older men with the hacking coughs produced by lifetimes of breathing in coal dust and cigarette smoke. Danny was restless. It wasn't his sort of thing at all. He would have liked to have found a boozer and spent a couple of hours drinking, but we had agreed that we would just visit pubs in the evenings.

Baz spent a lot of time looking at the engine and reading a small technical manual he found in a drawer. I could see him stare enviously at some of the launches we passed with their powerful rear motors. He said, 'I bet they are dying to let it rip.' The speed limit on the Broads had been set at four miles an hour to stop the banks getting eroded by waves from fast craft. Mostly people kept to the limit, but on the bigger expanses of water we did occasionally see somebody open the throttle on a big boat. These rare events usually provoked angry shouts or fist waving from any others in the vicinity.

It took us most of the day and into the evening to get to the mooring near Great Yarmouth. We were all tired when we arrived. We tied up and didn't bother to shave or wash, we just found a quiet old-style pub which served pie and peas. We ate, had a couple of pints and a chat with the locals about the best way of getting into the town, and then got back and bunked down ready for an early start next morning. I got everybody moving early and we just had bacon sarnies for breakfast. I knew there would be plenty of opportunities to eat later in the big seaside resort.

I didn't know the resort at all, but Jase had been there a couple of times with his parents. He said, 'It's the east coast version of Blackpool, not as big or crowded, but lively. You get lots of Brummies here and quite a few from London. Lancashire and Scots accents are rare, why come here when Blackpool is so close. There they get coach loads down from the Glasgow when the factories close for the fortnight's summer holiday.'

'You been there then?' I asked.

'Just a day trip. Dance and boozing hot spots are best avoided at night, lots of drunken fights.'

'I can't believe that about Glaswegians,' I replied.

Danny gave me one of his looks. 'Not fucking much,' he said. 'My uncle Bill was with that lot in the war. For some reason they were all in the Gordon Highlanders. He described them as a great fighting unit, both at the front and on leave. Wild men! Punch up and piss up artists par excellence, he called them.'

Then he said, 'You're a bit quiet.'

'Just having a think,' I replied.

We had spent the late evening drinking through some of the bottled ale we had brought down and watching the late June sunset over the water. The holiday had been a revelation to me. I realised how little I knew of the world outside my own small mining village and its adjacent grimy industrial town. It was all sowing the seeds of restlessness and dissatisfaction which would weigh on me in the coming years. I realised I had to do something to change things.

We left the boat early and were on our way into Yarmouth just after nine. It looked like being another blistering day. The bus driver told us the last bus back was at 9pm. If we missed it it was a three mile walk or a taxi.' We disembarked at the central bus station and wandered towards the sea front. The place was typical of an early sixties' seaside resort—still thriving, with boarding houses and hotels full, and lots of day trippers, especially at weekends. Though car ownership had started to increase as purchase tax on them had recently dropped from fifty to twenty-five percent, they were still expensive and only about a third of families owned one. The bulk of the population made its visits to the coast by train or coach. These were still the days when a working men's club or works club would hire sixty coaches and deliver two thousand adults and kids to the nearest resort. The stall holders loved it as business was great during those times. In addition to the sea food, ice cream, rock and candy floss, the penny arcades also did a roaring trade.

By the time we got to the sea it was just starting to get busy with boarding houses disgorging residents after breakfast and most of the families heading for the beach. By eleven, some coaches had arrived and the crowds along the front swelled considerably. We wandered along taking in the sights, drifting through the amusement arcades. We had long ago learned that the slots and other contrivances with brightly flashing lights were just machines for taking money off mugs. We circulated, looking at the machines and watching people put money in. No one seemed to notice that the users always lost. It was the old 'gamblers fallacy' operating on a small scale—next time they would win! I couldn't work out what was wrong with people—why couldn't they see it? Baz was like me, he never put anything in a slot machine. He had a relative who had undergone some sort of breakdown after being passed over for promotion and after that had put a small fortune in sixpences into the 'one arm bandits', as they were known. He played feverishly for hours on end every evening. It was some sort of mania which eventually left him impoverished in retirement, as most of his salary was squandered and a big balance in his savings account dwindled to nothing.

Baz hated the things. I just couldn't see the logic of throwing money away like that or of any other type of gambling. Danny was different; he occasionally tried his luck at the stalls such as the darts or shooting and the cranes in the small glass kiosks where you could grab a prize and try to drop it in an opening. I had watched this over the years and seen people almost do it, but I had never seen anyone win a prize. I had realised long ago that the entertainment came from seeing people lose. It applied in all fields. Later I came upon gamblers elsewhere, late on in restaurants or hotels who had lost big at the races, sometimes simmering and almost boiling up as though they needed a fight to get rid of their loser's frustrations. How did they feel? Exploited mugs? Stupid? Was it something deeper? It could be. My observations in casinos later on told me that there was something strange about a lot of gamblers. I could see them white-faced, sweating, gambling feverishly with no sign of enjoyment unless it was the masochistic pleasure of being humiliated in public as a pathetic loser.

These were the obsessives. Lots of people just gambled occasionally as part of a night out, expecting to lose a few quid —it was no big deal. Others were there for the 'very artificial' glamour. Even small provincial casinos occasionally entertained celebrities and I suppose people could dress up to the nines and fantasise that they were in Monte Carlo rubbing shoulders with the rich and famous. The one thing I did like about casinos was the food. The gambling side of things usually made so much money that the food available was usually cheap and of a high standard. Not that the top table types used those facilities. The very attentive staff at those tables saw to it that sandwiches were supplied, gratis, whenever required. The uneducated in these matters would probably think 'how civil!' Cynics, such as I, saw it as an excellent method of keeping the punters at those tables as long as possible and thus assuring an uninterrupted flow of money, usually in the casino's direction. But this was the early sixties, just bottom rung gambling in penny slot machines in Yarmouth. I had no interest in making the arcade owners even richer than they were.

We drifted along slowly through the sultry afternoon. We had sampled ice cream and hot dogs and had finally moved past the amusements. We bought a large bottle of lemonade and headed for the beach. It was empty at the top end. We lounged on the sands. I wondered about having a swim. I had my trunks on under my jeans but no towel, but that was no big deal as on a hot day like this I would soon dry off. It was June and the North Sea would be cold, fourteen Centigrade, but the afternoon would be the best time to brave the chill.

A group of young women meandered down onto the sands. They wore loose coats and chiffon scarves over their bouffant hair styles. Although the beach was empty, they sat down a few yards from us chattering and giggling. They pulled out some sandwiches and a flask from one of their bags and then some towels which they sat and lay on to enjoy the sun and the sights. The main sight being we four.

I said, 'I'm off for a swim. I took off my tee shirt and jeans and trotted off, down to the sparkling sea. I was aware that eyes were on me, so once waist deep I plunged straight in and struck out in my powerful crawl. I had never been taught to swim but was fast due to my shoulder strength. A coach down at the local baths had watched me and tried to get me down to the local swimming club. He had said, 'You've got a lot of raw power, but your technique is poor, you're only doing a two-beat crawl. With a six or eight beat you would be a lot faster.' I didn't know what a two-beat crawl was. He explained: 'You are only kicking your legs twice during your arm strokes.

138

You are surprisingly fast but that's just raw strength. If you could increase your leg beats it would be easier and faster.' He explained that I would have to spend hours in the pool just doing the leg kick pushing a float and then coordinate it with my arm movement. Hour after boring hour just did not appeal. I could swim fast now; why spend a lot of time just so I could swim a bit faster?

The water was freezing and took my breath away but after a couple of minutes and some furious strokes I had acclimatised and started to enjoy it. After about twenty minutes I emerged and made my way back to the group. I lay out on the sand soaking up the sunshine and dried off fast apart from the light-weight trunks. But they were canvas, and I knew they would be dry before we moved on. Danny had laid himself out strategically in a spot which enabled him to glance at the women occasionally without being too obvious about it. Baz and Jase had taken their shirts off. Jase had the thick-set build which often denoted strength. Baz was like me, with the muscular definition and broad shoulders which usually denoted power and speed. Big Danny was blond and burned easily in the sun. He was almost six foot six and had a big raw-boned build. He kept his shirt on and had pulled out an old cap which covered his forehead down to his eyes.

After a while and with much noise, the young women decided to go for a paddle. The dark-haired leader of the bunch shouted across. 'Can you keep an eye on us stuff, we won't be long.'

Baz replied, 'Any money in the handbags?'

She laughed and they pulled their nylons off and made their way to the sea.

Danny waited till they had got out of earshot and said, 'That little blond has been giving you a real eyeballing. When you were walking back, she said to her mates "look at the muscles on that!" I don't know how an ugly looking fucker like you does it.'

I laughed and said, 'If being an ugly fucker attracted 'em you would be knee-deep all the time.'

Baz and Jase snorted with laughter and Danny said: 'Fuck off! At least we know it's not the size of your cock that pulls 'em.'

Baz joined in, 'OK, we all know you've got a twelve-inch love truncheon, the only problem with it is, it's still in the wrappers!' We all joined in the laughter, but I knew that Danny was only really attracted to a certain type—they had to be at least five feet ten, very dark and severe looking. They were few and far between. Danny got the urge but would usually rather have a few pints and a good smoke rather than waste his time emptying his balls into some cock-happy fat-slag that he didn't really fancy. Baz always went for blonds with big tits, and I wasn't sure about Jase but suspected his needs were on the pervy side of the line. Personally, I just wanted to be helpful, and if some juicy-Jemima wanted me to assist in relieving her sexual tensions and satisfying her needs, I was of that callow age where I was all too happy to help out.

After a while, the girls came back laughing and giggling. The brunette called across, 'That water's bloody cold, I don't know how you could stand it just wearing trunks.'

'Who was wearing trunks?' I shouted back.

All the girls giggled at this. Two of them had pale red hair and looked like sisters to me. They seemed to be engaging in secretive words as they looked across. One of them asked where we were from and it turned out that they were from a township called Wath-on-Dearne which was about fifteen miles from us, up the Dearne Valley. They started to pull out sandwiches and crisps and other food and started to eat, and after a while the brunette called across, 'Do you want some? We have lots. We'll only throw it away if it doesn't get eaten.' We drifted across and helped them to demolish the food. They had made loads of salmon, egg, and fish paste sandwiches. They even had a pack of sausage rolls and biscuits.

I found myself sitting next to the little blond who seemed very attentive and intent on satisfying my every need. She was about five feet four and a natural blond, attractive but a little on the heavy side, which appealed to me. I had realised ages ago that for some reason or other blokes went for different types of women. I didn't know why. Perhaps the girlfriends had to resemble mothers, or some other type encountered in childhood. I found myself left cold by the thin, especially the tall and thin, but I knew others who would date nothing else. The girls chattered to each other and to us the little blond seemed to be moving closer and closer to me and focusing her attention more and more on my lordly form.

It turned out that they all worked in a factory making electrical goods. They got a basic rate plus so much per completed item. The arrangement was called 'piece work' and the fast and skilful girls could earn decent money. The work was obviously as boring as hell and the general plan most of them had was marriage, preferably to a high earner, followed as soon as possible by pregnancy and release into a life of domestic bliss. It wasn't always the case. A few were determined or had to keep working. Sometimes it was driven by a heavy cigarette addiction or even by booze or gambling. Others had decided that they wanted to go one better than their fellows and were aiming for a semi on one of the new private housing estates which were just starting to be built in the early sixties.

I had a chat to a couple of brickies I had met about the new houses. Their opinion was that they were small and crap in terms of the materials used, compared to the council houses they had been building in the fifties. I noted as time went on that although standards were brought in during the 60s and 70s, they were never made mandatory and were abandoned in 1980. The result was that dwellings became smaller and smaller in terms of floor space and the building materials used were the cheapest that the construction firms could get away with.

The little blond was very much into the marriage, cosy nest, longing for a suitable mate, class category, and was bubbling over with sexual yearning and promise. She kept looking up at me as though I was some sort of god, or possibly husband to be in shining armour. I found myself trying to distance myself and not engage too much. On one level I was sympathetic but on another I was wary. I had seen too many of the youth of the

141

village sort of drift or be pulled into marriage without too much thought. It hit them very often after the honeymoon. They realised that there was somebody else there who put a considerable damper on the free agent situation they had enjoyed before involvement. Most made the best of it and settled down to raising kids and paying hire purchase on the fridge and on the interminably long list of other home necessities which the good lady of the house thought they needed.

Occasionally the blokes bailed out after a couple of years, usually if there were no kids involved. I realised it was a spectrum. At the bottom end were 'the grunts', 'the basics', whose only concern was gratification of immediate appetites. Usually, tobacco and booze were at the top of the list with gambling often high up there. I had occasionally been to the bomb-hole hovels they lived in. The places were almost always dirty, chaotic with papers, plates left where they were put down, usually near very old and dilapidated furniture. There was usually a cooker of some type and little else.

It seemed to me that most people just drift, life seems to descend on them with no plan or vision with the most pressing need being dealt with as it came up. Among the more switched-on types there was a sort of half-plan or some idea of direction but little in the way of specifics. This, as I realised later, was something that the intelligent were good at. It wasn't always class, but you stood a far better chance of being in tight control of your destiny if you were from the upper orders. But sometimes even here the wasters or the dim managed to fuck things up and end up on their arses, although even these usually had soft landings provided for them via family or school connections.

Even in early youth I had made my mind up that if life offered different directions or possibilities to me that I was going to be the one to choose them. I was not going to go with the flow or run with the herd. Getting married to some nice young woman to the approval of aunties and all the rest who wanted to see you stuck in the same quagmire that they had slipped into, was not for me. Thus, although she was gagging for it and I could see the two of us possibly bonking at some stage, I withdrew and kept it as distant as possible. I didn't want to hurt the girl's feelings but, on this occasion, I just couldn't do it. All the previous ones were different. Sex was required but no long-term relationship. It was satiation of basic need. Lots of crap was talked in the village when relationships went wrong of the 'he used her' variety. It was always the blokes of course. In my case, and I may not have been typical, I thought it was about 50:50. As a connoisseur of the quickie since my fifteenth year, I had come to realise that not all women were candidates for sex, although when they were on heat the struggle to abstain from sexual pleasuring must have been intense.

In those days the details of intercourse were never spoken about openly; it was 'dirty', or at least that was a common mother to daughter propaganda line. The outward image presented by most was of virgin purity ranging down to nice girls who would never do 'that sort of thing'. There were a few who had worked out different priorities with lots and lots of sex very high on their agendas. It was almost as though there was a menu, sex was a commodity to be enjoyed and they chose it, while many did not. I got the impression that the large numbers who didn't must have been tormented by the agony of sexual frustration. Of course, there was always masturbation, or 'wanking' if you were male, but no one ever did it, or admitted to doing it. The view expressed in the hilarious Scouting for Boys, still to a large extent held sway. In that noble tome it was described as a borderline mental illness and called 'self-abuse'.

I later discovered that very different rules applied to the upper and lower orders. Those running things pretty much had free rein to indulge their sexual appetites no matter how perverted. The lower orders were supposed to remain monogamous, sexually unimaginative and limited. Exotic sexual pleasure was not for the working class, even ordinary sexual pleasure was to be disdained and severely rationed. Divorce was a disgrace and difficult to obtain. The workers could

143

indulge, certainly, but without contraception—they had to produce the next generation of servants and fodder for the factories, mines and forces. If it hadn't been for that necessity something as delicious as sex would probably have been banned for everyone apart from the upper classes.

By now it was late afternoon, and the beaches were emptying as the day cooled. Baz suggested that we should go and find a boozer. It was early but we found one near the front which advertised live music. I was wondering how to play it without showing blondie up or hurting her feelings too much. After a couple of drinks, the girls had managed to insert themselves in between us. It became clear what the red heads had been discussing—one had decided to have Baz and the other Jase. The Brunette was obviously attracted to Danny who was now quizzing her about how much she earned.

I eventually managed to have a quiet word with the blond and told her she was very attractive and if only I didn't have a serious girlfriend at home, I would have been really interested in getting to know her a lot better. I felt that lying about the girlfriend would let her down lightly. Her face brightened at the first part of my remark but fell at the second part. After that she seemed to get more and more interested in the booze. Quite early everybody had had a lot to drink apart from me. I had been drinking small bottles of Guinness while the others had pints. The girls were drinking barley wine, which was a very strong beer, but it had warmth due to the alcohol and lacked the bitterness of northern beers. These features made it an acceptable drink for a lot of girls.

Inhibitions loosened and they eventually invited us back to their caravan where they had a lot more drink awaiting. As we left, I muttered something about making a phone call. 'I won't be long. I'll catch you up,' I lied, and walked round the corner in the direction of a call box. After that I made distance between us and headed back to the boat. I had a sandwich when I got back and got down for an early night. Much later there was a hell of a racket as Danny and Baz arrived back supporting a very drunk Jase who had made the mistake of sampling some of the barley wine without realising that it was about twice as strong as ordinary beer. They all staggered aboard, dumped Jase on his bed and headed for their bunks.

I got up at eight and started to cook breakfast. I made sure it was as greasy as possible with loads of bacon, sausage and fried bread. Danny appeared and grabbed a mug of tea and went to the back of the boat to drink it and have a fag. Baz then emerged, not too worse for wear and looked appreciatively at the frying food.

After a while Jase came in looking very pale. He looked apprehensively at the lard smothered fry up and said, 'Don't do me any, I'll just have some toast.'

'Too much to drink?' I said. Jase just took a glass of water and sat on a bench, sipping it slowly.

Baz said, 'They all got pissed apart from me. The girls had a big bottle of vodka, and we were drinking it with coke. Silly twat there thought he would try a few barley wines as well. I paired up with one of the red heads. Danny was talking to the brunette. Jase got dragged off by the other red-head but she wasn't too pleased and threw him out.'

'What happened?' I asked. 'Brewer's droop?'

'No, worse than that. He spewed up. He grabbed her knickers and filled 'em with spew.' We fell about laughing while Jase just sat there looking morose and green about the gills.

After breakfast I asked what they would like to do. Danny said, 'Let's just have a quiet day sailing down the broads.'

It was after ten when we set off, we found ourselves on a big lake chugging slowly past lots of small sailing boats and other narrowboats with occasional launches. Most kept to the low speeds required but occasionally some show-off speeded by. Jase clearly did not enjoy the rolling motion which that produced in our craft. The idyllic day drifted by, and we eventually found ourselves on the river Waveney and almost crawling along due to the narrow nature of parts of the river. We had corned-beef sandwiches at two, but Jase left most of his; he still looked pale. After a while he grabbed one of the dog-eared western novels from the shelf and said, 'I'm off for a crap.'

Danny said, 'Yeah, tha' needs it after the stink tha's been makin' wi them big farts!'

Jase made his way down to the bog and locked the door. Just then I could see a village approaching with a big and crowded waterside pub. I asked Danny to take the tiller, and adjusted the engine till the boat was just crawling along. I said to Baz, 'Let's walk down the roof.' We got above the lavatory compartment. I said, 'If we reach down, we can unfasten the catches and then lift the panel. Give Jase some air. We are mates, aren't we?' Baz grasped the idea immediately and we reached down on either side and opened the retaining clips and then slowly raised the panel. We timed it perfectly and drifted by the crowd of drinkers just as the panel came up exposing Jase, sat on the crapper with his trousers round his ankles. One or two of the drinkers looked a bit puzzled, but after a few seconds a big cheer went up. Baz and I took a bow. Jase just stared blearily at the crowd till we had moved past.

Jase re-emerged after a bit, 'I suppose you thought that was funny,' he muttered.

I said, 'We had to get some ventilation down there, mate. The stink was so bad down this end that we were getting ready to abandon ship.'

Jase muttered something inaudible and said, 'I'm off for a kip.'

He wandered down to his bunk and lay down fully clothed and was soon snoring.

I said to Baz and Danny, 'Are you going to see the girls again?'

Danny said, 'Nah, not my type.'

Baz said, 'I got mine's address. I just might get across and see her.'

'I don't suppose Jase will be welcome,' I laughed.

Baz said, 'You would be OK with the blonde, she really had her sights on you. I can see you in the parlour talking to her mum about wedding cake.'

Yes, I thought, that was the problem. She was a bit too keen and nice. I didn't want a long relationship and I didn't want to hurt her feelings, but I also didn't want to be thinking back fifteen years down the road, with three kids and a council house, 'How the fuck did I get into this!' All the pressures were there, and the game was loaded against the poor innocent males, but I was going to wait for something I really liked the look of before I committed.

Chapter 16

Saving the bookie's daughter, class hatred, and the beginning of my enlightenment

It was Wednesday. We drifted down the various waterways. Danny was getting bored and would have liked to have been back in some saloon bar chatting to the local numpties or playing snooker. Baz and Jase still seemed to like the place. I was still enchanted by the beauty, the willows drooping down over the gently flowing water and the various sedges which crowded the banks. The various types of waterfowl and other birds were amazing. The place had a sort of enchanted harmony which I had never experienced before.

Back home it was the stark and functional buildings of the mines and factories, the pit and factory chimneys and the all-pervading soot which belched from the furnaces and domestic fires.

We had become used to how it looked—conditioned, as the psychologists called it. The bleakness, the grey waste tips and spoil heaps. The stark dereliction with shabby grime-stained buildings which had been built only for purpose, with no thought whatsoever for an environment which was pleasing to look at. Scrap equipment, slowly rusting and with peeling paint, dumped here and there, old tyres, piles of broken glass or bricks or rusting cans. It was all so depressingly normal for those of us living there.

I made a comment about the difference between the Broads and the pit townships.

Danny said, 'It's pretty round us when it snows!'

It was true, but just for the first day of fresh snow. After that, the snow got blacker and blacker with flecks of soot from the surrounding chimneys and domestic coal fires. The more I thought about it the more depressed and discontented I got with where I lived and what I was doing. I couldn't see a way out, but at least I was seeing things through fresh eyes.

We chugged on. It was getting into late afternoon and Baz was steering while I was at the front of our craft. We approached a wider stretch of the river and headed towards a mooring where several narrow boats and couple of launches were tied up. As we got closer, I could see an older man and a young woman on the biggest of the launches. They were having a furious row. I caught fragments. The woman was almost screaming, 'You can't tell me what to do!' and similar. The man seemed to be making a few pointed remarks about appropriate behaviour. The argument got more heated as we got nearer, and I could see people on the shore and on the other boats looking at the pair. Suddenly she screamed, 'I'll show you,' and leapt off the launch into the river. Jase looked across blankly and Danny sat back drawing on his fag saying, 'Silly fucker!' She flailed in the water and went under. I realised immediately she couldn't swim and dived off the narrow boat. I was at the point she had disappeared in about five rapid and powerful strokes.

I looked round and could see a dark mass under the water. I reached down and grabbed it and pulled, it was her hair, the woman's head emerged. I struck out for the bank on my back, pulling her along. She was spluttering but she was breathing. I got her to the side of a low, stone-built quayside and several hands reached down. She was too shocked or dazed to reach up, so I got a hand under her arse and gave a big shove till they got hold of her. She was dragged upwards, and I reached up and pulled myself out. With the adrenalin rush I hadn't felt a thing but now I realised I was feeling cold.

A couple in the crowd said, 'Well done' to me and the man who I recognised as the bloke she had been arguing with said,

'I will take her back to the boat to dry out.' He turned to me and said, 'Please come as well, we will get you some dry clothes.' I shuffled along after them leaving a trail of water on the cobbles of the waterside path.

The owner of the launch was called Jack Ray; he welcomed me aboard. His dripping daughter went into her cabin to shower and change. Jack took me into the day cabin and after taking a close look at me said, 'Get a hot shower and I will sort some clothes out. I think they will fit. Forty-four chest, is it?'

I replied, 'Should be OK. Forty-four can be a bit tight these days though, I am heading to forty-six.' He took out an expensive looking pair of slacks and shirt and sweater from a wardrobe. I towelled down after the shower and put his gear on and emerged into the day cabin.

He said, 'I have turned the heating full on. I have made you a drink, its coffee laced with brandy, that should warm you up.' He went on, 'That was very quick thinking. I can't thank you enough. My daughter is like her mother, headstrong and with a hysterical streak. It's a good job we weren't on a train station, she might have jumped on the track. Are the clothes OK?' he asked.

Fine. The slacks are a little loose round the waist, but they are the right length. This shirt and sweater are really warm. I will get them off when my gear has dried out.'

Jack laughed and said, 'You will do no such thing, that gear is yours, it fits you pretty well. The shirt is Egyptian cotton, and the sweater is Cashmere.'

This meant little to me, I had never run into garments made from anything other than ordinary cotton, which usually shrank when you washed them, or wool which usually tangled and looked crap after a few washes. As for trousers I took a thirty-two waist and thirty-two inside leg. Those he had given me were a comfortable thirty-four waist, but they were OK.

He said, 'In a couple of years they might be too tight—you find that after your teens, waist size increases rapidly.' He went on, 'Where are you from? You sound like you are from somewhere near me.'

It turned out that he was based west of Leeds and ran a dozen betting shops called Ray-bet. He told me he was into bookmaking in a big way long before the act which legalised it in nineteen-sixty. He said, 'I knew it was coming and I was ready and set up shops straight away. I cleaned up, but I had made a lot of money before that. It paid for the boat; do you like?'

'What I have seen of it, very much,' I replied.

At that point his daughter shuffled sulkily into the room wearing a dressing gown and with a towel round her hair. She went across to a drinks shelf and poured herself a large whisky. I could see that her hand shook as she poured it out. Jack dryly said, 'This is my daughter Melanie. You've met already but not been introduced. This is Dave,' he said to her. 'He pulled you out of the water and probably saved your life.'

She looked at me and half smiled and said 'thanks' and went on. 'Don't get on at me again. I thought it wasn't deep. I could see the bottom. I thought my feet would touch it.'

I said, half to myself, 'Refractive index.'

Jack gave me a piercing stare. Melanie said, 'What?'

I explained. 'Water bends light. It makes water look shallower than it is, people drown because of it.'

'Oh,' she said disinterestedly, finishing her drink. 'I feel cold, I am off for a lie down.'

I said, 'I'd better think about getting back to the narrow boat, the lads will be wondering what has happened.'

Jack replied, 'Don't worry about that, I have sent a message that you are alright and that I will catch up with them later and drop you off. I recommended a pub about six miles down the river. We will see them later.' He walked to the galley and came back with half a chicken with a few tomatoes and olives, and some cheeses and bread and butter. He said, 'Tuck in, I bet that swim made you hungry.' He asked if I would like a beer or some coke to wash it down. I asked for an orange juice. I wasn't too sure what the little green things were, I had never seen or tasted an olive till then. Jack said, 'Sorry about the olives, you can only get 'em in tins over here. I eat 'em all the time when I am in Spain. The fresh ones are vastly better than these.'

He went on, 'Tell me about yourself. I took you to be an

average bloke by your clothes, but you know about refractive index, and you were very quick thinking in getting Melanie out of danger.'

I replied guardedly, 'You were right, we are a bunch of ordinary lads on holiday. We worked together. My education is a bit better than theirs. I managed to get into a grammar school. We are all from a mining village in Yorkshire.'

'West Riding then?' he said. I nodded and he continued. 'Same Riding as mine then, but its big. There are a few pits near us, and miners are some of my best customers. There are lots of textile mills, but they are in decline. They can't get the labour because their pay is shite, and they can't compete because in Asia labour costs next to nothing. So, the gamblers from them tend to be two bob each way merchants. But you're not ordinary, I can tell. In my line I spend a lot of time weighing people up. It's useful to be able to spot the fiddlers and the devious; you might be from an ordinary background, but you are far from ordinary.'

I think he realised that I would open up a bit if he told me more about himself. So, he gave me a potted history. 'My old man worked down a pit near Barnsley—it's shut now so you've probably never heard of it. I was the eldest of three and at Barnsley Grammar and was one of the top three in the top class and I was the star at maths. The old man got killed underground just after I was 15, so we went from being comfortable to impoverishment overnight. I left school straight away. A couple of the teachers were dismayed and tried to encourage me to continue either via night school or the Workers Educational Association.

'I tried a few factory jobs to get money to help out at home, but they all wanted to pay a couple of quid a week, so, much against the old man's wishes I signed on at the pit. They got me a job with the surveyors, and I got day release which was useful. Lots of mathematics in surveying. I was there almost eighteen months and was thinking I could easily make it into management and become a chief colliery surveyor, but there was a methane outrush on a face near where I was working, and three miners got asphyxiated due to lack of oxygen. We walked out down a roadway as the rescue team were coming in. I had a blinding headache. Somebody took some air samples and worked out that the oxygen content must have dropped to about seventeen percent and that we were traveling out in an explosive mixture. Luckily, there were no ignition sparks, and the air flow diluted the plug of methane, and we didn't lose consciousness, but it was a nasty experience.

'I heard that the manager halted production on all faces till the firedamp cleared. It didn't take long luckily. He had the rescue team looking for pockets of gas and after that he had the deputies in doing a full survey of the roadways and faces with their lamps, but everything was alright, it was just one of those freak happenings that you sometimes get down mines. It wasn't alright with me though. Surveying is one of the safest jobs underground, but I had almost been killed. I gave it some thought, and a mate got me a job at his dad's bookies. It wasn't legal then, but I was quick with numbers, useful for working odds out and working out the winnings.

'The only downside, and it was the one thing I didn't work out in advance of leaving the pit, was that I was no longer exempt from National Service. The pits were classed as protected occupations like farming. Technically I was now listed as an office worker and at eighteen I got called up into the mob. I had done German at school so after basic training I was assigned to the Pay Corps, and I got sent out to Germany with the army of occupation. Lots came out after they finished saying that National Service was a waste of two years and the only thing the army taught them was how to skive. I was quick to see the opportunities, which weren't exactly the ones the top brass wanted people to see. I started to run a book and was tripling my army pay taking the bets in no time. I did some loan sharking. Lots of the idiots had blown their pay by Wednesday or Thursday and were desperate for a drink or a smoke. They started by tapping their mates up, but they rapidly got fed up as they never got paid back. I used to lend them four shillings and get paid five shillings back on Friday.

'I didn't want the money in a bank account because if anybody found out the army would have been asking awkward questions. In Germany, after the war, they were desperate for pounds or dollars as their currency was worth shit. Lots of 'em used barter or cigarettes as currency. I hit on a nice side-line buying up good quality cameras. They were superb compared to the British crap. I bought 'em very cheap using pounds and cigarettes and managed to get the things shipped back by various routes. I took some back myself when I got leave and got mates to take the things back and drop 'em off at home. By the time I finished I had well over a thousand quid and was a corporal. The officer types in charge were a mixed bunch. In a lot of the regiments, they were boneheads, but they tended to be smarter in the Pay Corps and tried to persuade me to stay in, with all the usual bollocks—sergeant within two years and a good chance of finishing as a warrant officer. I told 'em I would think about it. The army was my first direct experience of the British class system. I learned to hate the bastards. Some I met formed the same opinions and went on to join the communist party or similar. What a waste of time! I just decided to get rich and live life on my terms.

'I went back to work for the bookie, and he got into some financial bother because he didn't lay-off a big bet. I bailed him out and moved in as a junior partner. I saved, but he had a wife with expensive tastes so after a bit I was senior partner. I also learned about the dodges, the 'crooked' trainers doing things like improving a horse which had been nowhere in previous races and then putting a big bet on it at long odds.' He looked hard at me and said, 'Do you bet or follow it?'

I laughed. 'I know some that do, and they are usually skint.'

'Good lad,' he replied. 'I knew you were smart. If you did follow it, you would have seen occasions on-course when the odds tumble all of a sudden. That's just after the big bet has been put on, usually just before the race. The fraternity call it 'a springer'. Lots rush off and get a bet on knowing that horse has got a very good chance; they get poor odds compared to the crooks that put the big bet on, and that drives the odds down further. A fifteen to one shot can become 2 to 1 on favourite in a few minutes. There are lots of fiddles like that—horse racing is bent. Unless you have an 'in', betting really is a mugs game.

'When the recent act legalising everything came in, I had just bought my partner out and I rapidly expanded. It was exactly at the right time, for the first time in ages ordinary people had some spare cash. They have started to buy cars and even houses. That's why I have this boat and a top of the range Jag, and a few other nice things.

'My big mistake was the daughter. I got a local lass pregnant as a teenager. We had a shotgun marriage and she moved in with my mother. After a bit she pissed off down London leaving me holding the baby, literally. She was a very good-looking piece and thought that entitled her to something more than bringing a kid up in semi poverty in a pit house.

'Don't get me wrong, I have done my best with my daughter, but she is too like her mother, spoiled because I have overindulged her and hot headed with a tendency to have hysterical outbursts of the sort you saw if she can't get her own way. I keep on trying to steer her in the right direction, but I work fifty to sixty hours a week running the shops. She has started to knock around with the local horsey set. She doesn't realise that they despise her, and me, despite the fact that I am wealthier than all of their parents by a good bit. I have never lost my accent, I'm proud of it, but she is only a bookie's daughter— and a bookmaker, however wealthy, is not socially acceptable. She is tolerated because she has the sports car, lots of money and a couple of horses, but they use her as a convenience and leach on her money. That's what the row was about. A group of 'em are going skiing, and they wanted her to drive across to the French alps with them and some gear, and their skis on her roof-rack. It also looked as though she would be paying a lot more than her fair share for the chalet they were going to hire.

'She has never skied and never driven abroad. They have all been there before. I made some enquiries and found out that quite a lot of the young kids go in the winter holidays, but most go by train with their skis and other gear and stay in hostels.

The train trip is part of the adventure. I suggested that they share the costs equally, hiring a big van and taking turns driving. Her bloody car is just not suited to winter driving up in the Alps. I know what it's like up in the mountains in winter from my army experiences. I learned to ski in Germany, and I know how exhilarating it is. Of course, it is all very middle class out there now. Working class kids don't go because they have never had the chance, it's not that they can't go, they just don't know it's there. There aren't many practice slopes near Blackpool or Bridlington are there? Also, secondary modern schools don't have sports like skiing or rowing as options.'

Jack interested me. He had lots of views on how things were set up in Britain to keep things as they were and favour the upper classes. He had a lot more experience than me and had thought things through a lot further, but I was gratified to find somebody at long last who had similar thoughts to mine. He asked me if I would meet up sometime after the holidays. He said, 'I owe you, and I would like to chat, and it might be useful if you could talk some sense to Melanie. Her head is anywhere but where it should be. I tried private schools for a bit but she didn't like that. She has inherited one characteristic from me. She hates being patronised. She had a slight accent and a couple of the teachers were on to it. Subtly mocking, talking about enunciation and received pronunciation etc if she didn't quite get the vowels right etc and similar. She blew up after one teacher had a go and told her exactly where she could stuff her snobbery and snobbish attitudes.

'The headmistress demanded that she apologise but Melanie told her to get stuffed and packed her bags and got the train home. Pity, because deep down she is a bright girl and could have got to university. As it was, she went to the local Grammar after I did a bit of string pulling. She wasn't interested but got a few O-Levels and went into the sixth but came out with an A-Level in art. Her two terms at the boarding school smoothed her accent out—there is almost no trace of it when she is out. At home, if she loses her temper, she swears like a market trader and the accent creeps back.

'Anyway, we had better set off and catch your mates up.' He took me over to the controls and showed me how to use them. He said, 'This thing is powerful and sea-going if it needs to, and after this week I will get it sailed up the east coast. I have a berth in Bridlington and like getting down there on Sundays to relax. I usually stay overnight and drive back before the shops open on Monday morning. This thing has four cabins and eight berths. The fittings are top of the range. I would never recommend anybody getting a boat unless they use it a lot. They are money pits, but that's alright, I have lots of that.'

At that stage Melanie emerged and sat sulkily in the day cabin.

I smiled and said, 'Dried out ok?'

She smiled back somewhat nervously and said, 'You must think I'm really stupid doing something like that.'

I said, 'People can be hot-headed and do things without thinking. I have an auntie—she has flaming-red hair and a temper to match. She was getting some lip from her middle son who is a natural rebel. She lost it and picked up the nearest thing to her and flung it at him. The thing happened to be a carving knife which stuck into the door about two inches from his ear. When she realised what she had done she was horrified. She could have killed him.' After that Melanie relaxed and we started to chat naturally. I saw Jack give me a sidelong glance; he had a smile on his face.

Our chat was light-hearted, and I had her laughing a couple of times with my irreverent banter, however at one point I saw her face cloud and made a note to steer clear of discussions about that topic. At one level I liked her, particularly when she was just herself, but on others, especially when the spoiled brat petulance started to show through, I was put off. Jack had a word later and asked what I thought. I told him frankly that she was OK, but the pouty episodes were an off-putter.

He said, 'Yes, you see what I am up against. I don't have the time, but it would be really useful if you met her occasionally. You are really grounded in life's realities; you are a bit like me as a young kid. Some of your sensible views might rub off on her.'

The launch was moving at a much higher speed than the narrow boat. I could see the wave rocking the reeds as we passed. Jack laughed and said, 'Don't worry, I know what I am doing. Normally I stick strictly to the allowed speeds. I am not going anywhere near flat out, like the idiots do who damage the banks.' We eventually arrived at the pub which he had recommended, and he went inside with me. Melanie stayed on the boat. We found Danny and the others.

Jack said, 'I owe this young man a big favour. You are all drinking on me tonight and no argument. I will arrange for something for you to eat as well.'

My first instinct was to refuse but I saw there was no point. The landlord came across while we were chatting and said, 'Any problems, Mr Ray'. It was obvious that the bookmaker was very well known there and had a lot of standing.

'No. Just the reverse Les,' he replied. 'This young chap dived into the river and pulled Melanie out. She had a bit of an accident. These young men are drinking on me this evening and can you do some food. Your pork pie and some of your sandwiches should do. Make sure there is plenty—they are big lads. Just open a tab and I'll settle up next time I am here.' The landlord nodded. Jack took me on one side and said, 'I want to see you again. Don't be embarrassed and don't try and avoid it or put it off. Here is my direct number. Give me a ring on next Monday evening when you are back home.'

The landlord arrived just then with four pints and said, 'Just wave when you are ready for a drink, and I will send one of the girls across. I will get you something to eat. It will be about half an hour, will that be all-right?'

I said, 'Fine, but don't go to too much trouble.'

He laughed and said, 'Nothing is too much trouble in this pub for Mr Ray.'

Chapter 17

A turning point

There is a tide in the affairs of men, which, taken at the flood, leads on to fortune.

William Shakespeare

We woke up on Thursday morning in good spirits. We had all had a good feed and I had downed five pints the night before, which was a lot for me. Danny had guzzled eight. He said, 'We'll have to bring you down here again and we'll moor near the launches in case some rich bint falls in and needs rescuing.' The 'treat' had done us a big favour in that our money had started to run out and we would have had a miserable Friday night with just enough for a couple of pints. It was Thursday morning, and we knew that we had to head back to Potter Heigham. They left the navigation to me. I estimated that with no undue delays we should be back there at about nine that evening if we kept moving, or we could moor somewhere and carry on the next day.

We decided to go straight back, we could get back just in time for a few drinks. The next day we could pack, clean the boat out and get ready to travel back home and have a final really good night in the pub. Jase's dad said he would be there early, and we could expect him about eight a.m. or there-abouts. He had told us to be packed and ready and on the quay side.

I set us off and negotiated a couple of awkward stretches which could have taken us the wrong way. When we got on the long waterway which would take us back to our starting point, I handed the tiller over to Danny. He had picked up a peaked sailor's hat in Yarmouth and we headed back with him looking like a cross between Popeye and Captain Bligh. Occasionally he shouted silly nautical sounding commands, sometimes to us and sometimes to passing boats. He was really in the holiday mood as were Baz and Jase. I was much more subdued.

I sat at the front of the boat deep in thought. I had realised that most people don't actually think. They find themselves in certain situations and adapt to them and make the best of it. It all seemed very natural to them—a sort of pre-ordained ordering of society with little need or opportunity for change. I reflected and integrated these latest experiences into my growing picture of what life was and what working class existence in the Britain of the early sixties meant. We arrived at our destination at almost ten and then moored up and wandered over to the nearest pub. The place was quiet so after a couple of pints we wandered back and sat drinking the last of the beer we had brought and watching the sunset and the slow transition to darkness.

The next morning, we had a huge fry-up using the last of our eggs, bacon and tinned spam, beans and tomatoes. After that we set to cleaning the boat.

After a couple of hours Joe turned up and said, 'Any problems?'

Danny said, 'No, we really enjoyed it thanks.'

Joe took a quick look round the craft and could see we had cleaned it up well. We told him we were planning to get off early. He told us that he would be with us at eight sharp the next morning to have a quick look round and he would bring the deposit. He said, 'Don't worry about the beds. I get a couple of girls in, and they change the sheets and leave fresh towels.'

We thanked him and got on with our chores. As he left, he said, 'Nice to meet you lads. I was a bit concerned when you turned up, being on the young side, but you are clearly a sensible lot and have had no groundings or collisions. We sometimes get them, but to be fair its often with the dopey older types who don't seem to have a clue about steering, speeds or which bits of the broad are too shallow to sail over.'

Joe left us to it and Danny said, 'I'm looking forward to a good drink tonight. We're back home tomorrow and its fuckin' work on Monday.'

Around mid-day we had finished, and everything looked good on board, so we set off for a last wander round. I was fascinated by the old houses and church because of the big pebbles used for the walls. An old chap was cutting the grass in the church yard, and he told us, 'The big, rounded stones are flints. They are incredibly hard and resistant to wear. If you build like that all you need is a bit of re-pointing every few decades, where the cement gets weathered. If you build from sandstone the whole thing decays and the stone needs replacing and that's an expensive job.' I was aware that old buildings always used local materials. Round us, everything was limestone, which looked great until coal started to be burnt by everybody in the area. This turned the limestone black due to a combination of soot and the sulphur-based acid given off.

I meandered along, not saying much, still deep in thought from time to time, thinking about how this rural idyll compared to where we lived. I had picked up enough to realise that Norfolk was still largely an agricultural area and there was a lot of poverty. I knew that in some respects the set up was semi-feudal, with most of the labourers living in tied cottages. Here the rents were low, but the cottage was owned by the landowner and if you got sacked or left employment you had to leave the cottage. When you retired or got ill, sometimes the owner would graciously allow you to stay, but some showed their gratitude for years of long, faithful and low paid service by shuffling their responsibilities off onto the local council housing service. The work force was poorly unionised and generally kept their heads down and kept their gobs shut and kept on the right side of the farmers, clergy and landed gentry.

I had talked to one old timer from round us who had started working on the land as a youngster around nineteen hundred.

He had tales of grinding hard work and long hours especially around harvest and ploughing seasons. He told me about how the fillings were scraped out of apple pies and new fillings put in because it was cheaper to use the old unused piecrusts than bake new pies, and about strength being kept up by them being allowed two gills of the strong harvest beer with their mid-day meal. The beer was usually brewed by the farm.

There were other differences. I noticed that fewer of the men smoked cigarettes, and that the consumption of them seemed to be frugal, almost reluctant in nature. It was evident that far fewer of the women smoked. I realised that in mining at that time earnings were high and that the brewers and cigarette manufacturers were only too delighted to foist their wares on the mining communities and that lots of the wives were also only too delighted to assist in helping their husbands to burn through their wages and push cash in the direction of the purveyors of these delights. The government was also immensely gratified at the huge tax revenue this generated from those areas. It wasn't that the mineworkers were stupid—they knew what was happening—but the majority view was: if I've had it they can't take it off me, and they, unlike the labourers in Norfolk, had the cash to indulge in these pleasures. They worked in an industry with a high casualty rate—the focus was very much on today because tomorrow you might be dead!

Around two we found a fish-shop, and we all had fish and chips. I said, 'We can probably get a sandwich at the pub later. All we have left now for supper is a block of cheese and a pack of cream crackers.' After that we wandered back to the boat and got down for a kip prior to getting ready for the pub.

We got there at about half past seven and the place was packed as it was the last night of their holiday for many there. We got a tray and got four pints and grabbed a table near the door. Luckily, many of the family groups were sat outside where harassed looking parents sorted out the high spirits and needs of fractious kids. The folk group appeared shortly afterwards, and I made my way round to the serving hatch and ordered four basket meals. Two of chicken and chips and two of scampi and chips. These were served on a paper napkin in a small wicker basket. One or two of the classier pubs round us had started to do them and they were considered the height of sophistication by some. I got back with them just as the group were about to start.

I had been brought up in an era where the music allowed by the BBC monopoly was bland, and about 30 years behind the times. I disliked folk or folksy music but listened analytically. The lead singer seemed to affect a mock nineteenth century country accent and sing down his nose. His compatriots were worse. The locals who had grabbed the tables near the stage loved it, but after a bit there was lots of chattering from the disinterested holiday makers at the fringes, most of whom much preferred the semi-pro singers and groups who circulated round the clubs in the industrial north and midlands. In those places no one talked over the singers, who were generally pretty-good, and certainly not over the groups who would just turn the amplifiers up if anyone did. The folk lot, being purists, didn't have the advantage of electronic enhancement, but they battled on with a few angry glances and comments from the afficionados at the front. At the end they seemed pleased because they got a round of uproarious applause from a crowd that was bent on having a good time on this final night away. I joined in, cheering, because at last the racket had ended.

I had noticed a youth at the rear of the pub who was looking in our direction; he seemed particularly interested in me. I pretended not to look at him but could see his reflection in a mirror—he was definitely interested. At the break he went outside. I followed him, careful not to be noticed. I shadowed him as he headed down, taking cover behind the large trees at one side of the grounds. He went up to another couple of youths just round the side of the pub near the towpath. He said to the two who were waiting, 'He's in there but with three others and they all look pretty hard.' The biggest of the two said, 'If I could get him outside, I would show him. Nobody has it away with my Lana.' I realised that somebody must have spilled the beans about my liaison earlier in the week. The boyfriend had found out or worked out where we would be and had turned up to have a crack at me.

The three were engrossed. I sized them up. They were big, strong, farm-boy types. The one who was shouting about doing me was, I judged, a loudmouth, more shout than action. The other two did not seem to be massively switched on. I reckoned that none of them would have the fighting experience that I had picked up round the boozers and dances of South Yorkshire. At weekends particularly these could resemble the wild west if it really kicked off, and you had to know how to handle yourself. The other choice was to stay away from these 'dens of iniquity'; lots of the 'nice boys' did so. If you did that you missed out on the steaming hot totty which always seemed to be attracted by the testosterone filling those places.

With characteristic arrogance I stepped round the corner of the pub and said, 'You talking about me?' I could have gone back into the pub for backup but that would have spoiled the fun.

The loudmouth turned round and said, 'You're the bastard that had it off with my Lana.'

I don't take kindly to being called a bastard and many would have started throwing punches straight away. I knew, though, that if I could wind him up, if it kicked off, he would be swinging wildly with not much intelligence. I also knew that the easiest punch in the world to avoid was the haymaker.

I laughed in his face. He stepped forward, but I made sure I was just out of range. I said, 'She seemed to know what she was doing. She's a big girl, very big.' I smirked salaciously. 'And when I rammed it up her she was begging for more, not screaming at me to get off.'

At that he snapped and pulled his arm back thus telegraphing the punch that was to come. An eight-year-old would have seen it and dodged it. I jinked to one side and his fist flew past my ear. I stepped in close, dropped my head and butted him hard, smack on the nose.

He staggered back, blood streaming down his face. I

stepped back. The other two had been caught as much by surprise as had my assailant. One stepped forward, perhaps with a half-hearted notion of backing his mate up. I raised my fists in a professional looking stance and said, 'You want some, pal?' He stepped back, obviously deciding that he didn't. I said, 'If I was you, I would piss off before my mates come out. They haven't had a fight all week and are dying for one to kick off.' They turned and left, half supporting the bleeding loudmouth, walking towards an old, battered van which they climbed into. After a few moments the engine spluttered into action, and they drove off.

I wandered back into the pub. Danny saw the mark on my head and said, 'What have you been up to.'

I smiled and said, 'I had a bit of a workout with one of the local yokels, full story later. Let me get 'em in.' One thing I hadn't mentioned was when my clothes had been delivered back to the narrow boat washed and ironed courtesy of one of Mr Ray's minions, I had found a couple of fivers in the top pocket of my denim shirt.

I wandered up to the bar and ordered four pints and some cheese and ham sandwiches. My head was a bit sore where it had made contact with my opponent's nose. I had expected that. A head butt is very good at stopping somebody in his tracks, but I had found out previously that it hurts your head as well. I got back to the lads and Danny pointed at the sarnies and said, 'How much?' I replied, 'Don't worry, these are on me.' I slipped to the bar and got another four in just before the folk quartet arrived for their final stint. Everyone seemed in an uproarious good mood, and we left as the group ended to get an early night prior to being picked up the following morning.

We got up early and had some cheese on toast and had a final clean around. Joe turned up at twenty-to-eight and had a look round. He was happy with how we had left the boat and told us that we would all be very welcome to use one of his craft again. We piled out with our cases onto the boat side. We could see Jase's dad's van trundling down the road towards us.

Joe said, 'Oh I nearly forgot. Here's a letter from Mr Ray.' He passed it over. The note was brief. All it said was, *Thanks again and remember what I said about seeing me when you got back.* Underlined and in capital letters were the words *MAKE SURE YOU DO!* I had thought about it and was reluctant. I did not want to trade on the bloke's gratitude. However, it was obvious that he was going to be persistent so I made my mind up then that I would comply with his request. Perhaps this was fate, a turning of the tide, a new path opening up before me with a new direction possible, out of the awful seemingly pre-ordained rut I was stuck in.

Chapter 18

My real education begins

I climbed into the back of the van and slept most of the way back, on top of our gear. Jase's dad had business to attend to and he thrashed the old van as hard as he could. On some stretches of road, he was managing sixty-five miles an hour. He got us back home in less than four hours and dropped us off at the transport café at the edge of the village, and then hared off to his meeting in Barnsley.

We drifted in and all had sausage egg and chips with pint mugs of tea. We arranged to meet up later and made our way to our individual homes. Back there, Liz was having a fag and reading the *Daily Mirror*. She said, 'I hope you've had something to eat. I've just seen to Jed and I'm not starting again. If you've got any washing, put it in the basket.'

I went upstairs and took out the shirt, sweater and slacks that Jack Ray had given me and insisted that I keep. I put them into the small alcove which served as a wardrobe for me. It had a rail across it and a curtain in front of it, both put up by Jed after we had moved into the council house. He had gone off to collect money from some of the houses where he had cleaned the windows, but where the occupier was out when he did them. He would undoubtedly call in at the local and have two or three pints before getting back and then taking Liz out to watch some act and play bingo at the ex-service men's club closest to where we lived. Not that the district was short of them.

There were four big working men's clubs within a mile of us and a small one used by the colliery management and foremen. In addition, there were three large public houses. All satisfying the huge thirst of the almost three thousand men at the local colliery. When the pit eventually shut, the area was left with a small pub and one working men's club with a hugely reduced clientele. The brewers must have been crying in their beer at the huge loss of income in this and all the similar heavy industrial areas in the north.

The attitude from my parents was, 'Oh, you're back then.' I avoided Jed by getting out of the house before he came downstairs. A Saturday afternoon drink for him was always followed by two- or three-hours' sleep. I eventually heard him moving about to start his evening ritual of having a shave and getting dressed in his Saturday best. Liz was similarly engaged. She did mention the Broads in a half-interested manner, and I grunted something back in similar vein.

She said, 'You'll be able to see to yourself. There's some corned beef or cheese if you want a sandwich later.'

I said, 'I'll be out.'

She said, 'Don't be late, you know what he's like.'

I knew alright. At eighteen I had asked about having a key but was told no chance. Keys meant power and he was going to show me exactly where I stood in that house. I was one rung down from a lodger, and there on sufferance, tolerated purely for my generous contribution to the household income.

This meant I always had to be in before Jed went to bed. Which was usually about half an hour or so after he got in from the boozer. One night I was detained by a particularly sexually voracious young lady and got back at about eleven-thirty, which wasn't late but they had gone to bed full of booze. The back door was locked. I spent about ten minutes hammering on it. If he heard me, he ignored it and stayed where he was. I was just on the point of smashing the kitchen window to get in but remembered a small top window was open at the front. I jumped up on the sill and could just reach the handle of one of the big windows. I lifted it and was able to let myself in.

The next morning, I was out at work early due to a message about some emergency at one of the pits. As it was Sunday it was Jed's day for a lie in and then down the big working men's club to pay his sweepstake. Dinner was always at about two, when he rolled in from the boozer, smelling of beer and fags. The result was that I missed seeing him. I got in from my emergency shift at six p.m. with instructions to be back at six the next morning. Fortunately, the pit canteen was always open, and I had some sandwiches and a couple of steak pies while I was there. It was also fortunate for Jed as I had made my mind up that if he said anything about the door being locked or was sarcastic in any way, I was going to give him some back, and if he reared up, I was going to give him a good hammering and then try and find digs somewhere else quick. He would have been about forty-two then and wasn't in bad shape apart from his wind which was increasingly being affected by his smoking, but I was taller and heavier than him by then. I remembered the old religious instruction lesson and the ten commandments: 'Honour thy father and mother.' I smiled grimly, wondering if there was a version saying, 'Honour thy father and mother unless they are twats.'

I got out for a couple of pints and expressed my simmering anger to Danny and Baz. They were open mouthed. Baz said, 'Tha's joking. I've had a key since I started work at fifteen.' Danny said, 'There's one under the plant pot down our garden but I never need it, our back door is never locked till we all get in.'

As things turned out I didn't see Jed for a couple of days, which was just as well for him. Liz tried to justify locking the door saying, 'What if somebody broke in.'

I said, 'To do what? There's nothing here worth stealing! And you know that if I was late, I would lock the back door after I came in.'

She picked up on my anger though and tried a different tack saying, 'He *is* your father.'

My terse and vehement reply was: 'Is he!' With strong implications that being a father actually involved acting like a father, it wasn't just a title. This made her feel uncomfortable because she was well aware of her own deficiencies in the

171

maternal department. This gave her the strongest hint that she should drop the topic, which she did.

I had spent my first ever week on holiday. It was good, it had given me time to think, but now I was more dissatisfied than ever. Thus, on my first day off I phoned the number that Jack Ray had given me and got put straight through to him. After cursory greetings I started to talk about getting a bus up to see him, but he said, 'Don't be daft, it will take you an hour and a half to get up here. I will pick you up in half an hour, look out for a black Jag.' I told him I would be on the A1, just outside a big pub at the entrance to the village. He drove up on time and took me back to his office at his biggest bookmakers and sent out for sandwiches.

He said, 'Me and thee are going to have a long chat, but I will be disturbed from time to time.' For the next two hours he questioned me closely about my background and what I was doing. I explained that by the end of next year I should have a Higher National Certificate in Chemistry. He knew all about them. He told me that a cousin had got one and worked for ICI up in the northeast. He said, 'He is well on the way to a degree with a heavy focus on analytical chemistry. They were brought in to give industry a good supply of analysts on the cheap. The UK lags and always has lagged other leading industrial countries in producing graduate engineers and scientists. I remember reading that at the start the first World War we had just three hundred graduate mechanical engineers. The Germans had six thousand. It's bloody amazing that we won.'

He went on, 'You will find that my view of how this country is run involves extreme cynicism. But I am an outsider, perhaps outsiders always feel that.' I looked at him quizzically, so he expanded on his views. 'I have made a lot of money, but in an area that is frowned on, partly because of church influences. They are a boring lot and seem to condemn anything which brings a bit of excitement or pleasure into ordinary people's lives. Sex, gambling and drink seem to be their main targets. For some reason smoking seems to get through the net, but I suppose when you see various royals and people like Churchill hard at it, that would be a tough prohibition to bring in. Of course, these prohibitions don't and never have applied to the nobs. They have always done whatever they liked whilst treating any of the lower orders who wanted to join in with considerable viciousness.

'Things have loosened up though. They had to as the work force got more skilled and we moved away from a semi feudal country controlled by the Whigs, which was the party of the great landowners. That lot had Draconian laws to protect property, people could be and were hanged for things like stealing a silver spoon. The juries were eventually so sickened that they started refusing to convict, so that was changed. You must have done things like Rotten Boroughs at school, and only males with property being able to vote and the drastic repression of early attempts to unionise. The same repression in Europe triggered revolution, which still scares the shit out of the upper classes. They all remember what happened in Russia in nineteen-seventeen. Voting and trade union rights were slowly wrested from the gaffers. The two world wars helped and now you can vote and join a trade union. Even women can vote,' he said, chuckling to himself.

'Here they loosened restrictions just enough to stop it kicking off and they were lucky because they had a growing empire which gave very able people, who might have developed into a British Lenin, huge potential career prospects and a chance to accumulate fortunes due to commerce. Also, there was the possibility of high position abroad, which in this country were reserved exclusively for the sons of the top families. They had it all tightly sewn up. The top positions in the church, the law, the services, universities and parliament almost always went to those from the top families. Occasionally, somebody who was exceptionally brilliant might make a breakthrough from the middle classes. I always wondered how they would fit in socially; with amused and patronising tolerance I would suspect.'

I listened intently. It became apparent that Jack had acute analytical intelligence combined with a near photographic memory. He went on, 'All the levers of state are very much under state control.' He smiled and said, 'I didn't say controlled by the state, oh no, we're not communists. Occasionally you get some naïve idiot in the church hierarchy who wants it to behave in a truly Christian manner. They are usually rapidly rubbished or sidelined or even made a bishop in some disease-ridden colonial hell hole.

'Do you believe that the BBC is independent?' he asked.

I replied, 'Well, it's very stuffy and you very rarely hear working class accents. It might be independent, but it's hardly representative of all classes.'

Jack gave me a sharp look and said, 'Smart reply, I knew you weren't just one of the herd.'

He went on, 'Think about this one: A.J.P. Taylor, the noted historian, was writing about the BBC in the *Oxford History of England*, and he pointed out how the powers that be had tackled the new phenomena of Broadcasting. With TV now coming in in a big way people are forgetting how popular 'steam radio' was. Especially during the war. Here it was decided that you had to have a licence to have a radio receiver to fund the BBC. In the USA it has always been funded by advertising. This has the great advantage that people tune into programs that they want to hear and not those that the authorities think that they should hear.

'American TV and radio are, and always have been, much more entertaining and livelier than the very stodgy stuff we get here. Kids here tune into radio Luxembourg to listen to pop music. Here they just don't broadcast it apart from a morsel now and again on radio or TV. In theory the BBC is independent, but Taylor was on about it in connexion with the very controlled and one-sided reporting of the General Strike in 1926. It has always stuck in my mind. He said this: "Reith managed to preserve the technical independence of the BBC, not yet a public corporation. He did so only by suppressing news about the General Strike that the government did not want published. This set a pattern for the future: the much-vaunted independence of the BBC was secure so long as it was not exercised."'

Jack cracked out into laughter. 'Hilarious, eh? And subtle. In Russia, old Stalin would have shot the lot if they said something he didn't like. Here it was pressure applied behind the closed doors of gentlemen's clubs and similar places. The illusion is: independence! Nobody gets shot for being independent because nobody is. All very effective. Far more so than the thuggish approach in totalitarian states.' I smiled, shaking my head. What Jack was saying to me was priceless in sharpening my perspective of how things worked in this country. He said, 'Interesting, eh?'

He said, 'I want you to do something for me. It will put money your way but it's a bit complicated. You said you're nearly through an HNC—well keep on with that just in case what I have in mind doesn't work out. You don't drive do you, not much opportunity I suppose. So, first, I will get you through the test fast. A few lessons and I know one of the local examiners—he loses regularly at one of my shops.' He winked, 'Second, I would like you up to the house a couple of times a week. Melanie liked you; you are different from the posh-brat dross she knocks around with. She never listens to me but perhaps you can get a bit of sense into that pretty skull. Get her to see things as they are and how that crowd just tolerate her because she has a car and lots to spend, courtesy of an over-indulgent father.

'Third, when you can drive, I have some courier work in mind as well as your duties with Melanie. I am sure I can trust you. The work can be hazardous. Sometimes you will be carrying several hundred quid, maybe even a couple of thou' if it's a big meeting. It might not be a problem because you don't fit the image of a regular courier. The big danger is inside information from somebody who works for me. I keep 'em in the dark as far as I can, and most are loyal. OK, they might work the usual fiddles, and I expect that, but one or two are very sharp and I wouldn't trust 'em as far as I could throw 'em. I heard about your run in on your last night, so you can handle yourself. I will take you down to a gym I know about. They do weights and some boxing and wrestling but the bloke who runs it is one of the roughest characters I have ever met, he will pass some of his combat skills to you. You will like him, he has done a few jobs for me, mainly debt collecting. It's amazing how they pay up after a visit from him.'

Chapter 19

Hard men, soft men, idiots and throwbacks

I fell in easily with Jack's plan, partly because my little group was breaking up.

Danny had learned to drive a lorry at work, his dad had paid for more lessons, and he had just got his heavy goods licence. After a while he got a job with a long-distance haulage firm, and we saw him less and less.

Baz had been fed up for some time. One day he walked into the Swinger and said, 'We're having a party next Sunday at our house. I've signed up for nine years in the Army and I will be going to Aldershot on Monday to start training.' After a few months he got posted to Germany and I didn't see him again for a couple of years.

Poor old Jase had started to booze far too much. He had bought an old banger and one night crashed while overtaking. He spent weeks not feeling well and complaining to the doctor. He was losing weight and I was worried. One day one of the regulars at the pub brought a message saying he had died. An autopsy showed that he had splintered a rib which has penetrated his lung. The hospital had missed it, but the pathologist seemed to think damage was blindingly obvious on the X ray. I heard that Jase's dad was considering suing, but I never heard what happened.

Thus, we drifted apart. I suppose it was inevitable. I was different, and we all knew it. We had enjoyed some good times and some teenage rough and tumble. We had always come out on top. I was always the one who could think things through and push us in the right direction. We had drunk together, and our small band had explored the vast realm of womanhood, but with different outcomes and different conclusions and intentions regarding future relationships. I could see Dave and Baz both being married within a couple of years; I had no such intentions. I could see it happening eventually, but it was going to have to be to someone very special. I wasn't going to go for looks, they would be a bonus. I hadn't hardened my views up yet but did admire the hardworking tidy German hausfrau types. I wondered if piercing intelligence should be a priority but knew that all the old, wise heads in the village held to the view that if you ended up with a clever-one she would run rings round you, and you would end up working to her agenda and not yours.

One old sweat had ended up in charge of the sixteen Lancashire boilers at the local Colliery. I had to take samples from them when I first started laboratory work. It was a pain in the backside, cracking valves which were stuck half the time due to corrosion, and then avoiding spurts of scalding water forced out by the pressure. He was one of the most taciturn blokes I have ever met. He had joined the regular army in nineteen-twenty-six after the miners were forced back to work after six months on strike. They had objected to cuts in pay and increases in hours. The TUC had backed them in the short-lived General Strike, but that had rapidly crumbled, and they were left to fight the establishment on their own. He was still bitter about it but had come to the important conclusion that in life you could only count on one person and that was yourself. Bill didn't smoke or drink, he lodged with a widow in the village, and spent his spare time on his allotment and gained immense pleasure breeding canaries.

Bill hardly said two words during our first few encounters. Eventually he opened up. He could tell, because of some of my terse comments, that although I was part of the staff structure, I certainly wasn't a gaffer or even worse in his view, 'a gaffer's bum boy.' His wry view of the world certainly coloured my own thinking and helped develop my frame of reference. His service had placed him in bases stretching from Malta to Singapore. They were always very conveniently near bars and brothels which were only too keen to help the squaddies spend their pay. He had a low opinion of much of woman kind. He pitied the whores because he knew they didn't have much choice, especially in the far East where girl children were often sold to 'madams' by impoverished parents. He had never used one. Early on he had seen troopers come back after a drunken night out and finding a few days later, that after having sex they were paying for it with a dose of clap or worse. 'Gonorrhoea,' he mused. 'The lads said it was like pissing pins and needles. I didn't want any of that.'

The women he had absolutely no time for were the group who could be seen in the local pubs and clubs most nights. He observed them occasionally after being persuaded by a dutiful nephew to join him for a shandy and a chat. He observed and contrasted the shrieking, smoking, bingo playing drinkers to the women he knew while growing up in the village. For the latter it was a hard life—unremitting toil, as he described it. Washing done by hand and cooking on a coal fire often for husbands and sons on different shifts. No hoovers or any type of labour-saving equipment. No fridge, so almost daily visits to the local shops to ensure fresh food was available. No wonder they were dying early, mainly in their sixties and seventies. They were like their blokes who worked down the pit, just worn out.

In respect of the former, he had one theme, which was, 'Where's the money coming from?'

He would say pointedly, 'I know how much their husbands earn, I get the same. I know what rent and other stuff costs. You can see their kids, dull eyed because they just aren't getting the right food, whilst they are smoking, drinking and bingo-ing down at the club.'

I knew what he meant, but it was just a small minority who were like that. I knew of some who lived for their kids, one in the next street to us had put two daughters through sixth form and then through teacher training college. He had restricted his personal expenditure to one razor blade per month to do it. It was part of life. People had the freedom to choose, and some chose self-gratification—it was up to them, it was their money. However, the consequences of what they did was also their responsibility. If they ended up in poverty in a rented house in a run-down district somewhere with kids who wanted nothing to do with them, they could not complain.

I took Bill's views on board; different perspectives were useful and the more the merrier. I was finding out that some people had very narrow world views due to very limited life experiences. The one fairly naturally following the other. I was still drifting through that vast sea of life's happenings. Eventually I would choose, sifting and sorting till I had a plan and firm direction. Thus, I wandered easily along the path that Jack was providing for me. It was summer and I had just finished the HNC. The tutors at the college wanted me to go on and do the part-time course leading to the Graduate Membership of the Royal Institute of Chemistry. If Jack hadn't appeared on the scene I might have, but I decided that after 4 years of day release, doing 9 am to 9 pm, two days a week, that I would give it a rest. If things didn't work out, I could always go back to it later.

Jack had arranged with one of his employees to pick me up at work each night and have an hour driving the car he had sent. After a month he said, 'I think you are ready, we will put in for a test.' In the fortnight before the test, he paid for a double lesson on Saturday and Sunday. He explained that this was so they could familiarise me with the routes used by the driving examiners. My instructor was a retired colliery engineer who could not have been better. He practiced the set pieces like the three-point turn and reversing round a corner. He said, 'Tha'll pass lad, unless tha's really unlucky. It's much easier at thy age, tha's quicker. I had one lad at seventeen who got through after just four lessons. I've had women over forty who failed after fifty hours instruction.'

It was as he said, I sailed through, and Jack started to introduce me to his managers. He took me down alternative routes and taught me to be alert in case I was being followed. We always parked away from the betting shops, and he led off saying, 'Follow me, don't let anybody see us together. The trick is to be inconspicuous, dress in boring old gear. Every-body knows me, that's why I never carry much cash. When I was younger and greener, I did, and a couple tried to rob me out-side my first shop. I always parked in the same place, and they tried to jump me as I got out of the car. I had a leather bag, but it had some big ball bearings inside the lower pockets. I swung it and I downed one; it must have been like being hit with a brick. I jumped into the car and got away. That's another thing, the money will be in a money belt—you can carry a bag. If they snatch it all they will get is a bag stuffed with a few bags of washers and magazines or something similar.'

After my driving improved a little, he took me to a disused aerodrome and introduced me to a wild-eyed character who he introduced as Stan. The instruction which Stan imparted was all about driving extremely fast at high speeds and doing things like handbrake turns, driving on the wrong side of the road and the wrong way up one-way streets. My instructor had done some racing and had worked for the flying squad. He had been invalided out with dangerously high blood pressure. After I got to know him, he told me that he had been pre-scribed medication, which he did not take. He had instead stopped boozing and smoking and lost four stone in weight, and that sorted it.

He explained, 'I got fed up with all the bullshit and corrup-tion. Whoa! Bent coppers! Hardly ever happens according to *Dixon of Dock Green*, does it? Believe that if you want! One thing that used to annoy me was that the senior officers obvi-ously knew what was happening. They could see the big cars some were driving and if you have a foreign holiday four times a year and are buying an expensive house and jewellery; where is all that money coming from?'

I said, 'Do you think the top lot were on the take?'

Stan said, 'No. It was peculiar—they seemed unwilling to

confront it, to admit it was happening. It might just have been that they thought maintaining the reputation of the institution was more important than a few notes exchanging hands lower down the food chain. Anyway, I thought it was getting more and more widespread, so I bailed out. I found out that I could work myself up into such a rage before my blood pressure was taken that my nose used to bleed because it was so high. The doctor at my medical was very concerned, and I got out with an invalidity pension, paid immediately. I thought if you can't beat 'em join 'em. If you like, my pension was my brown envelope. How's that for police corruption? All perfectly legal and above board and signed off by medical experts.' He grinned. 'I went back to doing what I enjoyed. Fast driving mainly. I'm in a rally team. The reflexes are slower so its second division, but it's still lucrative. I occasionally get specialist driving jobs or ones like this.'

Stan pushed me hard, putting me through my paces till a lot of it became second nature. He eventually had words with Jack and said, 'I can't do much more with him. He has fast reflexes, he is a natural and has that wild, risk-taking streak when he is behind a wheel, which would have made him a good racer.'

Jack seemed pleased and said, 'Now the driving's sorted out, I have somebody else I want you to meet. Are you free on Wednesday evening about seven?' I said, 'Yes,' and he arranged to pick me up at six forty-five to take me to the place he had in mind.

Jack was fairly non-committal on the way there. He said, 'I know you are strong and fit and you've done a bit of boxing. Useful, but what Cannonball will teach you will make all that look like a vicarage tea party.' I looked quizzically at him, and he said, 'Joe "Cannonball" Crookes is the toughest man I have ever met. He runs a back-street gym. He joined the Commandos, under-age in nineteen forty-three. He was posted to the far east and ended up in Japan when hostilities ended. He was up for discharge, but he had got interested in Japanese martial arts, so he stayed on. He really liked the ordinary people there. He learned the language, travelled round and visited dojos on all the big islands. He became a judo expert and learned some of the banned ju-jitsu techniques. Things like leg and spine locks, banned because they caused too much damage if they are applied over-enthusiastically during practice sessions. He roughnecked with an oil company for a bit and ended up in the Singapore Police.

'After we took back control after the war there was lots of trouble, little law and order, and gangs running bars and brothels for the foreign sailors. There were lots who had wallets stolen and who were beaten up after getting drunk and fighting, with murders happening all too often. There were shortages and it was a big port so there was lots of crime. The Singapore police had hand-picked squads of very rough lads and they went in for some highly effective dirty fighting techniques. They needed to, after a bit the locals realised what they would get if anything kicked off and pulled back. The crime was there but it worked within accepted limits, there were lines which it was unwise to cross. It was a good life for him, but the colony started to move towards independence, so our man got out. He had a spell in some tough mining camps in Australia and after that he got a boat to Chile and worked his way up through South America until he got to Los Angeles. In the USA he worked as a bodyguard and as a bouncer. He was always restless. He did some lumberjacking and ended up in Canada doing a bit of prospecting. He has been back here for about five years. He bought the gym and does some part-time all-in wrestling and manages a couple of wrestling pairs who mainly do the Northern circuit.'

Jack parked up a dingy alley next to a warehouse and led me through a battered door which was badly in need of a coat of paint. The door wasn't locked. It led into a spacious gymnasium. A couple of the blokes nodded to my guide who was obviously well known there. I looked around. There were lots of barbells, dumbbells, chest expanders and the like. I could see various benches along one wall. Laid on one of them a muscular type was pushing a heavy looking barbell up and down, grunting with the effort. Two handlers stood in close and lifted the bar off when he could do no more. In the middle was a large piece of canvas pulled tight by ropes at the edges. Half a dozen men with different coloured belts were practicing judo throws. I recognised the activity from the television as it had recently started to be shown as a novelty sport on ITV. At the far end were a couple of rings which could be used for boxing or wrestling.

Jack took me up some stairs to a small office which over-looked the training areas. Cannonball Crookes was stood at the window looking out into the alley. He turned as we walked in. 'Nice car, Jack,' he said. 'You've changed it since the last time you were here.' I noted the 'Jack', there was none of the very respectful 'Mr Ray' which I usually heard. It was obviously a meeting of equals. He wore a smartly cut suit. It was obviously tailored, it would have to be, no readymade suit from Burtons would ever come near to covering a physique like that. The gym owner was about five feet four in height and almost the same in width. He was built like a coal bunker with a physique obviously packed with considerable power. His nose showed fight damage and he had a couple of small scars on his fore-head. A short pale blond crew cut topped the face, and below it were a pair of ice blue eyes. He looked the part, just as Jack had described—he was obviously an extremely tough customer.

'This is the lad I was telling you about Joe,' he said. 'What do you think?'

The piercing eyes looked me over. He said, 'Tall, good shoulders, athletes build. He should be fast, but you can never tell till you get 'em in the gym. Some don't like the discipline.'

'Can you do an intensive job on him?' said Jack. 'He can handle himself, but as you know punch ups in bars and outside dance halls are a doddle. I want him to be able to handle pro-fessional thugs.'

Joe said, 'No problem, if he has what it takes.'

Jack needed to get away, so I was left in Cannonball's cap-able hands. He said, 'I will show you around, and you can meet some of the boys.' A few more had come in and my host said, 'Don't say anything about why you are here. You will find places like this are a mix, usually a few hard men, sometimes on the edge of crime. There are the soft men – who would like to be hard—and the usual bunch of idiots who don't do a lot, but they like the vibes in places like this. They like to belong.

'You will do some strength work with weights, and some Judo. You will find that's good for shoulder strength and fitness and your trunk will get a lot stronger. I will let you do some sparring so you can block or dodge a punch and we will have some one-to-one sessions. That will be unarmed combat techniques, the ones that work to disable an attacker. You OK with all this?'

I affirmed that I was. 'I wasn't just doing it to please Jack. It was something I had always been interested in.'

He said, 'I don't usually do the unarmed combat. If somebody knows it, loses his temper and cuts loose, he could kill somebody. I don't teach those techniques to idiots, but Jack Ray is vouching for you, and talking to you I can tell you're level-headed. OK, let's have a look round and meet the boys.'

As we walked down the stairs a small kid came in and headed for the changing area. He was young and beetle browed and had a sort of gormless look on his face. After he had disappeared, Cannonball smiled and said, 'We have one or two like that, young Wilf, or 'Wanking Wilf' as the boys call him, or 'the throwback', the only bloke in the world whose bollocks hang upwards!'

'Do they?' I asked.

'Dunno, I've never looked' he replied, chuckling to himself. 'The lads in the gym say so, but they are a load of piss take artists, as you will find out when you hear some of the insults they throw at each other. It's all part of the banter, no ill intent, but if you have any unusual physical feature, they will home in on it and take the mickey. Wilf is one down from the idiots. He seems to think that by coming down here and just breathing the air that he will get a physique like Charles Atlas. He occasionally picks a dumbbell up and does a few reps, nothing too strenuous of course. Most of the regulars on weights here realise that to get bigger and stronger you have to train till it hurts. Those that don't like the pain usually pack it in fairly fast and take up ballroom dancing or darts or something. It's the first test. Some can hack it, but many can't! We will see how you go on.'

Chapter 20

I Sing the Body Electric

We walked round the gym. Cannonball took me across to the weightlifters and body builders. A short barrel-chested bloke seemed to be in charge. He looked to be in his mid-forties. He wore a gymnast's vest and track suit bottoms. He had no sign of any fat on his face or on his very muscular arms.

My guide introduced me. 'Gordon, I want you to work out a strength and fitness routine for this young man. He will be joining you. I want it intensive, about an hour three times a week. Do the basic leg stuff but concentrate on arms shoulders and trunk.' As we walked away, he said, 'Ex-P.T.I. He was in during the war, did fitness training for the Commandos. There is nothing he doesn't know about fitness or physical culture.'

We walked on towards the judo mat. It was much the same there. The lean-faced leader of the group wore a brown belt. There were a couple with blue belts, several more with green, orange and yellow ones, and a pale, weedy looking, novice in a white belt. They were moving about the mat, practicing throws of various kinds. Joe said, 'Doug, I have a recruit for you. He will be joining you for the two senior practices after I have given him some tuition. The judo man nodded and said, 'Will you be getting him a judo suit?' Joe nodded.

At that moment, a couple of wrestlers emerged from the changing room and climbed into the ring. They did some stretching and bounces against the ropes, followed by a few rolls on the canvas to warm up, and then started on the wrestling which was the 'all in' type, including elbow smashes and drop kicks and similar. At one point one turned in for a throw but failed and dropped to his knees. The other seemed to smash his elbow down on the other's skull. The recipient rolled on the canvas moaning and holding his head while the other jumped on the lower rope and held both hands up in victory, playing to an imaginary crowd.

Cannonball said, 'I manage these two. You might realise that most of it is pre-rehearsed, even the fouls and leaning out of the ring to gee the audience up.' He smiled grimly. 'It's amazing, some people take it seriously and think it's like boxing, but its virtually the same bout every time. They throw a bit of variation in and sometimes they do round two where round one should be. Bookies don't take bets on all-in wrestling, too many people know who is going to win and in which round!' He winked and smiled as he said it.

I had seen the sport on the television on Saturday afternoon and had always assumed it was genuine. I asked if it was all choreographed like that. 'Most of it,' he said. 'You can't smash somebody in the face with an elbow without them expecting it. It would cause far too much damage. Most wrestlers circulate in pairs, all the moves are practiced again and again. It's a form of athletic showmanship, not a contest to see who the best wrestler is. The punters love it, they think it's real. I was in one bout where a woman was so enraged at the dirty stuff that she grabbed a bottle and was going to throw it at the wrestler who had done the pretend fouls on his best mate. I snatched it out of her hand and told her to calm down. I had a word with the lads after over a drink and suggested they make the fouls less convincing. We all had a laugh, but one of them shook his head in disbelief that anybody could be so stupid. Ha, but yes, they are! The great gullible public! They fall for it every day through adverts, hire purchase deals, by believing politicians. The thing is, and I'm sure you've realised this: never run with the herd! If the silly buggers want to run off a financial cliff or damage their health with booze or fags, let 'em, it's a free county, but don't join in.'

My host walked us over to some heavy punch bags and a punch ball suspended from a beam. He said, 'Jack told me you've done a bit of boxing.' He rummaged in a box and pulled a pair of gloves out he told me to put them on and then expertly laced them up. He held his palms up and told me to use my normal stance and jab into his hands as hard as I could. I threw about half a dozen hard jabs. They slammed into his hands, but he didn't move. He stepped back saying, 'Not bad. Crisp, hard and on target, long reach, and you're a southpaw. Are you left-handed?'

'No,' I replied. 'I've been asked that before. It just seemed natural when I started, so I was told to stick with it.

Cannonball said, 'It's an advantage. Most boxers are right-handed and lead with the left, saving the right for their power shots. They don't like facing awkward southpaws, they're not used to it, whereas southpaws almost always face fighters who aren't, so they are perfectly used to the right handers in the ring. And with that reach, you will be able to tangle them up and keep 'em out.' He laughed. 'I bet you have difficulty getting jackets with arms long enough.'

I said, 'That's right, but till now I didn't think it was unusual.'

'Your reach looks to be thirty-eight inches. Only about one bloke in forty has a reach like that. If you ever wanted to go pro, you have a lot of natural advantages.'

He paused, then said, 'OK, I like what I see. If you work hard, we will make something of you. It takes a lot of self-discipline, but I have the feeling you will be OK there.' He told me to come down in shorts or other training gear and said he would fix me up with a judo suit, a judogi. He said, 'They are thick cotton with a reinforced collar, based on the sort of thing an ordinary Japanese peasant would have worn in the old days.'

He said, 'Mr Ray fixed it up with me to get you home. My handyman Cyril will give you a lift in the van.' He led me into a back room filled with oddments of equipment, broken benches, tools and paints and lubricants and similar. Cyril was bent over some old rusty weights, cleaning them with a wire brush. Joe said, 'You ready Cyril? This is the lad I want you to drop off. Do it now and then you can get off down to the boozer. I will see you tomorrow.'

He turned to me. 'Tomorrow it's weights, and then a bit of judo tuition from me. The Judo lads have senior practice nights on Tuesday and Friday. The mat can take about ten pairs. I told 'em I would up the size if they could get more members, but it always seems to be around fifteen or sixteen. They each pay me a small mat-fee; it helps with heating and lighting costs. It's the same with the weight lads—there are about thirty of them. Judo runs a junior section on Saturday mornings, which is popular but not many seem to make the swop from junior to senior. I have a ladies fitness section three times a week, in the mornings, and a yoga group uses the mat on Sundays. It's all useful income. I'm not greedy and I own the place, so it's just lighting and a bit of heating in the winter and maintenance. I still do some wrestling, not quite top-flight, but I get on telly about once a year, and I do special jobs for Jack occasionally. Before he puts that sort of work your way, he wants you fitter and stronger and tutored in some of the dark and dirty fighting arts that I picked up.'

We said goodnight and Cyril led me down to the large van which he used for moving gear and transporting equipment. Cyril was a big bloke with huge forearms. He said nothing as we drove, apart from the occasional grunt as I gave directions. I wondered if he had been a fighter but found out later that he had been pulled out of a terminal decline by Cannonball who had helped him after his wife died young and he was drinking himself to death. He had got the sack from his job as a foreman joiner and was on the streets when he was taken in, sobered up and sorted out. He would drink all day if he had the money but had come to an agreement that he would only get into the pub at nine. This meant his intake was limited to five or six pints, which was probably a life saver as before that he had been doing fourteen or fifteen pints a night.

As he dropped me off, Cyril said, 'I will be here at six every night to take you to the gym.'

I took to the training regime as though I was made for it. It was fascinating. I had done P.E. at school but there was never any sort of skill tuition or discussion on training. If you got good at a sport it was because you had the physique for it and did it a lot. Thus, footballers kicked and headed, runners ran, and cricketers bowled and batted. Those who were tops at it, usually by virtue of playing the sport a lot in the evenings, were picked for the school teams. In some sports, such as rugby union and athletics, coaching was frowned on as it smacked of professionalism. If the ordinary types got too good, it would undermine the reputations of the ex-public school types who ran lots of the sporting organisation. The cherished status of 'the amateur' had to be protected at all costs so that the plebs would look up to these types as exemplars who by virtue of 'effortless superiority' demonstrated why they were and should remain in charge.

The ex-army P.T.I. running the weights section seemed to know everything about the human body, its limitations and how to push it to its maximum potential. I could understand this because an army must take in all types and get them to a high level of fitness in a few weeks. Some recruits were sporty and there already, but others, being in poor shape through never bothering to do anything much more than stroll down to the pub and play snooker or darts, had a few weeks of hell to face.

Gordon hated smokers and smoking. He had seen how it held his recruits back. Gasping for breath after a run and then gasping for a fag as soon as they got changed. He had hated it during the war, long before the Doll report which confirmed the link between smoking and lung cancer. After that he got even more fanatical about it and wouldn't allow it in the gym, which was unusual for the nineteen-sixties because people still smoked everywhere. In pubs, on busses, and even in hospitals and doctor's surgeries. He was also hot on diet, pointing out that to train hard lots of high protein food was needed. He also recommended lots of fruit for the vitamins and minerals they contained. It seemed to come as a surprise to many of the wallies at the gym that you couldn't get very muscular on a diet of beer, fags and chips. He kept on pushing the diet stuff at me —at least a pint of milk a day, plenty of eggs and tinned fish like sardines, because all of them were cheap.

He told me about body types. I had never heard of them in the science or P.E. lessons at school, but he patiently explained that there were three basic body types, and these determined how big you would get. He sized me up and said, 'You will be OK, you are pretty mesomorphic. They have the power physiques suited to boxing, sprinting and similar. They put muscle on fast. If you look across at the weight lads, you will see a couple of thin lads. They are ectomorphs, good at endurance sports like long distance running but they will never ever get anywhere near being muscular. The third type are the endomorphs—those with heavy builds. If they don't train, they are the ones who get really fat. If they do train, they are the heavyweight weightlifters or wrestlers.'

He told me that he always sized the lads up when they arrived at the gym. 'Some of 'em come after seeing the advert about being a seven stone weakling and having sand kicked in their faces. I quietly explain that although they will get quite a bit stronger after a few months, their natural builds will probably limit them to a thirty-six chest and maybe eleven-inch biceps. That's if they train hard and heavy. In your case your top limit will be about a forty-six-inch chest and fifteen-inch biceps. But never expect to run a mile in less than five minutes or break a record for the shot put. What you do is work hard with the gifts you have. Luckily you have the natural fighter's build—you will get strong and be very useful in a rough house if it comes down to it.'

I said, 'What about you?'

He laughed and said, 'I have a non-standard build—short and powerful. My endurance is unusually good for my size. In the army I could march all day carrying a big pack. Don't be too rigid about it—the three types I spoke about are pretty broad categories. You get a mixture of all three in some people.' He explained that he was basically endomorphic, but had trained and worked exceptionally hard, and though big and hugely powerful, he was very fit and fast for his size.

I absorbed all the new knowledge and started to look at people in a new light. I could see instantly that the top marathon and ten thousand metre men were ectomorphs. Thin in build and thus made for endurance. I could see that the big shot putters like the British champion Arthur Rowe were endomorphs. Footballers were a mix, they seemed to be partly ectomorph and partly meso. The more mesomorphic types with the powerful legs seemed to be the forwards who could produce the powerful shot at goal while the wingers seemed to be lighter ectomorphic types. It seemed to be a trade-off. In boxing I noted that some of the slimmer types could last the fifteen rounds, but it was always a points win and never a knockout. The more powerful fighters could produce a knock-out and they needed to do that, because if a fight went the distance they were struggling and puffing and blowing and usually on their last reserves of stamina by the time it ended.

Gordon had a jaundiced view of the vast majority of the population, which were those who did not train or do some sort of sport. He snorted, 'Boozing, smoking, bad diet! Twats! Ok, if they have hard manual jobs they will last a bit longer, but if they don't, God help 'em. Lots of them are knackered by the time they are forty. Big and fat and daft and heading for an early funeral because they don't know and don't want to know. Lots of them kid themselves that something like a round of golf at weekends will mean that they are fit. I once did some work on fitness for golfers at a top club. The top ones who played every day had some level of fitness. They were amazed at how much their drives improved by doing some arm and shoulder exercises with weights, but it didn't really catch on, especially for the weekenders. They walked round the course, often with a fag in their gobs, kidding themselves they were athletes. They usually finished up at the clubhouse and drank half a dozen pints and had a few more fags. No wonder heart attacks are common on golf courses!'

I eased into the weight group and improved rapidly in strength, putting on half a stone but managing to look leaner. Gordon said, 'It's because you are losing some body fat. Your arms and chest are getting bigger, as are your thighs, but its muscle going on and fat coming off. After six months I was stronger than all but three of the group. Our leader had told me, 'It often amazes people, but they can frequently double the poundage they are lifting in four months. Somebody who struggles to bench-press eighty or ninety pounds when he starts is often doing a hundred and sixty in no time at all. That's not exceptionally strong, it's just that most of the population are physically very weak through not working their muscles properly.'

Cannonball had me doing some sparring and work with the light and heavy punch bags. After a few months he commented, 'You've come on no end and now have a hell of a punch. Are you sure you don't want to try some pro boxing? After half a dozen amateur fights and the right training, you could try out with some of the bottom ranking pros and see how you went on.' It came as no surprise to him when I turned down his generous offer to manage me.

The real revelation to me in the fighting arts was the unarmed combat and the judo he tutored me in. We had lots of sessions on the mat. He taught me how to take a fall and went through the throws. He said, 'At this stage just concentrate on one throw and one counter throw and build on it. Then build a combination, moving from one throw to another and from a throw learn to move immediately into groundwork.' He tutored me in groundwork or *Ne-waza*. This consisted of powerful hold downs and strangles, plus choke holds and arm locks.

He said, 'The bloke who put judo together was a professor of physical education called Kano. He studied at the old jujitsu schools and took just the stuff which could actually be practised and built it into a form of jacketed wrestling. He missed out some of the nasty stuff which could produce severe disability. He just left in the armlocks against the elbow joint. I will teach you the nasty ones he left out, but make sure you never use them on the mat. Jackets give wrestling more scope. In real life people wear clothes and you can get a better grip than the Olympic style wrestlers. They can throw if they can get an arm round your neck or waist, but they are limited. If you watch it, you will realise that they most often use take downs to ground by grabbing the legs. There are quite a few jacketed styles of wrestling. In Cornish, for example, they sometimes use harnesses like in Icelandic Glima wrestling. Judo evolved with people doing it wearing more or less what were their everyday clothes.'

Once he was satisfied that I knew what I was doing he started me with the judo group. I found that my strength and fitness was a big advantage and though only a tyro I found that I could easily cope with the lower grades and was soon throwing them. Initially, the higher grades caught me with their long practised and skilful techniques, but I found that after a while I was being thrown rarely as my reflexes built up natural avoidances, such as slipping off the hip or moving a leg out of the way, and by thrusting the hips forward powerfully to counter the forward momentum of the throw. We had long sessions practicing different throws. These moves were called *uchi-komi*. Moving in, twenty times to the left and twenty to the right in turn and just lifting your partner off the floor without completing the throw. The main practice was called *randori*. Here we formed two lines sorted in grade order and had four minutes with each opponent trying to throw each other. If the throw went to ground, groundwork followed naturally. At the end of each practice the man at the top end of one line moved down to the bottom. Thus, opponents changed every time until the final contest which was between the two highest grades. It was usually six or seven a side, and the effort to complete the line was considerable and far more than I had experienced playing other sports such as football.

After a few months, Cannonball said, 'I can see you are getting bigger round the shoulders and chest, and I bet your trouser size has gone up.'

I said, 'Yes. I have moved up from a 30 to 34.'

He laughed and said, 'That always happens in Judo and wrestling. The trunk is worked incredibly hard and the muscles round your gut thicken and get a lot stronger. You can forget about any prospect of becoming a male model!' He told me that he would put me in for the next grading. These were competitions where judoka fought each other in order to move up the ranks as indicated by their belts. He said, 'You are way above white belt standard. We will see what you do.'

A few weeks later, he took me down to a big old place near Birmingham. It had previously been a big Baptist church. The mat area was huge and split into two. Over a hundred aspiring blokes had turned up and we got changed and waited our turn. There were over twenty white belts, technically ungraded. We were called out two at a time. We faced each other and at the command *Hajime*, or begin, we moved in and took our grips on sleeve and lapel. I turned in immediately as Cannonball had instructed and my opponent flew over my leg and landed flat on the mat. '*Ippon!*' shouted the referee, which meant a ten-point win and the end of my first contest.

The second white belt was big, about sixteen stone I estimated, and was a tougher proposition. I managed to stumble him to the ground, but he managed to end up on top and tried to move in for a hold down. Cannonball had taught me a smart defensive move though. He said, 'Control it, let 'em come in between your legs then take hold of both sides of the right lapel about four inches apart and then bring the lower arm over the neck. It gives you a really powerful strangle hold, very effective against lower grades. It will take them by surprise.' I let the big bloke come in. He obviously thought he was onto a winner. I grabbed his lapel and, in an instant, applied the strangle. He turned red in the face and his eyes were bulging. After a few seconds he tapped in submission. The referee once again shouted *Ippon*. I had two wins and had been on the mat less than two minutes in total.

The two black belts running the grading called me over and one said, 'We will put you in with the orange belts. You are well above yellow belt standard. One or two wins and you get orange, three wins and it will be a green belt.' My first contest was tough. My opponent was clearly experienced. It nearly went to time but near the end I managed a throw and was awarded a *wazari* or seven points, winning the contest on time. The second was ridiculously easy. Once again I managed a clean throw early on and was awarded an *ippon*. The third contest was interesting. My opponent was big and square jawed. He came in with a high grip and his thumb gouged into my mouth. I could tell by the look on his face that it wasn't an accident. He then tried a leg sweep, kicking hard on the shin with no intention of throwing. His game was clearly intimidation.

Cannonball had shown me a throw and told me not to use it in *randori*. He said it is called a *maki-komi*. You pull his arm in hard and wrap your arm around it and dive down, winding him round your body. It needs full commitment. The big problem with it is that if you land on your opponent, they can get badly winded; you have to make sure you go down by their side and don't land on them. I had practised the throw during the *uchi-komi* sessions but had never used it in *randori*. Square jaw came in again with his high grip. I grabbed his arm, violently pulled it hard and wound in for the *maki-komi* as strongly as I could. He went down with a crash. The ref shouted *ippon!* By 'accident' I had landed hard on top of him. I got up but he was laid there gasping for breath. After a couple of minutes, they got him up on one knee and then on his feet so that he was able to bow and leave the mat.

I had got my three wins and after demonstrating a couple of throws in the theory part of the exam was the proud holder of a judo green belt or 3rd Kyu. The Kyu belts went up in decreasing order from 6th to 1st Kyu, which was a brown belt. Kyu meant pupil or student. After brown belt there was a difficult transition from first Kyu to first Dan or black belt. After that the Dan grades went up in ascending order, Dan roughly translating as master. At that time in Britain, first Dan was a rarity and second Dan almost unheard of, especially in the north or midlands. A sprinkling of higher grades was to be found in long-established London clubs such as the Budokwai, the oldest British club, which usually provided the bulk of contestants in international competitions.

I could tell that Cannonball was pleased. He said on the way back, 'Don't get too cocky, but keep at it. With lots of these at lower levels they don't do weights or any fitness training. What they do is turn up at the club a couple of times a week for a pull round on the mat. Some blokes work shifts and only turn up every second week or two weeks in three. You will note that a few of them smoke and usually can't wait to light up when they get outside. I tell 'em it buggers their wind up and they'll struggle if a contest goes on past three minutes, but what can you say, they are addicts and they enjoy it.'

My tutors kept me under pressure. Jack Ray had made it clear what he wanted. He knew all about the low life which operated in the North and Midlands and knew that if I was trained in the right way, I should be able to get out of scrapes and that people would be reluctant to tangle with me. I was still working in science and becoming a skilled analyst, but I was still unsure which way I wanted to go. I could pack it in and go full time for Jack and was hugely enjoying the workouts and getting incredibly fit and much stronger. I needed time to think things through.

Chapter 21

Rejoice, oh young man, in thy youth.

I avoided getting too close to any of those who trained at the gym. I respected some more than others; these were the grafters, those who strained every fibre to force that last repetition out while doing weights or who got stuck in hardest on the mat. All were from ordinary backgrounds and had gone to Secondary Modern Schools and left at fifteen. A few had done National Service, but most had gone into factories or the mines. Some worked for themselves as builders or painters or similar. I came to realise how invaluable education was. My own had been limited but that extra year at grammar school meant that I was streets in front of the rest of the blokes at the gym. It wasn't about intelligence, it was about luck or opportunity. Some of those who had drifted in the gym's direction were thick as pig-shit. I couldn't work out why they had bothered, but Canonball was glad to take the fees and would give useful pointers if asked.

I could see the effects of body type and natural gifts on the results which training produced. In the weights section we had one hugely built endomorph who held the gym record of three hundred and thirty pounds for a bench press. A couple more could do in excess of two-sixty. I was in a group of about half a dozen who could do around two hundred and twenty pounds. There were some who struggled with a hundred and fifty. The training was non-scientific. Most did three workouts a week and tended to aim for at least ten repetitions. Gordon had asked whether I was interested in building muscle or strength. I asked him, 'Aren't they the same thing?' He told me that the body builders did lots of reps with light weights, this built muscle but also lots of vascular tissue which pumped the muscles up when full of blood. He said, 'In a muscle show they pump-up before they go on, with press-ups and similar, and keep pumped by flexing during their posing routines.'

I told him that I had little interest in building huge useless muscles. I knew that they reduced speed in combat. I was, however, interested in being as strong as possible. He explained that I should reduce repetitions and train as heavy as possible. The main thing was to warm up to avoid tearing muscles or ligaments and then aim for five repetitions to start. He said that the following sets of repetitions will reduce. If you do four sets you might be doing five, four, four, three or similar. I did as I was told and found that although I wasn't putting much bulk on, my bench press crept up to two-thirty and then two-forty. He also told me that weight training wasn't much good for fitness—that the judo and the boxing I was doing mixed with skipping and some running were needed for that.

I absorbed everything he said and rapidly moved on to my next judo grading. I managed to progress to blue belt, but the event left Cannonball shaking his head. The black belt running the show obviously wasn't keen on letting people into the higher grades. There were nine green belts. He made all of us fight all the others. I managed seven Ippons and a draw, as did the powerful bloke I drew with. The black belt hummed and hawed a bit and said, 'I wanted eight wins and was only going to let one of you through, but I suppose you have both done *just* enough,' and awarded the two of us the grades.

In the car on the way back Cannonball said, 'I have seen people get their black belts with far less effort than that.' Three months later he put me in for brown belt and I sailed through it, just needing four wins against other blue belts.

Having achieved first Kyu, or brown belt, he took me on one side and said. 'You are ready for some advanced tuition in unarmed combat. You already know how seriously it would be viewed if you tried a judo move against an untrained opponent, unless you were being attacked of course. The judo association has strict rules. You would lose your license and be banned from all registered clubs.' The judo licence is the document issued by the British Judo Association, on which grades and progression were recorded. He arranged for me to be down at the gym when only he was there. He said, 'This is serious. Lots of this stuff was developed by the Singapore police to deal with gang members. Other moves are from Japan and my time in the commandos. You are never to use any of it unless you are in danger from somebody who has a weapon of some sort.'

He started off with using the hands as a weapon. The edge of it, used to chop down in vulnerable areas. Forming it into a claw and pushing it in the eyes. Straight fingers into the throat or solar plexus. He said, 'With all of these you should temporarily disable an opponent. You can cause permanent damage and if you go for the throat you might kill 'em.' He had me practicing all the moves against the punch bags in the gym, and then against him wearing a padded jacket and face protector. I did it till it was almost second nature. He built it so there was always a throw to finish things off. He explained, 'You might stop 'em, but then you need to slam 'em down hard so they don't get up. If they are real thugs, once they are on their back go in with the boot hard. Into the groin or crunch down on the collar bone. It's all about having a plan and doing it automatically, you don't think about it; thinking takes time, it slows things down.'

He moved on to knife defences. He pointed out that an unarmed man against a knife was at a severe disadvantage, standing almost no chance, but someone who was unarmed and who had mastered the defences probably had a fifty-fifty chance. He showed me blocks and locks, how to chop down on the wrist, and a throw which just used the legs and went in low under a knife. He asked me if I had seen movies where a knife man came in swapping the blade from hand to hand as he came in. He said, 'Do you know why they do that? Obviously, in a film its flashy, good for the audience. The idea comes from a notion that if a knifer comes in holding a blade in one hand and you have a belt or a coat or something, you can wrap it round the arm and wrist on the side he will come in on. The blade swopping is so you don't know which is his knife hand—the one he will use. It's all very good on film, but if you are right-handed, hold the knife in your left till the last moment, then swap it into your other hand. If you are throwing it from hand to hand as you move in, you might drop it.'

As time went on, I could tell that he was warming more and more to me, and thus showed some offensive moves that I would almost certainly never need or use. He showed me how to snap a neck and how to use everyday objects as weapons. He pointed out that combat moves shown in books bore little resemblance to reality. He said, 'If you keep practicing the drills till they get automatic, that gives you some chance. However, there is a big difference between some thug running into a place waving a knife—that is for effect; it is done to intimidate and cause fear—and the professional killer, who would never do that. The weapon would be concealed till the last moment, up a sleeve or in a rolled-up newspaper.' He said, 'In the Commandos we were told not to stab sentries in the back. You might hit a bone or a bit of harness or a buckle. The Sergeant-major in charge told us to take sentries out by creeping up behind, grabbing the collar or helmet, and sticking the knife in the side of the neck and pushing forward. That severs the blood vessels and pipes in the neck. Lots of blood, but they don't make a sound and they never get up.'

By now I was calling him Joe when just the two of us were around—the others called him Mr Crookes or Boss. He was different, he didn't buy into all the establishment bullshit about Great Britain and the superiority of the British or other white races. He was incredibly knowledgeable about Japan and told me a lot about the place and the culture. He said, 'For a start it is made up of loads of islands—over six thousand in total with about 500 populated. The place is very different from here. There are about sixty active volcanoes. The islands run in a chain from about latitudes 30 to 45, so it's a bit milder than here. The culture is very old and draws a lot from China, but it differs in that like us they are a vigorous island race and like us they are good at war.'

I told him I had an uncle who had fought them in Burma and that what he thought about the Japs was unrepeatable.

He replied, 'I would have agreed with him till I went over there, then I learned first-hand. The ordinary people are great, hard-working and very disciplined. They don't like foreigners and hated it if one of their daughters married one of them. It didn't happen often, but they would just cut the girl out of their lives. Regard her as though she was dead.'

He went on, 'You should read a book by a bloke called E.J. Harrison, called *The Fighting Spirit of Japan*. Get the pre-war one, he cut a lot out of it in the post-war edition—the chapters which described Bushido and the military code and culture, which he admired. He was a bar room brawler who arrived in Yokohama at around the turn of the century. He took up judo and spent years there. The key to understanding them is in realising that there were centuries of feudal warfare between the different clans. The actual feudal period here was short, but there, with the islands and mountainous geography of Japan, it was exceedingly difficult for a single clan to gain and keep control. It had been done a couple of times but eventually a lord called Tokugawa Ieyasu managed it in 1600. In 1603 the emperor gave him the title Shogun. The British translate this as Military Dictator, but that's not what the word says. It has two characters *Sho* which means first and *Gun* which means war; he was First-in-War. He wasn't just a crude military dictator, he was a politician. He set up a system of checks and balances which kept the local lords or Daimyo and their Samurai under control. The emperor and court were revered but had little money or power. They spent their time doing art, poetry and other aspects of Japanese Culture. Military affairs and policing were left entirely to the Shogunate. It kept things stable and war free for two hundred and sixty years.

'An American fleet arrived in 1853 and Admiral Perry

strong armed the Japanese into accepting a trade treaty. At that stage the military technology and weapons in Japan could not have withstood an attack, but they learned very fast. By the late nineteenth century they had developed modern steel and other industries and were building iron clad war ships. In the 1904-5 war, much to everybody's surprise and perhaps even to theirs, they destroyed the Russian fleet. This caused a considerable re-think in the West about Japan and its military potential. Some people started to realise that that nation was very smart and not just a bunch of quaintly dressed, sword waving clansmen. They continued to build up ships and skills and fought on our side in the First World War, some of their destroyers even did some excellent escort duty in the Med in the last half of the war. By the Second World War their navy was formidable.

'However, the superior attitude of the west persisted. For example, in WW2 American naval experts could not believe that the Japanese had developed a torpedo of the range and power of their type 93 Long Lance, simply because the West had developed nothing comparable. All that despite the fact that their ships had seen the things in action and knew they could travel more than ten thousand yards. This was about twice as far as US torpedoes and the warhead on the Long Lance was at least twice as big as any in the Allied navies. It's simple if you think about it. A torpedo's range is determined by the amount of fuel and compressed air it can carry. The Japanese realised that a huge increase in range could be achieved if you used compressed oxygen. It was dangerous, but they worked at it and perfected the technology.' He laughed and said, 'I sometimes think that wars are won by the side with the fewest idiots and not by those with the best troops.'

He could tell I was really interested and he in turn kept on pushing me until he was satisfied that I would be more than a match for the type of thug that I'd meet on the racing circuits. He was also keen for me to finish the Judo training as a black belt, which would have been the first one that his little club had managed to produce. He had never bothered to grade—if he had he would have been well up the black belt ranks.

I could also tell that the weights crowd were giving me sidelong glances. They knew somehow that I was getting special training. I hadn't said anything, and Cannonball certainly would not have, but organisations leak. Perhaps Cyril had said something. I kept hard at it with the weights and Gordon was really pleased with my progress. The muscle boys seemed a little puzzled as I seemed to have got stronger than most of them but not with the bulk which comes of building lots of blood vessels into the muscle tissue.

The training continued with lots of piss taking at people's performance. One youth who was lopsided and had a limp as a result of a motor-cycle accident was fondly nicknamed 'the throwback'. Wilf got lots of it along with another big daft bloke called Charlie Cutler. Charlie was an avid fan of the various bits of special equipment which were advertised in Health and Strength and in the other muscle magazines. They usually promised big improvements fast. Iron circles with a harness on for squats, levers to attach to bar bells, weirdly shaped bars, were all purchased by Charlie at various times and brought to the gym. Then, after a couple of weeks, during which the promised huge improvements did not occur, they were discarded and left in a pile with the old unused weights and kettlebells.

Charlie was big, with a lumpy build and fleshy arms. The standard joke was to tell him how good he looked. He was compared to Steve Reeves, and they used a tape to measure his dimensions. Holding the tape doubled up at the back of his arm to convince him the measurement was a couple of inches bigger than it actually was. Charlie had a little moustache which used to sort of bristle when they fed him the bullshit. 'Look at that Charlie, tha's got a 47 chest and 17 round the biceps. He sort of flexed his biceps, bristled, and said 'Come on, guys.' But everybody kept a straight face and everybody agreed—'Big Charlie, another nine months and you will be in for Mr Britain.' It didn't make him train any harder, but he was often to be seen flexing and looking in one of the long mirrors at the end of the gym, not quite believing what he was seeing.

After a few months one of the older members of the weights

group, Les, told us that he was getting married and invited us all out on his Batchelor night. Les was the second biggest in the Gym when I had started. He was nearly sixteen stone and was eating his heart out to do well in the local annual body building competition. He had entered a couple of years earlier and come a disappointing fifth out of ten contestants. Shortly afterwards I heard a conversation about steroids which had just started to come into the Northern part of the UK. Les got hold of some via a contact in the big gym in town. Within four months he had shot up to eighteen and a half stone and was vastly bulkier than he had been when I started. Several of the others started to think about buying the stuff, which went under the name Dianabol.

Gordon was very wary about it. After a lifetime of getting big naturally, it seemed unsporting to him. I didn't like the idea. I read up on it and found there were lots of potential dangers. Over the years it came in more and more. I eventually came to the view that it was probably impossible to get an Olympic medal in the strength, speed and endurance sports unless you were on something. There was lots of bullshit about being clean, which usually meant that you trained on steroids and came off them just long enough before the event for it not to show in a test, or you were on new stuff which wasn't being looked for, or you used masking agents. The chemists, especially in the communist countries, were working overtime and it showed in the medal tables.

Other things came in, such as blood doping, which meant taking blood a week or so before the event and centrifuging it so that you got a liquid, rich in red cells, which were injected back into the athlete just before the event and increased oxygen uptake. It caused mild amusement when a top sprinter had his gold medal taken off him. He had come off the steroids as usual in plenty of time for them not to show, but unfortunately the blood they had taken out of him and then put back in before the race still contained enough of the stuff to show up and get him banned. Unlucky really, because all of those in the final were probably at it, but he timed things wrong.

Eight of us accepted Les's invitation—Gordon, four of the biggest lads in the gym, me, Charlie and 'wanking' Wilf. The event was on a Thursday, not on the Friday because it was the night before the wedding. Les told us that his bride to be had explained in no uncertain terms what would happen if he turned up at the altar hungover. On the day, the nine of us met outside the Gym. Les had hired a minibus and just in case things got a bit wild he had arranged for us to be dropped off in the next town—he didn't want any comeback if something kicked off in his own back yard. Gordon arranged a 'kitty' and we all stumped up. They knew I wasn't a drinker and would alternate halves of Guinness and bottles of tonic water. We got there at seven and the driver dropped us next to the train station and we arranged to be back there at eleven-thirty. I could tell that something was afoot. Gordon wasn't a drinker either. Neither were Charlie or Wilf, but they had the notion that Guinness was good for body builders and were going to drink half pint bottles of the stuff. All the others were regular drinkers and could down a gallon with not too much difficulty. The plan was to have a good drink and finish off at about ten with a Chinese.

We went to the bar. I saw the landlord take a quick second glance—he had never seen us before, and he was looking at some rough looking lads with very big biceps and wide shoulders. Gordon asked me to give him a hand. He ordered five pints and four bottles of Guinness, and to my surprise two double vodkas. He took a look round and said, 'Take a swig out of one of the bottles.' He also took a swig. He then poured the vodka into each and said, 'Take them across to Wilf and Charlie with their glasses and come back here.' I did as I was instructed and realised that the plan was to get the two of them pissed. I went back and returned with four pints and Gordon brought the rest. After a bit he said, 'Bloody hell, its good this Guinness. Got some real bite. That's a real man's drink, what do you think Charlie?' The intended victim growled a response from under his bristling moustache, indicating that he agreed. Time passed, with the lads talking the usual bollocks and having a laugh.

The drinking continued. We had four rounds in the pub and then moved to one opposite to a Chinese. It was busy there, but we had another round. By this time Wilf was sitting there with a happy grin on his face having had five double vodkas and five bottles of the black beer. At the sixth round Gordon just got Wilf a Guinness but Charlie, who was much the bigger of the two, got the usual double in his. Charlie looked a bit odd by then, rather as though he was trying to get his brain to work but was finding it difficult. He picked the glass up and downed its contents in one big swallow, then jumped up, stood rigid and walked outside. Gordon followed him but came back after a couple of minutes. Les said, 'Is the silly twat alright?' Gordon replied, 'I think so. He got outside, and then spewed up in the gutter and then set off at a trot towards the bus station. He will probably get a service bus back—its fourteen miles and will take him ages, but they run every half hour. If we pass him trotting along the road later, we can pick him up.'

Shortly after that we piled into the Chinese and got a table for eight. We ordered a round of drinks and most of us ordered curries. We got the incoherent Wilf a milder dish. The meal was served, and we got stuck in. Wilf just sat there with a silly grin on his face, not eating. It was coming up to eleven. We had all finished apart from Wilf and were sorting out payment. All of a sudden, Wilf slumped face down into his plate of noodles. I pulled him back up; he was paralytic. The noise level from the little Chinese waiters went up considerably. We had all heard tales of trouble in Chinese eateries and people running off without paying and staff running out after them waving meat cleavers, but Gordon hurried across to the till and paid. Wilf was still sat there looking stupefied. It was jokingly suggested that we left him there. However, we knew the police would be called and he would probably spend a night in the cells, and it could bounce back on us. It was agreed that we get him back to the minibus. I wiped his face with a napkin and then picked him up and slung him over my shoulder. His head bounced against the door as we exited, but he didn't seem to feel a thing.

We wandered across the main square looking for the

minibus. We could see a policeman on one corner of the open space. He was preoccupied looking down an adjacent street at a rowdy group pouring out of a pub and wasn't aware of us until Gordon said, 'Excuse me.' He was a young kid of slim build and probably at the minimum height required to join the force. He turned round, and his face dropped. He could see he was surrounded by a group of very muscular types with rolled up sleeves and bulging biceps who looked like they could be trouble. Gordon said, 'Sorry to bother you officer, we're strangers here and I wonder if you could point us to the bus station.' A look of relief swept over his face. He pointed and said, 'It's just down there about three hundred yards.' He looked at the body hung over my shoulder. I said, 'He was taken ill. We think it was the Chinese food. I could leave him with you.' The officer was less than keen. We departed along the narrow street he had indicated.

I said, 'Anybody else fancy carrying him for a bit, he's getting bloody heavy.' They all thought it was a big laugh to decline. A few minutes later we could see the bus. Gordon looked at his watch and said, 'We're just on time.' He asked the driver if he had been waiting long. The reply was, 'About ten minutes. I always get to the pick-up point a bit early in case they have got fed up and are waiting.' We got Wilf aboard and he sat, still stupefied, slumped in his seat. He was the first drop off. Gordo and I carried him to the door and sat him on the step. He rapped hard on the door and then we turned and legged it. As we jumped back on the bus he said, 'Wilf lives with his mother. I'm not facing her bringing him back to her in a state like that.'

Les duly got married and everybody agreed that we had enjoyed his bachelor night, apart from Wilf who couldn't remember anything about it. Charlie said he enjoyed it, but he seemed a bit odd. He might have had some glimmer of an idea of what we had been up to. Les said his bride was pleased. 'She thinks that you lot are 'uncleansed'. She was worried that you might get me drunk and then dump me on the late train to Edinburgh or some similar jolly drunken jape.'

A few years later I met up with some of the boys for a drink. I told them I always liked going out with them because with all the bulging biceps it would soon be over if a punch up started. To my surprise they said, 'No, we're no good in a fight. We always liked going out with you, with all that unarmed combat stuff and judo we always knew that you would sort it out. We felt safe with you. We called you Deadly Dave.'

Chapter 22

The seedy side of life

'Strippers should be role models for little girls. If only for the fact that they wax their assholes.'

Sarah Silverman

My first introduction to the professionally nude female was just after I started work. One of the older men there seemed to be obsessed by sex. He was called Doug or 'Doug the Deve', *deve* being short for deviant. The sad fifties severely limited the opportunity of males in the UK to have any sort of encounter with the naked female form. Doug had got round this by joining a photographic club. These outfits periodically hired female models for artistic purposes. Supposedly taking the form of tastefully posed nudes, no shots of genital areas were allowed. This was avoided using G-strings or strategically placed objects or camera angles. I asked about his collection and was told by one of the older men who had seen it that I should not expect beautifully produced albums. There were shoe boxes full of prints which gave the impression of the photographs being taken rapidly and then ripped from the camera and developed as quickly as possible, without trimming the edges.

Doug was preoccupied with sex, constantly probing for details of the sex lives of the younger blokes he worked with. He seemed particularly interested in those with new girl-friends. I got the picture during one dinner break when we were playing cards. Sex reared its head; it always did when

Doug was there. There was some bragging and kidding about staying power. Suddenly he said, in all seriousness, 'OK, how long is the longest you have ever stayed on the job?' Various figures were thrown out with each of us upping the ante.

It got to me, and I thought quickly and said, 'About an hour and a half.'

'How did tha' know?' he said scornfully. 'Did tha' time thee-self?' He told us that he had managed two hours solid, without de-cunting, which caused snorts of laughter. We asked him how he knew, and he said, proudly, 'I got on the job just as the church clock struck ten and got off as it struck midnight.'

He mentioned that each year he went down to the Windmill Theatre to see one of the nude shows. He eventually invited me down with him. I was concerned about the cost, but he said, 'Don't worry, I drive down and drive back the same night. All you need is the money to get into the theatre.' I was curious and I had never been to London, so I agreed.

We set off early in his old Jowett Javelin. The car was his pride and joy and had only done about thirty thousand miles. It had been one of the last to be manufactured and at one and a half litres was quite powerful. On the way down he explained how the show worked, with some fill-in acts before the arrival of the naked ladies. He was obviously very curious about my sex life, but I had been warned and was non-committal about it, just responding in general terms and avoiding the specifics when he probed.

We arrived at around ten-thirty in the morning. The theatre was near the centre of London, near the National Gallery and adjacent to Soho. After parking we ate sandwiches in the car and had coffee from his flask. He walked me to a café in Soho which he was obviously familiar with. He ordered two mugs of tea and took us to a table in the window. I was fascinated by the cosmopolitan nature of the people in the café and in the streets —I had never seen anything like it. There were lots of Chinese and other types who were clearly non-European. For the first time in my life, I saw black people. Up to then my world had been totally white—the only variation coming from the Scots

212

and Irish and occasional Pole who had arrived during the war and who had moved into the mines afterwards.

He seemed absorbed by the happenings at the end of an alley across the road. Two women stood there chatting and smoking. Occasionally one or other of them would walk down the alley with one of the passers-by who had stopped to have a word with her. Doug eventually explained. 'I've been in this café several times before. They are a couple of prostitutes. You can see the blond one unbuttoning her skirt as she walks down the alley with her customer. She is never away longer than twenty minutes. They aren't particularly busy now, it is early. I sat here once during an evening after a cup final. She managed seventeen clients in three hours.'

Just before one p.m., Doug got up and said, 'Hurry up, we have to join the queue.' I swallowed the last of my tea and followed him as he rushed towards the theatre. To Doug's annoyance there was one bloke already there. I stood with him for a few minutes and then asked when the show started. He replied, 'The doors open at two.' I said, 'I am not standing here for an hour. I am off to the pub over the road.' I went across and had a pint and some salted nuts and once again enjoyed the amazing variety of humanity to be found in the capital. I left the pub and wandered back to the Windmill at about five to two. By then the queue had extended to a massive half-dozen. I was somewhat out of place as all the rest were middle-aged types. I walked over and re-joined Doug who was getting a bit agitated. He said, 'Gimme your money, gimme your money.' I handed the entrance fee over and another couple of minutes ticked by. At two the doors opened, and we moved to the ticket kiosk. The bloke in front bought his ticket and slowly walked towards the doors marked 'stalls.' Doug rushed to the kiosk as soon as he had turned away and thrust the money forward saying, 'Two, please. The money's right.' The woman nonchalantly peeled off two tickets. Doug snatched them out of her hand. He then took hold of my arm and hurried through the other door leading to the stalls. He then raced down the aisle, while the first ticket purchaser slowly progressed down the opposite side. We got to the ends of our respective aisles at the same time, but Doug sprinted to the middle and claimed the two centre seats in the front row. He looked at me with a look of triumph on his face as the portly bloke who had entered just before us took his seat alongside Doug. I couldn't see the point of what he had done—we would get a good view from any seat at the front—but he seemed to think that what he had accomplished in getting the two centre seats in the front row was something extremely smart.

After a few minutes the show started, with a comedian. There must have been about two dozen men in the place by then. The comic seemed bored, his routine was old and corny and ignored by all present. He left after a bit and an accordionist appeared. He wasn't bad but he was also ignored. Then the nudes came on. Doug was riveted to the sight of bare flesh. I was interested as up to that point in my life I had not had the privilege of seeing much in the way of the naked female. The girls were tall and had good figures and nice breasts. They might have been pretty, but it was hard to tell with the make-up they had on. I was slightly disappointed though, mistakenly thinking that they might move or dance in an exotic fashion. I found out later that the series of nude tableaux, with unmoving figures, was how the owners had got round the obscenity laws. What we were seeing were a series of artistic poses. The men viewing the stuff were so sex starved or repressed that they found it a huge turn on.

After the nudes there was a break, but most of the audience sat unmoving in their seats. Then the show started again. It was a repeat of what had been shown previously. A few of the audience had left during the interval and a few more had come in. I noticed that during the support acts several were reading papers. When the nudes started everybody but me was riveted by the sight. I noticed that a couple of blokes in the side seats were sat with macs over their knees. I couldn't see clearly but I thought they were masturbating under their raincoats. At the end there was another break. It was about half past five. I asked Doug if the show changed. He said, 'Oh no, it's on five times altogether, it finishes at ten.' I said, 'Well we have seen it twice, are we off?' He replied, 'I am staying to the end.' I said, 'I'm not. I'm off to the pub for a sandwich and then I will have a wander round.' He said, 'Make sure you are back here and outside before I come out.'

After I had eaten, I had a walk round Soho, which was fascinating. Walking past dark alleys, sleazy looking clubs and various types of eating house—I had never seen so many different kinds. There were Chinese, Turkish, Indian and many others, the spicy exotic odours emanating from the places was an education in itself. I had never fully appreciated what the word cosmopolitan meant until my visit to that small world. There were more women about now who were very obviously prostitutes, and often with dodgy looking characters hanging around them which I surmised were pimps or minders. One or two of the prostitutes were young but most were middle-aged, and a couple were decidedly elderly. All seemed to have heavy make-up with lots of mascara and eye shadow and all of them seemed to be smoking or holding cigarettes. All of them seemed to pose rather interestingly with them. I realised that they were being used as one of the tools of the trade. Here was smoking with a hint of eroticism rather than the matter of fact almost mechanical consumption of the things which usually occurred when the nicotine levels in the blood fell and triggered the craving experienced by the mass of ordinary addicts.

I got back to the theatre just as they were starting to come out. Doug eventually emerged and we walked back to the car. 'What did you think?' he said. I thought it was pathetic, but didn't want to upset my chauffeur, so I said. 'Interesting.' In some ways it was, and added to the rich picture I was forming about what motivated people. My view of humanity and the way things were organised and controlled moved another couple of notches into the negative. We got back to the village in the small hours. I slept most of the way. Doug dropped me off at home. I was ready for bed.

I had gathered from snippets of our conversation, like, 'I

hope she's ready', that vigorous sex with his wife was very much on his mind as a first priority before he would get any sleep. I couldn't work it out. He had obviously found the experience hugely sexually stimulating and couldn't wait to get back to excise his lust. To me the poses had all been rather tame. I much preferred the smouldering sex which could emanate from some of the suggestively attired young ladies in our village when they were out on the prowl.

About a year later I had my first encounter with actual strip artists. The law must have changed or something because Phil, who was one of the regulars at the gym, told us that a strip venue had opened up at one of the big pubs in a local pit village. We were dubious at first, but several of us turned up to have a look. There was no entry fee, but the organiser had put a hefty surcharge on the beer. The act started with a singer, who everybody ignored. Then a second spot, this time a comic, who everybody ignored. It reminded me of the Windmill. Then the girl came on. Her dance was slow and heavy on the tease. She performed to records, taking the outer layers off, then gloves and black stockings and suspenders. At the very end she whipped her bra off and we got a glimpse of large pendulous tits which she then grabbed and moved backstage. The G-string stayed on because back in those early days it would have been illegal to take it off.

After that Phil, who was now 'Phil the Perv', kept us 'abreast' of what was happening. The various acts were booked for Thursday to Saturday. If there was a particularly juicy one, he would pass the word on and some of the guys would go down to witness the action. Phil came down to the club one Friday and said, 'You gotta come down for the Saturday show—it's the hottest thing I have ever seen.' He said it with a smirk, which made me wonder, but we were sufficiently curious to turn up on Saturday and get a seat at the front. The act ran through twice with each performer coming on twice. The stripper came on and had a good figure and moved very lithely and professionally round the small stage. She performed to a large tape recorder rather than records and it looked as though the music had been arranged professionally. At the end she revealed her smallish and very well shaped breasts and was in no hurry to cover up. This was very much appreciated by the connoisseurs of the fine arts who frequented the place. One of the lads said to Phil, 'That was OK, but I wouldn't call it hot.' He said, 'It all happens in the second spot, just wait and see.'

We got some drinks at the interval and a bloke came in, climbed on the stage, and went to the rear where the acts were. He wore the sort of black jacket and waistcoat and striped trousers usually worn by barristers. Phil could see me looking and said, 'He runs the show. It's the landlord's son, very posh. He's a homo, the landlord sent him to public school. He couldn't afford it for the younger son—he's at the grammar school.' 'He looks a lot out of place in this dump and in this village,' I murmured. After a couple of minutes, the bloke, who was called Godfrey apparently, came out and minced quickly out of the room. After ten more minutes the acts started again. The singer was ignored but the comic was a mature woman with a low-cut dress and tits like torpedoes. Her crude humour and amazing breasts went down very well amongst a Saturday night crowd who by now had had a lot of ale. After one particularly suggestive joke she wiggled her weapons at the audience. One diminutive and very well-oiled bloke thought it was an invitation. He climbed onto the stage and made for the big boobs with arms outstretched. The woman picked him up by his collar and belt and threw him off the stage. That got a loud cheer. She bent forward and took a low bow. That got an even louder cheer.

After a bit the stripper appeared. I could see Phil smirking. It might have been in lewd anticipation or something else, there was just something about his smile that wasn't quite right.

She swung into the act which was a little more suggestive than the first-time round. We hovered in anticipation but nothing out of the ordinary happened. Les said, 'What a waste of time.' Phil smirked and said, 'Wait.' Right at the end the comic and singer came on, the three of them all linked arms and joined in a song for the finale, it was Frankie Vaughan's 'Give Me the Moonlight'. The stripper then stepped forwards and finished the last few lines on her own. They were, 'If there's anyone in doubt who would like to try me out.' With that she whipped her wig off revealing that it wasn't a her at all, it was a balding male. There was uproar. The stripper vanished, and the singer launched into another song. I thought for a moment that tables would get turned over and pint glasses would start flying at the stage. After a while, things calmed down. Phil said, 'I was talking to 'her' on Friday. She is on hormones to change her into a woman and doing the stripping to earn the money for the final op that changes her completely.' It was my first encounter with transsexuality.

As time went on the controls got more and more lax regarding strippers, and eventually they were taking all their kit off. It hadn't stopped the local 'Watch Committee' from ending the stripping at the boozer we occasionally visited. They were very concerned about the effect it might have on local morality and sobriety and it had been put to the landlord that if he didn't end it, they would oppose his licence renewal at the next quarter sessions. If it had been me running the pub, I would have faced them down and taken it to court.

Watch Committees oversaw policing and were composed of local councillors and other elderly worthies who were usually small-minded and self-righteous and a couple of centuries behind the times. They disappeared in that form at the end of the sixties, because it was pointed out that the members of the Committees would watch the 'dirty' films coming into the town and then decide if the public were to be allowed to. They made themselves a laughingstock because of it. They were swept away by the rising tide of permissiveness which was starting to run through Britain. Various forms of quite ridiculous censorship lingered, with local authorities proceeding on the personal views and prejudices of their members. Recommended classifications were overthrown. A ludicrous example occurred somewhat later with the comedy classic *Life of Brian*. It was banned or issued with an X certificate by thirty-nine local authorities after it was released. If it had been me running the cinemas, I would have given it a U classification as family entertainment and one of the funniest comedies of all time.

I suppose the landlord had decided not to rock the boat with the authorities and in any event interest in the striptease was clearly declining. The youth of the village had been exposed to the joys of seeing naked breasts for twelve months and the novelty was wearing off, so I suppose he might have been running the strip show at a loss by then. I suppose that sort of thing and the ludicrous, small-mindedness connected to it, helped shape my libertarian outlook on life. I deplore censorship of any kind. But this was that fevered period of the mid-sixties. Religiously driven sexual repression still hung heavily over education, and the media was prohibited from showing anything overtly sexual. As far as the churches were concerned, sex was sinful, an act to be indulged in not for pleasure but purely for procreation.

Strip shows continued, and continued to become raunchier. The requirement to keep a G-string on seemed to be put aside. I noticed that now it was no longer a novelty the art form declined and almost vanished in my locality, eventually being replaced with the very sad pole-dancing. The last strip I saw involved a young and thin girl with almost no breasts. I had called in for a drink at the pub after training and got there late one Sunday afternoon just before last orders and could see the audience drifting away as she performed. I stood at the bar, half interestedly looking at what she was doing while chatting to the barman. She was near the end of the act now and just a few die-hards remained, and by the look on her face she wasn't very pleased. She removed the G-string and danced towards a table and did a couple of high kicks which seemed to gratify the lads directly facing her. On reaching the table she picked up a beer bottle and started to suck the end as though it was a dildo. An appreciative murmur ran round the sparse audience and some of those who had left turned and surged back. She then danced into the middle of the floor and stood with her legs wide apart leant back and inserted the bottle into her hole.

She took it out and dropped it on the floor in disgust, gave the audience a V-sign and stormed off. The subtext of her actions was blatantly obvious: that will teach you to ignore me, you bastards!

After that, strip shows virtually disappeared from pubs in the area. They did survive in private venues and were a popular form of entertainment at bachelor nights. I noticed that here they had become raunchier and raunchier, with the girls using various sex aids to add spice to the performances. They had to, in order to maintain interest among the increasingly sexually liberated youth who now comprised the bulk of the punters. The days of strict wearing of G-strings had long gone. The poor old Windmill closed a couple of years after Doug had taken me down on his annual pilgrimage to see the show. The staid nude poses were unable to compete with the increasingly sleazy strip shows and massage parlours that were opening. In sixty years, we had gone from a culture so repressed that the sight of a well-shaped ankle could induce sexual frenzy, to one where we were starting to find even the most lascivious displays of flesh rather boring.

Chapter 23

Beating the odds

'Last year people won more than one billion dollars playing poker. And casinos made twenty-seven billion just by being around those people.'

Samantha Bee

I was going out more and more for Jack, usually carrying several hundred pounds between betting shops and to other people, mostly in the racing fraternity. I could tell that he wanted me to pack my regular job in and go full time for him. He could also see that I was hesitating and was smart enough to see it was about security. I was earning more working for him part-time than I was getting as a young chemist. He didn't force it, but on one occasion he said, 'Have you got twenty quid?' I passed it over without questioning him. Two days later he came back with two thousand and said, 'Your winnings.' It was a huge amount in the mid-sixties. He had put my twenty and a hundred of his own on a complex bet which had paid out big. He had cleared ten thousand and told me, 'It's a rarity for me to bet, but I had some inside info on three horses.' After that he said, 'What about going full-time with me? You will earn at least three times what you are getting now.'

I was still slightly reluctant, but I agreed, partly because what I was doing as an analyst was tedious. I was down at his house now on a regular basis and it was clear to me that he hoped that I could sort Melanie out. He was guarded, but I was sure that if a relationship developed, he would be pleased. The big problem was that Melanie was a spoiled and screwed up brat. Her mother pissing off and an overindulgent father hadn't helped. She was reasonably intelligent but was in with the wrong set who were a horsey lot connected to the local fox hunt and pony club and similar. She had persuaded me to learn to ride. I was over thirteen stone by then and needed a powerful horse. At best I was competent on a horse. She was rather good. I could take a jump and fortunately could take a fall when I came off.

I accompanied her to various social events, doubling up as an escort and minder, and went out riding with her. The posh set were wary of me. They didn't know anything about me, and I was careful not to give them any information. They went out of their way to be sociable and now seemed to treat Melanie with more respect, especially after one dinner when I was walking her back to the car. She was in a very expensive red satin ball gown, and I was in a black dinner suit. Some Hooray Henry made an obnoxious remark as we walked past them. He said, 'Perhaps we should ask the bookie's daughter.' We were next to a fountain in the grounds. I picked him up by his crotch and neck and dumped him in the water. He climbed out and stood up spluttering and said, 'You barstard!' I grabbed him by the neck again and pushed his head back under the water. After a while I pulled him up and said, 'What did you say?' The immersion had sobered him up and a look of fear had entered his eyes. I said, 'Listen, prick, in future you had better learn to mind your manners.' I took him by the lapels and pulled him in close till he was up on his toes. I was tempted to stick the nut on him, but just held back. That would have been overkill. I looked into his panic-filled flabby face and said, 'Anything else to say?' He could feel the strength of my grip and see the anger in my eyes. He didn't reply. I let go of him, turned, and walked off with Melanie.

On a couple of occasions, she persuaded me to come out with her with the local hunt. I didn't hold with hunting. I had run into foxes and cubs as a kid and thought that they were charming and intelligent animals. I was prepared to go because it was all part of my learning curve. I kept my gob shut and observed. It was clear that rigid class structures operated. On the face of it the set up was open, but after a while I realised that if you wanted access to the top levels of society, even at county level, you had to ride. After that you were judged on land ownership, money and above all on family. The wealthy farmers were very much part of the setup but generally second division because they sullied their hands with work. There were crossovers, with many of the riders also shooting and often fly fishing as well.

It was clear that family connections were overwhelmingly important. If you had the wrong background, you would never get into the inner circle. Having lots of money was not enough. Jack probably had more than most of them, but he was a book-maker, which was no sort of background at all. Melanie couldn't see it—she had all the trappings, the right accent, a couple of horses, a field with a stable and a part-time groom, a sports car, and so on, but there were unwritten codes, and she did not fulfil the requirements stipulated by those codes. It was a question of breeding. At the lower levels all sorts hunted, from builders to businessmen. The posher young ladies were often partial to a 'bit of rough', especially if the males exuded physicality as I did. I was gratified to find that lots of post-hunt shagging seemed to take place in horseboxes and stables. I could see early on that I was being eyed up by various women of various ages.

On one occasion I was asked if I could drive one of the very wealthy and very posh women home. Her pretext was that she had sprained her wrist and couldn't handle the vehicle. I didn't mind and welcomed the chance to get behind the wheel of her big Land Rover. We set off and she gave me directions. Eventually I found myself on a dual carriageway with one side blocked by cones which went on for miles. She leant across and started to stroke my crotch, and said, 'You can't stop now.' This was true as we were crawling along at about fifteen miles an hour. Pretty soon she had liberated my straining member. She then leant across and took it into her mouth. I stiffened behind

223

the wheel, trying to keep part of my attention on the car in front. She was obviously very expert in the ancient art and kept me on the edge for ages.

Eventually she sat up and said, 'Pull off here.' It was a deserted country lane and it was just starting to get dusk. She made it very clear exactly what she wanted and eventually I found a deserted wooded area and backed her car into what looked like a small path. She was on top of me almost before we had stopped and was riding up and down my shaft where I sat. Deep animal moans came from her throat. We had orgasms almost at the same moment with her screaming at the top of her voice. Afterwards she sat back in her seat adjusting her clothes. After a couple of minutes, she resumed normal conversation as though nothing had happened.

I put the car into gear but couldn't get much traction. I said, 'We must be on soft ground,' and got out for a look. We were in a muddy area, and I thought 'wow.' As I had backed in, I had stopped about nine inches from the edge of a steep sided drainage ditch. If I had reversed another foot, we would have slid nine or ten feet down into the thing. That would have taken some explaining, I thought. I looked round and picked up stones of various sizes and pushed them under the wheels. After that we were away easily and back on the road. I saw her a couple of times after that at hunt events, but she was always very aloof. I found out later that she was ultra-careful, because infidelity would lead to divorce from an impotent husband. On the one hand, when on heat, her body was screaming for sex, but on the other she could not risk losing the wealth and status which depended almost solely on her marriage. I logged the experience and added it to my collection but could not help thinking that Rudyard Kipling was onto something when he wrote the line, 'For the Colonel's Lady an' Judy O'Grady are sisters under their skins!'

Being a landowner was hugely important in horsey circles. It usually qualified you to be a hunt member and wear the scarlet coat permitted for master and ex-masters, and favoured individuals and hunt staff and whippers in. The ladies wore black coats with coloured collars. There were strict rules about types of boots and what sorts of tweeds the under eighteens were to wear. All carried a hunting whip which was never called a crop—this was also made to strict specifications. I was fascinated by the complex culture and by what was assumed to be known about the etiquette surrounding the sport. This was rarely discussed outside family or intimate social gatherings. A series of traps seem to have been laid for the ignorant. A mistake, such as calling a whip a crop, instantly identified you as an outsider.

Melanie seemed to be oblivious to the huge amount of information being transmitted around her by gesture, facial expression and tone of voice. She regarded herself as one of the crowd, but it was obvious to me that many of those there did not. The attitude towards her seemed to vary between amused toleration to the blatantly superior and patronising. I didn't even try to point it out but reported back to Jack who said, 'I know. One of my big fears is that she will be wooed by some well-to-do waste of space with no money. The next step would be to target me for it after they get married. I would have no choice but to say no, probably followed by divorce and by Melanie blaming me. It would be bad. If I agreed to some limited funding, I would then see it disappear and then have the hand held out again and again for more. What would you do? I hate the idea of having some waster son of a landed gent leeching on me permanently. Why can't she dog on with one of the betting shop managers, or you, or somebody similar.'

I just shrugged. 'Nothing I can say, really. I just hope it doesn't happen. I suppose you could put it round that you were in financial difficulties, that would deter the buggers.' Jack shot me a sharp glance and smiled. I said, 'Another thing would be a trust which paid her a small allowance with full control passing over to her on your death.'

He nodded. 'I thought about that one but it's difficult. If some waster incurs big debts in both their names and then pisses off, she could be really lumbered.'

He went on, 'I see you've been chatting to my accountant. I

told him to fill you in on how money works; its important. If you have cottoned on to things like trust funds you are on your way. Have a word with him about how the stock market works. That's a form of gambling I like—you can actually win!'

He changed the subject and told me that he would be abroad for a week or so seeing to some business interests and said, 'I have a big job coming up. Normally I would see to it myself. I need you to courier over twenty thousand in cash to a contact in the Isle of Man. I can't tell you what it's about, but they have just built a casino over there; they have other gambling interests elsewhere and this one can't go through the books. All you need to know is that there is nothing criminal in what you personally are doing.' He gave me a knowing look and said, 'There shouldn't be any problem. I have booked you into the casino hotel for a couple of days. Take a dinner suit and have a look round, tell me what you think. Whether it seems to be running smoothly, and whether things seem efficiently organised. Keep the money in your hand luggage on the plane—it's a short flight—and get a taxi from the airport to the casino and pass the money straight over when you arrive.' He showed me a photo of the contact there. He continued, 'It goes to him and nobody else, understand?' I nodded. He explained, 'Normally I would send it in several smaller amounts, but this is urgent. Just keep your wits about you.'

I had a word with Cannonball before I left. From the way he screwed his face up I could tell he wasn't happy. He said, 'It's a big risk. The slightest leak would put you in danger. That's enough money to buy six or seven decent sized houses. To be right you shouldn't even have told me. If this gets nasty you will be dealing with the big boys and not some cosh-boy on a racetrack. He took me into his office and unlocked a cupboard. He took down a metal box from the top shelf and unlocked that also. There were various bits of gear stowed carefully inside the box. I could see a derringer pistol and knives of various types and several metal star shaped objects.

I said, 'Are those Ninja throwing stars? Shuriken!'

'Yes,' he said. 'I brought a few back with me from Japan.

These are old, pre-Edo period. I found them in a junk shop in Tokyo. They were rusty. I cleaned them up and even learned to throw them at one of the martial arts schools. There is lots of myth about them, like them being poisoned, but their main purpose was to injure or disorientate the enemy. If you are bleeding from a nasty slash on your face or body from one of these, you are distracted and easier to take out with a katana or tanto.'

He pulled a small metal cylinder out of the box and pulled a pin out at one end. He let go at the same time and the cylinder telescopically expanded into a thin rod about thirty inches long, which he deftly caught. He said, 'Clever, eh! Not exactly orthodox but some of the blokes I worked with in the police out in the far-east carried them. These are modified with a small weight at the end. Useful against somebody with a shorter weapon like a knife or iron bar. If you crack it against a face or knee it is bloody painful. Too fragile to be much good against a sword but in most other circumstances it will give you an edge, especially against three or four.' He passed it over and said, 'Practice with it. The trick is to pull the pin and then catch and use it straight away. Most people won't have seen one and it will give you the advantage of surprise. Pass it back when you return—it's a memento of some wild times out east; with luck it will stay in your pocket. They are legal but if anyone asks about it tell them it's a magician's wand or something. Most of the customs or police officers won't know enough about 'em to know any better. But your main weapon is your brain—be wary, keep your antenna up, look out for people watching you or following you, be alert at all times.'

My martial arts mentor then proceeded to show me how his contraption could be used most effectively, pointing out the parts of the body least easily defended and those susceptible to maximum pain. He reinforced the lesson with a few swings and whacks against one of the old, heavy punch bags. He passed it over and said, 'Give it a try.' I was surprised how light and wieldy the implement was. The ingenious bit was the small weight at the end, which due to its length and when swung at the end of an arm would build up a lot of momentum in the weight and deliver a powerful cracking impact as it struck a skull or collar bone, or as it came up between the legs. He said, 'If you leave the pin in and just grip it hard, it will magnify your punching power no end. Somebody as powerful as you should be careful though—if you use it like that you might break a knuckle as well as their jaw if you punch 'em very hard.'

Two days later I was on my way. I set off early using back roads and picked up a flight at Manchester airport to the island's small airport at Ronaldsway, situated in the south about six miles from the seaside town of Douglas, which serves as capital of the island. The casino/hotel complex had a very nice sea-view site. Jack told me that he had booked me a double at the front of the hotel with its own bathroom. He said, 'I have stayed there and it's a mistake to book one of the rooms at the back overlooking the car park. If you do that you will be kept awake till 5 a.m. by the stream of bloody taxis arriving to pick up at the big rear entrance, despite the double glazing and heavy curtains. You just hear car doors slamming all bloody night.'

I parked the car as close as I could to the terminus. I had the money in a small suitcase, which I would carry as hand luggage. My gear was in another slightly larger case which went as baggage in the plane's hold. I got out of the car and looked around, but nothing seemed out of the ordinary. I hurried through the terminal and did the minimal check in required for an Isle of Man flight, and was the first to board the plane. The thing seemed old and dilapidated to me. An old RAF type who took the seat next to me, told me that it was a Douglas Dakota which had been sold as war surplus. My informant said, 'Don't be put off by the way it looks, they are very reliable aircraft.' I replied, 'They? It's this one I'm worried about!' RAF chuckled and said, 'It will probably still be flying ten years from now.'

The flight took little more than thirty minutes and we landed amid drizzle and low cloud. I raced off the plane and grabbed my large suitcase. There was a bus service to Douglas, but it would be twenty minutes before it set off. I looked around and could see four taxis in the rank. I noticed a car waiting with a couple of others in the pick-up area near the exit, with a couple of blokes stood by it, smoking, and a driver inside. They seemed to take just a little too much interest in me and what I was doing. Instinct is a funny thing, but my antennae were picking up strong danger signals. The two blokes who were standing looked like some of the heavies I had run into on the racetracks. Both had trilby hats pulled well down over their faces. Their driver wore a cloth cap which was also pulled well forward to cover his face. I took a good look. I wanted to be able to recognise them again. I noticed that one had a broken nose and a small dark moustache with a very pronounced jaw line. His companion looked agitated and had an easily remembered ferret face with thin lips and an oddly twisted mouth. I put him in his thirties and his moustached companion in his early forties.

I thought quickly. I went to the first taxi and said, 'I want to go to Douglas but wait a minute, don't take another fare.' I turned rapidly and approached the driver of the second cab and gave him the big case and passed a fiver over, saying, 'Deliver this to the reception at the Palace Hotel. He looked at the money which was about five times what he would have got as a fare and said, 'Right, sir,' touching the peak of his hat with two fingers. I said, 'It's urgent. Go now!' The cabbie caught the tone in my voice. He jumped into his vehicle and pulled out of the rank and set off. I walked back to the first cab. I noticed that I had caused some consternation amongst the heavies, both of whom were getting rapidly into their car.

Their actions confirmed my suspicions. I climbed into the second cab and told him my destination. I had thrown a spanner in the works! The heavies might be after the money, but they now didn't know if I had it or if it was in the big case I had deposited with the other driver. However, although they couldn't be sure, they had correctly worked out that I was unlikely to let the case with the cash in it out of my hands. Thus, as we left, I could see them pull out and start to follow us. I noted that the road was quiet with few vehicles on it.

I said to the driver, 'Much police activity here?'

He said, 'Bloody hell, on the Isle of Man? It has almost no crime and if there is a car about it will be heading across to Ramsay. There was some sort of incident reported outside there about twenty minutes ago. The car usually based at the airport left about five minutes before you came out.'

The thought of a possible staged incident or false report, to draw the police elsewhere, flicked through my mind. I kept on looking back. The car was closing on us.

I said, 'The island is pretty quiet then.'

The driver said, 'Yeah, it must drive younger blokes potty. After the TT fortnight in May when the place is packed, we have a sedate holiday season with lots of families and older types filling the boarding houses. Then for eight months the only exciting activities here are drunken driving and shagging other men's wives.' He chuckled at his own joke, but I had other things on my mind.

The road was deserted and the car behind was started to overtake. I glimpsed the three as it sped past—the driver was expressionless, moustache looked grim and ferret face had a wild look on his face.

Their car was now in front. It braked and then braked again, causing my driver to slow down considerably. It then pulled half out so we couldn't pass and braked again.

'What is the silly bugger trying to do?' said my cabbie. We had really slowed down by now; I knew exactly what they were trying to do. I took hold of Canonball's telescopic wand in one hand and the small suitcase in the other and braced myself. The car in front slammed the brakes on and the taxi driver braked but ran into the back of it at about five miles an hour. Moustache and ferret face started to climb out of their car. I was faster though and leapt out of my side. I could see that they were both carrying heavy steel tyre levers. My driver just sat there looking shocked. I extended the wand and then did exactly what they didn't expect. I ran towards them. My tactic caught the thugs by surprise—they had been used to situations where fear would do most of their job for them. They didn't expect much trouble from a young kid. I slashed downward with the wand at moustache's head, he moved out of the way with a boxer's reflex, but the weight came down hard on his shoulder. He dropped the tire lever and cursed. I slashed at ferret face's knee and heard a satisfactory crack. I then swung the wand up between moustache's legs. He couldn't avoid that one and doubled up in agony. I swung again at ferret and caught him on the side of his head.

With that I legged it and hopped over a gate and sprinted through a lightly ploughed field towards a small wood. I heard a crack, and something whizzed through the air near my head. It was obviously a bullet. Another crack and something caused the case to almost jerk out of my hand. I heard a raised voice: 'You cunt! What did I say about bringing a shooter! If you kill him, we could swing for it!' My mind was racing. I guessed that as the robbery had failed my attackers would want to be out of the way as soon as possible rather than pursuing me on foot. The bit of country I was in could maybe have been crossed in a Land Rover but not in their saloon. I wasn't taking any chances though. I sprinted harder, and a few moments later I heard their car start and speed off. I ran on as fast as I could through the trees and to the top of a hill. I could see Douglas in the distance and jogged down a track towards the town. A few minutes later I heard a police siren. I negotiated a short stretch of lane and by then was amid the outer houses of the island's capital. I made my way onto a main street and could see a sign pointing to the beach. A couple of minutes later I was on the beach road and could see the hotel.

I entered the foyer and asked a porter where the manager's office was. 'I've got an important package for him.' He could sense the urgency in my voice and pointed to a double door. Through it at the end of a short corridor was an impressive looking door emblazoned with the words Hotel Manager. I knocked and walked in. A secretary looked startled for a moment. I said, 'I'm expected. It's the package from England.' Just then an inner door opened and a shrewd looking smartly suited bloke with impeccably groomed grey hair came out. He grasped the situation in an instant and ushered me into his inner sanctum, saying to his secretary. 'I am not to be disturbed for any reason.'

He said, 'Have a seat. You look a bit hot and bothered.' He turned to a cabinet. 'Can I get you a drink? You look as though you need one.' I accepted a large still orange. 'When your suitcase arrived without you, I thought you might have run into difficulties.'

I rapidly outlined what the difficulties had been and said, 'Don't worry though, the money is here,' and passed the case across with the key for the small lock. 'Can you check it please and then confirm you have received it.'

He opened a safe in his office wall and then opened the case. He did a rapid check of the large denomination bills. He picked one bundle up and pointed to a small, neat hole. He looked at me quizzically and said, 'Bullet? It looks like the leather and the paper stopped it. You might have been lucky there.' He finished counting, then said, 'I'm satisfied it's all there. Forty bundles of five hundred. I'll get a clerk to do a detailed count later and have the damaged notes replaced.'

He turned and picked a phone up. A couple of minutes later he was talking to Jack, confirming receipt of the package, and said, 'But there were difficulties in transit.' He transmitted the story using coded language and then passed the phone over. I heard Jack's voice saying, 'Don't say anything, it's an open line. We will chat when you get back, but you're OK?' I said I was, and he replied, 'Good, just enjoy the break. I will see you in a few days.' I passed the phone back and a few more words were exchanged.

The manager said. 'My name is Olaf, by the way, Olaf Gunnarson. Icelandic originally, my dad came over here to work the boats during the First World War and stayed. Jack said you are to have the best of everything while you are here. If you would like to go and get showered, we can meet up, in say an hour, and I will give you the personal tour after we have eaten.'

I showered and changed. Events kept on running through my brain. I had been prepared for whatever a standard thug might hand out, but being shot at was something of a shock. My reflexes and the adrenaline rush had enabled me to deal with it, but it was an experience I wouldn't like to go through every day of the week. It was fine watching guns being fired in westerns or war films but when bullets started whizzing close to my frame it was completely different.

I met up with Olaf who took me straight to the restaurant. He led me through the main part to an obviously exclusive area at the rear. A waiter appeared immediately, and Olaf said, 'The menu in this part is very high standard, we have a top chef. This area is reserved for some very rich clientele. The food here generally is good and relatively cheap as are the drinks. We find that our money is made overwhelmingly from the gambling. The amount of money about is surprising. We aren't a top casino by any means. If we were in Monte Carlo or Biarritz or the U.S.A. the amounts would be huge but here, they are just large.' He went on, 'Try the lobster. I can recommend the Beef Wellington.' I looked blank. Olaf smiled. He said, 'Jack said you were a rough diamond from the mining villages. Let me broaden your horizons. When I first saw it, I thought it was just a big meat pasty. I had never heard of it either. It is a fillet of the very best beef coated in a mix of pate de foie gras and duxelles which are a mix of chopped mushrooms. It is delicious, take my word.'

I was persuaded and having tried it, agreed with him that it was. He also ordered an expensive claret and white wine called a Chablis and explained something about the vintages and terms like premier cru. He said, 'It sounds better than it is; it just means "first growth," or from the grapes picked first. Grand cru translates as great growth and means that the wine comes from a notable vineyard. It isn't really about the quality of the wine in the bottle. It may not be all that good if it was a bad year.' He had a word with the wine waiter who appeared a little later with a bottle of champagne. Olaf let the waiter pour and then tasted the wine with obvious relish. He pointed to my glass and the waiter filled it. He said, 'Give it a try.' After a few moments my host said, 'What do you think?'

I thought for a while and said, 'It's the first time I have ever tasted champagne and I can't compare it to anything. It is a bit like sparkling cider but far less sweet, but it has a far richer set of flavours.'

Olaf nodded and said, 'You must come back to one of our wine tastings. It is easier to compare it if you have tried some of the cheaper blends. The one we are drinking is called Pol Roger; it was Churchill's favourite. He was first served this wine at a dinner in 1928, the very beautiful Odette Pol Roger was there and after that Winston had a life-long preference for it. It is certainly one of the very best. During the course of my career, I have tasted some very good champagnes; make a point of trying Krug and Bollinger at some time if you get the chance.' I absorbed the experience like a dry sponge. It was an alien world, totally different to the one I had grown up in.

After coffee he showed me round the casino. He said, 'We run various events and are reasonably busy during the whole year. Some hotels on the island shut in the winter. We are full during the summer and packed during the practice and TT weeks in late May.'

The setup was interesting. A foyer full of slot machines led into a large hall containing twelve centrally located roulette tables. Nine were grouped together, two had more space around them and a final table stood in splendid isolation with a low rail round it. There were players round three of the tables in the first group and around one of those in the group of two. A couple of croupiers stood ready at two of the other empty tables.

Olaf spoke quietly. 'The busy tables are for the small-time gamblers. They buy chips in multiples of a pound, that's our smallest stake, but they go up five, ten, twenty, fifty, a hundred and we have some at a thousand pounds each, which are purchased occasionally if we get a high-roller in. The separate table is for the rich. The minimum stake there is a fifty-pound chip, which deters the small beer punters. Often, it's just the high roller, perhaps with friends and the croupier at the table. The table is there for show more than anything. The small stakes tables rake a lot more in over the year. But you have to have it, to give the place an air of class. It creates a lot of excitement if we get a big money guy in, but it's not often. They sometimes fly in, or a yacht calls in at the island. At the other two tables the minimum stake is ten pounds. That's a full week's take home pay for a lot of people.'

Side rooms contained blackjack and poker tables, and at one end in a slightly raised area were three tables. Two were empty but one had two elderly women playing and a flashy looking Mediterranean type with his much younger and tarty looking girlfriend as an onlooker. A small nondescript bloke and two other men who looked like solicitors made up the party.

Olaf nodded to the croupier as we passed and then stood looking on. He said, 'Have you played?'

I replied, 'I don't have a clue, never seen the game.'

He took me out of earshot and said, 'It's called chemin de fer or chemmy, have you heard of it?'

I replied in the affirmative saying, 'It looks complicated.'

My escort said, 'It's surprisingly simple. Aces count as one, two to nine have those values and royal cards and tens count as zero. All get two cards; the aim is to score nine. More than that you lose. The bank rotates, you can pass on it. If you take it, you have to cover the bets of the other players. You can take other cards. Simple mathematics says if your hand totals zero to four the odds are in your favour so take one, five to nine the maths says don't take any more. The casino takes a small percentage of winning hands.'

I said, 'Why do they call it that? It means 'rail track' in French.'

He smiled and replied, 'The game is one of the three variants of baccarat. This variant is called chemin de fer because it is the fastest moving of the three. When it was developed at the end of the nineteenth century the railways were the fastest thing around. The name stuck. The term baccarat refers to the worst hand you can get, which is two cards each worth zero.'

I asked about the players. He said, 'That table is reasonably high stakes. The two older women are Jewish sisters, who each own a hotel on the island. The greasy looking bloke with the tart owns a hotel and other property here and elsewhere. We think he might be Maltese or Corsican and have dodgy connections. The plain looking bloke is a multi-millionaire. He comes in almost every night. He doesn't seem to be interested in women and is bored or maybe guilty about something, morose about who he shafted to get his wealth perhaps. He has a few hours at the table and then wanders to the bar to have a steak sandwich and a bottle of champagne and a few more drinks. We usually put him in his taxi at 2 a.m.

'The two other men are a local boat builder and his accountant. The two sisters and the accountant are the astute players. The game in outline is simple, but the betting strategy is complex. The millionaire doesn't care, and the boat man is crap. The Maltese likes to act the part of Mr Big, he is a good player but will bet against the odds on a whim just to impress. We get others at the table. If they are inexperienced, they usually don't stay long. The point is that you play against the others round the table. The shoe contains six packs of cards so you can't count cards unless you have a mathematical brain like Einstein. There are other players who have their regular nights. We have a lot of tax exiles here, authors and the like who moved here because our income tax rates are lower than on the mainland. We get the once only types of course, those who are here for conferences or other events. They have perhaps seen chemmy in films, usually in very glamorous settings like Monte Carlo, and want to experience the glamour of playing. I remember one chap moaning that he had lost a month's salary after playing for just half an hour. His wife dragged him away before he lost another six months money.'

Just then a heavily jewelled woman in a silk dress and white fur stole moved to the table attended by a young man. He pulled the chair back and stood attentively slightly behind her. She was about fifty and I could smell what seemed to be very expensive perfume filling the air around the chemmy table. The croupier asked if he could get her anything to eat. I looked at Olaf who said, 'It's all part of the service. We take their money off them in the most civilised manner possible.' The croupier snapped his fingers and a waiter appeared almost instantaneously. Words were exchanged and a small plate of smoked salmon sandwiches were back at the table before the woman had removed her stole. She joined in the game, lit a cigarette and nibbled the sandwiches in between taking tiny puffs of the smoke between her lips, the plate being held by the young man who had accompanied her.

Olaf moved me out of earshot and said, 'What did you think about her?'

I replied, 'Obviously rich but she seems agitated, as though something is eating her.'

'Perceptive. She is the ex-wife of an American industrialist worth hundreds of millions apparently. She was a rising actress and one of the hottest things around. She was twenty-five when he married her, but a few years ago she started to fade a bit and he got rid and replaced her with a newer model. She went from being a member of the very top set—Monte Carlo, Biarritz, Switzerland, Rio, Paris, New York—to being a B-lister after he dropped her. Money isn't the problem for her—she got millions from the divorce—it's the loss of the very pampered and privileged lifestyle. She doesn't get invited to the very top race meetings or parties any more. She consoles herself with a series of younger men and trips to not so glamorous casinos like this where she is not known. Her play at chemmy is erratic. She can be brilliant, and the two sisters are wary of her, but she gets distracted and then throws money away in frustration. There is nothing stopping her from visiting the casinos she used to go to, but she can't stand it. Just being treated like the one of the crowd, rather than someone very special. Also, though still strikingly good looking, she is not the head turning stunner she was twenty years ago.'

We drifted back towards his office. He said, 'It's getting busier. I need to circulate. It's expected by the punters, you know the sort of thing, public relations, back slapping, being interested in people or seeming to be. I never forget a name or a face. Helpful in creating the right atmosphere with the punters and in dealing with the small minority who get their kicks by complaining or causing trouble. You must excuse me. If you want to try the chemmy I can get one of the croupiers to talk you through the loss minimising strategies, but I wouldn't recommend it—some of that group have been playing for years.' He laughed and said, 'Let me fix you up with some chips and you can wander round the tables and try your luck.' He took me across to the cage which sold chips and cashed them in. He had words and then passed a hundred quid's worth of chips across to me and said with a laugh, 'When you have lost those you can buy the next lot. But remember the two golden rules.' I looked quizzically at him, and he said, 'The house always wins, and gambling is a mugs game.' He waved and left, eyes twinkling with amusement.

I wandered round placing a couple of chips on red or black, sometimes winning, sometimes losing. I knew enough about probability theory to know that long term I was bound to lose. Various systems had been tried. A favourite was doubling up. With the zero on the wheel the odds for a win on red or black were slightly less than a half. Ignoring the zero the odds of four blacks or reds in a row happening were thirty-two to one against. Thus, some thought that each successive roll which produced the same colour was increasing unlikely, so if you doubled your bet each time on the same colour the odds would seem to suggest that eventually the colour you were betting on must show up. Unfortunately, longer runs of either black or red can occur. Therefore, because the roulette wheel has no memory and the possibility of the ball landing on zero or of you exceeding the table limit before you win, the winning system was flawed.

I always sort of admired a group of lads from my village. They had been working as steel fixers and had earned a lot of money picking up forty or fifty quid a week, which was huge in those days. The four put two hundred and fifty quid each into a pot and they went to a London casino at the end of their contract and bought a thousand-pound chip. They were going to make a single bet and then walk away with their money doubled or with nothing. They gave the chip to the wildest of them and he put the chip on red. Black came up and they walked away from the table without a word and spent the rest of the night having a laugh and getting pissed at the bar. The next day they were on the train home, but having gambled a thousand pounds in a single go at roulette in 1963, they thought the experience was worth it.

I circulated and the place got fuller. I realised that lots of those putting money on the tables didn't seem to be enjoying it. Some looked bored, others seemed glued to the tables, placing their bets and then watching the ball spin with the same fascinated look as that of a rabbit caught in the glare of headlights. One pair were particularly interesting. They fever-ishly placed the chips on the table. It seemed they were work-ing to some pre-determined sequence involving groups of four numbers. It involved leaving the winnings on the table but moving them to adjacent number groups. She was deathly pale, and he was pallid and sweating with a feverish look in his eyes. It struck me that their gambling had some sort of sexual content which I couldn't quite work out. Perhaps it was the excitement of a possible win coupled with the masochistic punishment inflicted if they suffered a heavy loss.

I had a word with Olaf about it later and he said, 'Very observant. I have seen everything having worked at many casinos. From the occasional big win and very big loss to people who are dying, who walk in with their last few thou-sand and put it on a single number, lose and then order a bottle of our most expensive champagne to be sent to their rooms and then overdosed, washing sleeping pills down with it.

'The bill was always picked up by the hotel who figured that the dead punter's losses at the table would more than cover any costs. Everything was kept as hush hush as possible and at least here we don't expect some desperate type to lose his shirt and then wander outside and shoot himself with a .22 pistol.' I looked at him quizzically. 'That sort of thing was looked out for at some of the top French casinos. They sometimes managed to intervene, they gave the loser a stiff drink and some money and kicked him out and banned him from the place. I suppose here they might wander off and jump into the harbour, but at least that's not on our premises and we don't get tiresome squads of police running round afterwards and the resulting reputational damage. We need to avoid that because some of the puritan elements here would like to remove this "cess pit of the sins of the flesh" from the island.' He laughed. 'The people running things here are realists like me. They can see the huge amount of money that this place is bringing into the local economy.'

I finished the night with sixty-three chips. Just before I left, I put them all on black and won. I went to the counter and pushed the hundred and twenty-six chips over and said, 'Cash them in but give it to Olaf—it's the casino's money.' Maybe I have some sort of character failing, but I always felt uncomfortable owing people, unless I could pay back.

Chapter 24

The Scouse Maiden

'Liverpool girls are as sharp as razors!
—Believe me son, razors aren't even close.'

Anon

Olaf had words with me after breakfast. 'The tellers told me that you cashed in your chips with a profit for the casino. There was no need to do that, you know; it was just a little bonus for what you did for us and to compensate for the danger you found yourself in. We didn't expect that. There must have been some leak of information. The way that things were set up it can only have come from Jack's end. He is looking into it.' He continued, 'There is a big amateur boxing match here this evening. It's a biennial thing: the Island against Liverpool. We have a strong club and an annual match with the scousers, it's there one year and here the next, and it's our turn to host. A couple of ABA champions are fighting each other, and it should be good. You can sit in the VIP box with me and a few others. I think you will be interested in the sights. It will be a nice end to your visit before you fly back tomorrow.' I gleaned from his tone that the sights would be those other than hairy blokes punching each other on the chin.

We met up later. He looked superb in a very well-tailored and obviously very expensive dinner suit. I didn't look bad in my off the peg one. But I was sat with the boss, being fussed around by three or four very attractive waitresses. I was oblivious at the time but soon found out that people notice, and some people were seeing me as more than I was. The fighting was enthusiastic, with lots of guts shown by everybody who took part. The last bout finished at 10 p.m. I had been told that there would be a few hours of partying before they made their way to the harbour to get the special early ferry which left at 5 a.m., disgorging its happy and fatigued cargo into the city about three hours later. The boxers sat around with red wheals and bruises on their faces, having a hell of a good time, probably drinking for the first time in a while after getting into peak condition and trying to make the weight in their various categories. They were surrounded by family, friends, fans and various hangers on. The older contingent, which was made up of the coaches and various officials, tended to sit together and somewhat apart and talk about things like the national picture in the amateur ranks, rule changes and the rapidly approaching Olympic selections and who was likely to turn pro after it or even before it. The gambling hall was full, with the lower stakes roulette tables doing particularly well.

I absorbed the sights and sampled the various sense impressions. The thing that was particularly striking was the way that many of the younger women from Liverpool were dressed. The theme amongst the younger, unattached women, seemed to be one of as much sexual provocation as they could get away with without being arrested. Thus, lots of make up with very short skirts and high heels were the order of the day. Some took it to extremes with slit skirts and very low-cut blouses or wanton looking St. Trinian type schoolgirl outfits. They all exuded sex appeal in large quantities. The bouncers looked on in amusement or with quiet appreciation; they had seen it all before. Some of the portly and respectable middle-class types just looked at the sex parade with jaw dropping amazement. I knew one or two women back home who liked to look tarty, but they never got anywhere near this on the scale of the deliciously lascivious.

I said to Olaf, 'Obviously some good Catholic girls in tonight.'

He smiled and replied, 'Yep, very good, but harder nuts to crack than you might think. It always strikes me that there is a battle between the raging hormones and the repressed culture with this lot. The base line is, they want a husband. And remember, they look after each other ferociously. Watch out if you get chatting. If you do, the first barrier is the language—if they are mainly from the port area the accents will be as thick as treacle and they are fast, with words you can't waste time trying to work out what they mean.

'If they say something is Baltic it means cold, as in the Baltic. La is short for lad, its gear la means its good stuff lad. Plazzy means fake, the word's a contraction of plastic. Some words are obvious like ma and da. Some have wider use and are heard in other northern towns, like scran for food and kecks for trousers. They will probably like your accent, your natural one I mean—you sometimes slip back into it with the occasional 'wun't' or 'dun't' when you don't need to be communicating clearly. They like northerners and generally hate Londoners or any sort of posh boy. A lot of that comes from the Irish culture which permeates Liverpool. In the wars there were huge numbers of merchant seamen from there and they remember what their dads and grandads said about how things were then and how they were treated in other ports, and by the officer middle and upper classes. Belfast, Hull, Bristol, Glasgow and Newcastle were fine, it was the South coast ports and London, they weren't so keen on. There were exceptions of course. I have heard stories of scousers getting drunk with scrumpy rats in Portsmouth and the scousers being very impressed.'

I looked at him quizzically and said, 'Scrumpy rats?'

Olaf grinned and said, 'The term was applied to a small number of sailors—usually with the purple noses you see with some very heavy drinkers. Don't ask me about the technicalities, but there were scrumpy houses near the docks in some southern ports. They just sold crude scrumpy, cloudy cider and full of tannin and other stuff and fully fermented so the alcohol was over eight percent. It had a low rate of tax for some reason, and was a cheap way of getting very drunk with an awful hangover thrown in. The scrumpy rats used to get off their ships and make straight for the places. I know one heavy drinker from up here who had four pints of the stuff and the worst hangover he had ever experienced afterwards. Lots of scouse sailors and dockers are very heavy into the bevvy as they call it.'

After the boxing I left Olaf and drifted into the bar area. I was running the events of the last few days over in my mind, having a last drink before bed. I leant on the bar chatting to the barman who had been instructed to serve me whatever I wanted and charge it to the casino. I ordered a tonic water. He looked at me and said, 'We have some twenty-five-year-old malts sir.'

I smiled and said, 'Thanks, but I don't like taking advantage.'

He smiled and shook his head and said, 'You are a rarity, sir.'

He moved away to serve another customer and I turned round to survey the scene. There were lots of people milling about or sat in large circles smoking and drinking in the adjacent lounge. One or two were dozing. It would be five hours or more before they had to board the early ferry back to the port. Some casino regulars were coming in, I had been told that they tended to be night-birds especially on Fridays and Saturdays, and I was aware that lots of them left the place as late as four or five a.m.

I continued to look round and became aware that one youngish woman was looking straight at me. The look could only be described as smouldering. I looked back, trying not to show much interest, but the package on display was hard to resist. She was about twenty-five, I guessed, blonde and about five foot four. She was dressed in the provocative St Trinian's style of the films, with a school tie knotted loosely around a half-opened blouse which showed the top of a low-cut bra and a pair of very inviting tits. Below that was a very short, pleated school type skirt and some wonderfully shapely legs surrounded by wickedly black nylon stockings. I could just see the ends of the black suspenders which held them up. A half-smoked cigarette dangled from her lips, and she was looking at me in a sort of half-scowling, truculent, challenging, half-inviting half-haughty, half-fearing rejection sort of way.

She also exuded sexual attraction and imminent need in an incredible manner. I realised that I wasn't going to have an early night, or not one that was going to involve much sleep.

She took a long drag at the fag and walked forward and stubbed it out in the ash tray on the bar. She turned to me and said, 'I saw youse in the boxin', in the posh-box. Are youse some sorer gaffer?' Her accent was incredibly thick.

I replied, 'Nope, I did a big job for the boss and got an invite. My first time here.' I could see that her defences dropped quite a bit when she realised that I was a northerner like her. Well not quite like her but at least I was more acceptable.

She said, 'It's the second time I've been across here. It's always borin' after the boxin' ends, angin about waiting ter ge' back, and yer dog tired next day.'

She moved closer and the vibe was telling me that she fancied me rather strongly, which was more than mutual.

I took a long breath and said, 'I've got one of the luxury rooms. If you want, we can go up and you can have a kip, or we can chat and have a drink or play cards or something.'

I saw a deep glint of something which looked like pure lust fill her eyes. She said, 'Oright, the sumthin' sounds OK.'

I said, 'We don't want your reputation ruined being seen walking off with some stranger. Have a slow walk through those doors and round the corner and wait next to the lift. I will be there in a minute. I'll get a bottle of champagne.' I caught the eye of the barman and said, 'Change of plan, can I take advantage? A bottle of champagne and a couple of glasses as quick as you can.'

The barman grinned, and the bottle of Bollinger in an ice bucket and the glasses were there in a few seconds. He winked and said, 'If you want another sending up just ring down.' I picked them up and walked to the lift.

She had lit another cigarette and was standing near the wall by the lift doors smoking nervously. I took her hand, walked to the door, pressed the button and we both got in.

She said, 'I was thinkin' you might do a runner.'

'Nope,' I replied. 'Not my style, no way to treat a lady.'

We got up to the top floor. The corridor was empty, and half a dozen strides took me to my room. I opened the door and ushered her in, then walked to the small table and put the champagne down. I took my jacket off and laid it across the easy chair. I turned, loosening my tie as I did so. She had taken her blouse off and dropped her skirt to the floor. The next minute we were kissing passionately as I tried to undress with one hand. A moment later she was fondling my bulging cock and looking gratified at the size of it. She pulled me towards the bed and tore her panties down as I left the debris of my dress shirt on the carpet. Her urgency was incredible, pulling me towards her in desperate need and guiding my cock into her wet and receptive pussy. She gasped with pleasure as I started to fuck her as she wrapped her legs round mine. She was moaning now as my thrusts came harder and stronger.

I knew enough about sex to know that a key in the art of lovemaking depended on the male delaying his orgasm until the woman had been pleasured. In this case delay wasn't needed. She rapidly had a massive orgasm, screaming at the top of her voice as she did so. I followed shortly afterwards and just stayed there looking at her and said, 'Wow!'

She said, 'God, I was gaggin' for it. But don't think you've finished, big boy.' She looked round the room and was impressed. 'I've never seen a room as big as this in a hotel.' I grinned and jumped off the bed and opened the Champagne, pouring us both a glass about three quarters full. We lay back and sipped the expensive wine, looking out of the window at the moonlit sea. She said, 'You're not a whipper outer then, youse shot it right up me, but don't worry I'm on this new birth pill.' After that she got on her knees and in the most natural and unembarrassed way started to suck my cock.

The member once again got very hard and this time she mounted me, gliding up and down and stimulating her clitoris. I lay there enjoying her expertise. After all, I was just a simple country boy and had a lot to learn, and boy was I learning. After a short while she started to moan again and was soon rapidly and violently pleasuring herself like a wild animal.

Prolonged and deep gasps came from her mouth as she had another orgasm and slumped against my chest.

After a while she rolled off and reached for her cigarettes. She lit one and drew deeply on the long cylinder and then lay back looking very relaxed. I poured her some more champagne, and we began to chat.

She said mischievously, 'Wo sora bloke takes a girl to bed without knowing her name?'

We caught up on the introductions and she told me her name was Bernie, short for Bernadette, and that she worked as a typist for a big insurance company in the city.

'Catholic then?' I said.

'Don't talk to me about them twats,' she replied.

After a bit of probing, she explained her animosity. I told her that I had grown up in good old atheist South Yorkshire, and that for everyone making a church attendance there you probably had a thousand people visiting a boozer. She liked that and told me about her upbringing in the Catholic part of Liverpool. She was a natural rebel and an early developer. She said, 'I had me first bra at eleven and that seemed to cause interest among the nuns who taught me.' When she was thirteen an older friend of hers told her that an older priest at the church was bumming his sacristan. 'I didn't know what it meant,' she said, so her friend got her to sneak back into the church after a service. Everybody had left and the sacristan helped the priest to robe up and after the service disrobe, followed by some rapid homosexual sex. She witnessed the act herself and was shocked. After that she gave the church set-up a lot of thought and decided it was riddled with hypocrisy.

She said, 'A bit later at school where I was taught by "the Sisters of Mercy," a nun waded into me with a big board ruler screaming at me after I back-answered her. It came down hard on my head, so I smacked her in the gob and walked out. Luckily, I was fourteen then and the summer hols were coming up and I was fifteen in August, so I left. They tried to make a big thing about it and the nun lied about hitting me, but there was a big bruise on me head and the other girls said she done it so they couldn't touch me. They tried a back door rubbishing campaign. Lots of gossip and looks from some of the women, but I stopped having anything to do with it. Another Catholic lapsed due to the 'Christian' teachings of the sisters of Absolutely no bloody Mercy. What a bunch of sanctimonious arseholes.'

I smiled to myself, thinking how lucky I had been to have attended a non-religious school. We did the bare minimum to fulfil the requirements of the 1944 act, which said that each day should start with an act of collective worship. We sung a hymn to a badly played piano and said the Lord's Prayer parrot fashion with little understanding. Then the headmaster got onto the interesting stuff about games and Christmas stuff or similar. It was the first contact I had ever had with a Catholic and she had thankfully decided to lapse into the arms of the gods of pleasure, with me as the present provider of it.

She finished the cigarette and turned towards me and slid my cock between her lips again and started to do things to it that I had never experienced before. The semi-flaccid member suddenly leapt to attention. Bernie rapidly moved from sucking to riding me hard again with me laid on my back. She got me to squeeze her nipples, and this caused her to ride me harder, almost in a frenzy, till she orgasmed again. After that it was more Bollinger and we relaxed chatting once more. I briefly explained what I did, and her chief interest seemed to be in the sort of money it paid. She said she was a senior typist and did some secretarial work now and hoped to get a job full time as one of the secretaries to the various managers. She told me that she wasn't prepared to drop her knickers to get promoted, as one or two others had done. She was good at what she did and thought she would move up the ladder soon but was not sure which way to go.

She said, 'I gerra lorra interest from blokes and the choice seems to be get myself a big daft la from the docks. Then have kids and do what mi parents did, with him down at the boozer every night, and to Liverpool for the home games on Saturdays with his mates and a nice council house with all the others. The last thing I'm havin' is six kids, all at a fuckin' Catholic school, with the priest callin' round for a cuppa and cake and the weekly half a crown. The sex would be alright I suppose with a young bloke, or I could go for one of the older managers and live on a nice estate and learn to talk posh and get to Spain for me hols, but I don't really fancy some fat bloke fifteen years older than me puffin' and blowin' after ten mins, when we were at it.'

I sympathised, wondering if I was now in her sights. I changed the subject and asked her what she thought about this newish group called The Beatles. She said they were alright, but she was a Billy Fury fan.

The conversation transposed into her eventually getting on all fours while I fucked her from the rear. I could tell from her uncontrolled moans that this was particularly satisfying.

She looked at the clock. 'It's half past three, have we been at it that long? I could tell you were an animal as soon as I clapped eyes on you.'

I laughed, saying, 'I think this bedroom has a couple of real animals in it.'

She smiled and got into the shower and then dried off and then did her make up. I made her a coffee while she was getting ready.

'How do I look? she said as she finished her hair.

'Great,' I replied. She really did.

'Not like I've been fuckin half the night then?' she said with a smile.

'Nope, you look as fresh as a daisy,' I responded.

She looked at the clock again. 'It's twenty past four. I'd berra get down and find the others, they might be gerin worried.'

I said, 'Do you want me to walk you down.'

She smiled gratefully—wonderful teeth and lips, I thought —wonderful in all respects. 'Nah,' she said. 'Youse might be from the Yorkshire wilds but you are a real gent. Some blokes are, some aren't.'

I took her to the door. She looked at me sort of sadly and said, 'Thanks, you were terrific in bed and god how I needed it, but we are just ships that pass in the night.' With that she gave me a long passionate kiss and then turned rapidly and left. I never saw her again.

Chapter 25

The contract

I grabbed three or four hours sleep and woke up feeling great. I had a shower and went down to breakfast. My flight back wasn't till three-thirty, so I had lots of time. As I was finishing, one of the staff came to my table and said, 'Mr Gunnarson would like to see you as soon as possible after you have finished eating.' I nodded and the young man walked off. I assumed it would be some sort of routine matter. I ate in a leisurely manner, enjoying both the great food and service. After that I drifted towards Olaf's office. His secretary waved me straight in. The manager was on the phone. He looked up and waved me in, pointing at a chair.

He finished the conversation and in his usual smooth and polite manner asked if he could get me anything. A serious expression then clouded his face as he said, 'I'm afraid a situation has developed following the attempted robbery. After it, Jack got on the case with urgency. He found out that the leak about your trip had come from one of the young women in his main shop. The oldest story in the world. She was a bit on the dowdy side and had been seduced by somebody who targeted her because of her position and after that manipulated into passing the vital information about the large sums of money and where it would be delivered. Getting large quantities of attention and lots of cock all of a sudden had scrambled her brains and she wasn't thinking straight. Apparently, she had listened in to conversations between you and your boss. She had been told it was all about getting gambling information and wouldn't hurt anyone. Once she realised how she had been

251

used she was very helpful. Jack found out that her manipulative boyfriend worked for a gang based in Manchester. Their specialities are safe cracking, armed robbery, prostitution and cigarette theft and smuggling, with a lot of fencing thrown in. They sell stolen jewellery abroad through contacts in Italy. The bloke who runs it is a half Italian psychopath called George Gilberto. He uses the name Gilbert. He is well known, and half-feared, half-respected in the underworld. They call him Big G.

'All that is fine. That's the world we operate in, but he has a no-brain hot-head of a younger brother called Franko. He was the one who took the shot at you after they failed to grab the money and who was bollocked for it by the heavy who had been sent with him to do the job and keep him out of bother. Apparently, there were developments after your encounter. They got back to Manchester in quick time by a private small plane. Big G was furious at the failure and was not told about Frank carrying a shooter, apparently. After a few hours Frank collapsed. The crack you gave him at the side of the head caused a hairline fracture and bleeding into the skull. They managed to save him, but he nearly died, and Gilberto has vowed to put you in a wheelchair or kill you. There is a contract out and a team of heavies are on their way to give you a working over which will really fuck you up if they catch up with you. There is no point in trying to reason with a psycho like that. Despite the fact that you were defending yourself in a nasty situation, it's a family honour thing. He can't back off now; he would lose face and that is something you just can't do in the underworld.

'But don't concern yourself. Jack is sending a friend of yours across—he should be here within the hour. He will escort you back and a couple of my bouncers will escort you to the airport. After that he has a few things planned. I am sure you will get a full briefing very soon.'

I shrugged, receiving the news with equanimity rather than concern, knowing that I could easily hold my own in difficult situations.

Olaf went on, 'Big G is a nasty piece of work, but he does not run one of the really big crime firms and he has enemies in the underworld. Jack thinks he can use that against him.'

A short while later I was pleased to see Cannonball's huge frame striding through the hotel foyer. He shook hands and had brief words with Olaf, and then turned to me and said, 'Grab your gear, we are off.' Olaf had made his car and driver available, and we were soon at a small private airstrip and boarding a single engine plane which could hold four passengers. We were very rapidly aboard and on our way.

'Next stop Belfast.' said Joe. He explained that via a circuitous route back home any pursuers would be left guessing. 'Once back I have something arranged. You will be out of circulation for a bit. That will take the heat off because it will cost Gilberto a lot of time and money if he keeps his heavies on the job. They will withdraw and then wait to find out where you will be and then plan an attack. Don't worry about anything. While I was out in the Far East, we dealt with far nastier gangs than Gilberto's mob. It's just a question of being careful and making any attempt by them very costly to them.'

A few hours later I was being introduced to someone dressed in a saffron robe in an isolated wood somewhere in Herefordshire. It turned out that he was the abbot of a small community of Buddhist monks who had been given a long lease on the wood. The owner of the wood lived in a small, isolated manor house located in low hills just the other side of the wood. It was all very new to me. I knew little enough about Christianity and virtually nothing about this even older religion.

Cannonball explained he was using one of his old contacts from his young and wild days. He said, 'Just look on it as a few weeks holiday. You will learn an awful lot.'

He had given me a brief run down about the setup on the journey across. He told me that the place was ideal because of its isolation and wild rural setting. 'Even if big G's thugs found out where you are, and if they managed to get through the isolated country lanes, they would find themselves in a wood

253

inhabited by a group of about thirty monks. No information would be divulged by them, but even if they did manage to get through the wood and up to the big house, they would not enjoy the experience. The owner of the place is the most unusual man I have ever met. Name of Baldur Hector Rolf Balestier. At public school his nickname was 'Strange'; you will realise why when you get to know him. Those closer to hem refer to him as BB. You will rapidly find out two things about him – he is tremendously knowledgeable and one of the most intelligent men you will ever meet. He is also completely unconventional in his beliefs and in the way he operates. If you chat, never repeat yourself or waffle, he hates that. Sometimes he will have worked out what you were going to say before it gets out of your mouth. No wonder his nickname was Strange.'

We were shown into a library by a small dark man.

'One of BBs Gurkhas,' said my guide after he had gone. 'All his staff are Gurkhas. Some served with him during the war and a few younger ones are sons or nephews of those men, but they were in the regiment later on.'

After a few moments the great man walked in. He glanced at me and then greeted Cannonball. The two could not have been more different physically. The older man was small, compact and wiry with no evidence of fat on his face or anywhere else. If anything, he had the malnourished appearance sometimes seen in ascetic religious types. I immediately got the impression of someone who lived a life of severe self-discipline.

He greeted my companion with deep and sincere warmth.

'It has been a very long time since our adventures in the jungle, my friend,' said the older man with a wistful smile. 'It is still the case that my debt to you from that episode can never be repaid.'

For a moment I thought Cannonball looked slightly embarrassed, but he grinned and deflected the remark, saying, 'If you hadn't been leading, none of us would have got out.'

BB turned to me and said, 'This is the young man you have been telling me about.' My escort did the formals, we shook hands, I had the impression BB was analysing every move I made and every word I spoke. He ushered us into a dining room set out with a cold buffet. Gesturing to the food, he said, 'I am sure you are hungry.'

Cannonball led the way and was soon tucking into a huge plateful of cold meats. I had taken a smaller amount and less meat. BB ate sparingly, his main dish seemed to be a small bowl of pale soup, accompanied by a chunk of unbuttered coarse brown bread.

After the meal our host ushered us to a large study. A log fire was burning in a large grate and several leather armchairs were set around it in a comfortable semi-circle. We sat and BB said, 'I will have drinks brought. Wine, beer, spirits—we have a large selection.'

My huge companion said, 'Some of that green tea you used to have would be very nice.' Turning to me rapidly, he said, 'You ought to sample it, it is amazingly refreshing.'

I picked up on the subtleties and repressed my desire for a pint of cold, foaming, draught ale and said, 'Yes, I would like to try it.'

Our host's facial muscles hardly moved but from the slight glint of his eye I thought I discerned a slight look of approval at my choice.

We sat back enjoying the tea. It was totally new to me as all we ever had at home was the cheap Indian tea then marketed as Typhoo Tips.

BB leaned forwards and said, 'I think a brief council of war is called for.' And turning to me he said, 'You may know that thanks to my parent's interest in the Norse legends my first name is Baldur. Also, it was the name of one of my grandfathers. But please call me Hector. I much prefer the name of the great Trojan warrior to any of the others.' Our host continued, 'This matter concerning this gangster will seem very large to you, but I can assure you it is trifling, a mere skirmish in life's struggles. The basic psychology of that art was worked out by the great master Sun Tzu in his essays on the Art of War.' He asked if I had read the work. I shook my head and Hector stood and strode over to one of the shelves and picked out an old quarter leather-bound volume. He strode back and placed it in my hands saying, 'Please read it. In my opinion it surpasses even von Clausewitz, the great Prussian military thinker, and remember his great work *Vom Kreig*, or *On War*, was written in the period around the Napoleonic conflicts. Sun Tzu wrote his essays about five hundred years B.C.'

Joe remained silent. I took my cue from him and listened intently as our host expounded on the matter under consideration. 'Information is vital. We must find the enemy's weak points and exploit them. His resources are limited, so we will damage his staff and equipment. The cost will give him pause for thought and his hirelings will be increasingly reluctant to enter the fray. We will not place you in situations where a surprise attack will be possible simply by you not having any sort of regular routine. A couple of months here will sharpen your combat skills to the extent that if they come upon you by chance, your response will be deadly if needed and very damaging if not. I understand from my large friend here,' gesturing towards my tutor, 'that they are already probably more than adequate.'

Chapter 26

Transformation

Bushido—the code of the Samurai requires self-discipline, loyalty, and honour which demands courage and surprisingly, compassion.

D. T. Suzuki

I stayed with Hector for sixty-seven days. I wasn't conscious of it at the time, but he was putting me through a period of intensive physical and mental training. I realised later what a privilege it had been. I was also flattered after getting back and talking it over with Joe when he said, 'He must have thought you were worth the effort; that almost never happens.'

Hector was always with me at meals and in the evenings, constantly probing, explaining and testing me through question and answer, which inevitably led to more questions. My knowledge of the way the world works leapt exponentially and all the way through he provided lead ins to other areas of knowledge which I might like to pursue when I had less pressing business to hand.

My days were spent developing close quarter combat techniques. The first session was on the mat with a squat muscular Japanese gentleman. Hector had told me that he preferred to be as anonymous as possible. I was to call him Sensei, which translates as teacher, and he had the very high grade of 5th Dan at judo and was an expert in those deadlier techniques which had been removed from the sport in its infancy. We practiced the throws and locks which would all result in severe injury to an opponent until he was satisfied that they were becoming automatic. He went on in subsequent sessions to show me the banned striking techniques which had been garnered from the various Japanese martial arts schools. He was a man of few words but said in his halting English, 'Be very careful, these can kill if used by man of strength like you.'

Hector filled in the details later, explaining that during Japan's very long feudal period schools had grown up which taught every aspect of armed and unarmed combat. Swords, knives, spears, bows, etcetera. Efficient methods of killing using the weapons was taught, as well as defences against attacks with those weapons. He said, 'Some of the arts were obscure, bordering on the esoteric. For example, one Sensei even taught the art of avoiding knives thrown at the defender. You see how thorough they were. Every possible aspect of warfare and weaponry had been thought about, systematised, and trained for. The problem with the various schools was that there were so many of them that it would take several lifetimes to master their Katas or sequences of basic forms. You have done a couple of katas in Judo—those concerned with throws and the one concerning hold downs, locks and strangles. You would have had to learn the Nage-no Kata or series of types of throws for your first Dan. It contains fifteen throws performed to the right and left, and as you know it takes considerable effort to master it.'

I had a couple of hours every day on the mat with my teacher doing the moves again and again until they were locked in, and I would react automatically to any form of knife, club or other striking attack. Some defences against swords were included, but my Sensei said, 'Katana not used in this country, but defence good to know just in case.'

After a break, I had another session with a Scottish instructor. Again, he wasn't very chatty about his background, but I gathered from my host that he had taught his skills in a Commando school and had worked with the French Foreign Legion and some police units in the Far East and other units which he didn't talk about.

My host told me he was called 'Ice' in the foreign legion. He was ice-cold and methodical. Hector said, 'He has certain psychopathic traits, but he is well aware of his nature, and he is controlled. He knows all too well that to get out of control is counterproductive and can put you at a disadvantage or in danger.' I looked puzzled. My host said, 'Think of this: in a fight you lose your temper, which causes an adrenalin rush. If you disable your opponent in a few seconds that is fine. But after the adrenalin there is a crash, with fatigue and loss of fighting spirit and even desperation and the temptation to run.'

'Ice is never ruffled and is very fast and methodical. He always maintains the attack in the most efficient manner possible even if he gets wounded; an admirable killing machine, if you are in that line.'

Ice went through the basics of small arms use with me and had me shoot several hundred rounds with different types of handgun and showed me how to take the gun from an opponent at close quarters, when unarmed. He instructed me in the use of various rifles, including positioning and tactics. His speciality was knife fighting; he showed me how to kill and disable opponents and which knives were best for which purpose. I learned fast and towards the end he said, laconically, 'If ever you want a job after your present difficulties, contact me. Sort of in the personal security field.' I just nodded in acknowledgement but took what he said as a huge compliment.

I enjoyed the physical training and learning the new weapons skills, but what was most invaluable were the long discussions in the evenings in the library, during which Hector imparted his huge insights into the way the world worked. He seemed to have read every book ever written on military campaigns and tactics and virtually everything else. He dissected past campaigns analytically, pointing out what went wrong and what succeeded. He explained how weapon advantages due to developments of new alloys or manufacturing techniques had happened, how armour, mounted and mobile warfare and armies were organised. He pointed out that as courageous and disciplined as troops were, they could not succeed in the long run without weapons, equipment and food, and these in turn depended on the industrial capacity of the countries at war. He said, 'A prime example is Italy in World War Two. There was lots of jaw jutting and posturing from Mussolini, but Italy was doomed right from the start due to its relatively poor level of industrialisation.'

He talked about the ancient campaigns involving the Greeks and Persians and others. Of the genius of Alexander the Great, and Napoleon and the flaws which arose due to them overreaching themselves. He was hugely fond of the early campaigns of the Greeks and explained why they succeeded in large wars and in small campaigns such as the retreat under Xenophon from Babylon, after most of their leaders were killed. He said, 'It's still there! One of the ancient works which survived. It's called the *Anabasis* which loosely translates as the march up country. Ten thousand Greek mercenaries marching through deserts and mountain passes, under attack most of the time, until they reached the Black Sea.' He was misty eyed as he described the action of the three hundred Spartans and other Greek allies in delaying the huge army of Persians under Darius at the coastal narrow passage known as the 'hot gates', in Greek *Thermopylae*, or *thermo pylae* as it would have been then.

He was just as well-versed in Asian warfare, both ancient and modern. He could talk endlessly on the Mongol wars, or the interminable Civil wars in Japan, and had studied their successes and failures in the twentieth century wars. He explained, 'The Japanese are a hardy, intelligent and vigorous island nation, in many ways not dissimilar to the British. A critical difference was in viewpoint. The Japanese were determined to keep outsiders out, while we developed sea power as a result of warfare and then went on via exploration and a need to trade in order to supply our small land to find ourselves in possession of a huge empire almost by accident. This led in turn to a crass viewpoint that the white people who had spread out over the globe were in most respects superior to these "little yellow men", as they were described. It seems that our leaders had forgotten that the Japanese had fought on our side and that we even requested a squadron of their ships to assist with convoy duty between Suez and Britain, and that the assistance was invaluable and their ships and sailors were highly regarded. If you read recent histories all that seems to escape mention.

'In the Second World War we eventually overcome them, largely due to the huge industrial and manpower capacity of the Americans and by learning the hard way, in the field. The Australians were particularly effective against the Japanese and certainly outfought them in the New Guinea campaign. We were doubly fortunate that the USA had the resources to develop penicillin, which saved a lot of lives in nine-teen-forty-five and afterwards, and those needed to develop the atomic bomb. If Japan had not surrendered, it would have cost the allies hundreds of thousands of casualties and millions of Japanese to invade their mainland.'

Our discussions were wide ranging and by the end of them I realised that I was starting to think and analyse the world and my place in it in a completely different way. Hector taught me to look at the whole and not just at the little portion of events which were affecting me. He was disparaging about all inform-ation fed to the masses whether by radio, the papers or the newly emerging television. He said, 'The civil service has masses of data, it's there, but not easily accessible, they know exactly how many industrial workers are killed on site or who die subsequently or develop cancers or other diseases due to working in coke works or chemical plants etc. How many are killed and get injured in mining, fishing and construction and so on. The unions also know the facts, but either don't make a big fuss or, if they do, it somehow doesn't get reported or is just mentioned in passing. Knowledge is power, and if you hang on to it, it gives you huge advantage in politics and in the various propaganda arms of government.'

I wondered if he was pushing some sort of revolutionary agenda, but he rapidly explained that totalitarian states were far worse. He said, 'In the final analysis it is a compromise. What I am saying is, don't believe the pap fed to the masses. It contains bits of truth—usually heavily shaped and edited truth which suits the establishment with careful omission of key details. All I am doing is advising you to always look at all aspects of a scenario. Do you run a state in our rather subtle and paternalistic manner, or do you murder the millions who stand in your way, like Stalin, Hitler or Mao.'

He said, 'Never take anything on trust, sift the data, only accept it if it hasn't been massaged in some way by alteration or omission. Form your own views, never run with the herd and please don't ask me personally about the big picture—I am still thinking things through.'

He went on to give a piercing analysis of my situation and how to deal with it. He took me to a wooden panel and pressed a hidden catch. The panel slid open and Hector ushered me inside. Inside the room were thousands of books. My host saw the questioning look on my face and said, 'More than thirty thousand.' He showed me round the sections. Many of the volumes were leather bound and obviously very valuable, while others were more recent, but all were hardbacks as far as I could see with many in slip cases. The books were obviously in sections. I could see histories, dictionaries, all grouped together. Poetry, philosophy, theology, science and much else. Some names on the covers rang a bell with me, others I had never heard of. I was led round the shelves. Some volumes were lifted out with Hector giving a summary of their origins and what they were about.

Hector said, 'This is mainly for reference. The volumes I use regularly, and my favourite poets, are in my study. I have tried to collect a fair cross section of all the great works produced by the great minds.' We ended at his literature shelves. He said, 'Most of the world's notable literature is here, but let me show you this. He led me to a section containing small volumes. 'Here we have the surviving material from the classical world. It illustrates the nature of our problem. The works are published by the Loeb Classical Library Foundation—there are about five hundred in total. James Loeb was a German Jewish philanthropist who thought that all the ancient classical works

262

should be accessible and in one collection. They are translations with the original Greek or Latin on the facing page. These volumes are all we have. They represent less than one percent of the writings of the ancients. Unfortunately, most are lost, including most of the works of the great poet Sappho. We do have eleven of the marvellous plays by Aristophanes and much of the work of the great philosophers Plato and Aristotle, but huge amounts were destroyed at the behest of the small-minded religious types who came later. If it didn't fit in with their very narrow dogma or moral systems, they were destroyed. What happened was a huge tragedy.' He picked two volumes off the shelves and said, 'These two volumes contain all we have left of the Greek writings on mathematics. Thousands or tens of thousands of scrolls must have been written, but this is all that remains.'

At the end of my stay, he said, 'You are as well prepared as I can make you. In many ways I have been selfish and kept you here too long. You were to be here a few weeks while the heat died down, but I found you intelligent and stimulating. Also, your disappearance would have wrong-footed your enemy. Now you have a critical choice to make: do you return and move about avoiding the enemy, or do you disappear—it could easily be arranged. I have contacts in Asia, Africa and India. Do you go on the attack? You could disrupt the gangster's organisation, or you could try to cut the head off the monster. I know what I would do, but it's up to you. Yet always remember the code of the Samurai: violence must have an honourable purpose.' He was about to turn away but said, 'It might be useful if you thought about who you were and how you thought a few years ago and compare it to what you are and how you think now. You are no longer just a cog in the great machine fed the convenient pap which the machine and its agents in the media churn out. You have the tools now to work things out for yourself. You can analyse and evaluate. Use these tools well.' He smiled mischievously, one of the few times I had seen him do that. He turned away and waved as he walked back towards his inner sanctum.

Chapter 27
Into battle

'On the shaky frontier of life, here I stand, on the borders of death'

From 'The Land of the Dead' by Warrith Olawale

I walked down the long path through the wood, deep in thought. I saw the occasional saffron robe as monks moved about their business. I had seemed to have grown immeasurably, not just physically; my thought processes had changed. I was no longer the naïve primitive of my not-so-distant, wild, early youth.

At the entrance I found Cannonball in the car waiting to pick me up. He looked serious. As we drove, he brought me up to speed on the situation.

'We hoped that your longish stay here would have taken the heat out of the situation. Unfortunately, Gilberto's idiot brother got out of hospital and three weeks later got drunk and crashed his car. He was back in hospital for a while but seems to be suffering from mental problems now. His big brother is convinced that it's all down to you though, and is more determined than ever to get payback.'

'No point in talking then,' I said.

'None at all,' was the reply.

We drove straight back to Jack's house, and we talked it over. I thanked him for his efforts but said it's up to me. 'Fortunately, I have choices, but I don't fancy Calcutta or Wagga Wagga. As I see it the only solution is to neutralise the threat. I can't involve others, but information would be useful on our psycho friend's operations and whereabouts.'

'I can supply that,' said Jack. 'He has been doing some probing, but I have been counter-probing. I know where Gilberto lives—a nice house in a posh suburb. He also has a flat above his big nightclub in Manchester. I managed to contact a builder who did a lot of work there and I have drawings of the layout. I sent a girl in from a detective agency I sometimes use, and she pretended to get drunk and 'accidentally' got lost in the club and wandered upstairs; she noted where the fire doors and alarms were and checked out his security. He always has men on the door and heavies inside within call. Stairs from the club lead up to his flat. He feels secure there.

'The next problem is where do you stay? They located your house and keep periodic tabs on it. If you move back in there you can count on a visit from his hit team. I can find you a place but if they know you are back, they will close in on you so that won't be much better. The secret here is never to get into a regular pattern of movement and to change where you are living often. Not satisfactory, but until this gets resolved the main thing is to stay safe.' I agreed and Jack said, 'You are welcome to use one of the stable-boys places over my barn and I know a small out of the way hotel that has a couple of caravans at the rear. Both will be reasonably secure.'

Cannonball said, 'The attic above my gym is available. It is warm and has a bed and a shower. I have stayed there occasionally when working late.' I thanked them both and accepted their offers on a temporary basis, but I didn't plan to let my predicament linger on and on.

I settled into an erratic routine working for Jack and staying at different locations. Sometimes I was well out of the way on courier or other business. I was always doubly careful to ensure I wasn't being followed and used small intercity air flights wherever possible.

I got back from a short trip to London one evening having planned to stay at the gym. I let myself in through the side door and slipped upstairs. A few of the regulars were in using the weights but no-one gave me a second glance as I climbed the back stairs. I could see Cannonball in his office. I waved as I went up to the loft bedroom on the other side of his premises. He waved back at me and turned to talk to somebody who I assumed might be a new customer.

I got a shower and had a nap for about an hour and then changed into a track suit before joining the blokes for a session on the weights. I was just lacing up my trainers when I heard a racket downstairs. I slid out of the door and could see half a dozen rough looking types carrying pickaxe handles, short axes, machetes and the like. I could see that one of them was Gilberto's younger brother and that he was waving a gun and almost screaming at the top of his voice, 'Where is the bastard?' Cannonball had emerged from the office and was confronting the gang. The weight trainers looked shocked and were gathered in a small defensive group among the weight machines.

I found out later that the new recruit to the gym who I had seen talking to Joe, just by the purest bad luck, had been one of Gilberto's ferrets. He had left as fast as he could after seeing me and got on the phone to his boss to arrange the visit of the thugs.

There were some hard lads among the gym's customers but none of them had ever faced armed gangsters. I realised that it would be up to my giant mentor and myself if I was to get out of this fix. Just Joe and me; good odds, I thought. I could have crawled along the gantry at the rear of the place and made a run for it down the fire escape, but that would only put matters off. This was a great opportunity to draw the dragon's teeth.

I could see that Cannonball had clocked my emergence. I pointed to the rear, and he lifted both hands in acknowledgement as though trying to pacify the situation. The thugs were sizing him up and even tooled up they were reluctant to take him on. I was the one they were after.

Cannonball said to Franko, 'We know who you are Frank. Use that gun and you could swing for it.'

A torrent of abuse resulted; it was obvious that the man was bordering on the unhinged. The raised voices suited me because I knew attention would be focused on the one shouting and also drown any sound that I might make. I picked a small kettlebell up and edged along a girder at the back of the thugs. I let myself down quietly hanging from one arm and then dropped to the floor landing on some horsehair mats piled at the rear of the large room. The rearmost of the gang heard me land and turned round just in time to be met by me swinging the kettlebell into the side of his jaw. He went down like a poleaxed bullock, blood pouring from his mouth.

The other five turned around, and the distraction gave Joe his chance. He grabbed Franko by the throat with one arm and gripped the wrist of the hand holding the gun with the other. This left four for me to deal with. I rolled under the next nearest to avoid the arm which held a short machete and swung the kettlebell hard into his knee-cap. He screamed in pain and dropped to the floor, writhing about holding his shattered leg. With two down the other three looked doubtful, then they looked at each other and rushed me. I threw the kettlebell at the first. It caught him on the shoulder, and he dropped the axe. I stepped forwards and jabbed my straight fingers into his solar plexus and he fell, gasping for air. I stamped down on one of his ankles and there was a satisfying crack. As I was dealing with him, I heard a shot followed by the sound of a bullet pinging off something hard.

The pickaxe man was next. He swung his implement back before bringing it down. I reacted instinctively as I had been trained. The best defence with a long weapon involved getting in close, thus removing the advantage which the extended reach of his weapon gave him, which I did. I wrapped my arm round his and slammed him down with a hip throw and then kicked him very hard a couple of times in his groin. He lay there, folded up in agony. I stooped and picked the pickaxe handle up and faced the remaining assailant with the chain. A look of panic swept over his face, and in an instant he turned and ran. He was fast, but I was faster. I caught him at the door and swung the pickaxe handle hard into the back of his thigh.

He stumbled and fell, dropping the chain. I picked him up and slammed his face into the wall. Then I took his arm into a lock and violently snapped it at the elbow. I punched him hard in the face a couple of times, breaking his nose, and knocking a couple of teeth out and splitting his ugly lip. I said, 'It will be a long time before you will be at it again, pal.' He fell to the floor in a dazed and bleeding heap.

I turned back towards Cannonball. Franko lay dead at his feet, his eyes bulging and his tongue sticking out of his mouth. His windpipe was heavily bruised and had obviously been crushed. Joe went down on one knee, looking ashen. I stepped forward to try to lift him. He winced and said, 'Don't. Ricochet! That madman pulled the trigger. I felt it in my back. I think it's hit a lung.' He grinned through the pain and said, 'I was just trying to disarm the idiot. After I got hit, I just kept squeezing his throat till he stopped moving.' He got to the floor, leaning against the wall, and said, 'It's bad. I've been around firearms long enough to know; it must have damaged a major blood vessel.' He looked at me. 'Two things. I know you will deal with Gilberto, that gives me satisfaction. The other is, look in my safe. It's hidden in the second cupboard on the backwall. The combination is 1-9-5-3. You can't forget it— Coronation year. Get what's in there before anybody else gets to it.'

He squeezed my hand with that still powerful grip, but he was looking paler and breathing very fast. After a couple more minutes he slumped down, his eyes glazed, there was a rattle of breath and he was gone. I took a moment looking down at his huge lifeless frame but knew there was no time to lament. Rapid action was needed.

The lads who had been training started to gather round. I said, 'Call an ambulance and make sure that that lot lying on the floor don't move. Then call the police; you haven't seen me. Give statements: the armed gang broke in and killed Joe. You all saw that. Apart from that, be vague, say there was a lot of shouting and a gun shooting, you just kept your heads down. Let them sort it out.' Three of them picked up some of the dropped weapons. One of the thugs had got groggily to his feet but was sent flying with a well-aimed punch from one of the muscle men and then kicked a few times to ensure that he didn't get up again.

With that I raced upstairs and opened Joe's safe hidden inside the battered cupboard marked 'used towels'. It contained a red deed box and several large envelopes. I swept them all into a gym bag and then got my clothes from the flat, raced back down the stairs, and left by the back entrance. As I drove away, I heard the bells of a police car approaching.

Chapter 28

Lex Talionis

My first stop was at Jack's office. I was surprisingly calm externally, but inside I was filled with a cold and deadly fury at the death of my friend. I filled Jack in on the exact details of what had happened.

He said, 'What are you going to do?'

I said, 'What do you think? I am going to pay a visit on big brother and give him exactly what Joe got.'

He sat down and said, 'This isn't advice I am just thinking aloud. As things stand, unless one of his thugs blabs, and they won't, he will get away with this. He organised it and he is more guilty than any of them but there needs to be evidence. Even with it he can afford the best lawyer and he won't get convicted. OK, he has lost his deranged younger brother, but he must have been half expecting that with the number of near misses that idiot has had in the past. This should take the weight off you, and he might be glad to call it quits once he hears what you did to his men.

'If somebody killed him out in the open in front of witnesses the charge would be murder. The perpetrator might hang, but it would more than likely be a life sentence. All are things that you might think about. He is probably not expecting retribution, but he always has a few goons about so he will be hard to get to, especially in a place where there are no witnesses.'

I said, 'I doubt that he will be expecting anything audacious. I have all the details of his house and the plans of his office. I think I might pay him a late-night visit.'

Jack shot a sharp look at me and said, 'The less I know the

better, but some people get a sadistic kick out of this sort of thing. I hope that's not you.'

I replied, cold as ice, 'No. This is about justice.'

I hadn't had the chance to look at the contents of Cannonball's safe. I got my bag and handed the contents to Jack. I said, 'Can you sort it out? Joe seemed to think it was important.' Jack nodded and took possession of the red file and the envelopes.

I spent some days in reconnoitring Gilberto's house and his workplace. I decided that the club would be the better location to pay him a visit. I realised that he probably felt more secure there than at home. I discovered that on Friday afternoons he got deliveries of money from his various rackets and then locked himself in the upstairs office and sorted the money out for payoffs and the like. At about 8 p.m. one of his prostitutes would arrive and after an hour with her he would sit back relaxing, drinking and watching TV, with his men also drinking and relaxing downstairs. He was left undisturbed after the girl departed till the next morning. I turned the options over in my mind until I finally had a plan which I thought would work.

After my reconnaissance, I phoned Jack and he asked me over. He said, 'The file contained some items picked up by Joe during his time out east. There is a dagger called a Tanto, with some notes—apparently it is a very old and very valuable example of that type of weapon. There are photographs and nearly three thousand in money and a will and here's the thing —Joe had no family. He left everything to you apart from two small mementos, for me and Hector. They are small Japanese ivory carvings—looking at the craftsmanship and style I would think that they are also very old and valuable. I think he must have seen something in you which reminded him of himself as a young man.'

The Gym was shut up for a week as a crime scene. As soon as the forensic lot were happy, I reopened it. I had words with Cyril, the ancient bloke who had been the cleaner and caretaker there since it opened and set things up so he would run it for a few weeks.

After that I did a recce of Gilberto's place. The front entrance was manned by bouncers during the evening and locked during the day after the cleaners had left. The ground floor windows all had internal steel shutters. A fire escape ran down from the second floor into a side alley, but the end, which was about fifteen feet up in the air, was designed to be lowered in an emergency and to make any entrance by that means difficult. I noted that the fire door was made of steel. It seemed that Gilberto was very security conscious. However, no place is impregnable. The weak spot seemed to be the flat roof. There was a maintenance hatch there to allow access to the roof from below. I noted that the alley alongside the club was narrow, little more than a car width. On the other side of the alley from the club was a furniture warehouse, mainly containing damaged or second-hand items. I wandered into the place one morning without being challenged and found a ladder on an upper floor. Ideal, I thought.

A day later I walked in wearing paint spattered overalls carrying a couple of eight-foot builder's planks and went upstairs to the top floor. I got hardly a second glance from the staff, who were sparse in any case. I moved the planks up some back stairs to the roof along with the ladders. Everything was set up for a late evening visit on the coming Friday.

When the day came, I slipped into the furniture place just before it closed and made my way upstairs being careful to avoid being seen. I waited till the few staff that worked there left, and the lights went off. I would have to wait for several hours and settled down in an old armchair, making myself comfortable until the evening. I was cold and methodical. I had everything planned and knew that the best time to go in would be around ten. Gilberto would be full of booze and in his mind, he probably still thought of himself as the predator and I as the prey, but he was in for a very severe shock to that mindset. The way it worked for him was that trouble was deterred by the physical presence of the large bouncers. They were rarely called on to get physical. At the end of a long day, they would probably be in the club winding down, knowing that nothing would get past them and up the stairs to their boss's office. I did not expect them to be particularly alert. They would have just been paid and were probably more focused on how to spend their money than on security. I could see Gilberto's window from my vantage point and could see the flickering of a television. It was 9.45 p.m. Time to move, fast.

I made my way to the roof and manoeuvred the ladder till it was upright and against my feet and then lowered it slowly using my rope till it was across the gap with just over a foot resting on the building on either side. I calculated that the alley below was about eight feet wide. I pushed the planks along the rungs till I had a solid path from roof to roof. My clothing was black. In addition to the rope, I had Joe's tanto and a screwdriver, and a cosh and cord in my battledress pockets. I walked quickly across the gap and over to the maintenance hatch on Gilberto's roof. I levered the catch open and lifted the hatch and listened—all I could hear was the TV blaring. I doubled the rope around a projecting corner of the opening and lowered myself into the flat. The room was a small bedroom that smelled of sex and booze—obviously the site of Gilberto's earlier exertions. I listened at the door but there was nothing but the sound of the television. Suddenly the channel changed. It sounded like he had switched over to get the news. Now it was all about speed.

I opened the door slowly and silently and burst in. He was sat with his feet up and a glass in his hand. He looked round with a startled expression which changed to one of terror as I leapt forward. I grabbed him round the neck so he couldn't shout and slid the tanto across his mouth, saying, 'Make a wrong move and I will slice your cheeks wide open and cut your tongue off. Now put your hands on the table and I will explain a few things to you. Move a muscle and you will lose a lot of blood.' Gilberto went very white and then complied.

I went on. 'Since my encounter with your brother in the Isle of Man you have had a team out after me. I am not sure whether you were told that the demented bastard pulled a gun and started shooting at me. However, your actions resulted in

274

the death of my very close friend Joe Crookes, and actions have consequences. Joe crushed your brother's throat before he died so that score is settled, but you were the one that started the events that led to Joe dying and you are going to pay. I am just being very clear on all of this. I could have just slit your throat when I grabbed you, but I want you to know what is coming your way. Now, I am going to move this knife forwards half an inch. If you have anything to say, say it. Keep your hands flat on the table. If you try to shout, I will pull the knife back till it slices your jawbone.'

There was a large mirror opposite the table, and I could see him looking around wildly for some means of escape. There was a desk a few feet away with a phone on it and an old-fashioned bell push, presumably to summon assistance or service. He rapidly realised from the power of my grip on his neck and his position that his only option was to talk. I moved the tanto out of his mouth just enough for him to begin speaking. There was a satisfactory smear of blood from both corners of his lips where the razor-sharp blade had been resting.

He spluttered, 'What you want? I got money, I pay you. Your friend dead, my brother dead, we call it quits? I got over four thousand in the safe and some diamonds.'

'Where's the keys?' I said.

'In the lock,' was the reply.

I said, 'Unfortunately, Joe said he expected me to deal with you. I could cut your cock and balls off and leave it at that. But you wouldn't leave it, even with no balls. I would always be looking over my shoulder for payback. Have you heard about the way the Japanese do suicide?'

He looked around wildly again, sputtering. 'If you think I gonna kill myself, you crazy.'

'It's just something about the way they do it,' I said. 'They slit the belly across with a knife like this—it belonged to Joe, you know. Antique. After the first cut they pull the knife up. Excruciatingly painful they say, but they have an assistant who chops their head off with a katana when they make the belly cut, so the pain is brief.'

I suddenly pulled him back in the chair with my hand over his mouth and plunged the tanto in deep and sliced his gut open and then sliced upwards in the traditional manner. He went white and groaned with the awful pain and then slumped in the chair, moaning, with blood spurting out of the cuts. After a couple of minutes, he stopped breathing.

I went to his safe and took about half of his money, leaving the diamonds and the rest because I wanted no indications that there had been a robbery.

I poured a couple of bottles of vodka over the body and scattered the contents of a paper file over it and spilled some cigarettes around and pushed a couple of bottles of whisky over on his desk and then lit the liquid. I exited the office fast and was up the rope to the roof in a flash. I pulled the rope up and shut the hatch, pushing the catch closed so it would appear as normal as possible. I kept low and was over the planks to the other building on the far side in a matter of seconds. I pulled the planks and ladder after me and moved down into the furniture repository with them. I could see that Gilberto's office was now burning furiously. With the music and other noises from the club, no one seemed to have noticed yet, but it wouldn't be long. I left one plank in a cleaning store and pushed the other under a decrepit looking sofa.

I reasoned that the fire service would think it was some sort of accident and I knew that if anything was left of the body there would be no bullet holes or bone damage to indicate foul play. I also thought that even if the C.I.D. got involved, they would not be wasting too much time on a low life type like Gilberto and that it would take an exceptionally smart detective brain to work out what had happened and who had been involved.

I dropped down into the side street from a first-floor window and slipped off into the darkness. Soon there was quite a racket from the club as people ran out, and I could smell smoke. If anybody was in the vicinity, they would be focused on what was happening in the next building. I had parked my car several streets away. I walked back to it slowly and then drove back to the gym and had a shower. About an hour later I got a phone call from Jack. He told me that one of his contacts had phoned to tell him there had been quite a bad fire at Gilberto's club and he had burned to death in his flat.

'Oh dear, what a pity,' I said, and put the phone down.

Chapter 29

New Horizons

For the next few days, I led a very boring and normal life. I went to Joe's funeral. Some of the roughnecks from his past turned up and most of the lads from the gym. An army chaplain from his old regiment did an adequate job but was a bit too heavy on the religious stuff for my tastes. At the booze up afterwards, his old sparring partners filled in some of the gaps about the wild times of his younger days. It was obvious that they all held him in very high esteem. After that I spent most of my time down at the gym, getting into the swing of things as the new proprietor. I did a bit of tarting up and bought some new boxing gloves, weights and other equipment. It was all much appreciated by the regular lads.

A detective from C.I.D. had done a bit of nosing around after Joe's death, but the lads just stonewalled him and I couldn't help—I hadn't been there, had I. Well, that was the official line, and nobody was going to rock the boat or challenge it.

Jack was Joe's executor and about a couple of months later he called me to his office. He said, 'The probate lot have been remarkably quick, and I have all the documents here. My solicitor will see to things if you sign the documents. I can hand the money over and the properties will become yours. He said, 'There is a letter from Joe, and Hector would also like to see you, at your convenience.'

I signed the papers and picked up Joe's letter. It was brief and typically to the point. It started by saying, 'You will only be reading this if I am dead.' There was a brief history of his life and then it went on to detail his assets. The letter instructed me not to be sentimental about disposing of them or about his early death. It went on, 'Jack, Hector and me, are impressed by you. You have lots of talent and probably a lot more than you realise. So here is my advice—get out there in the big world, and I mean outside Britain, and have a look round and see what you think and what you can learn, follow your instincts. You might end up running a brothel or in a monastery. I don't think either is likely. Never run with the herd and never let people pressure you into living a life you don't want. Find yourself, your true self. Out there, life is shit and full of cute operators who want to bully or induce people to do things that suit them or the outfit they work for. There are good times to be had—treasure them, be loyal, and above all else be lucky. If there is an afterlife, we will have long chat and a pull round in the Great Dojo in the sky when you make it up here, bye for now. Cannonball.'

I turned, took a long breath and pocketed the letter, and then turned back. Jack gave me a quizzical look but didn't ask about the contents of the missive. After a while he said, 'Well, Big G turned out to be not so big after all; terrible accident.' He said the last two words in a semi-amused tone, looking straight at me as he did so. He said, 'We can get on with our lives now. You can keep on doing work for me or you might like to con-centrate on your new gym.'

I said, 'I would like to have the chat with Hector, but I'm thinking of selling the gym and having a break to do some travelling. I was thinking about buying some rental properties to get an income while I'm away.'

Jack laughed and said, 'Why not come in with me? Fortuit-ously I am moving into business properties and private rentals. I could manage whatever you buy. We could keep it separate and simple, with the rents going into your account.'

It took me about five seconds to think about it and agree. I ended up with five terraced houses and a large late Victorian house which we converted into six flats. I also picked up a fisherman's cottage in a small village on the top side of Whitby.

It had a nice sea view and I intended that as a bolt hole should I need one in the future, but for now it would be used as a holiday cottage and then shuttered up during the Winter season. When everything had been sorted out, I arranged to go and spend a few days with Hector.

I arrived at the little car park in the outskirts of the wood and was escorted once again through the wood where the occasional monk was to be seen doing monkish things. I wasn't too sure what to expect from the hugely erudite, orientalist sage. What I got surprised me. Hector obviously knew what had happened but did not want to talk about it or moralise about murder, revenge killing, and whether it was justified. I got the feeling that he neither approved nor disapproved, and just viewed Gilberto's demise as just a natural and very satisfactory event in life's pattern. It turned out that what he intended was an intensive discussion on his own world view. He hoped that by imparting the conclusions of how the world systems worked and interacted, he would provide a path or paths for me to move on in a fruitful and life affirming way from the events of the last few months.

He started his discourse with a question: 'Do you have any idea how many Batchelors degrees were awarded in the USA and in the UK in 1950?' Seeing my look of surprise he said, 'Let me answer my question. In 1950, the USA, which then had a population of slightly less than one hundred and fifty-one million, produced 432,000 people with a Batchelors degree. The UK which then had a population of slightly less than fifty-one million produced 17,300 people with that degree. If we scale the figure up by a factor of three to compare us with the USA population, we can see that we would have about 52,000 graduates. Pro rata we produced only 12% of the graduates they produced.' I looked at him in bewilderment. Hector smiled and said, 'Bear with me. You will eventually see where I am going.'

He went on, 'Just a few more examples—I could give you hundreds. What is your view of British science and engineering?'

I murmured, 'We are a world leader, aren't we?'

Hector smiled and said, 'Not an easy one to answer. Let us say the impression given by the powers that be does not reflect reality. You have some background in chemistry—what do you think of the British standing there?'

I said, 'We all learned about the great British pioneers like Davy and Dalton at school, and numerous examples are quoted. I suppose it is natural, really, teachers wanting to express pride in the achievements of its nation's scientists. We were fed stuff about discoveries by people like Perkin of the first synthetic dye, and other British discoveries such as Brearley's discovery of stainless steel used to get mentioned.'

He said, 'In terms of academic research into science we are very good. Up to 1960 we had eleven Nobel prizes in chemistry, the USA had twelve and Germany twenty-one. Germany had nine in physics, we had thirteen and the USA had sixteen. I think it is a fair assumption that over the next sixty years the USA will move well ahead due to the huge amounts of money they are now starting to pour into engineering and science. By the way, the examples you quote about Brearley and Perkin were actually accidental discoveries and not the result of any systematic research program. Brearley was trying to find a steel that would resist erosion in gun barrels. His high chromium steel wasn't suitable, and it was dumped. After a while he noticed that the stuff lying in the yard did not rust and that eventually led to its use in cutlery and so on. Perkin, who was working under the direction of a German professor, tried to synthesise quinine. That failed but he noticed that a black residue produced during the experiment was the purple dye he called mauveine, which made him rich.

'We didn't capitalise on the discoveries in any major way, but the Germans and later on the Americans certainly did, by virtue of large scale and well-funded, systematic programs. It may be the case that Perkin patented mauveine, but the Germans discovered and patented most of the rest of the synthetic dyes. I suppose what I am saying is never take anything at face value. It suits the powers that be to project an image of great scientific and engineering capability here, but they have always spent as little as they could get away with in those areas. There are other great cultures out there who have different ways of looking at things, and experiencing what they have to offer can be a very life enriching experience.'

We chatted for hours over the next few days, Hector continually returning to what he called, 'the system'. It was clear that he viewed everything done by the human race as a huge system, with thousands of interlinking smaller systems contributing to the overall picture. He picked out examples such as religious groupings and asked me what their function was. He had a completely different way of looking at things to most people. He said, 'The first thing you need are facts. Organisations such as churches are often not too keen on disseminating the factual data about their origins and internal finances and organisation to the acolytes.' He kept on drumming it in. 'Virtually everything involving groups of human beings can be viewed as "a system". This applies to small groups such as a family or bigger groups such as schools, courts, armies, and nation states. And this is central: view each system in terms of its inputs, outputs, and its fundamental function. This may be very different to the function which they like to portray themselves as having.' He picked out Christian groupings such as the Catholics and Church of England and asked, 'What do you think their fundamental purpose is?'

I said, 'I don't suppose it's spreading the word of Christ and encouraging people to live by his example?'

Hector smiled and said, 'You are learning. I am sure there are some simple and godly priests within these organisations who actually believe that the Bible is the word of God and try to do that. However, if you dig out the usually obscured facts, you find out things like the Bible was cobbled together out of a large body of writings which were produced in the early centuries after Christ died. You discover that there were various candidates for inclusion in the Bible, and books like Revelations only made it in by the skin of their teeth after much furious debate, and that the New Testament only took its present form after the council of Rome in 385. You discover that the layout is not in the order that the documents were written. That Paul's Epistles or letters were written first. You also find out that about half of these epistles are believed to be forgeries. Biblical scholars and the upper levels in the churches are aware of this and cloak the facts in obscure language. The non-Pauline epistles are referred to as pseudepigrapha, an obscure word meaning false writings, in other words—forgeries.

'You also become aware that passages in the Bible were altered or modified or omitted in order to make sure that they agreed with the authorised beliefs or dogmas which were being developed by the churches.

'If you look at the church structures, you may form the opinion that disseminating Christianity is an accidental byproduct of the activities of parts of the church. You may start to think that what you have are very wealthy power structures who spend most of their time energy and money in trying to maintain or increase the power and influence of their organisations and that their activities are fundamentally political and not religious. However, it's up to you. Build up a good knowledge base and then look at the actual inputs and outputs of an organisation. Never swallow the propaganda lines which they use to describe their activities and further their interests.'

He laughed and said, 'A bit heavy, eh? But all I am trying to do is to get you to look at the world critically and analytically and perhaps give you some insights which will enable you to do that. There are formal tools, 'systems methodologies', some mathematical and some based on amassing data and viewpoints from multiple perspectives and forming an overview of a system or activity.

'Another example—what is your view of smoking cigarettes? The practice seems firmly embedded in our culture, despite growing evidence that it causes cancers and other early deaths through premature heart attacks and strokes. Would you view it as a civilised and relaxing adult pleasure? Or perhaps as a viciously addictive activity, cynically used by the government to raise huge revenues by exploiting the pursuit? Or an activity which turns your lungs into the receptacle for the cancer-causing tars produced by destructive distillation of the tobacco leaves?'

He laughed again. 'The Government and tobacco companies would obviously prefer it if you subscribed to the first point of view. All are valid ways of looking at the practice—looking at all of them and not just one is the way to go, it gives you a sort of rich picture and moves you beyond the blinkered viewpoint of those who adhere to just one viewpoint. That is the way of the fanatic—rigid belief in just one possibility/dogma/belief system/legal code. In history we see examples of endless murders of those who have deviated even slightly from the approved path, usually by those who will not tolerate any departure from the prescribed official line.'

Hector continued to probe, question and lecture. His knowledge was vast. Insights into language, linguistics, politics, mathematics, psychology and various sciences were imparted and absorbed by me. He always included suggestions on further readings. Later in life I came to realise that the works suggested were seminal in those fields.

After one particularly intensive discussion he smiled and took a long hard look at me, and said, 'I think you are ready to depart.'

We had one final dinner during which he told me something of himself and his family background. He had inherited money, which he despised, from a father who ran large colonial estates, mines and factories. His ancestry had a strong academic and free-thinking strand. He said, 'The state always seemed to be suspicious about our activities, but my ancestors were always smart enough to keep just on the right side of things.' He continued, 'In your case you have clawed your way up from a class in which sons tend to follow fathers and daughters follow mothers in treading the same route through work and through life. Supporting the same football teams, going down to the same pubs, working in the same mines or factories and so on, and the establishment likes it like that. A few make the breakthrough and you had no advantages; the system is stacked against you and those like you. If they do get higher qualifications they usually end up in the lower or middle ranks of their professions and are usually delighted to have done that, while the sons of the public school educated, top echelon, effortlessly slide into the prime positions as though by divine right, often with huge self-confidence which is not matched by similar huge ability.'

He went on, 'Oh, I went that route, but was a trouble causer, a questioner of the status quo. They don't like that and were glad when I was accepted into university at sixteen. I got a first in just two years, again ruffling feathers, and went on to study at the University of Paris and then Berlin and then at MIT. He looked up, Massachusetts Institute of Technology—ferociously good at Maths and Science, that place. Razor sharp minds. I did terrific courses on relativity and cosmology there.

'Perhaps in some sense you were lucky—a wild boy with wild friends, from a tough mining village, impelled by chance into new and somewhat dangerous areas. However, people saw things in you, and you had the chance to develop high level combat skills, accumulate some money, perhaps due in some measure to myself. You saw something of how the real-world works. You are now thinking about life and how the world operates. Your world view has changed. You now have the physical and some of the intellectual skills which will make you the master of your situation and not just a cog in the great machine. You can leave here and do whatever you wish. If you want to return at any time, I will be here. The monks in the wood, which I have loaned them, provide me with the benefit of a secure buffer to the outside world.'

After breakfast the next morning I departed for London. Hector said, 'Just get to a major travel centre. Have your passport and a means to get money abroad. Toss a coin. If its heads go left, tails right. Let the fates decide.'

After a few days I found myself in a pub in Earls Court, chatting to a tall, attractive, athletic Australian woman. She was wonderfully articulate and was filled with the wild spirit of restlessness and need for adventure. I had never met it in a woman before. She was bumming round the world after university. She explained that she had done Japan, India, Egypt and most of western Europe. Her next stop was Argentina then Brazil and then on to the US and Canada before she finally went back to Oz. We really got on and I had thought about visiting the Andes as one of my possible destinations. I found out she was departing for Argentina on the following day, and I thought –what the Hell?—and after a moment I found myself saying, 'I'll come with you.' The big Sheila laughed and said, 'OK.'